teaching
mr.cutler

robert currie

teaching
mr.cutler

COTEAU BOOKS
WWW.COTEAUBOOKS.COM

Edited by Edna Alford.
Cover and book design by Duncan Campbell.
Cover photo by mad cow Studio, Regina, Saskatchewan.
Author photo by Larry Hadwen.
Printed and bound in Canada at AGMV Marquis.

National Library of Canada Cataloguing in Publication

Currie, Robert, 1937-
Teaching Mr. Cutler / Robert Currie.

ISBN 1-55050-205-0

I. Title.
PS8555.U7T33 2002   C813'.54   C2002-904096-5
PR9199.3 C8 T33 2002

1   2   3   4   5   6   7   8   9   10

COTEAU BOOKS
401-2206 Dewdney Ave.
Regina, Saskatchewan
Canada   S4R 1H3

available in the US from:
Fitzhenry and Whiteside
195 Allstate Parkway
Markham, Ontario
Canada   L3R 4T8

The publisher gratefully acknowledges the financial assistance of the Saskatchewan Arts Board, the Canada Council for the Arts, the Government of Canada through the Book Publishing Industry Development Program (bpidp), the Government of Saskatchewan, through the Cultural Industries Development Fund, and the City of Regina Arts Commission, for its publishing program.

This book is for my former students
from whom I learned much
and for the good teachers
of whom there are many.

One

Maybe if he hadn't asked for volunteers, things would have been easier. If he'd been able to look out at the faces in front of him, the lesson barely begun, those faces already shifting to boredom, the same blank expression slipping over all of them, that dead look in the eyes. If he could have accepted that for what it was, a common condition of high school life, he might have learned to slide along, the safe and simple way, with nothing changing, nothing at all, but he was young and still thought that change must always be for the better.

Brad Cutler had arrived early for the first day of school at the end of August. Long before any students would be there, at seven-thirty in the morning, he'd driven into the staff parking lot, nosing the car toward the caragana hedge, its branches neatly trimmed for the first semester of the new year. He'd had a nervous stomach, switching off the car radio, silencing the raucous voice of Great Big Sea's lead singer in one song he didn't like. "Consequence Free." There were always consequences. Make sure the students understood that, and he'd be okay. Sure, he knew he would. He'd swung around in the seat, only two other cars in the lot, sprinklers already turning beyond the crescent, the lawn freshly cut and sparkling in spray and sunlight. He'd gazed at the building, its lower bricks an arc of darker red where they'd been drenched by water from the sprinklers, the centre tower rising into a bright prairie sky without a single cloud.

Better get a move on. He'd checked the dashboard mirror, his cowlick sticking up again, smoothed the collar of his only decent dress shirt over his new blue tie – he hated wearing ties, hoped these teachers didn't wear them every day. Swinging the door wide, he stepped out of the car. He knew he could get through today all right, thought he could – he'd just be assigning lockers, handing out books and collecting student fees – but he wondered how he'd be doing in a month or so. That would be the real test. He stared a moment at the school. Below the tower, the main entrance to the building was immersed in shadow. Well, time to descend into the belly of the beast.

He remembered trying to laugh at his little joke, but all he'd felt was bile rising in his throat.

And now here he was, months later, looking down at Parker Stone in the front seat, his face a mask whose expression lingered always halfway between boredom and hostility. Behind him sat Bert Peale, looking more bored and more hostile too. Both of them big, good-looking kids except for the sullen twist of their mouths.

When Brad stopped speaking, the only sounds in the room were feet scraping at a back desk, the radiator hissing on the side wall. He'd better try something else. Should he tell them about Mr. Roy, his English teacher back in Outlook, who used to loan him books about kids coming of age, *The Lark in the Clear Air, True Grit, Catcher in the Rye*? No, that wasn't going to do it. Try Miss Wilson.

"When I was in high school," Brad told his grade twelve class, "I had this teacher, Miss Wilson. She used to gush about Shelley. His poems were exquisite, he was the grandest poet who ever lived, he'd fallen on the thorns of life, but he rose above it all." Brad paused. "She wouldn't have noticed that awful pun either. Rose above the thorns. Oh, no, she was too busy going on about his greatness. The way his poems sang with glory, we'd never hear such beauty." He paused, looked at the faces in front of him. "I hated Shelley before I'd read a single poem."

They were staring at him now, wondering, a hint of life in their eyes.

Danny Litowski raised his hand. "I thought we were gonna do *Hamlet.*"

"We are. But I get the impression that some of you feel about Shakespeare the way I used to feel about Shelley."

"Oh, no, Shakespeare's different. There's lots of drama, and everybody gets killed." Melinda Harper, brown-nosing as usual. Those behind her looked at her and rolled their eyes.

"Shakespeare's boring," said Bert Peale. His hair was clipped so short, the skin on the top of his head shone beneath the fluorescent lights that flashed off his wire-rimmed glasses and the stud in his ear. In the desk in front of him, Parker Stone sat motionless, his eyes angry, staring straight ahead, focused somewhere else. Brad sometimes wondered if they hadn't spent too much time studying the fashion ads in *GQ* and *Esquire,* staring at the scowling models, every one of them a rebel with a sneer. Were they acting tough and bored, or was that the way they really were?

The other kids were jumping in now. Well, he'd raised the lid himself, he'd have to ride it out, good and bad.

"I hate reading stuff I never understand. What's the point? It's a total waste of time."

"Nobody talks the way they do in Shakespeare. What a bunch of crap."

"You always know the hero's gonna get it in the end. Why bother reading the whole thing?"

"Yeah, Shakespeare sucks." That from Bert Peale. Naturally.

"Page after page and all they do is talk. Bo-ring!"

"I kind of like the language." It was Lori Campbell. When the boys in front of her turned toward her, she shrugged and added. "It's colourful, you know; I like it."

"Well, I don't," said Bert. The heads swung from her to him. Except for Parker Stone who was still turned around, looking at her, or, perhaps, through her at something else. He was such a moody kid, always hard to read.

Brad had to reel them in, get them back on task.

"Well, you don't have to like it, but you do have to know it." He paused. "Though I wish I could make you like it. I'll try. But I'm not going to gush about how great it is."

Thirty-one of them, and maybe two or three were looking forward to *Hamlet*.

"It's a play," he said. "Shakespeare wrote for the theatre, and the Elizabethans liked what they saw. They paid their pennies to get in."

"Hard to imagine, eh?" Bert again. In front of him, Parker seemed to be staring at a spot on the chalkboard where nothing was written. Now he just looked glum.

"True, though. People flocked to the plays. And stood under a hot sun to watch them, stood for hours. Groundlings, they were called, pushing in around the stage on three sides because that was where the action was. And they were part of it."

"How do you mean?" Exactly what he wanted to hear; thank you, Lori. She might have ragged hair that was dyed a brilliant red today, but it didn't affect her curiosity.

Red hair made him think of Kelly, Kelly with her wide smile that left him weak in the knees, sent his temperature soaring, Kelly leaning toward him –

He realized that he was grinning, grinning like a fool, yeah, and blushing too.

"Sorry. I...lost my train of thought."

"Yeah," said Bert Peale, "the choo-choo train run off the rails."

Better ignore him. Get things going again. Quick. "What was that, Lori?"

She was staring at him, too, but she said, "The ground-lings. How were they part of the action?"

"It wasn't like today. The audience in the dark and every eye drawn to the actors on a bright stage. Back then, it was all daylight. If you were an actor, you could see the audience all around you, every one of them just as clear as Brutus looking at Mark Antony. There they were, you couldn't just ignore them." The class was back with him, most of it anyway. Parker still seemed to be studying a spot on the chalkboard. Bert Peale looked as if he were sulking. "The actors tried to bring them into the play. With soliloquies for example."

A hand went up. Nelson Ahenakew. "Yeah, some guy thinking out loud. That always looks so phony."

"Not the way the Elizabethans played it. The actor was surrounded by audience. He was talking to them, giving them the low-down on what really bothered him. Then there were asides, quick, off-the-cuff remarks to the audience. It made them a part of things."

"You want to explain that?"

"Sure. An example. The first play I ever saw in college was *Come Blow Your Horn*. Neil Simon. Anybody heard of him?"

"Yeah, guy who wrote *The Odd Couple*." For someone who liked to grouse, Bert often knew the answers.

"Right. Well, this play was done as theatre-in-the-round, a lot like Shakespeare's day – the audience seated all around the stage, and I was in the first row. In one scene, this father's complaining about his son who's always late for work in the family business because he's up most of the night chasing women. This father's hot-tempered and he starts pacing back and forth in front of his son, ranting like mad: 'You're no good. You can't get out of bed. That's the trouble. You're a bum!' All of a sudden he wheels around and he's maybe a yard away, staring right at me. He yells, 'A no-good bum. You agree?'

"Well, I was stunned. There he was, talking to me. Me! I didn't know what to say, damned near fell off my chair." Brad paused, looked at his students, many of whom were smiling at him. "Somebody in an Elizabethan audience wouldn't have missed a beat. 'You're right,' he would have shouted. 'A lousy bum.'"

They sat easily at their desks, waiting for more. Most of them, anyway. Bert Peale was frowning at Walter Buchko beside him, but Walter was listening. There was a slight smile on Parker's face, but he looked as if he might be thinking of something else.

"I guess what I'm trying to say is that Shakespeare wrote for a live audience. If what he wrote seems dead on the page to you, you have to get it off the page. Try to visualize it as a play, imagine what the actors are doing when they say the lines. And how they say them."

"How we gonna do that?" Neil Wallace. His first words in

at least two weeks. For some reason, Neil always reminded him of Homer Simpson on tranquilizers.

"I guess it's my job to help you. Help you see what's going on, hear the emotion in the words, understand the characters."

Now he had come to the part that scared him. The students were waiting, some of them sprawled in their seats, all of them watching him, and he could almost hear his father saying, "Things don't pan out with teaching, don't come crawling back to me. You had your chance."

He took a breath, let it slowly out. "*Hamlet's* one of Shakespeare's longer plays, a lot of different scenes. Some of them should be fun to do in class." There was a little stir among the students. Uneasiness? Disbelief? He wasn't sure, but he noticed that Parker Stone never budged. That Bert Peale was glowering at him.

"I don't mean like great Shakespearean actors with every line memorized, but there are things we can do with a few words and some pantomime. It'll help you understand the play – and make it more interesting. So when I call for volunteers..." Strange, Bert Peale was smiling now. "Of course, if you're nervous about acting, if you're kind of scared to get up in front of everybody, why, that's normal. You should volunteer anyway."

Oh, man, he thought, I hope this is working. He let his eyes run up and down the rows. Faces lifted toward his own, some of them open and friendly, a few closed, Parker Stone staring at his desk, Bert Peale looking back at him. Were any of them willing? He'd get lucky now or maybe blow it for the whole year. Yeah, and that could mean forever. Screw things up and they wouldn't hire him back.

He took a deep breath.

"I need four of you to try a little scene. Today – now." He paused, heads dropping, eyes suddenly averted. Wait a minute. Bert was flicking a hand at him. Was this possible – a breakthrough at last?

"Good for you, Bert."

"Hey," said Bert, his smile wider now, "I didn't volunteer."

"I thought you raised your hand."

"No effing way!"

"Bert!" Louder than he intended.

"Aw, come on," said Bert, "I didn't say no f-word."

Mind games, eh? Better not lose it, Brad thought. No sense stopping now, no need to panic, this could still work. "We'll need four people for this bit. The rest of you can read the first eight pages of the introduction. Let's see, out in the hall, let's have...Walter...Danny...Will...and...Parker." Parker. Oh, man, where had that come from?

He closed the door behind them, said, "Thanks for 'volunteering.'" Three of them grinned at him, but Parker stood, gazing at the wall beside his head, no sign of emotion on his face.

"I never volunteered," said Parker, ice riding the current of his voice.

"I was just kidding."

"Yeah, but you dragged me out here." Parker looked at him now, his eyes cold. "I didn't want to come."

Damn, it was going down the drain, all of it.

"I guess maybe I did drag you out," said Brad. Don't give up now, he thought. That'd give his old man a chance to say he knew it all along. Have to push on, somehow get them to try it. "I thought this would be fun – it'd make the class better for all of us. I picked you four because I figured if anyone could make it work, you guys could."

Parker glanced away, looked back at him, did not speak.

Brad waited. Knew everything was up to him now. "If it's not something you're game to try, fair enough. I'll see if I can get someone else."

"Well," said Parker, "maybe I could try it."

"I'd appreciate that," said Brad. "How about the rest of you?"

"Fine with me," said Walter Buchko. Even with his thin goatee, he looked like a little kid, eager to please. The other two nodded their heads.

Brad gave them the few words of script he'd copied out, the two rulers from the chalkboard rail, explained the scene and how they'd play it, ran them through it twice there in the hall.

"Pretty good," he said, though he was concerned about Parker, who seemed to be concentrating, yet moving in a daze. "You guys try it once more while I go in and set the class up for what's going to happen." They can do it, he thought, Parker too. Yeah, they can do it – if they don't freeze.

As he entered the room, his students looked up, some from their books, some from chatting with their neighbours. He moved his homemade lectern out of the way, carrying it to the far wall. Bert Peale continued whispering to the boy behind him. "Okay," said Brad. "Here's the situation. You have to imagine that we're on the ramparts of a castle in Denmark. It's around midnight. Kind of hard to picture, eh, with the fluorescents beaming down, but in Shakespeare's day, sunshine made the stage just as bright as this basement room. Now the guys are going to do this scene mainly in pantomime. Notice how much you learn before a single word is spoken, and be ready to talk about it afterwards.

We're going to see a couple of castle guards and something strange is going to happen."

"I'll bet," said Bert.

Brad decided to let it go. He walked to the door and swung it open. "Give us half a minute of silence," he said to the actors, "then do it." He hurried to the back of the room, slid into an empty desk, and waited. The students were quiet, attentive, leaning forward in their seats, and he – he suddenly realized – was holding his breath. He let it out as Danny strode into the room, the ruler shoved through his belt like a sword. Danny'd be okay in front of the class; he liked attention.

He seemed to be shivering as he walked, his hands tucked into his armpits, his eyes darting left to right. He stopped walking, turned toward the class, staring above their heads, squinting at something he couldn't quite make out in the distance. He gave his head a little shake, began walking again, turned at the far wall and walked back, pulling his hands from his armpits to rub them together, patrolled toward the door, turned before he reached it, stopped again to look into the distance, puzzlement spreading across his face. And walked slowly on.

Then Parker entered, moving even slower, stepping on the balls of his feet, his body slightly stooped, his head swinging from side to side. With his mop of curly brown hair, his lively eyes, the kid was actually handsome when he wasn't frowning. He stopped, cocked his head as if listening to something behind him, his hand falling on the hilt of the ruler-sword in his belt.

The room was absolutely still, a few of the students hunched up in their seats, leaning toward the front of the room. Even Bert Peale was watching. They're doing it, Brad thought, they're going to make it work. And Parker's got it just right.

Parker took two slow steps toward the class, stopped again, peering straight ahead. Just as Danny reached the far wall, Parker jerked his head around, drawing his sword as he yelled, "Who's there?"

Danny wheeled toward him, his own sword swinging in a huge arc. "Nay," he shouted, "answer me: stand and..." He faltered, rushed on: "unfold thyself."

Parker raised his sword in front of his face, tipped it toward Danny, and grinned as he spoke, "Long live the king!"

Danny, too, seemed suddenly relaxed. His sword hand dropped as he squinted toward Parker. "Bernardo?" he asked.

"He." Parker nodded his head and put his sword away. Danny scuttled toward him, clasped him by the hand, squeezed his shoulder, slapped him on the back. Something not quite right here. A sudden glance at Brad.

Oh, oh, groping for his line. Just one more, you can do it.

"For this relief," Danny said, his voice loud but tentative, then flooding with assurance as he finished, "well, thanks!"

Not quite, but it would do.

Then the two were pantomiming a moment's conversation before Danny turned away and Parker began to walk the ramparts. He blew on his hands, rubbed them together, shoved one deep into his pocket, the other hovering above his sword. Behind him, Danny's sword leapt out again as Walter and Will stepped through the door. But when they seemed to question him, Danny put his sword away and pointed toward Parker before leaving the room.

"Holla!" shouted Will, spinning Parker around with the sound of his voice. Parker's sword was trembling in his hand. Will added, "Bernardo!"

Parker took a step toward them. "Say, what," he said, "is Horatio there?"

"A piece of him."

Then Parker was shaking their hands, glad for the company. Pantomime again. Walter, standing between Will and Parker, seemed to be explaining something, perhaps telling a story. A story that didn't impress Will, who shook his head, laughed into the palm of his hand. Then Parker held up his own hand, silencing Walter who stepped backwards, as Parker leaned toward Will. Parker's lips were moving, his finger shaking in front of Will, who listened quietly, then shook his head. And laughed again. Parker was in tight now, nodding his head, explaining something that Will couldn't or wouldn't accept.

Suddenly, Walter's hand was between them, rising above the class, his eyes bugging at what he saw, his mouth falling open. Parker followed his sightline, a look of dread flashing over his face, but determination, too, as he grabbed Will, turning him toward whatever it was they saw. Will raised his eyes, his mouth flopping open, his body shrinking away until he was jammed against the chalkboard. Parker was pointing up, but his eyes were on Will as he pantomimed a speech, just a hint of a sneer on his lips.

My God, Brad thought, he's marvellous. You can see the sarcasm, almost hear the words: "How now, Horatio! you tremble and look pale: Is not this something more than fantasy?"

Brad stood up, walked to the front of the room. "Great work, guys," he said. "Maybe we should give them a hand." And the class was clapping, their hands beating together with pleasure. The four boys were themselves again, shuffling to their seats. Parker, he noticed, had his head down, but there was a twist of smile on his lips until he noticed Bert

Peale sneering at him, and he slouched into his desk.

"Now, think about what you saw," Brad said. "How much did you learn even before the first word was spoken?"

Half a dozen hands shot up.

"It was cold out."

"And real dark. They couldn't see very far."

"The guard was nervous. He kept looking for something to happen."

"Not as nervous as the other guard," said Pam Wheeler. She reminded Brad of a coiled spring, so much energy contained in such a small body. "Man, he was freaked-out."

"Good," said Brad. "Now, if you were really on your toes, you might have noticed something rather strange there."

"Well," said Lori Campbell, "the acting was pretty strange." When everybody laughed, she added, "No, just kidding. You guys were really good." Her eyes swept over Will, Walter, Danny, but they lingered on Parker. Then she was looking at Brad again. "How do you mean – strange?"

"Strange – unusual. Something unusual happened there – while we still had just the first two guards on stage."

They were all looking at him, bemused. But not one of them with dead eyes, not even Bert. No, he looked angry.

"What we were seeing here," Brad added, "was the changing of the guard."

"I got it!" Neil Wallace again, twice in one day. "The wrong guard spoke. Parker. The guy coming to relieve."

"Exactly. The guard on duty's supposed to issue the challenge – he can't see who's coming, so it's his job to challenge anyone who comes along. Why did the other guy do it?"

"He's scared." Neil was on a roll. "Man, he's freaked out of his skull."

"Correct. So, right from the first words of the play,

Shakespeare establishes the atmosphere of uncertainty and fear that exists in Denmark, that will carry on throughout the play."

"That's cool," said Melinda Harper. She spoke quietly, almost as if musing to herself, but not so quietly that Brad wouldn't hear.

"The thing I find strange comed later," said Allan Chow. He was the only Chinese boy in the class, recently arrived from Hong Kong, a perfectionist – despite his tense problems – who only answered questions when he was sure he was right. "The three of them seed something awful. Like a horror movie."

"Right on, Allan," said Brad. "But before we get to that, think about Will. He was playing the part of a man named Horatio. Horatio's going to be important in the play. What did you notice about Horatio?"

"He was laughing at them. Walter and Parker was trying to tell him something, but he don't believe them."

"It was just a big joke to him," said Melinda Harper.

"Horatio's a scoffer," said Brad. "He needs to see to believe. Now if you'll all turn to Act One, Scene One, we'll read a few pages and find out what it is he sees, what it is that horrifies them all."

The students opened their books, quickly flipping pages.

They want to know, thought Brad, they're with me. For a while at least.

Then he noticed Parker Stone sitting motionless at his desk, his copy of *Hamlet* closed before him. He was staring at Brad, his face expressionless. Behind him, Bert Peale was sneering. Around them, many of the others were already looking bored.

Two

"You ask me, he's just another spoiled rich kid," said Maurie Pack. He taught chemistry and seemed to think that most things could be solved by an equation.

"Could be," said Phil Simpson, who was as lean as Ichabod Crane and taught history. "His old man's a doctor, gives him anything he wants."

"I'm not sure that's true." Sue Burton raised her head from the current affairs journal she'd been reading in the staffroom. She was a bright and cheerful woman, perhaps five years older than Brad, but at the moment he thought she looked angry. It was the second week of classes, and he knew most of the teachers now.

"What about that Toyota he bombs around in?" said Maurie. "He sure never bought that working at the A & W." Maurie had a small bald spot exactly on the top of his head, and unruly brown hair that usually failed to cover it. Brad wondered if that was why he often acted as if the world owed him an apology.

"Okay, it's his father's car. Maybe he is a little spoiled.

Only child of a single parent." Sue's voice had a snap to it. She was never afraid to take anyone on.

"You talking about Bert Peale?" Brad asked.

"No," said Maurie, "Parker Stone. They're both jerks."

Sue looked angrier. "Parker's no jerk. He's a good kid. You said it yourself, he works at the A & W."

"Sure. And spends every penny on himself. Totally self-centered."

Sue stared at Maurie a moment before speaking. Maurie reminded Brad of a fire plug; he was stocky, squat and red-faced. "Aren't most kids to some degree self-centered?" she asked. "It's a fact of life in adolescence."

"Ah, Burton," said Maurie, "you should've been a social worker."

Phil laughed. Not a bad looking guy, Brad thought, except for his chin. Give him some of mine, we'd both be better off.

"Social work and current affairs," said Phil. He grinned at Sue. "Why don't you stick your nose back in your magazine? Ha. As if you need further instruction on affairs."

She didn't miss a beat as she picked up her magazine. "Better a current affair than an ancient one, eh Phil?"

She was blushing, though, Brad noticed. Whoo, he thought, these people sure do go at it. He wondered if all schools were like this. He was struggling with his classes, muddling along as best he could, and still surprised at the jibes that flew across the staffroom. Between people who genuinely seemed to like each other. Anywhere else and someone would be screaming sexual harassment.

Nothing about teaching was quite what he'd expected. He remembered his first trip to Moose Jaw after he'd been hired for the job following his internship in Rosetown. Having crossed miles of flat prairie, he'd driven through a city of hills and dips and liked it right away, a population of 33,000, not too big for a country boy from Outlook, a park just a block from Main Street, more parks on the edge of town, a river and two creeks making him feel right at home. He wasn't so sure about the school.

It was late August when he made his first visit to Lawrence Collegiate, hoping for some early orientation. Coming up the steps from the crescent in front of the school, he stopped and stared at the building. Three storeys of solid red brick and a bell tower rising high above. On the west side, a new wing of lighter brick, it looked as if it might contain a gymnasium. Above him, many of the windows had been bricked in. Like something under siege. The bell tower, he saw, contained no bell – resembled, in fact, a gun turret overlooking the crescent and the football field behind him. Yeah, the whole thing seemed more like a fortress than a school. Feeling suddenly puny, he hurried inside.

In the hall he met a teacher who introduced himself as Doug Gunnars, the guidance counsellor. He was friendly enough, but in a hurry, late for an appointment to work out a new timetable for a student who'd failed two finals in June.

At the end of the hall there was a sign that said Office. When he opened the door, he saw a big man leaning on a long counter and talking with a young woman who seemed to be sorting through a stack of index cards. What he noticed about her was her hair, a bright red, brighter than auburn, so bright it looked as though it had been dipped in paint, wild tangles springing at right angles from her head, as if it were at war with her skull and determined to break away in every direction. Rebellious hair, he thought. Then he noticed her body, oh, man, straight out of *Sports Illustrated*, the swimsuit issue.

He rubbed the scar on his chin, pulled his hand quickly

away. Put him in the same room with a pretty girl, he could almost feel it pulsate.

"Help you?" The man had spoken. Brad wrenched his eyes off the woman. This guy was a good four inches taller than Brad, must be at least six foot two, dark complexioned, his arms below his short-sleeved shirt meaty and covered with curly black hair. The chequered tie around his neck looked as if it might choke him. He was maybe fifty years old.

"Yeah, sure. I'm Brad Cutler. I was hoping to see the principal." He paused, worried that he might sound like a kid. "Would that be you?"

The big man laughed. "No, sir. You want Mr. Workman. He's busy right now. In the inner office." He made it sound like something special, the Oval Office in the White House, maybe. "I help you?"

"I was hoping someone might show me around."

The big man straightened, stood back from the counter. Six foot three, Brad thought. He knew that he himself was slim, but next to this guy he felt positively skinny. "Want a tour, do you?" the big man asked.

The woman ducked her head. Brad found himself staring across the counter at that volcano of red hair erupting above her shoulders.

"Yes, if you've got the time. I'm the new teacher. Brad Cutler." He extended his hand.

"Oh, sorry. Little slow on the uptake here. Name's Schwitzer. Herb Schwitzer." He shook Brad's hand. "This is Miss Irving."

"Kelly," she said, a big smile on her face. He wondered if she were laughing at him. Or at Schwitzer.

"Let's see now," said Schwitzer. "You'd be English, right?"

"What? Oh, English. I teach it, yes." He knew he sounded like an ass.

"Good. I'll show you your room."

The big man, it turned out, was the vice-principal. He took Brad on a quick tour of the school's three upper floors, rows of battered metal lockers at each end of every hall. There were classrooms on every floor, plus a Home Ec lab on the top floor, Chemistry and Physics labs on the second floor, library and staffroom on the main floor. Schwitzer pushed open the door beside the staffroom. "Computers and copier in here, staples, copy paper, foolscap, that kind of thing," he said. "Now, let's go down to the basement. I'll show you your room."

Oh great, thought Brad, the basement.

They went down two flights of stairs, the landing between them dark and shabby, he noted, the stairs scuffed and worn in the middle. They pushed through glass doors and turned to the first door on the left. "Here we are," said Schwitzer, "the combat room."

"What?"

The vice-principal looked suddenly embarrassed. "Sorry," he said. "That kind of slipped out. Staffroom joke is all. Teacher in here last year had a few problems."

It was nothing but a large rectangle, beige ceiling tiles, beige walls, a beige tile floor – over concrete, he guessed from the feel of it. In the back of the room, he noticed, the concrete had heaved, the flooring tiles cracked and bellied up around it, a few of them missing. Above his head the ceiling was stained from an ancient leak. On one side wall there was a patch of fresh plaster where a hole had been repaired but not yet painted over.

There were no desks, no pictures, no windows. The only

decorative effect came from two radiators standing some-what crookedly against the side wall, silver paint peeling off to reveal a coat of rust beneath, and in the back corner of the room, a wooden cupboard which had pulled away from the wall, one door torn from its hinges.

"Well," said Brad. "Kind of empty, isn't it?" It was like a stage with no set and no actors, drab and cheerless. Man, and he'd have to make something happen here, yeah, something other than combat. He wasn't going to be the next staffroom joke.

"Don't worry," Schwitzer said. "We'll have thirty-five desks in here by opening day."

Thirty-five, he thought, hoping he hadn't shuddered. "I suppose I can put up some posters."

"Sure thing. No tacks, though. Caretakers don't want holes in the walls. Got some gummy stuff in the office. Won't mark the walls."

Brad looked around the room, wondering what it would be like when it was filled with students. He felt a shiver in his stomach, heard his father telling him he should have picked farming, should've stayed home, he'd be the fourth generation of Cutlers on the farm. Reminding him it was too late now, the farm was gone.

"Mr. Schwitzer," he began.

"Herb. Call me Herb. Mr. when there's kids around."

"Uh, Herb, the kids, any of them ever complain about being stuck in here without a window?"

"No. Used to be the woodwork room. Switched places with the English room under the gym. Teacher said it was tough try-ing to get through a poem when there was a basketball game going on overhead." He grinned and added, "Thump. Thump. Thump. Doesn't match up with your iambic pentameter."

"I guess I'm lucky then." He tried not to sound sarcastic.

"You bet. Straight English too. Come on up to my office, I'll show you what we've got for you."

As they started up the stairs, Brad noted glumly that his room was right beside the boiler room. Yeah, real nice, he thought, double, double toil and trouble; fire, burn, and caldron, bubble. A minute later, however, when he bent over the vice-principal's desk to see his timetable, he was pleased. One grade twelve, one grade eleven and two grade tens in each semester. The two grade ten classes would cut down the amount of preparation he'd have to do.

"Not bad," he said. "Thanks. This my copy?"

"Sure is. Have a seat." Herb Schwitzer motioned to the chair in front of his desk. He stood up, marched deliberately around his desk and closed the door, then sat down again. "Your first job?"

"Teaching, yeah. I always worked on the farm at home, you know, driving the tractor before I was old enough for a license. Worked a winter at Lake Louise too. As a lift operator."

"Living the good life on the ski hill, eh? Maybe I should've tried that myself when I was younger." The vice-principal leaned back in his chair, his hands folded in his lap. He was staring at his hands. "Mind if I give you some advice?"

Discipline, Brad thought, he wants to know if I can handle problem kids. "Not at all," he said.

"Things change. When I started out in this system, I was at the Tech. Tough school. I was supposed to help coach the football team. Sal Necker was the coach – and the vice-principal. Football practice started a week before classes began. That first practice, I'm on the side-lines, watching the kids doing calisthenics. Sal comes over to me, we're just standing there, both of us looking out onto the field. All of a sudden he reaches over and grabs my arm. Squeezes my muscle. 'You're a big, strong guy,' he says. 'Any of these kids give you a rough time, knock 'em around a bit. Make it hurt. You show 'em who's boss, they won't give you any shit.' That was all. He walked back onto the field, never did look at me. Only advice on discipline I ever got."

Schwitzer leaned forward, placed his elbows on his desk, and studied Brad's face. Brad guessed that he was expected to say something. "I don't think that would...."

"Course not. Good advice then, maybe, but times change. Kids today, they know you can't touch them. Lay a hand on them, someone's screaming for a lawyer." Schwitzer sank back into his chair. He seemed to be staring now at a file folder on his desk. Brad could hear the clock beating out the seconds on the wall behind. Titch. Titch. Titch.

"I was wondering," Brad said. "You have any advice on discipline?"

"I do." Schwitzer raised his head. "First-year teachers come in here, full of idealism, they love their subject, going to make the kids love it too, going to be their friend. They get an education fast – the teachers, I mean. Little buggers run some of them right out of the profession. Fact number one: these kids will do anything you let them get away with. The good kids too. Anything."

Brad knew Schwitzer was studying him, managed to restrain a shudder.

"I kid you not. Absolutely anything. The fellow with your timetable last year. Shy. Had trouble looking people in the eye. Spent most of his time writing on the board. One kid used to pick up a dirty chalkbrush, sneak up behind him and blow chalk on the back of his jacket. A line of yellow chalk. He had to know what they were doing, but he didn't know how to handle it. So he used to pretend he didn't notice. Made himself a laughing stock. Selling used cars now."

"I –"

Schwitzer raised his hand. "Wait. Most young teachers think they know everything already, but you asked. So I'm going to tell you what I know. Fact number two: kids in a class like that aren't happy. Usually miserable, in fact. You run a tight ship, maybe you'll never hear them thank you for it, but they'll be a hell of a lot happier. Fact number three: get yourself a reputation, teaching's a lot easier. You can concentrate on your subject, start to enjoy the job." Schwitzer glanced at his gesturing hand, lowered it quickly to his desk. "Just trying to level with you."

Brad thought about his internship in Rosetown. Kids pushing all the time, anything to get under his skin. "I want all the help I can get," he said.

"Good. What you do is come on strong. First kid who's half a step out of line, you nail him quick. With words, you understand. Put him in his place. Keep him after school. Whatever. Same thing in every class. Show them who's boss. It's not exactly combat down there, but you can bet they're going to test you. Keep it up a month, they'll know you won't take any crap. You'll have the right kind of reputation. Then you can relax, really get into the teaching."

Schwitzer paused, watching him. "You start off being Mr. Nice Guy, we'll be advertising your job by November."

Brad felt a hard knot tightening in his stomach, hoped he didn't look as nervous as he felt. This was just the kind of stuff his old man would love to hear.

"Not trying to scare you off," Schwitzer said. He took a

deep breath. "There's something else that happens. Once in a while. Teacher gets run ragged his first year or so, kids drive him up the wall. Finally, decides he's got to do something or get out. Becomes so bloody miserable, hammers out the detentions, heaps on the sarcasm, finally gets some order, but he can't shake the memory of those first hellish years. Stays miserable because deep inside he's scared it's all going to fall apart. Kids are quiet in his classes, but they hate his guts. Could care less about what he wants to teach them." Schwitzer paused, two fingers on his right hand tapping out a beat on his desk. He looked down, dropped his hand into his lap. "What I'm trying to say is we want you to be a good teacher."

"I appreciate that," said Brad. "Thanks. I'll do my best." He sounded like a kid himself, but hell, that was what he wanted too.

"Something else: this is an academic school, you'd be surprised how many of our students go on to university. Yeah, a lot of good kids in this school – and some jerks, too." Schwitzer grinned. "Matter of fact, we usually manage to distribute at least one jerk to every class. But no matter what they're like, miserable, bitchy, smart-asses, you've got to find some way to like them – every one of them."

He paused, as if wondering whether to continue. Brad thought he looked almost embarrassed. "One other thing: Mr. Workman likes to keep an eye on new teachers. You don't want to cross him."

In the staffroom now, almost two weeks of teaching under his belt, the argument about Parker Stone finished, Brad looked down at Sue Burton skimming through her journal, a trace of a smile playing over her lips. He liked her. She was, as usual, stylishly dressed, wearing a cotton shift today, rich with autumn colours that made him think of Indian summer. She had a plain face, a shade too round perhaps, but when she smiled, he was certain *plain* would be the last word anyone would use to describe her. He took the chair beside her.

"You have Parker Stone last year?" he asked. When she nodded, he said, "Anything I should know about him?"

"You've got him now, have you, Brad?" He liked the sound of his name on her lips.

"Uh-huh. I don't really know him though." Yeah, he never had a clue what the kid was thinking.

She closed the journal, laid it on the coffee table. "You having problems with him?"

"No, not exactly." With Parker – sure, and the rest of them too, but there was no way he was admitting that to anyone. "I think maybe he's the one with the problem."

"He's in my form room this year, but I've only taught him once – grade eleven, second semester. He's a pretty good kid. And very creative. Didn't seem especially troubled." She paused, as if considering something else. "Lonely, maybe. He's an only child. Mother died when he was small. Cancer. Father's usually working – that could be a problem. Like Phil said, he's a doctor. Orthopedic surgeon."

"Well, ooh la la." It was Phil Simpson butting into their conversation. What was bugging his ass, Brad wondered.

"That doesn't make him spoiled, Phil. He didn't jerk around. Worked hard, as a matter of fact, made the honour roll. First semester, he didn't do quite so well. I think he had a crush on Angela Maddox. Couldn't keep his mind on business." Brad nodded. That was maybe still the problem.

When Sue looked up, he followed her eyes to the table

where Dutch Van Hoek was playing solitaire. "Then, too, he was pretty busy with other things. I think he was mainly interested in football."

Dutch Van Hoek slapped another card on the table. "Well," he said, "we don't have to worry about that this fall, do we?" He stood up and strode from the room. Phil rolled his eyes.

"What was that all about?" Brad asked, but the bell rang and it was time for class. Sue shrugged and got up to stack her coffee cup with the others in the sink.

Three

B rad had spent three full days at school before classes began, trying to get himself organized and a few lesson plans prepared, though his stomach was jumping with nerves and he hardly knew what to prepare. He didn't see Mr. Workman, the principal, until the staff meeting the morning of opening day.

Workman was a tall, cadaverous man with stooped shoulders and sunken cheeks, who sighed as he slid into the chair behind the teacher's desk while the teachers sat in the student desks before him. Doesn't look threatening, Brad thought, but Herb Schwitzer had said not to cross him. Workman introduced the new teachers, ran over policies governing attendance and discipline, plus procedures for handling late students and keeping track of textbook rentals. Teachers were expected to turn in the money they collected by four-thirty every day. He directed them to the file folders with their names in the upper right corner. Dance duty and detention schedules were there. And everything else they needed to know. Seems efficient, Brad thought. There were sheets for people to sign up for noon duty (optional with extra pay) and for extra-curricular activities (no option there, and no pay). Vic Pendleton, the senior English teacher, had already advised him to volunteer as an intramural house adviser; he'd be so busy his first year, that would be enough for him to handle. Vic was portly and pushing sixty, a round ball of energy, who – despite his weight – actually looked a bit like William Shakespeare.

Brad noted that students were divided into four houses for intramural activities: Browning, Tennyson, Shelley and Keats. Kind of nice, he thought, working in a school where they honoured poets. Hope the kids appreciate it.

Workman announced that after the coffee break, the teachers would hold subject meetings and he assigned the rooms for each meeting.

"One other thing," he said, reading from a yellow page in his hand. "The detention room's running four nights a week this year. Tuesday to Friday." When his announcement raised a chorus of groans, he looked up. Smiling. "If you don't like staying Friday, imagine how the kids will hate it. The schedule's posted in the staffroom, as well as in your folder. Make a note of your turn and don't miss it." There was a sudden thrust of steel in his voice.

"Remember, Mr. Schwitzer is the only one who sends kids to the detention room. The rest of you look after your own problems." He dropped the yellow page into his folder. "If there are no questions at this point in time, we'll take our break now. Doughnuts in the staffroom."

Brad didn't see him again for a week. Then he was sitting in his room with a few minutes to go in the fifth and last period of the day, wondering why his students wasted so much time staring at the clock as it groped its way toward three-thirty and the final bell. They all had questions to answer. A few questions. Finish them now, they wouldn't have homework. He was watching the minute hand simultaneously click and jerk ahead when he heard static on the intercom. A late announcement coming.

"Are you in there, Mr. Cutler?" Hard, flat tones distorted by the cheap speaker, and then a chill on the back of his neck. Workman's voice, of course, but for a second it had sounded just like his father, when he was angry and struggling to control his temper.

"Right here."

"Good. I'll see you in my office at four o'clock." More static and the snap of the intercom being turned off. Followed by the bell and the hubbub of students making for the door.

Brad glanced at the clock on the wall, at his watch – it was right on time – then pulled his literature text from his briefcase. Maybe he could get something ready for tomorrow before he went up to the office. He turned to James Thurber's "Secret Life of Walter Mitty." Lucky kids, he thought, getting to read "Walter Mitty" for the first time. That was something they'd really like. He'd read it in different voices, emphasize the fun in it. Yeah, give it a good reading, then ask the right questions, get them to think a bit. Wasn't that his job? Easy as that, eh? Huh, as if anything with thirty-four kids was ever easy.

Wonder what Workman wants?

Better read the story over, make up some good questions. He closed his door and began reading aloud, trying voices. Make the real Walter Mitty kind of soft and wimpy, but in his dreams give him a deep voice, slow and cool. Mrs. Mitty would have to natter on, a high, quick voice with just a squeal of frustration now and then. He tried Mrs. Mitty, but it didn't sound right. It sounded, in fact, like the metallic voice of Mr. Workman on the intercom.

Write out some questions then.

There was a rubbery taste in his mouth. He looked at the tooth marks on his pencil, a drop of saliva clinging to the eraser, and laid it down. He wasn't in any kind of trouble, was he?

Then he was thinking of that wet August after grade ten, the crops late, some of them down from a hard rain, his father worried, agitated, saying this was the year he quit school and stayed on the farm – where his future was, and he hadn't been smart enough to keep his mouth shut and walk away. "Fat chance," he'd said. "I'm going back to school."

"The hell you are. You already know too much of that useless crap they want to teach you. I need you here. On the farm. Every day."

He felt his backbone stiffen, his voice rising. "I'm going back to school."

"Bullshit, you are! They'll turn you into some kind of fruitcake, reading poetry, all that shit."

"Fuck you. I'm going back to school." He was turning away even before he finished speaking, but not before he saw the colour drain from his father's face. How could he have sworn at his own father? He kept walking, expecting a blow to fall on his shoulders, but behind him there was only silence.

It was useless. He couldn't concentrate on Walter Mitty. He fingered his collar, felt a wrinkle chafing his neck beneath the tie. Most of the guys didn't bother wearing ties to school. No reason why he should keep it up. A short-sleeved casual shirt, tan cotton pants, they'd be plenty good enough.

He got up, walked up and down the aisles, checking to see if any of the desks had writing on them. He saw a heart with an arrow sticking through it. The arrow looked more like a penis, skinny but erect. Inside the heart someone had written, "Diana does it with class." Someone else had drawn a line through "with" and replaced it with "in." He pulled a kleenex from his pocket, spat on it and wiped the inscription off. He'd have to keep an eye on all the occupants of this desk, see if another drawing appeared, figure out what period it was done. The other desks were clean. He walked the aisles again, shoving desks a few inches this way or that until the rows were straight. Sat down at his own desk. Heard his thumb drumming on the cover of his text. What a waste of time. He'd go upstairs, maybe have a coke before he saw Workman.

With a frenzy of red hair, Kelly nodded him toward the inner office. He stepped through the half-open door and saw Workman slouched behind his desk, a copy of what looked like a manual open before him. Without raising his eyes, Workman waved Brad toward one of the three chairs in front of his desk. "Just checking through the Board's new policy manual," he said. "It still takes two years of effective teaching before they give a teacher tenure."

Was that meant for him? Brad wondered if he'd ever be good enough to earn tenure. That might get his old man off his case once and for all.

He sat down, his eyes drawn to the framed photograph on the wall behind the principal, a huge aerial view of the school and the houses around it, captured apparently shortly after sunrise, the east side of the school ablaze with light, dark shadows stretching to the west. Dark and ominous, he thought. In front of the school, the grass shone with dew.

"It looks almost pristine," said Workman. "Looking at it, you'd never guess all the life that's contained within these halls."

He was studying Brad now, his eyes dark in the hollows of their sockets. "So, Brad," he said, "how would you say you're managing all that life in your own classroom?"

"Oh. Pretty well, I guess." No need to mention any problems.

Workman seemed to be grinning now, his lips twisted upwards at the corners, but his eyes were cold. "Fellows in the staffroom had a little joke about that basement room of yours. Called it the combat room. Chaos room would've been more like it. New teacher – couldn't handle kids. Didn't last eight months before we had to bring back a superannuate to finish up the year." Workman paused. No sign of a grin now. "We'll expect more from you. A lot more."

"Of course." What was he supposed to say? "Herb – Mr. Schwitzer said to clamp down at first. Let them know who's boss right away." Workman was staring at him, his elbows on his desk, his fingers clasped together, his chin resting on his thumbs. "And," said Brad, "that's what I'm trying to do."

"Yes. Fair enough." When Workman spoke, his mouth opened above the knuckles of his fingers, but his chin never lost contact with his thumbs. "Teachers are expected to control their students, but the school as a whole is my responsibility. I like to keep an eye on everyone, see how they're doing. Or, rather, an ear. I can put the intercom on reception mode and get a fair idea of what's going on in any room."

Sneaky bugger, Brad thought, he's been listening to me. My God, what's he heard? Me yelling at Bert Peale or Parker Stone? Trying to get Angela Maddox to talk?

"We had one teacher used to stroll into his room ten minutes late after the long break. No need to mention names. There'd be quite an uproar until he got there. A lot of horsing around. Then you'd hear a voice saying, 'Here he comes,' and things got real quiet right away. He'd come in and start off his lesson just as if he wasn't ten minutes late."

I've yelled at others too, Brad thought, not just Bert and Parker. What's he going to think?

"Well, it was time for a change," said Workman. There was a hint of a smile on his lips, though Brad wasn't sure at first if that's what it was. The man looked like a corpse that an undertaker had been trying to groom – but unsuccessfully. "The next time he was late, I had a few words with his class over the intercom. 'You be quiet now,' I said. 'Here he comes.' You could almost see the stunned looks on their faces – it sure was quiet when he walked in. I could hear his footsteps. Just as he was going to put the class to work, I let him have it. 'Thirteen minutes late, Mr. Winslow.'"

Bruce Winslow, thought Brad, science teacher, the guy who looks like he sleeps in his clothes.

"I told him why didn't he come on down to the office right now. There was this little grunt from him – surprise, I suppose, then the sound of his footsteps and the door closing. And a big burst of laughter from his class." Workman was definitely smiling now. "He hasn't been late since."

"Yes. Well," said Brad, "I don't think I've been late for class." Workman continued staring at him. "Not more than a minute or so."

"Good for you. That's been my impression too."

What a crappy way to run a school, Brad thought, and he likes showing up his staff.

Workman lowered his hands from beneath his chin, his thumbs propped against the side of the desk, all eight fingers spread on its surface. "This is an academic school," he said. "We get students from the best families in town, people of some influence. Doctors, dentists, lawyers. People who know how to exert pressure on the school board. Their kids are not the troublemakers."

Oh, and Bert Peale wasn't a troublemaker? Brad kept his mouth shut.

"If you have any discipline problems, if you need to make a point with your class, you pick someone whose parents aren't going to show up here in the office the first thing next morning. Go easy on the doctors' kids." With his hands propped on his desk, Workman levered himself from his chair. "No need to offend the doctors, eh? You do a good job for us, we'll bring you back next year. Maybe give you a chance at tenure."

Brad realized that he was still sitting, almost leapt from his chair.

"Nice talking to you," Workman said. "We'll have another little chat in a month or so."

In class the next morning, he twice caught himself looking at the intercom. They were taking up questions on *Who Has Seen the Wind,* and he could picture Workman in the office, leaning smugly against the intercom console, waiting for him to do something wrong. He should probably skip Bert Peale, but of course that's what Bert would want.

"Number one, Bert. What shows Brian's innocence with

regard to his understanding of God?"

"That's easy." Bert snorted. "He thinks God has to go to the bathroom."

"Good. Anything else?"

Bert shook his head and sneered.

Behind him sat Angela Maddox, a slim and pretty girl except for her eyes, grey circles around them, the pupils dark and dull as charcoal. Might as well try her too.

"Angela?"

She raised her eyes, but she was looking past him, not at him. She sat motionless a few seconds before she spoke, "I had the same as Bert."

He could never get anything out of her. "What about you, Parker?"

"The same as Bert too."

"What's going on – you trading homework back and forth?" He felt his voice rising, glanced again at the intercom.

"Don't go accusing me," said Bert. "You got no business."

"Me neither," said Parker.

He would have sworn Angela was staring at the intercom, but her eyes were dead. He wondered if she were on drugs.

Sue Burton was one of the first teachers Brad had met when he came to Lawrence Collegiate. He'd been nervous about his new job and he guessed it showed.

"You'll like it here," she said. "It's an academic school. A lot of good kids."

Later that first week, he was sitting in the workroom preparing lessons at noon when she came in to use the copier. Phil Simpson was busy at the computer in the corner.

When Brad glanced up from his daybook, he noticed she was wearing a blue denim jumper. On her, it looked like a gown. She said, "You've got a few days under your belt. How's it going?"

"Okay, I guess. Don't exactly feel relaxed yet, though."

"It'll come." She smiled at him. Sure she was older than he was, but maybe only four years, and when she smiled it didn't seem to matter much. "You hang in there, you're going to love this job."

He felt like talking, felt like talking to her. "When I was hired, I wondered about the name. Lawrence Collegiate. Hoped it might be named for Margaret Laurence. Then I noticed the spelling."

"There are probably schools named for her. Should be. In Manitoba, maybe." She laid her master copy on the table and took a chair across from Brad. "Afraid this one was built long before she was born."

"I figured as much."

"Still, it's a famous writer. You wouldn't think they'd name a school for him. I hear there was a real storm of controversy when *Lady Chatterley's Lover* came out in this country. Must've intrigued the school board."

"D. H. Lawrence? You're kidding."

"Well, yes," she said, "I am." There was that smile again. It was as if he could feel the room begin to tilt. "Lawrence of Arabia. At least he was a writer."

"And a great soldier. The perfect W.A.S.P." Phil Simpson had turned toward them from the keyboard, the printer beside him cranking out a page of type.

"What?" Brad asked.

"When they built the school in 1910, it was just the Moose Jaw Collegiate. Needed a new name when other high schools came along. Back then this was a very English town. Chapters of the I.O.D.E. everywhere you looked."

"I.O.D.E.?"

"Uh-huh. Imperial Order Daughters of the Empire. T. E. Lawrence seemed the perfect hero to the Brits who ran the town."

"A little history lesson, eh?" said Brad.

"Hey, I'm a history teacher." Phil grinned at him, then cast a sardonic look at Sue. "If they'd known Lawrence a little better, they might not have picked him." He turned away, lifted his sheet from the printer and left the room.

Brad was puzzled, but Sue only shrugged. He said, "You must be an English teacher too."

"History. And the occasional grade ten English when my timetable doesn't work out."

"Been here long?"

"My fifth year," she said. "The first year was the tough one."

"I've noticed. When's it going to get better?"

"Let's see. October of my second year I realized I wasn't working all the time. It was a bit of shock."

"Something to look forward to," said Brad. "Right now, I feel like I'm always running full out just to stay about two minutes ahead of my students."

"You must be ahead of them." She grinned. "I heard some grade eleven girls talking in the hall. They seemed to like the view. Nice buns, they said."

Maybe Shawna Carter, she was always hanging around.

He wondered if he were beginning to blush. At least Phil wasn't around to see him. "You're putting me on."

"No, no. They were right. I checked myself. Real nice."

He knew for sure he was blushing now. Pictured the scar vivid and white as his jaw flushed around it. "I'll remember that the next time I'm writing on the board."

"You're doing a good job, Brad." Her face was serious now. "They like the way you read to them."

"You're making this up?"

"No. They talk to me. When you read, things come alive."

"Good literature," he said, "doesn't need me to make it live." He shook his head. My God, but he sounded pompous.

"True – for good readers." Even when she was serious, without a hint of that killer smile, there was something about her face that lit the room. "Some of them need all the help we can give them."

Brad nodded his head, pleased despite himself. It was a sign that he might be in the right profession after all. He was soon telling her how he'd come to be a teacher.

"It's kind of weird, you know, my mom taught for years, and I never once thought about taking education. But then I had this great English teacher in high school, Mr. Roy. He used to slip me books after school, *My Name Is Aram, Stop-Time, The Travels of Jamie McPheeters* – I loved that one – it was like meeting Huck Finn all over again. He told us once if you really want to know something, you've got to be ready to teach it. Then he gave us this poetry assignment, ten poems we might have to teach. He'd pick the kids to do it. No advance warning either. I was petrified."

"That bad, eh?" said Sue.

"Absolutely petrified."

He had huddled in his seat, his head ducked behind the student in front of him, praying that others would be chosen, relieved when they were. Then Mr. Roy had said, "Only one left. 'Stopping by Woods.' Any volunteers?"

And his hand had gone up.

Before he could kick his brain into action and yank his hand down, Mr. Roy had seen it and called him up. As he slid out of his seat, he could feel a little wobble in his knees, but he made it to the front of the room with the copy of the poem, laid it on the lectern, held it there with uneasy hands, glad to have something to hang on to.

He raised his eyes from the poem. His classmates were spread before him, watching him, curious and attentive, but strangely unfamiliar. He'd never seen them from this angle before.

He took a deep breath, hoping to fill the hollow left where his insides had collapsed. When he began to read, he heard someone else's voice coming from his mouth, but it wasn't high and squeaky, it was gruff, it was all right. By the time he reached the poem's last line, the repeated line, "And miles to go before I sleep," his voice was as soft and solemn as a funeral eulogy.

Now what? The nine others who'd been called on to teach a poem had kept their eyes glued to the lectern, had told the class what they thought the poem meant, had finished with a note on its theme, had rushed back to their seats.

Brad looked again at his classmates. What the heck, he knew them all, they were his friends.

"If we assume the narrator is Robert Frost, why would you think he might stop his horse like this out in the middle of nowhere?"

Len Masonchuck grinned at him, then raised his hand and said, "He's having a look around him. The woods are lovely, eh?"

Brad looked at Wanda Gavronski.

"He's taking a break," she said, "having a little peace and

quiet before he does whatever he's got to do."

"Is that it?" asked Brad. "Or is there more to it?"

And then his best friend, Jack Pritchard, who used to raft with him on the South Saskatchewan River, Jack, who never said anything in school except "Do we got to take this down?", good old Jack raised his hand and said, "There's more going on. It's the darkest evening of the year. I'd lay money, the guy is real depressed."

At the end of class, Mr. Roy had drawn him aside. "Good job on the Frost poem, Brad." He paused then, as if deliberating about whether to say more. "You know, I always thought you might make a good teacher, but to tell the truth, I think you may already be one."

"Strange," said Brad to Sue Burton, "I actually volunteered to teach the poem, and, well...somehow I got through it okay. You know, when I went home from school that day, I already knew what I wanted to do with my life." He realized he might be saying too much and decided to shut up.

When the bell went at 3:30, Brad stayed at his homeroom desk, hoping to make a dent in the thirty-four descriptive paragraphs his grade tens were just finishing. Give them something he was going to mark and at least it kept them quiet. Except, of course, then he had to mark them. He was well into it before all the students had dropped their papers on his desk and hustled out. Then he felt someone looking at him. He raised his eyes from a sentence weighted down by adjectives. Willie Thornton was still sitting at the back of the room, his chin resting in his hands, staring straight at him.

"What is it, Willie?"

"I was wondering," said Willie.

"Yes?"

"My paragraph's not so hot. Could I maybe take it home?"

"Sorry, Willie. It's an in-class assignment. To show what you can do working against time. I'm going to read them all, make suggestions, then you can work on it at home. Make all the revisions you want."

Willie sat with his chin still cradled in his hands.

"Don't worry, Willie. I know it's just a first draft. But you're a writer, this will be good already."

Willie grinned, got up from his desk, and shuffled toward the door. Brad waited till he was almost there.

"Willie?"

"Yes, Mr. C."

"You play football?"

"No. Volleyball." Willie grinned. "Suits my frame better." He was long and lean, all bones and gawky angles.

"Parker Stone playing volleyball this year?"

"No. He's football."

"Any good?"

"I don't see that many games; we play a lot of tournaments on Saturdays. I saw a couple last year, though, and the opener this fall. I'd say he's pretty good."

"Running back?"

"Oh, no. Parker's a linebacker. The guy loves to hit."

Brad had another thought. "What about Bert Peale?"

"Yeah, he plays. Not much for school activities though. It's all he does." Willie glanced toward the door.

"Thanks, Willie. I suppose you've got a practice now yourself."

"Yeah, right away."

"Spike one for me."

"Uh-huh." Willie gave him a tired look, and he realized he wasn't being cool.

Brad sat for a moment, staring through the empty doorway. Then he picked up another sheet of foolscap. Small writing, the letters crammed together, the capitals not even half a line tall. He grimaced and bent his head to read. As he worked, he circled errors and omissions with his green pen, scrawled a few suggestions for improvement in the margin. The other teachers always used red for marking. Green ink, he hoped, would make it seem like the advice of an editor, not the criticism of a teacher. He tried for at least one positive statement on each paper. Sometimes it wasn't easy. They were short paragraphs; if he stuck to it, he might finish in one sitting.

Three hours later, he was done. He piled the papers in a file folder, locked it in his filing cabinet. Six-forty. Be dark soon, too late for a walk down by the river. Wait a minute, football practice would be over. He'd have a coke before he went home, maybe catch Dutch Van Hoek or one of the other coaches in the staffroom.

When he walked past the staff mailboxes, he saw that the room was empty. Maybe he'd skip the coke. Then he heard the toilet flush in the men's room, and turned toward the Coke machine. He dropped four quarters into the slot, heard gears shift, the Coke can thunking into the tray below. There were footsteps behind him.

"You got an extra quarter?" It was Dutch all right.

He dug into his pants pocket. "Here you go."

When Dutch had his coke, they sat across the table from one another. Dutch pulled off his Lions cap, a smudge of grime and sweat colouring his forehead.

"You look as though you've been working hard."

"Damn rights." Dutch took a long pull from his coke.

"Not as hard as the kids, though. We're not gonna lose the final this year because we get worn down in the fourth quarter." He raised the coke, tipping his head back for a longer drink, his Adam's apple rising and falling on his thin neck.

"Another good team, eh?"

"You bet. We're going all the way."

"Parker Stone one of the good ones?"

"Shit!" He stopped with the coke halfway between his lips and the table, glared at Brad, raised the coke and drained it. "Parker Stone." He lifted the empty coke can to eye level, glaring at it now instead of at Brad, slowly crushed it in his hand and pegged it past the recycle box into the garbage. It clanked against the metal can. "Lemme tell you about Parker Stone. He comes out in grade nine, just a little guy then, but he can tackle. Rides the bench at first, but before long we're getting him into the game. Grade ten, grade eleven we've got him starting, backing up the line. Kid's good as anybody we've had the last six, seven years. This fall he plays the opener, must've made a dozen tackles. Then he quits. Christ, how're we supposed to build a program that way? Invest three years in a kid and just when it's paying off he lets the program down." Dutch stood up. "I got to get a shower."

"You know why he quit?"

"Sure. His old man's a fucking doctor."

The next day, during the long break between periods two and three, just as Herb Schwitzer announced a short staff meeting for three-thirty, Brad took a seat in the corner of the staffroom beside Sue Burton. She was someone not afraid to say exactly what she thought, nor to listen either. He liked talking with her, guessed she was his favorite person on staff.

"You know," he said, "I spent most of last week looking over my shoulder to see if Mr. Workman was creeping up behind me."

"He'd be pleased," she said, smiling. Her smile, he thought, would have lit all three floors of the old building. "You probably spent an inordinate amount of time staring at the intercom on your wall too."

"You've got that right."

"Some days you can't help thinking it's a huge ear hanging there on the wall. An ear that sometimes speaks." She smiled that smile again.

Except for the smile, she looked rather ordinary, light brown hair no more special than his own – shit-brindle brown, he'd heard her describe it once to Phil Simpson. He liked that attitude. Maybe she was older than he was, but did it really matter? Besides, he could be wrong; she might be only two or three years older.

"Actually," she added, "I don't think he spends a lot of time at the intercom. He probably knows Herb doesn't approve." She laid her index finger on his wrist, tapped it once, stirring a shiver in his arm. "Eventually, you learn to forget about the fact that he may be listening. You have to teach the way you want to teach."

"Yeah, I think I'm figuring that out. There's one thing, though. What is it with Workman and doctors?"

Her finger still lay on his wrist, warmth spreading over his arm. She raised her hand, replaced it in her lap. Her voice was low. "He likes things to run smoothly. No bumps in the road, nothing to disrupt his days. You may have noticed he's not the most secure of individuals."

"Maybe I'm catching on," said Brad. "His inner office, it's a good place to hide. He's afraid of doctors?"

"Doctors, lawyers, dentists. He thinks they're the ones the school board listens to, and he doesn't like confrontations with the board. Two years ago there was a bad one. He took the whole board on, told them they weren't teachers, they didn't know what was best. Then the director sided with the board. It was a nasty scene. Now he expects you to let things ride with certain kids."

"Which explains why Bert Peale is such a pr – jerk." Better watch his mouth.

Sue laughed and said, "Exactly. He knows he can get away with things. What a lesson, eh?"

"What about Parker Stone? He doesn't seem to push it."

"No," she said, "he wouldn't."

"I was talking to Dutch last night. He said Parker quit the football team."

"Dutch won't be happy."

"He sounded steamed, all right. When I asked why Parker quit, all he said was his old man's an effing doctor."

"I don't know," she said. "Austen seems reasonable." He realized that she was suddenly blushing. "At parent-teacher interviews. I've talked to him. Dr. Stone. He supports the school – and Parker too." She stood up. "The bell's going to ring. I've got a projector to set up." She took two quick steps away from him, but turned back. "Ask Herb. He usually knows what's going on."

He wandered up to Herb Schwitzer's office at quarter after five that afternoon. One thing about Herb, he was a workhorse. You could count on him to be around long after most teachers had cleared out for the day. Brad found him at his desk, marking what looked like a set of algebra papers.

Herb looked up when he tapped on the open door.

"Grade nine algebra," Herb said. "With the cutbacks, I'm doing a class each semester." He grinned. "Marking's a snap compared to English."

"The math guys are pretty happy. You don't suppose Mr. Workman would like to pick up one of my English classes?"

"Not a chance. You in here to dream, or you got a problem you want to talk about?"

"Parker Stone. Something's going on with him. Dutch said he quit the football team. Blamed it on his father – the effing doctor. Which isn't quite a direct quote."

"I get the picture. Dutch's got his usual case of tunnel vision. Sometimes thinks the main purpose of this institution is to provide a home for his bloody football team. Got to support the program, you know."

"Parker get tired of Dutch or something?"

"Nope. Kid liked Dutch – they all do – and he loved football." Herb sighed. "Might as well tell you. Kid had some girl problems last year. Got dumped, as a matter of fact. After that, football was the thing that kept him going. When you're mad about something, you don't mind the chance to hit people."

"Yeah, I suppose so." Brad hurried on. "You heard anything about what happened this year?"

"Oh, yeah. He quit all right. Not his own idea. Old man made him quit. Worried about his hands."

"What?"

"Doesn't want him getting tromped on, fingers getting broken. Figures the boy is going to be a surgeon some day. Just like himself. Guess the kid is acting out. Surgery, you know, not a big thing in the life of your average high school football player."

"Parker goes along with this?"

"Dr. Stone's a fine man, but he likes things his own way. Yeah, likes them the way he likes them."

"I haven't met him yet."

"Gives you something to look forward to at parent-teacher interviews."

"At least I know where Parker's coming from, why he's been so moody." He wondered if there was more than that, the way he always looked at Angela Maddox. Was she the one who'd dumped him? Had to be.

Herb Schwitzer gazed steadily at him before he continued. "Kid's got some things to work out. You can't do it for him, Brad."

"Yeah, but it helps to know what's eating him."

"Helps to know when to cut your losses too." Herb's eyes were on him, his gaze solemn, heavy. Then the weight seemed to shift. "Remember Kenny Lowe, eh?"

Four

He should never have told Herb about Kenny Lowe.

The trouble had started early in September, with his grade tens, the class that came just before the lunch hour.

Maybe he would've managed it better if he hadn't already run into problems that morning. He'd asked Angela Maddox about Brian's relationship with R.W. God, B.V.D., and she'd looked up at him as if he were some kind of gnat buzzing around her head. "I don't know," she said. He looked at her a long time, her eyes dark and sombre, turned away from him. He was sure there was a deep current of feeling within her, but it was underground, out of sight, where he could never touch it.

Finally, he went on to the next student, asking Parker Stone where the B.V.D. might've come from.

"I don't know," said Parker.

He asked Della Neudorf then, got only a shake of her head.

Before the period was over, he tried again with Angela: "What about Mr. Hislop? Why's he thinking about resigning as minister of the church?"

"I don't know," she said. "Doesn't matter anyway."

"Sure, it matters. It matters to Hislop."

"Not to me," she said, her voice without a trace of emotion.

"Well, Parker, what are Hislop's reasons?"

"I don't know," Parker said. "Doesn't matter anyway."

This had happened a lot, he suddenly realized, the two of them saying almost the same thing.

"What's with you two?" he blurted. "A pair of bloody Bobbsey twins."

Parker had looked surprised, embarrassed too, perhaps. There'd been no change of expression on Angela's face, no expression at all, in fact. What was wrong here? How was he ever going to get through to her?

Now he was with his grade tens, still feeling uneasy, on edge. Somewhere along the way, Herb had warned him that a lot of his problems would come from the grade tens who were feeling confident after surviving their first year of high school. Grade twelve was still a long way off. They were ready to push the boundaries now, ready to test him every way they could, but, hell, they'd been easier to handle than his grade twelves.

The grade tens had been reading "The Tiger's Heart," a story about a lone man who'd gone into the jungle with a single-shot rifle to track a tiger that had been attacking village livestock, and he'd given them some questions for their notebook, questions to get them thinking about courage and character. Most of the students were busily writing in their notebooks, but not Kenny Lowe. At the back of the room, Brad could see him with his head bent as if it were weighted down by the huge metal stud in his nose. No, he wasn't working; he was studying his ruler which was balanced on the edge of his desk. Above it, he raised a Pink Pearl eraser, held it perhaps a foot above the ruler, sighted through the opening between the thumb and forefinger that held the eraser and let it drop. It hit the end of the ruler which leapt into the air, then clattered to the floor.

"Kenny," he said, "you've got some questions to answer. Get to work."

Kenny opened his text and ducked behind it. A few heads were raised around him, students watching him till they were assured he was back at work. In a minute Kenny leaned from his desk, retrieving his ruler and eraser from the floor. Once more he set his ruler on the edge of his desk, sliding it out until it hung precariously over the side. Again he lifted his eraser above it, sighting once more through the coil of his thumb and index finger. Around him, heads were bobbing up again, students leaving their assignment to watch the action. A big grin spread across Kenny's face.

"Kenny!" Brad felt the heat in his voice. "Quit horsing around and get to work."

Kenny raised his head from where it was bent over the bombardier's sight of his coiled finger and thumb. He looked at Brad, locked eyes with him for an instant, then closed his eyes, and dropped the eraser, nailing the end of the ruler, flipping it from his desk. Before it clattered to the floor, the students around Kenny were whispering, giggling, their assignment forgotten. Brad knew it was time to think before he spoke, but he was roaring with anger and frustration.

"Kenny!" he shouted. "Stop being an asshole!"

Oh my God, he thought, *asshole,* I called him an asshole – and then the bell rang, but the students sat stunned and silent in their seats for perhaps ten seconds before they rose together and rushed from the room, Kenny in the midst of them, his head down so Brad had no chance to catch his eye or draw him aside.

Brad stared at the intercom, shuddering, turned to study the empty room, the five rows of desks slightly askew, a few crumpled balls of paper lying on the floor. He glanced at the chalkboard where he'd written the questions for tomorrow. That was it, then. They wouldn't matter now.

He opened his briefcase, dropped his books inside it, snapped the lock shut. Before he left the room, he paused at the door and took a final look at the room that had been his. The author photos that he'd affixed above the chalkboard looked down at him as if they wondered what he'd been doing there in the first place, someone like him, an interloper. He pulled the door shut and hurried up the stairs, looking straight ahead. A few students still lingering in the hall at the top of the stairs stepped aside as he came toward them. He could feel their eyes on him, sense the way they turned around to whisper as he passed.

He ducked into the staffroom. A flurry of red caught his eye as he pulled his coat from its hanger.

"You okay, Brad?" Kelly Irving.

"Sure."

He spun around, his hand dipping into his pocket for his keys. He hurried toward the outer door, students fading away before him, falling in together behind him, watching him, he knew, their voices low and excited. Were they pointing, he wondered. Did everybody know already?

He walked to the staff parking lot, slid behind the wheel of his car. His second-hand Taurus. There were payments still to make, student loan payments too, but he'd never make them now. He sat for a moment with his hands gripping the steering wheel, his eyes closed. He could feel a pulse beating somewhere deep in his head.

He'd really gone and done it now. Workman listening on the intercom, and even if he wasn't, he'd know all right, Kenny would be on his way home this very minute, complaining to his parents, telling them everything, they'd be phoning the board office, phoning the principal, demanding he be fired, get rid of the foul-mouthed teacher, this is no way to handle children, they deserve better than this. Fire him outright.

The Teachers' Federation, maybe they could help him. No, not a hope, not without tenure.

Drive, he thought. He started the car, put it in reverse, backed carefully in a tight half-circle, shifted gears and pulled into the crescent before the school. He could see a huddle of students on the sidewalk. They all seemed to be grinning as he passed.

He wasn't sure where he was going, but he knew there was no sense heading home to his basement suite for lunch. Anything he ate right now would be like tin foil in his stomach. He turned left on Main Street, drove straight up the hill and continued toward the overpass, swinging right, onto the Trans-Canada Highway.

Shit, he thought, he had to go and open his stupid mouth. A job he actually liked – well, some days anyway – something he was learning how to do, getting used to the kids, beginning to like them, some of them, and already it was over, he was finished before he'd hardly started. And what would he do now – the farm was gone, his father would say he'd had his bloody chance and blown it – would he go back to school next fall, try to get a job clerking for the winter, hook on with a construction gang in the spring?

He was heading east toward Regina, passing the old winery

that had gone into bankruptcy and was now used by the local packer as a deboning plant. Might as well throw his carcass in there too. Wasn't good for much else.

He floored the accelerator and let the car run. Down the long, sloping hill, over the bridge that crossed the stagnant creek, up the other hill and past the old motel, adultery heaven everybody called it, where sinners slipped out of town for a few sweaty hours of passion. Sinners. Yeah. There were all kinds of sinners, weren't there, eh?

He glanced at the speedometer, eased his foot from the gas pedal, kept driving. On his left, the land fell away toward the river, like the fields at home, sloping toward the ravine behind the barn and running down to the South Saskatchewan. Except, of course, it wasn't home any more. The day he'd left for his final year of university the old man had said he was pushing seventy now, there was nothing left to hang on for. He'd put the farm up for sale. Sold it in the spring. And now Brad's job was shot to hell, but there was no going home to the farm.

He thought of his raft then, anchored in quiet water by the ravine, where he used to play as a boy, sleeping on it some nights in the summer holidays, waking up with the birds all a-twitter in the last hour of darkness, watching daylight come, the sky a little paler than the bank above him, then greyness spreading everywhere, grey trees growing out of the shadows, grey ripples appearing in the massive dark river, threads of grey mist rising, and then at the top of the far bank the faintest band of light, and you knew the sun was almost up. Sometimes he wished it was the Mississippi and he was Huck Finn getting as far away from his Pap as he could go, fleeing downriver with a black man, running nights on that monstrous big river, the whole expanse of water to themselves, the only sign of life on shore the distant spark of light from a candle in a cabin on the edge of the woods somewhere. Sliding along beneath the stars, enchanted by the slow magic of the river – all of it gone now, yeah, and maybe only fiction in the first place. But, oh man, what fiction!

Highway flowing by, the steady hum of tires, pavement running on for miles, fields of stubble beside him, flatlands and empty sky stretching to the horizon. Except, in the northeast, the sky was white with smoke, huge clouds hanging over the stacks of the potash plant. Should've been an engineer. Work with chemicals, solutions, know how to extract active ingredients. Wouldn't matter what he said then.

He rolled down the car window, felt the autumn wind beat against him, his collar lifting, slapping at his neck. The wheel solid in his hands. Staring at the road running straight ahead. What the hell, eh, what the bloody hell.

He thought about his mother, how proud she'd been coming in to Saskatoon for his convocation last May, taking a fancy room at the Bessborough, proud that her son was going to be a teacher, but embarrassed too, telling him his father couldn't make it, he had to overhaul the hay baler before the farm equipment auction. And now he'd have to write her in Victoria, tell her what had happened. Give the old man a chance to gloat.

But that wasn't fair. The old man would be sick to think that he wanted to go back to the farm and now he couldn't do it. Maybe if they'd been able to talk, but his father was so old, already nearing fifty when he was born – at last an answer to his parents' prayers, their only child a boy. Oh, yeah, some answer. They'd named him Hiram Bradford, Hiram for his grandfather who'd died two months before he was born, Bradford for the family patriarch who'd home-steaded beside the South Saskatchewan, survived his first winter there in a cave he'd dug out of the river bank with nothing but a spade and an axe. Brad knew he had the wide shoulders and narrow hips of both men – he'd seen their pictures – but he wasn't like them in any other way. He remembered that homestead cave, low and dark and musty, a pile of loose dirt by the back wall where a section of the ceiling had collapsed, remembered playing in it as a child, his father telling him this was no playhouse, this was a part of history.

Yeah, a part of history that was gone from him forever.

He must have driven half an hour before he pulled into the left lane, slowed down for a crossroad that joined the two halves of the divided highway, and turned back toward town.

Workman could go to hell for all he cared, let him freeze his ear to that bloody intercom, but Schwitzer, he'd better tell Schwitzer.

When he pulled into the parking lot, the doors were crowded with students heading back to class. He ducked his head and pushed through them, hurrying into the office. There were three students waiting at the counter.

"Brad!" Kelly Irving again. She glanced quickly at the students. "Mr. Cutler, is everything all right?"

"Mr. Schwitzer in?"

"Yes. You better go right in."

When Schwitzer saw him, he waved him into a seat and pulled the door shut behind him. "What's the matter, Brad?"

Brad sat a moment, breathing deeply, wondering if he should just keep his mouth shut. Then blurted out his story.

He kept his head down, staring at Schwitzer's desk as he tried to explain what had happened. "And," he finished, "I called him an asshole."

He could hear ragged breathing filling the small office, his own, of course, but Schwitzer's too, he was sure. And the clock ticking on the wall. He looked up and found Schwitzer's grey eyes holding steady on him. Grey and calm.

"Brad," said Schwitzer, "we can't have you calling students assholes. True enough. Still, might not be as serious as you think. Could be nothing'll come of this. Mr. Workman might never hear of it. But if there's a problem, we'll deal with it. Meanwhile, maybe you should get over to the staffroom, have yourself a cold drink of water. Settle down a bit. Bell's going to go in a few minutes. We'll need you in your homeroom to take attendance."

Brad walked unsteadily from the office, past the desk where Kelly Irving sat watching every step he took. He could see that she was smiling at him, nodding her head – as if that would help.

Got to calm down, he thought and pushed through the office door into the hallway, shoving the door wide, almost hitting a kid who side-stepped away from the swinging door. There stood Kenny Lowe, a shocked look on his face.

"Oh," said Brad, "sorry."

"No problem."

"Not this." He wasn't making sense. "This too. But before – I'm sorry I called you an asshole."

Kenny stared at him, his mouth half open. It snapped shut. Opened again. "Oh, that's all right, sir. I guess I had it coming." Then he continued down the hall while Brad tried to comprehend the miracle that had just occurred.

In his furnished basement suite that night, poaching eggs in the skillet his mother had donated to the cause, he

found himself whistling. The tuneless whistle that he some-
times slipped into unawares when he was feeling good.
Kenny Lowe wasn't a bad sort, didn't hold a grudge.
Somehow he'd find a way yet to get the kid working.

He glanced down at the egg whites beginning to solidify
in the bubbling water, glanced around at his kitchen, a four-
burner stove, a new refrigerator, the huge Tom Thomson
print hanging over the kitchen table where he ate his meals,
sometimes losing himself for minutes at a time in the wilderness of Algonquin Park, white caps riding the multi-
coloured waves, one lone tree bending below scudding
clouds, dark hills in the distance. It was a good suite, he
thought, not a bad place to live.

Even his dad had liked it when his parents had come to
town for a visit before moving to the coast. The old man had
wandered around the suite, gazing at the half dozen Group
of Seven prints Brad had had dry-mounted and hung on all
the walls. He'd nodded his head in approval, before he
caught himself and said, "You shouldn't have to live in a hole
in the ground. A man ought to have a window where he can
look out on his own land."

It was like staring at the sunset. He was lying on his back,
blinking beneath the bright rays of red that shook and
shimmered above him. He could feel heat in his groin, a
trickle of sweat running toward the cavity of his belly button. Kelly Irving was seated on his thighs, her head bent forward, her mouth open, gasping. Suddenly she threw her
head back, a burst of electricity, red hair shaking sparks, the
sparks snapping off his bare chest, one detonation after
another, and there was Bert Peale rising from his desk, his

right hand thrust high into the air.

"Sit down," Brad said, but Bert Peale was standing on the seat of his desk now, his right hand sweeping toward them. Then Kelly was gone, vanished in an instant.

"Sit," said Brad. "Take your seat. Now."

"Maybe I don't feel like it." Bert stepped to the top of his desk, reached down and steadied Kenny Lowe, who was stepping up beside him.

Behind them, the other students were climbing onto their desks, leaning against one another, trying to get a better look. He could hear Bert Peale saying, "Just like I told you," could see Della Neudorf beginning to smirk, Kenny Lowe raising his arm to point. And there was Angela Maddox, her eyes, hollow and dead, looking through him, empty sockets, and around those gaping holes her face was just a skull. Beside her, Parker Stone, the flesh falling from his body, a finger of bone pointing right at Brad.

"Sit down! All of you!" But no one was sitting. They were jumping on their desks, all of them now bouncing together, soaring into the air as if each had a private trampoline.

"Please," he said, and he grabbed for Bert Peale, got him by the collar, the cotton bedspread tight in his fist. Breath hot in his throat, he lay coiled in bed, his chest rising and falling.

When his heart had stopped pounding, he lay back, taking a long, deep breath, holding it for a count of five, letting it slowly out, taking another, and another.

Lying there in the dark, he was back again with Mr. Sommerfeld, the first teacher to whom he'd been assigned by the College of Education. His first day in the class, Brad sat in the back of the room, observing procedures. Sommerfeld was tall and gangly, somewhat rumpled-looking, his hair grey and thick, jacket a dark tweed with round leather patches sewn on the elbows. He looked like a middle-aged professor, and within five minutes Brad could see that he didn't have a clue about how to handle kids.

Whenever Sommerfeld turned to write on the blackboard, spitballs filled the air behind him. When he turned around again to make a point, the students ducked their heads, pretending to scribble in their notebooks. Brad wondered if he should speak up and tell the teacher what was going on behind his back. He was an observer. Was he supposed to get involved? Then he noticed something else. The boy at the front of the row in which he sat was leaning out of his desk, his left hand loosely cupped and held before him. When the hand opened he saw that it contained a mirror. Brad looked at the mirror and saw small, squinty eyes, a straight nose with a large, red pimple at the corner of one nostril, a big smirk of a grin.

That was when he realized the boy was smirking at him. He could see the boy's eyes crossing, his tongue sticking out. The mirror wavered then, and the kid was cranked around in his seat, looking directly back at him, still grinning, the mirror flashing in his hand, casting a ray of sunlight into Brad's face. The little bugger. Damned if he was going to blink. He ought to walk up the aisle, give that kid a shake, grab the mirror out of his hand, hurl it into the garbage can. There was a murmur of sound, other kids noticing what the boy was up to, turning to grin, more spitballs flying. In the desk next to Brad's someone raised a ruler, held a spitball against it, pulled it back and launched the spitball toward the front of the room. It soared over Sommerfeld's shoulder, landing with a splat beside his hand which was poised above a sentence he was dissecting on the blackboard. Laughter erupted throughout the room.

Sommerfeld turned slowly around. The kids sat grinning

up at him, waiting to see what would happen. "You grade tens," he said, "you're worse than the grade eights I had last year. Any little thing and you forget what you should be doing. Now settle down and get back to work."

"Maybe we don't feel like it." It was the kid who'd fired the spitball at the front blackboard.

"Listen! You keep your mouth shut." Sommerfeld's face was crimson. Brad slid down in his seat, wishing he were somewhere else, anywhere else, even back on the farm with his father haranguing him in the machine shed. "I've had enough smart talk from this class." Sommerfeld was shouting now. "Enough crap. What I want is a little respect."

The room was suddenly quiet. Then one hand went up, its fingers closed around a mirror.

"Yeah?" Sommerfeld's voice was still loud and angry.

"We don't respect you, whatcha gonna do? You gonna cry?"

Brad could feel the sweat blooming in his armpits. He rolled over, staring at the clock radio beside the bed. Four-thirty. If he could get back to sleep, he could still catch another couple of hours. He flipped a cover off, squirmed around, trying to get comfortable.

It was weird the way it had happened, that damned smart-ass kid with his smart-ass question, but first he put up his hand.

He kicked away the covers, felt the cooler air flow across his limbs. He closed his eyes against the red glow of the clock radio dial. Think of something else, he thought. Think of Mr. Hadley.

The same kids, the spitballers, the smart-asses with their rulers, their mirrors, but you'd never know it. This was a different class and they were leaning forward in their desks, quiet, attentive. When Mr. Hadley asked a question, students were pumping their hands into the air, competing to answer. When the bell went, a few of them circled the teacher's desk, with more questions, more answers.

Brad waited until they were gone. He wasn't quite sure how to put it. He couldn't very well say that Mr. Sommerfeld had lost control of the class.

"You mind if I ask you something?"

"Shoot." Mr. Hadley was short and muscular, an air about him like you'd find on an athlete who looked forward to coming to bat in the bottom of the ninth when winning the game depended on him.

"These kids, I saw them – in another room. All they did was horse around. Couldn't've cared less what was going on. You had them paying attention. They looked as if they really wanted to learn something."

"Uh-huh."

"I can hardly believe it was the same class. How come they behave for you and...uh, in that other room...they just run wild?"

"I expect them to behave for me." He must have caught the look of disappointment on Brad's face because he stepped toward him, his right hand balled into a fist with which he gave Brad a quick tap on the chest. "I'm not kidding. In this business, you have to expect a lot if you want it to happen."

"But that little guy in the front row, he was just pure hell before. Big, ugly smirk on his face. He didn't look like the same kid."

"Tim, yeah, he likes to push the boundaries. But you get him started, he'll settle down and work." Mr. Hadley grinned suddenly. "Oh, what the hell. I might as well tell you.

Sometimes, it helps to get lucky. About the third day in here, he decides he's going to test me. Starts flapping with the smart mouth. I was sitting there behind the desk when he starts in. I've got kind of a short fuse, but maybe that's okay too. One of my education profs used to say, if your students make you angry, don't try to hide it, go ahead and let it out, kids will always understand honest feeling.

"I let it out all right. I was out of my chair, shouting at the little bugger, shaking my fist at him. Got right carried away. What I didn't notice at first was when I jumped up, the arm of the chair came off in my hand. I was waving it in his face. Must've looked like I was going to clobber him, smash that hunk of wood across his skull. Kid turned white as a sheet. Impressed the hell out of the whole class." He paused. "Something they need to know, you don't take any guff from anybody." Mr. Hadley looked suddenly embarrassed, shrugged his shoulders.

"The thing is, I kind of like Tim. Kid's got a good head on his shoulders, and most days he doesn't mind using it."

Four-thirty in the empty staffroom. Brad was at the corner table, typing his marks into the computer, wishing that Kenny Lowe had a better mark. Sure, he was short on self-control, at the mercy of his urges, with no attention span, but no grudges either. When it was interview time, he'd say something nice about the kid, let his parents know their son had a good heart. He heard someone at the coffee machine, sensed someone watching him.

He glanced up. That tangle of wild hair. Beneath it, green eyes staring at him, wide with sympathy.

"How you doing today?"

Brad ducked his head, typed another average. "Fine," he said, "just fine."

"The other day – you looked like a death in the family." He heard her walk toward him, pull a chair up next to the computer. He thought he caught a trace of perfume as she sat down beside him. Something foreign, maybe, something exotic. Paris, he thought, or Tangiers. She was so close he knew that if he leaned toward her he would touch her. "I was worried about you," she said. "You have a run-in with a kid?"

"Yeah, kind of. Got it worked out though. It's okay." He looked up from the computer screen. She was right there. Red splendour of hair. Deep green eyes that took him, held him so that he could hardly breathe.

"Your first year," she said, "it's a tough job." He felt her hand on his and almost flinched. "Come on," she said. "Let's go down to Shooters'. I'll buy you a beer."

Five

When they came through the door, after meeting in the parking lot, he was surprised by the high ceiling, large fans rotating slowly, black pipes and vents everywhere, hardly any smoke in the place. Then he noticed heads turning toward them, guys watching them walk toward a small table in the corner. They sure as heck weren't watching him. He pulled out a chair for her and slid in behind the table, his leg bumping hers, a heat wave against his shin. He pulled his leg away. He remembered his dream, Kelly riding his thighs, and hoped he wasn't blushing. The waiter was there almost as soon as they were seated, grinning down at her. When he brought their beer, Brad pulled out his wallet.

"No," she said, "it's on me." She paid the waiter and poured her beer into a glass, scooped up some of the foam with her index finger, licked the foam from her finger. Her lips as bright, as red as her hair. Yeah, he probably was blushing.

He took a quick pull from his bottle. "Hits the spot," he said. "Thanks, Miss Irving."

Her face fell. "Kelly, for Pete's sake. I'm not your maiden aunt."

"Sure. Sorry." He was such a dork. Set him down beside a pretty girl and he went all to hell. "Tastes good." Had he said that already? "New job, I'm usually so busy marking, getting lessons ready, I don't have much time for this."

"Uh-huh." She raised her glass to her lips, took a drink, her eyes steady on him all the time. Luminous green eyes.

"Busting my ass, you know, just to stay one day ahead of the kids." Yeah, if Workman knew how true that was, the man would send him packing. "You can't imagine how many things I have to teach we never even took in university." He knew he was starting to babble. "It's a struggle. Learning how to handle them. The thing is – I want to be good at it." He realized he was rubbing the scar on his chin and dropped his hand to his bottle. Bad enough having a big jaw without that damned scar calling attention to it. He continued lamely, "And I still don't feel relaxed in front of a class."

"Not relaxed," was all she said.

"Not yet, anyway. It's bound to come." He could feel the tension in his right leg, nerves taut as guitar strings. If her leg was close to his, she'd feel it thrumming. "Nice to just sit and have a beer."

"Brad," she said. "I want to tell you something." She wasn't looking at him now, but at her beer. She gave her head a little shake, hair shimmering around her face. He noticed her front teeth digging into her lower lip. Suddenly he understood that she was almost as ill at ease as he.

"I see you in the staffroom, in the halls," she said. "You never seem to relax. Always in too much of a hurry. I know what it's like, a new job and being nervous. But let me tell you something."

When she hesitated, clearing a circle with her thumb on the moist surface of the beer glass, he said, "Sure. Go ahead."

She pushed her glass away and leaned toward him. "I overheard Herb talking to Doug the other day. Doug Gunnars. Herb said you were working hard. Too hard. Said you were going to be a good one."

"Oh. That's good news. Hope he tells Mr. Workman."

"If," she said. "If you didn't drive yourself crazy trying to get everything exactly right the first year." Her face was only inches away from his. He could feel the heat radiating from it. "I know you're dedicated, Brad; a person only has to look at you to see that. But he's got a point. It's your first year, you can't do it all, can't get through to every kid." She was so intent on making him understand, her nose was almost touching his. He could smell the beer on her breath as she spoke. "Brad," she said, "you can't be the perfect teacher right away."

He laughed, but without humour. "Perfect? Hell!" He might as well tell her. What else could he do? "The reason I'm working my ass off is just trying to keep up with these kids. To keep up with them and keep them busy. So they don't figure out how little I know and start running wild. Honest to God, I'm just trying to survive." There, he'd said it. It was the truth all right, and now that it was out, what was she going to think?

She reached over and took his hand, tugging it away from his beer bottle. He could feel the fire on his fingers. Man, she wasn't at all like the girl he'd hung around with at Lake Louise that winter. Linda was always saying something crazy, or going on about his eyes; come on, he'd said once, he had two like everybody else; not that blue, she said, not dark as an underground river.

"It's okay, Brad. I think you're doing a better job than you can guess. I hear kids in the office. When there's no teacher around. They're not afraid to say what they think. They're never bad-mouthing you." She squeezed his hand, then laid it on the table. "You're trying hard, I know. Just don't try too hard. First year of teaching, the main thing you have to do is just survive."

She gazed at him, her look unwavering, her eyes warm with sincerity, with caring. She lifted her glass of beer and emptied it.

"I buy you one?" he asked. Her knee was touching his again, heat spreading up his thigh. He held his leg steady.

"No thanks," she said. "I just wanted to talk a minute, try to level with you." She chuckled, a low, warm sound, almost a growl in her throat. "You probably thought I brought you here with seduction on my mind."

"Oh, no. Not at all." He sounded like such a cluck. "You see," he said, "that was my plan."

He felt her hand under the table, squeezing him just above the knee.

"Next time," she said, "we'll save that for next time."

He asked about her the next day in the staffroom. "What you see is what you get," said Sue Burton.

"That's right," said Phil Simpson. "All that red hair, those magnificent bazooms, everything is real."

"As if you'd know," said Sue. She rolled her eyes for Brad to see. "Kelly's okay. Comes on a little strong, maybe. Figures it's her personal duty to make the world a better place."

"Not a phony bone in her body," said Phil.

"You know a lot about her bones, do you, Phil?" But she

was looking at Brad. "Why the sudden interest in Kelly?"

He could feel heat beneath his collar, knew that his neck would soon begin to shine. "Had a beer with her after work is all. Just wanted to get a handle on her."

"Love handles maybe, eh?" said Phil.

"Oh," said Brad, "I didn't mean that."

"Stuff it, Simpson," said Sue. "Don't get too serious there, Brad. I think she's got a guy at the air base."

"He moved away," said Phil. "Transferred out to Cold Lake."

Well, thought Brad, how about that? Uh-huh, mustn't let them see him smiling.

B rad was nervous about parent-teacher interviews. This was the time, Maurie Pack had told him, when the shit usually hit the fan. Today classes were cancelled for the afternoon. Interviews would run from 1:30 to 4:30 and again from 7:00 to 9:00 at night.

There was a nervous energy in the staffroom at lunch time, the noon break fifteen minutes longer, the staff bantering, a game of hearts going at the center table. Soon the older ones were talking about Rutledge.

"Who's Rutledge?" Brad asked.

"Used to teach here," said Sue. "An eccentric character, the guys are always going on about him."

"Eccentric is right. Rutledge hated interviews," said Bruce Winslow, who looked cluttered, thrown together at the last moment, reminding Brad somehow of an ashtray full of butts. "Absolutely hated them."

Me too, thought Brad. He didn't have a clue who was

going to show, or what would be bugging them.

"Especially in the fall," said Bruce. "All those half classes in art, there were so many kids, he wouldn't know all their names yet. This one fall he's talking to Billy Temple's father."

Phil Simpson looked up from the sandwich he was chewing. "You sure it wasn't Billy Webster's father?" They both laughed.

"One of them, anyway. Rutledge tells him he's sorry about the kid. Going to drop him out of art class. Just doesn't have a knack for drawing – or an interest either. That, and he's got a dirty mouth. Ought to wash it out with soap, then give him a good rinse with Javex. The kid's old man gets red in the face, looks like he's going to rupture himself. 'My son,' he says, 'my son never swears.' 'You don't think so, eh?' says Rutledge. 'I had to send him down to the office for swearing at a girl in class. Called her a effing bitch.' The guy went white as a ghost. Man, he was starting to shake. Almost had a stroke before Rutledge finally figures out he's talking about the wrong Billy. Rutledge said he never felt good about interviews after that."

"I can see his point," said Brad.

"Gunnars was the guidance counsellor back then too," said Vic Pendleton. Take away some of Vic's hair and about forty pounds, give him a goatee, he'd look exactly like Shakespeare. Which seemed appropriate since Vic was the senior English teacher, not a bad guy. "Gunnars used to hand out these green forms on any kids having problems. You were supposed to write some comments, behaviour in class, attitude – that kind of thing. He'd sit there inside the gym door. If any of those parents showed, he'd haul them over, go through the comments on the green forms. Only problem was he asked Rutledge to fill out a form on Jeff Marks."

Phil Simpson stopped chewing on his cheese and lettuce sandwich and let out a whistle. "What a kid. About as much self-control as a tomcat. Attention span this long." He held up his right hand, his thumb and index finger jammed together.

"Rutledge gave him the form all right," said Vic, "but Gunnars had so many forms coming in, he didn't read them all. Just put them in alphabetical order, so he could find the ones he needed. Mrs. Marks shows up, she's got Jeff with her. They sit down and Gunnars starts fishing out the forms." Vic started to laugh, his eyes crinkled almost shut, and half the staffroom was laughing with him. "Rutledge didn't bother commenting on the kid's behaviour or his attitude. He went straight to the bottom of the page where it said *Recommendation*. 'The kid should be neutered,' he wrote, 'to prevent propagation of the species.'"

"Gunnars almost had a fit," said Phil. There was a speck of cheese riding on the corner of his lip. "Of course, he couldn't let Mrs. Marks see what Rutledge wrote. He's shuffling forms like mad, getting something else on top, and she's asking, 'What did Mr. Rutledge say?'"

"Gunnars is real swift," said Vic. "He tells her, 'Mr. Rutledge feels that Jeff should put more effort into his school work.'"

"That sounds like Rutledge, eh?" said Phil. "He'd've told the poor woman if she wouldn't get a doctor for her son, a vet could do the job."

Brad found that he was laughing out loud. At least he wouldn't have anything like that to deal with in his interviews. Unless, of course, Bert Peale's parents showed up. That could be trouble. Yet he knew, too, it might help to talk with them.

"Rutledge never was one to hold back," said Phil. "Art

teacher before him was a bit of a wussie. Kids figured Rutledge was going to be the same. Maybe the second day, he's walking down the hall, this kid sneaks up behind him, showing off. Swings his leg as if he's going to kick him from behind. Only thing is, he gets a little too close. Rutledge feels something and spins around. There's this kid standing there with his leg up. Egg all over his face. Rutledge tells him he looks like a dog who lost his hydrant. Kid turns around, embarrassed as hell. Then Rutledge boots him."

"What?" said Brad.

"Yeah. Kicks him in the ass. Kid was lucky he wasn't on the stairs. Rutledge would've booted him all the way down to the basement."

Brad was surprised when Workman marched into the staffroom at 1:25 to tell them there were already parents in the gym, they'd damn well better get moving. He put on his blazer, retrieving it from the hanger where he kept it in case he might need to dress up a bit, pinned the little brass bar that said "Mr. Cutler" on his lapel, straightened his tie – the first time in weeks he'd worn a tie – dropped a file of paragraphs into his briefcase beside his day book full of marks and headed for the gym. Maybe, he'd get lucky and have time to do some marking between interviews. Might as well let Workman see he was always marking. No exaggeration there.

The gym was set up with a circle of tables around the circumference; taped to each table was a sheet of foolscap with a teacher's name, the names arranged in alphabetical order. Behind each table was a chair for the teacher, in front, two chairs in case both parents should show up for the interview. In the center of the gym were more metal stacking chairs arranged in lines leading toward each table. The idea was that if things were busy, the parents would keep moving from chair to chair until they reached the front of the line. It was meant to keep things organized, keep people from horning in at the front, keep them from getting angry.

Brad noticed a line of parents already waiting next to Maurie Pack's table. Uh-huh, kids must be complaining about their chemistry teacher. There was a woman standing in front of his table too. He hurried toward her.

"Please," he said, "have a seat."

"Oh. Yes, thanks." She sat down quickly, holding her purse in her lap, both hands clutching it. She was looking, not at him, but down at her purse.

"I'm Brad Cutler," he said and reached to shake her hand.

She looked up then, leaning toward him, extending her hand, but her purse began to slip and she grabbed for it, straightening it on her lap. Then she took his hand. He felt her fingers, rough and moist.

"I'm Shelley's mom," she said, looking quickly away.

Shelley. Shelley? He had Shelley Malone in grade ten, Shelley Coates in grade twelve. Stringy brown hair, high cheekbones, this woman didn't resemble either of them. Her eyes kept darting up to look at him, then dropping to the floor. Embarrassed about something. Shelley Malone was doing all right, had to be Mrs. Coates.

"You're Mrs. Coates then?" he asked.

Her eyes were wide. "No, no," she said, "Mrs. Malone. I'm Shelley's mom."

"Sorry. I've got two Shelleys." He grabbed his day book, opened it to the grade ten marks. Tried to sound calm. "If you like, I can show you exactly where her mark of 70 came from. It was an average of six different things – including one big exam on a unit of short stories."

"I don't want to trouble you. It's just...."

"No trouble. She's a hard worker, got 74 on that exam, above the class average. Her first mark was a 60 on a writing assignment. I read them the first part of a story and they had to write an ending. Since then, her writing's been getting better all the time." Brad had the feeling that Mrs. Malone wasn't listening. She had something balled up in her hand. He saw it was a paper folded and folded again. When she noticed him looking at her hand, she dropped the paper on the table, picked it up in both hands, slowly unfolded it, pressed it flat, her fingers smoothing out the creases.

"Shelley's report card," said Brad. "Is the mark not right?"

"What it says." She pointed to the line of type beside the English mark. "I don't understand why you'd say that."

Brad stared at the words beyond her index finger, trying to read them upside down. What the hell had he said? He had four classes, one hundred and twenty-three students; it was impossible to remember all the comments he'd made. He couldn't just grab it from her, could he? Why didn't she turn it around and let him see it?

He wondered if Workman would be watching him, but he didn't look up.

"Perhaps there's some mistake. We use a comment code. If the secretary enters the wrong code, the computer will print the wrong comment. On the report card."

He could see her lips shuddering. Then she began to speak. "Sure, school don't come easy for her. But she tries, she always tries."

"Of course, she does."

"Difficulties, you said, severe difficulties. Why would you say that?"

"What?" He reached for the report card, slid it from

beneath her fingers and turned the print toward him.

"No, Mrs. Malone." He reached toward her again, was almost patting her hand before he stopped himself. "It's a compliment. 'Perseveres despite difficulties.' Nothing holds her back. Shelley's doing just fine."

He could see that she was doubtful. She'd misread the comment, of course, but he didn't want to make her feel like a fool.

"We've got this comment code. 205 comments we can use on the report cards. Different comments for every subject. All set out ahead of time. They never say exactly what you want to say." This time he did reach out and lay his hand on hers. "Don't worry, Mrs. Malone. I know it isn't easy for her, but Shelley's really working. I'm proud of her."

"So am I." The woman was pretty when she smiled. She stood up, took a step away, then reached out to shake his hand. "Thank you, Mr. Cutler. Thank you very much."

The poor woman, he thought, she was frightened, frightened for her daughter. God, what right did he have to be nervous about these interviews?

During the rest of the afternoon, Brad noticed that most of the parents who came were women, many of them not quite at ease when they sat down across from him. More than once he heard laughter at Sue Burton's table, Sue and someone chatting as if they were merely out for coffee. She was a good teacher, he knew. Vic had said she'd won a Hilroy Fellowship, for a local history project with her students, researching the archives at the public library. He wished he were more like her – at ease with people and innovative too.

As the afternoon wore on, he kept looking up, wishing that someone would turn out to be Angela Maddox's mother and he could have a talk with her, but by 4:30 she still hadn't shown. There were more fathers at the evening session, but neither of Angela's parents bothered to come. He'd hoped they might tell him how to get some work out of her, maybe even tell him what her problem was. Dr. Stone hadn't come to interviews, nor Bert Peale's folks either. There were lots of people whose kids were doing well, but no sign of the ones he needed to see. Still, he felt giddy when he finally left the gym, the last one out, but not a single parent on his case. His feet were nearly dancing down the hall as he headed for the staffroom.

Maybe someone would still be there, finishing off the coffee. He'd done okay; he felt like talking.

Flinging open the staffroom door, he almost ran into that red shock of hair, Kelly Irving reaching behind her, her right arm fumbling for the sleeve of her jacket.

She really is stacked, he thought. What he said was, "I didn't think you'd be here at night."

"Wasn't my idea. Workman wanted the office open, and me in it."

Brad glanced at the empty staffroom. "Everybody sure cleared out fast enough."

"To the bar," she said, "some of them. You want to come along?"

"Well, I don't know. Here. Let me help you with that coat." He held it steady while she jammed her arm into the sleeve, then drew it up around her, felt the warmth of her shoulders, quickly dropped his hands to his sides.

"You can ride along with me," she said.

"Well, I've – sure. Why not?"

Crossing the parking lot, she caught her heel in a crack in the pavement and almost went down, but he grabbed her arm, held her steady. She stood for a moment, looking up at him. It was dark in the parking lot, but he would've sworn that she was flustered.

"That red Ford yours?" she asked.

"What? Oh, yeah." He glanced at his car and back at her. "I can drive myself, meet you there."

"You might as well come with me. I'll drop you back here afterwards."

She walked toward the small foreign job in the corner of the lot. Was it a Nissan or a Toyota? He couldn't see the insignia in the dark. He followed her, starting toward the driver's door. What the hell – he couldn't very well hold the door for her. She had the key. He stepped to the right side of the car, feeling awkward. Damn, he was the one who was flustered.

When he was seated beside her, he felt her reach toward him. Looked down. Saw her pop the car into reverse. "I like a standard," she said. "Gives me something to do with my hands."

While he was thinking about that, she cut the wheel, shot the car backwards, spun the wheel around, leaned toward him, shifted again, and peeled out of the parking lot with just a hint of squealing tires.

"Live fast, and die late," she said. "That's my motto."

Shooters' bar was about half full when they walked in. Half empty made more sense. There was no sign of the other teachers. What he did see, of course, were heads turning to watch them – her – as they walked past the shuffleboard to an empty table. Like a red fire, he thought, sweeping through the room. Drawing every eye.

She sat down and looked at the other tables. "They must've

changed their mind and gone to the Brunswick," she said.

"We haven't ordered. No reason we can't switch bars."

"No reason we need to either." She laid her hand on his arm. "Your turn to buy, I think. I'll have a Great Western Light. Got to support the provincial brewery."

Brad looked for a waiter. He could feel the warmth of her fingers through the sleeve above his right wrist. He raised his left hand, awkwardly, waving to the waiter. Held his other hand steady on the table. The warmth spreading along his arm. Heat in his belly, in his groin. God, he thought, any minute there'll be smoke coming out my ears.

When the waiter brought their drinks, Brad looked at her, her hand still on his arm. He shrugged and pulled his arm away, reaching for his wallet. He paid for their drinks and took a quick pull on his beer.

"It's not good, but it's local, eh?" He laughed.

"Come on," she said. "Beer is beer. You couldn't tell one brand from another in a taste test."

There was fire in her eyes when she spoke. Brad decided he would stoke the fire. That fire, anyway. "Tastes bitter to my sensitive palate. You better treat yourself next round – try a Coors Lite."

"Listen," she said. "I drink Great Western. Exclusively. The old brewery was going under. The workers would've all been laid off – till someone figured they could get a loan and buy it out, run it themselves. Quite a gamble. You have to admire their nerve."

Brad knew he was staring at her. Her green eyes blazed as brightly as her hair. Her jaw thrust forward, quivering slightly.

Oh, what the hell, he thought. "You know, when something gets your dander up, you're absolutely gorgeous."

She was just opening her mouth to speak, but she closed it now. Quickly. He heard a little snap of teeth coming together. She looked away from him, took a drink from her glass. A long drink. He watched the smooth skin of her throat tighten as she swallowed twice. The graceful rise of her Adam's apple where the skin curved down from her chin. Skin as smooth as a peach that had been rubbed clean of fuzz.

She was looking at him. "Maybe you're not the guy I thought you were."

"What?"

"That sounded like some stupid line."

"No, no. I..."

"A line," she said. "Worn-out. Dead. What you'd expect from some superannuated casanova on the make."

"Why do you say that?"

She shook her head, that red halo vibrating above her shoulders. She looked down at her glass. "Believe me," she said, "when the good Lord sticks you with a shape like mine, you get to hear every line in the book." Her eyes were steady on her glass. "Time after time. Every come-on known to man."

She lifted her glass and drank, but kept her eyes away from his. He guessed that maybe she'd said more than she intended. When she set the glass down, a flush was spreading upwards from her collar, a warm pink glow stretching toward her hairline. Skin the colour of a ripe peach now.

Hell, she was the one flirting with him last time. He leaned toward her, placing his hand firmly on the wrist of the hand that held her glass. "Well," he said, "all I know is – when you blush, you're beautiful."

She jerked her arm away. Then began to laugh. Threw her

head back and roared. At the next table Brad saw an older woman swing around, a look of disapproval on her face.

Kelly wiped her hand across her eyes. "You're so full of crap," she said, "I guess you must be harmless."

Brad had to be quick. "Hey, I mean well. But I'm not harmless. Wouldn't want you to make that mistake." He grinned at her, feeling good, knowing that he liked her, hoping that she liked him too. "You want to live dangerously – have another beer?"

"Sure, danger I can handle. Not bullshit. My turn to buy though."

"No, I'll ..."

"My turn."

Over their second beers they were soon talking about school. Talking freely now, at ease with one another.

"Angela Maddox is the one I don't understand," said Brad. "I can't get her to do a thing."

"That may not be your fault."

"I don't know. I see her after class, drifting down the lower hall. All by herself. It's kind of sad."

"That lower hall," she said, "it's so dreary down there, anybody by herself would look sad. It needs another bank of lights."

"Ain't that the truth?" He felt his mood lightening again. "And you can bet, Stan Wieler and his girl are down there in the darkest corner. Glommed on to each other like their only source of oxygen is each other's mouth. Every break someone has to roust them out."

"Wieler and Keeler," she said, "their own kind of love poem. What they need is Rutledge."

"You've got a Rutledge story too, have you?"

"Everybody has. When they put in the new music wing,

they built in risers with rugs on the choir room floor. To deaden the sound, I guess. Anyway, one day after school, Rutledge goes upstairs. Sloan's got an office between the choir room and the band room – Rutledge figures it might be just the place to sneak a smoke. There's a light on in the office, but the choir room's dark. He's almost into the office when he hears something, a cross between a grunt and a sigh. He looks down and sees these two kids in the shadows. They're making out, of course, lying side by side, stretched out horizontal on that new rug. Rutledge stands there a second, watching them, but they're necking up a storm, they don't even notice him. So he goes into Sloan's office, pours himself a tall glass of water at the sink. Walks out and stands beside them. Just about the time they begin to notice there's a third person in the room, he dumps the water on them. Soaks their jeans. 'Act like dogs,' he says, 'I'll treat you like dogs.'" She laughed, then shook her head. "Ruth Simpson and Neil Fraser, those poor kids. They fled into the hall, both of them with dripping crotches."

"That's it," said Brad, "the big guy repeating grade twelve. I overheard some kids talking about him. They called him Crotch Fraser."

"You got it," she said. "Schwitzer always says teaching would be a snap if he could just figure out some way to activate their brains and put their hormones on hold."

"Instead of the other way around."

"Raging hormones," she said.

"I've had a few of them myself."

"I'll bet you have." Her eyes were steady on his.

He held her glance.

"So," she said, "what brought you into teaching?"

It wasn't what he hoped she'd ask. "I dunno. Not cut out

for farming, I guess. Half an hour of seeding and I was ready to drive the tractor into the nearest slough."

She laughed.

"I had this great teacher in high school. Mr. Roy. He loved books – and kids too. Kind of got me interested. I think maybe I wanted to be like him."

"Uh-huh," she said.

He guessed she was looking for something more dramatic. "Care for another beer?"

She shook her head. Another red crescendo. "Maybe we should quit while we're even."

"We're not even. I still owe you one from the other day. When you gave me the pep talk."

"Is that what it was?" She chuckled. "Well then, I guess we'll have to come back again, won't we? So I can collect." She paused, then added, "I'm really tired, Brad. Not used to working nights, I guess. You want that lift back to your car?"

"Sure thing." He was already standing, pulling back her chair. "You know," he added, "when you look as tired as this, you're really beautiful."

She curled her hand into a fist and punched at him, but he side-stepped away, laughing. Her fingers barely grazed his shoulder.

It was a few minutes after eleven when she turned into the crescent in front of the school. His car was the only one left in the parking lot. She pulled slowly up beside it, stopped, leaned toward him, reaching for the gear shift. He heard it shift. But he felt her hand settle on his knee.

"Thanks for the invitation," he said. He sounded as if he had a frog in his throat. Started to clear his throat and thought better of it. "I had a good time."

"Me too, Brad." She was still leaning toward him, stretching now, that frenzy of hair touching his forehead, her lips instantly pressing his. A long, hard kiss that caught his breath deep in his lungs and held it there. She pulled back.

"Mmm," she said, "you better go."

He tried to keep his breathing calm, tried not to gasp for air. "You don't kiss," he said, enunciating carefully, "as if you're all that tired."

She laughed, but she slipped the car into reverse. "See you tomorrow, Brad." The interior light came on as he opened the door, the splendour of her hair startling him again in the sudden light. He got out and took a deep breath of air. Just before the door clicked shut, he heard her say, "Remember, Brad, you owe me one."

For some reason, he thought of Linda, the girl he'd worked with at Lake Louise. They'd hung around together all that winter, friends, yeah, but more than friends too, until the weekend in late March when they'd had too much wine, quite a bit too much, and finally fallen into bed together, the sex not entirely satisfying. After that they always seemed slightly embarrassed with each other, both of them relieved when the snow melted and they could leave the ski hill far behind.

With Kelly, he was sure, it wouldn't be like that.

Six

It was Thursday, the morning after interviews, and so much had changed. All he could think about was Kelly. When he came up the stairs into the main hall, he saw Sue Burton through the glass door on the landing. She was hurrying down the hall toward the staffroom, a distracted look on her face. Sue was nice all right, but she wasn't much like Kelly.

He stopped in front of the door, switching his lunch bucket into the hand that held his briefcase, reaching for the door.

"Lemme get that for you, Mr. C." A student stepped in front of him and pulled the door open.

"Thanks, Jay." He walked through the open door, walked past Sue who'd slowed her pace to watch him, who'd almost come to a full stop. He nodded at her and continued into the staffroom. No, not a bit like Kelly. He heard her footsteps behind him.

"That was Jay Marsh," she said.

"Uh-huh." He set his briefcase on the floor, his lunch bucket on the rack above the coat hangers. The same lunch bucket he once carried out into the fields. It looked kind of funny here, but he was used to it.

She was standing beside him.

"He opened the door for you. Jay Marsh. The one the cops are always pulling in. Maurie says he's a total shithead."

Brad shrugged. "We get along," he said. He turned to check his cubbyhole for mail.

Maybe some time he'd tell her. Jay was the one who kept him going on the bad days – and there were a lot of days like that. Jay always had a friendly nod for him in the halls, and he wouldn't even teach the kid till next semester. If Angela Maddox was more like Jay Marsh, if Parker Stone could be just a bit like Jay, maybe he wouldn't have so many bad days.

He'd heard them talking about Jay Marsh the first week of school, Maurie Pack going on about how the first chance he got he was going to boot the kid's ass clear out of school. Get him terminated. There'd been enough complaints about the kid that Brad had gone into the office to look up his picture in the rolodex. A good-looking boy. Curly brown hair, wide grey eyes, crooked front teeth that for some reason made him think of Huckleberry Finn. A neck on him like a wrestler. Or a football player. He'd heard Dutch tell them to lay off, the kid was his best running back.

It couldn't have been more than four days later that he had his own run-in with Jay Marsh. Literally. He was going home at five o'clock, had just glanced at the new display in the trophy case by the student lounge, was about to turn into the gym hallway when something struck him. His shoulder, chest, stomach slammed. As if a giant had hurled a side of beef at him. A whoosh of breath, and he was going down.

Backwards. Landing flat on his ass on the floor. It was cold, he noticed, the tile floor was cold.

"Holy fuck!" He heard a boy's voice. Tried to focus on the kid who was crumpling to his knees before him. Brad was going to speak, but he couldn't catch his breath. The kid's face was fuzzy, something out of focus here. There. He seized a breath of air.

"Are you okay?"

The lines were straighter now, broad face, eyes wide, full of concern.

"Yeah." He got another breath. "Okay."

The kid was shaking his head. "Sorry. I'm really sorry. Lemme help you up." He leaned toward Brad.

"Forget it," Brad said, but he didn't resist when the kid got an arm under his armpit and began to heave him off the floor. My God, the kid was strong. Brad came to his feet, his heels leaving the floor an instant, then settling down again, a little shaking in his knees.

"Oh, shit," the kid said, "I didn't mean to swear. Honest. Didn't mean to hit you either."

Brad took a deep breath, felt his insides begin to stabilize. "Rule against running in the hall, isn't there?" You pompous ass, he thought, smarten up. "Probably another rule – I should watch where I'm going."

"What?"

"You don't tell anyone we broke the rules, I sure won't." Brad reached behind to brush off his butt. The kid was standing no more than a foot away. He was breathing hard too, his mouth open.

"Sorry. I was thirsty. Running for the fountain."

"You run like that," Brad said, "you're going to gain a lot of yards. Linebackers be fighting to get out of your way."

The kid grinned, his whole face crinkling.

"Go ahead and get your drink," said Brad. The boy was still grinning, and nodding now, his head jerking up and down. Brad watched him turn to the fountain. "One thing," Brad said, "anybody asks how we met, you don't need to tell them."

"Deal." The boy grinned even wider, flashed Brad a thumbs-up sign and bent over the fountain.

Despite his reputation, Jay Marsh was a pretty good kid, Brad thought, somebody he liked a lot better than Bert Peale. He was always cat-walking around Peale, taking it easy, wondering how to handle the kid. So far it was working; he'd managed things without really getting into it with Peale. Yeah, just barely.

Then one day in grade twelve English they were talking about ballads, the way they were passed down from one generation to another, the way they might contain a kind of historical truth. He tried to get an answer out of Angela Maddox – with no more luck than usual, but the other kids seemed willing to talk. Even Della Neudorf threw in a couple of words.

At some point in the discussion he noticed Bert Peale sitting up in his desk, watching him. Bert, who usually slumped back, staring at the ceiling, or the clock, the look of boredom on his face sometimes giving way to disdain and arrogance. The day before, when walking the aisles while his students worked at their seats, Brad had stopped beside Bert's desk and suggested he should take an interest in things, try to answer a few questions. "Why bother?" Bert had said. "They're all so obvious." "Well," said Brad, "for you, I'll have to make them tougher."

Now Bert was actually raising his hand. He didn't look especially interested, but at least his nose wasn't stuck up in the air. "I got an example," he said. "This record my old man used to play. 'Reuben' – something."

"Sure. 'Reuben James.'"

"Yeah, that's it."

"Kenny Rogers sang it."

"No, I don't think so." Just a hint of scorn in his voice.

"The First Edition, maybe?"

Bert was staring at him, shaking his head, the stud in his left ear flashing under the fluorescent lights, his glasses sliding down his nose. "No," he said, "definitely not." What was going on here? The kid looked as if he wanted to spit at him.

"About a black man," Brad said. "He's like a father to this poor white kid, an orphan."

Bert sneered. "You don't even know what you're talking about, do you?"

Parker Stone lifted his head to stare at Brad.

Don't let him get to you, Brad thought. He took a deep breath, slowly let it out before he spoke. "It's an old song. Late sixties, maybe early seventies."

"It's about World War Two," Bert said. There was a smile twisting the corner of his mouth, but his lips were still contorted with their habitual sneer. "The Reuben James was a bloody *ship*. A real ship – it got sunk in battle with the Germans." Bert leaned back, smiling wider now. "To the cold ocean floor."

Parker was studying him, no expression on his face.

"Oh," said Brad. "That one." Just take it easy now. Same title, but a different song. By the guy who sang the one about the Battle of New Orleans. "You're right, sure."

"Course I'm right. I suppose you know that song too, eh?"

That was when Brad lost it. "Suppose you wipe that sneer off your face, you smug little –" He managed to stop before he said more.

The room felt like the inside of a time-bomb, the only sound his harsh breathing, everybody staring at him, even Angela Maddox. Bert looked startled for an instant, but the sneer crept back across his face. At least he had the sense to keep his mouth shut, the smart-ass little bastard.

The two of them were still glaring at each other when Lisa Sharma cleared her throat. "Mr. Cutler," she said, "Tom Dooley – would that be another one?"

"Yes. Yes, it would." Thank you, Lisa, thank you. He looked down and saw the brightness of her smile, relief flowing across her face. Not for any right answer either. Because she'd got things moving again. It was going to be okay. Somehow he'd make it through until the bell.

He glanced at Parker then, but the boy was turned in his seat, looking back at Peale.

Thinking about it now, he wondered if Peale had set him up from the start. Maybe. The kid was smart enough. It didn't really matter though. He was the adult here; he should have handled him better – hell, handled himself better. Letting the kid get his goat was one thing, letting him know he'd done it was something else. Then he felt a chill slide down his back as if someone had dropped a frozen coin inside his shirt.

Lord, Workman might have heard him on the intercom.

When Brad went into the guidance office that day at noon, Doug Gunnars was at his desk, doodling on his calendar pad, the phone cradled against his left ear. He glanced up at Brad, waved him toward the chair beside his desk. Brad watched him shading the areas where a series of looping circles intersected.

"Fine," said Gunnars. "I'll call again on Monday." He hung up the phone. "What can I do for you?"

Brad tried to keep it casual. "I was wondering about Bert Peale. You have any advice about how to handle him."

"Had a run-in, did you?"

Brad shifted in the chair. "Bit of a one." He hoped Gunnars wouldn't go telling Workman.

"Not surprising. Kid's spoiled rotten. Likes to jerk his teachers around. About all I can advise is to keep an eye on him all the time, never let him slack off."

Brad nodded, was starting out of his chair when he had another thought. "What about Angela Maddox? You know anything will help me get through to her?"

"Angela Maddox, eh?" Gunnars gave him a weird look, one he couldn't read. "You have a run-in with her too?"

"Not exactly. I just can't get her to do any work. She's not on drugs, is she?"

"No, I don't think so. You...uh, try talking to her parents?"

"They didn't show for interviews. I must've called half a dozen times – they're never at home. Not available at work either."

"Uh-huh. She's a troubled kid, I guess." Gunnars was no longer looking at him. He'd turned back to his calendar pad and was now drawing a series of tightly interlocking rectangles. "You have to keep trying. Maybe she'll come around."

It was a Friday that he'd almost throttled Bert Peale. That afternoon Brad strolled into the office after school, fished the detention book out from under the counter, opened it and began to check the list of names. A dozen people slated for detention, but Peale wasn't one of them. There'd be no chance to catch him now.

"Your detention tonight?" He hadn't noticed Herb Schwitzer come up beside him.

"No. Just wondered who was giving up their Friday night."

"When you're done, I'll take it down to 113." Herb was grinning at him. "See a lot of you in here this week."

Brad glanced at Kelly Irving. She was typing furiously, her fingers dancing on the keyboard, a huge smile on her face. He wondered if he had the nerve to ask her.

"Oh, yeah." He didn't want to sound like an ass. "Office is the hub of the school, I guess."

"These days it sure is. Well, I'll leave you to it." Herb pulled the door open and stepped into the hall. When it closed behind him, Brad watched through the narrow pane of glass as Herb turned toward the stairs. He was still smiling.

"Am I that obvious?"

The typing stopped. "Were you talking to me, Mr. Cutler?" She looked up from her computer, her fingers poised above the keyboard, her eyes wide.

"Yes, I was." There was no one else in the office. "But only because I couldn't jump your frame." As soon as it was out, he wished he had it back, but it was okay, she was laughing.

"Mr. Schwitzer's an observant man. You *have* been in here a lot this week."

"Good place to get things done," he said. "Besides, I like the atmosphere. When you're typing, you know, you're absolutely stunning."

She crossed her eyes, set them right, was abruptly staring past his shoulder. "Yes, Roger," she said, "may I help you?"

Oh, no, it'll be all over the school. That's all he'd need, the kids going on about him and Kelly. Without turning his head, he glanced to his right. Saw no one. Heard the sudden sparkle of her laughter.

"Gotcha, Brad."

"Yeah, you did. Remember though, revenge is the mother of invention."

"Who said that?"

"I guess I did." Now. Quit blathering. Ask her. "Scarecrow Theatre's doing a play tonight. A comedy. *Out of the Frying Pan*. It's supposed to be pretty good, but they'll still have tickets at the door." She was just sitting there, looking at him, a few tendrils of red hair tumbling down across her eyes.

Just when he realized he hadn't asked her yet, she said, "Am I supposed to ask you?"

"No. I'm asking you. You want to go?"

She nodded her head, hair falling over her eyebrows, and beneath them, red lips smiling up at him.

"Good. I'll pick you up at seven-thirty." He grinned down at her. "Really looking forward to this," he said. Then he decided he'd better get out of the office before Herb Schwitzer came back from the detention room. If Herb was still laughing at him, he didn't want to see it.

"One moment, Mr. Cutler."

When he swung around, Workman was at the door of the inner office, beckoning him with a long, skeletal finger. Brad stepped away from Kelly, blushing. Damn, he knew he was blushing.

"Close the door behind you."

As he swung the door shut and headed for a chair, he felt

uneasy, like a kid dragged into the principal's office. Man, he felt that way a lot.

"No need to sit. This'll be brief."

The bugger, Workman wanted him uneasy.

"You're a young man, first teaching job. You might profit from a bit of advice." Workman paused, the index finger of his right hand hovering by his mouth. He raised the finger to his right eye and smoothed his eyebrow before he spoke. "When you work for the company, you don't fish from the company dock."

"What?"

"You heard me."

"You mean Kelly and –"

"Every break I look up and there you are. Hanging around my secretary. This is an academic institution. We don't need that kind of thing going on here. You understand?"

He had taken a step towards Brad, was glaring down at him. The son of a bitch, if he thought –

"You can't tell me –"

"Don't! Not a good idea," said Workman, raising his hand like a referee about to flag him. "You think about it, now, give it some time, you'll know I'm right."

Brad spun around. Get out of here, he thought, quick, before you pound the pompous bastard.

"And shut the door on your way out."

Seven

The play was about a group of young actors trying to break onto Broadway. Brad was still furious with Workman; it took him a while to get into it, but eventually it had him hooked. Guys and girls living together in a huge apartment that they'd chipped in to rent because it was one floor above the suite of a famous Broadway director. A director who was much more interested in gourmet cooking than he was in seeing any play the kids might want to stage for him. Yeah, one generation making it tough for another. The kids were always trying to lure him up to their apartment to watch them act, but all he ever wanted was to borrow some cooking ingredients for his current culinary experiment. Fluff, maybe, but it was right about one thing: the drive you needed if you were ever going to catch a break. Might be a good one for the kids at school, he said to Kelly, a chance to watch characters a lot like themselves.

Might be he should forget about the kids at school, she said to him, leaning toward him, their shoulders touching above the arm of the seat. It was easy watching the play with her, her laughter bubbling up so naturally. They seemed always to laugh at the same lines, the same frantic bits of business on the stage. Except when she shifted in her seat, and her knee brushed his, stayed a moment against his, the audience roaring with laughter, and he had missed it, wasn't even looking at the stage. To hell with Workman, he thought, and put his arm around her.

Walking her to the car afterwards, he asked if she'd like to go for coffee.

"Sure," she said. "Or better still, why don't we go back to my place? I'll pour you something stronger."

"That'll be two," he said, opening the passenger door. "I already owe you one."

She was halfway into the car when she looked up at him, those green eyes shining through all that hair. "Maybe I want you in my debt," she said and closed the door.

She lived on the top floor of a three-storey apartment on Fifth Avenue, a white stucco building, black stairs leading up the outer wall to a landing on each floor. He stopped inside her door. A framed print. Verdant jungle growth, branches spreading, leaves, vines curling everywhere, and behind them, birds, animals peering through the greenery, their eyes dark and haunted – eyes like those of Angela Maddox, he thought – and beneath the birds and animals, the jungle breaking into fragments, smoke and the glow of distant flames, charred stumps and endless, barren hills.

"Some of them are already extinct," she said. "And still they're burning off the rain forests."

"Yeah, in Brazil. People are crazy."

"Not just Brazil. I'm writing letters all the time."

"Uh-huh. They're crazy everywhere," he said, but he was

looking at a smaller picture. Photo of a guy, not much older than himself, a flyer, cap shoved back, parachute slung over his shoulder, cocky grin on his face.

She was gazing at it too. He thought she looked wistful, but she gave her head a quick shake. "My God, but he was handsome, eh?"

"Was?"

"Is. Frank moved away this summer. I guess I haven't had the heart to take him down."

He glanced again at the photo. Yeah, somebody Workman would approve of.

She motioned toward the chesterfield. "Have a seat. Your choices here are kind of limited. I've got beer or rye."

"Rye's good. With lots of coke – if you've got it."

"A prairie wedding, eh?"

"How's that?"

"Some comedian at the Festival," she said, "claimed we drink so much rye and coke out here, it should have a special name."

"Not bad." Brad glanced around the suite. It was small, the kitchen and the living room running together, an easy chair backed toward the table and facing the chesterfield. He looked at the photo on the wall again. Neatly clipped moustache, short hair beneath his flyer's cap. He'd have a military look to him even if he were naked. Naked – yeah, lucky bugger must've been naked in this room lots of times.

There was the clatter of ice cubes in the kitchen. He went to help her mix the drinks. Wasn't she supposed to leave that to him, while she headed to the bathroom, looking back over her shoulder, a toss of all that gorgeous hair, a crooked smile, saying maybe it's time to get into something more comfortable? Oh, yeah, dream on.

She opened the coke, a hiss of gas, foam spilling down the neck of the bottle, soaking her hand.

"If you don't mind," he said, "I'll have mine in a glass."

She laughed and grabbed the washcloth that hung over the sink. "Good line." She was washing her hand, but she was looking at him, turning the full force of her eyes upon him. "You're really quite witty, you know."

"I wish. Kaufman and Hart."

"Pardon?"

"It's from a play we take in grade eleven. By Kaufman and Hart. Nice little love scene when this couple comes home after the ballet – kind of touching, but light."

"So she sprays him with coke." She topped up his glass with mix and filled another for herself.

"The other way around, actually. The line was hers." He took a sip. "Most of the good lines were hers."

"Ah. A realistic comedy for a change." The chuckle in her throat like the tinkle of ice cubes in her glass. Ooh, he thought, bad simile.

"When he asks her what caught her interest in him, she says it was the back of his head."

That sound again – if not ice cubes, then wind chimes rocking together. No, he was getting carried away.

"He asks her what happened when he turned around; she says, after a while she got used to it."

Yes, wind chimes in a spring breeze. A touch of hyperbole, sure, but who could blame him with that open-mouthed smile only inches away?

"Your face," he said, "I could get used to it."

She smiled, but she wasn't laughing now. "It's not your face," she said, "or the back of your head. Your eagerness – sincerity, I guess."

She was about to say something more when he bent forward and kissed her. Soft, pliant lips, a rush of warmth. He opened his eyes and discovered her watching him, an inch away. He stepped back.

"Sorry," he said. "It seemed like the thing to do." Flustered, he stepped away, sat heavily on the chesterfield.

She hadn't moved. "Maybe it was."

He took another swallow from his glass. It was a weak drink, the coke masking the flavour of rye. "Isn't this the time," he asked, "when you're supposed to say you want to get into something more comfortable?"

"Another line from Kaufman and Hart?"

"No, just an old cliché." He shook his head. "A real clunker."

She walked toward him, paused to set her glass on the coffee table. Then she was kneeling beside him, leaning toward him. "I *am* comfortable," she said. "Now." Her lips on his, pressing his, opening, the quick moist flick of her tongue.

D riving home, it was as if the car were steering itself. There was music playing, and he wasn't sure there was a cassette in the player. Next time, he thought, maybe next time. Yeah, and what would Workman think of that? He was just turning into the driveway when he remembered Bert Peale, those cool, haughty eyes, the smirk on his face. He felt his stomach tighten. It was strange, but probably a good sign, the first time all night he'd thought of Peale.

Monday morning he made up his mind about Bert Peale while driving to school. Maybe some people would say it wasn't the right thing to do, it would cause him problems later on. It didn't matter what they'd say. Maybe it wouldn't matter to the kid either. But it mattered to him. He had to like himself again.

He'd apologize right after attendance.

While the kids were straggling into the room, he took down the Emily Dickinson poster, replaced it with one of Edgar Allan Poe. He read over the announcements: All teachers should report to the staffroom at the long break for a brief meeting; period three would start three minutes later than usual. Brief is right, he thought. Better take the attendance: everybody present except for Angela Maddox, as usual. She'd be along in five or ten minutes.

Hope she doesn't come in at the wrong time. In the middle of it.

He ran the attendance sheet up to the office, saw that Workman's door was closed. He handed the sheet to Kelly, their fingers touching, a flash of heat in his hand, her ducking her head away, hair falling across her eyes, but not before he saw her wink.

No, got to get back down there. Do it.

He jogged down the stairs, walked into the classroom. A few kids chatting, some of them slumped in their seats, Parker Stone yawning, most of them quiet, period-one quiet – it took them a while to wake up. Angela Maddox was in her seat now, her late slip on his desk. He stood behind the lectern, leaned his hand on the tray at the bottom. Fibres of wood on the palms of his hands. Hand-sawed. Unpainted particle board. He'd made it himself. Something for them to stand behind during speeches, to give them confidence. For him to stand behind too. Come on, get it done.

He cleared his throat.

"Friday morning," he said, "we had a bit of a scene in here. An angry scene, I'd have to say. It never should have happened." Make it quick now. "I want to apologize, Bert. I lost my temper and I shouldn't have done it."

That was enough. He looked at Bert who sat motionless in his desk, saying nothing. A little twist of his mouth. Was it pleasure, maybe, or just the usual arrogance? In front of Bert, Parker Stone, looking wide awake now, seemed to be studying something on his desk, but his book was closed.

"Now," said Brad, "this morning we're going to read a poem called 'Annabel Lee.' Written by Edgar Allan Poe there." He nodded at the bulletin board. "Check those eyes. Looks kind of driven, doesn't he? Anyone here know anything about Poe?"

"'The Tell-Tale Heart,'" said Walter Buchko, "he wrote that." He shrugged at Tom Swenson across the aisle. "We took it in grade ten."

"They make horror movies," said Parker Stone, "from some of his stories."

"The man was nuts," said Bert Peale. "Crazy as hell – just like every other poet."

After school that day, he hurried down the hall and caught Sue Burton before she left her room. She wore a forest green pant suit, was marking at her desk. Even bent over a stack of papers, she managed to look stylish.

"Sue," he said, "you teach some grade ten English, right?" He knew she wouldn't mind his asking for advice.

"Last year I did."

"I want to try a novel unit. Been going through the class-room sets in the bookroom, but there's not a lot of choice. What do you think of *Breaking Smith's Quarterhorse?*"

"Have you read it?"

"Yesterday. I figure St. Pierre's got those Chilcotin ranchers dead on, the Indians too, but it's not exactly a kid's book. You think it'll work in grade ten?"

"It'll work if you make it work." She smiled, her smile so bright it always took him by surprise. "Try reading it aloud."

"The whole thing?"

"It's short. Won't take long. You can have some fun with the dialogue, show how stubborn Smith is, emphasize the humour."

He wasn't sure. "What about the courtroom scene with Ol' Antoine? His speech about Chief Joseph isn't going to sway the kids, is it?"

"I'll tell you what I do. There's a book by Dee Brown, *Bury My Heart at Wounded Knee,* Indian history with a chapter on Chief Joseph and the Nez Perce, shows exactly how they were betrayed – time after time." He could hear the passion in her voice. "Cheated, driven off their land, cold, starving. Tell the kids what happened, they'll understand where Ol' Antoine is coming from."

"Thanks. I'll give it a try." Hearing her advice, you just knew she had her heart in her job. "Book's in the library?"

"Sure is." All at once there was a different lilt to her voice. "Of course, I wouldn't mind loaning my copy to the right sort of fella."

He felt his face begin to flush.

She studied him, seemed to make a decision. "You know what you're doing?" she asked.

"What?" His hand was at his waist again. He knew all right.

"Rubbing your chin like that when you're embarrassed."

"Hockey injury." He was flustered. "Took a stick in the face. Back in high school. Too dumb to get stitches, I guess, just used a couple bandaids. Never figured how ugly it would get."

"It's not ugly, Brad." She smiled at him. "Matter of fact, it looks rather manly."

"Oh, come on."

"Maybe not on Joe Sakic, say – he seems like such a pretty boy – but on you it looks good."

"Burton," he said, "you are so full of it." But he was laughing, and so was she, laughing with him. "I'd be pleased," he said, "to use your history book."

He enjoyed talking to her, didn't want to end it here. "I got a charge out of that Smith character. Loved the names of his sons."

"Sherwood, Roosevelt, Exeter, and John," she said. "Good of him to let his wife name one."

So far he hadn't been able to get through to Angela Maddox in class, hadn't once gotten her to say anything meaningful. At first, he thought that she and Parker Stone were mocking him with their carbon copy answers, but then he realized that it was always Parker duplicating whatever she said. Parker, whom he'd caught more than once – his head turned toward her, gazing across the aisle with wide and wistful eyes. Then, after he heard about Parker being dumped, he was certain she was the one who'd dumped him, even more certain that Parker still had a crush on her, and he wondered if Parker's mockery wasn't his way of shielding her, protecting her from a teacher who maybe seemed conscientious at all the wrong times. Still, it didn't matter. She was going to fail her year if he didn't figure something out.

He waited till class was about to end, timed it so that he'd be beside her desk when the bell rang. She was already closing her notebook when he leaned toward her and said, "I need to talk to you." Without looking at him she shook her head and reached for her backpack, shoving the notebook inside.

"Just for a minute." Other kids were squeezing past him in the aisle. "Please, stay."

She looked at him then, responding with the slightest nod of her head, and lowered her backpack to the floor beside her desk. He wondered again if she might be on something, but there was certainly no smell of pot or liquor on her.

He waited till everyone else had left the room, Parker lingering in the doorway an instant before shuffling out. "Listen, Angela," Brad said, "I'm really worried you keep up the way you've been, you're going to flunk the class – and I know you're too smart for that. I looked up your marks from last year. You can handle this work if you want to. I know you can, but I don't know how to help you."

She looked at him, her flat gray eyes fixed and staring. He wondered how long she'd stare at him if he stopped now and said no more. Forever, was what it felt like. And yet he knew there was something there he had to reach, unseen currents stirring somewhere deep within.

"I don't know, there's something wrong here." He rushed on. "If it's me that bothers you, I'm sorry. But you've got to get beyond that – somehow you have to." She continued staring at him with empty eyes. "Or switch classes. People change electives all the time. You could switch into someone else's English. It's not too late – you'd just need to buckle down and go to work, do some catching up. You could do it."

She shook her head, leaned out of her desk, picked up her backpack, stood and started for the door.

"Angela," he said, "you have to take some responsibility here. You've got to help yourself."

"No," she said, her voice only a whisper. "Sorry." Then she was through the door and turning out of sight.

"Not half as sorry as I am," he called after her, but his words were loud and thick with anger.

Three days later she quit coming to school.

M onday he spent most of the noon hour in his room, the door locked for privacy, so that he could finish the marking that had kept him busy all weekend. Hurrying up the stairs to grab a quick coffee before the bell, he noticed a group of grade twelves huddled outside the office door. Something happening there, he thought, but he was tired, needed that coffee to get him going for the afternoon. Then he saw Parker Stone split off from the other boys, walking quickly away from them.

"Parker," he said, nodding at the boy, but Parker didn't seem to see him, was staring past him, hurrying past him. Brad watched him stride down the hall and push through the side door of the school. Running away, he thought, and he wondered where that idea had come from. The kid's eyes were wet. Surely he wasn't crying.

He turned and walked into the staffroom, going directly to the coffee urn, drawing himself a cup, the gurgling of coffee the only sound in the room. He looked up. A cluster of guys sat at the round table, slumped and motionless. They seemed inert, none of them talking. He turned to the chair against the east wall where Sue Burton often sat and saw that she was crying.

"What's wrong?"

"Angela Maddox." He could barely hear her. "She's dead."

"What?" He reached toward her, felt her shoulder shaking, saw that one hand was clenched between her knees. "What happened?"

She looked up at him through streaming eyes. "Talk to Doug." She ducked her head toward a wad of kleenex in her other hand.

No sign of Kelly, and the door to Gunnars' office was closed. There, beneath the poster of speed-skater Catriona Le May Doan, the poster that said, "Yes, you can do it," he paused, took three deep breaths, tried to steady his breathing, then tapped on the door. His knuckles felt like stone.

"Come."

Gunnars was at his desk, gazing through the window toward the parking lot. He shoved his chair back and turned to Brad. Studied him. "I see you heard already."

"She's dead – Angela Maddox?"

"Uh-huh." He'd never noticed it before, but Doug Gunnars was a lot older than he looked, a network of lines beneath his eyes, skin almost transparent over his cheekbones, flesh sagging around his mouth.

"What happened?"

"Suicide."

"No."

"Hung herself."

"But why would she do that?"

Gunnars winced. "What the hell," he said. "Isn't going to hurt her now. Pregnant." As Gunnars spoke he lifted a pencil from his desk, rolled it between his fingers, got a grip on it and began to shade in a square on his calendar pad. "Social worker said she was pregnant. Couldn't seem to handle it."

Parker Stone, thought Brad, was he the guy?

"God, you could've told me. I might've been able to help. You should've told me what the problem was." Was that fair, he wondered, could he have somehow helped her? "Man, I was blundering along, didn't know a thing. If I knew, I would've handled her better. Might've made a difference. Why wouldn't you –"

"Shut the hell up." Gunnars lifted his pencil from the pad and stared at it an instant. Suddenly hurled it against the wall. "You couldn't help her, I couldn't help her, the social workers sure as hell couldn't help her. All they could tell me was everything's confidential, I don't need to get involved, they told the police, let them handle it. Proper procedures right down the line – and who gives a shit? Now – when it's bloody well too late, when I can't do a goddamned thing – now, they let me know her old man was screwing her." He turned on Brad with ancient, weeping eyes. "Get out of here, will you? I need to be alone."

Brad backed toward the door, shaking his head in disbelief, his knees shaking too. The poor kid. Christ, and he'd been going on about responsibility, telling her she had to help herself. Yeah, help herself.

When he drove out of the parking lot, he surprised himself thinking of the ravine at home, the South Saskatchewan lapping on its banks, the raft that he and Jack had built tied securely to a willow, floating in the quiet water of the turn, a drifting island in that great river, the stars above him like countless candles.

He turned the car, not toward his basement suite, but toward the river valley on the south side of town, driving through the subway, following the winding road through the park until he reached the Burger Cabin. He pulled into the empty lot and stopped the car, headlights illuminating the log building, its door locked, shutters swung down over counter windows. Lifeless, closed for the season. Yeah, but it would open in the spring.

He slid out of the car, slammed the door behind him.

He crossed the pavement, stepped over the single line of chain between the posts that separated the road from the Wakamow trail. He walked quickly along the trail until it turned toward the river. It was dark now, but the path between the trees was a lighter grey than the bush beside it. He could see ragged caragana hedges growing wild beside the trail, hear a sighing in the branches of the taller trees, a sighing like you might hear at a funeral, people with faces buried in their Kleenex. Beneath his feet, the fallen leaves were still damp from last night's rain, the sound of his footsteps muffled and sombre. When the trail turned again, he knew he was near the river, long grasses rising almost to his waist along the bank. There was a bench here somewhere. He found it, a solid darkness half-hidden by the shadows, the grasses cut away around it and opening in a path that led toward the water. He sat down, the wood as hard and cold as a church pew.

The river was there, only a few feet away, without a current this late in the fall, a crescent moon riding the surface. Like a lamp someone had set adrift on the still water.

He buried his head in his hands.

Sensed the grasses beginning to stir with the breeze, brushing against one another, moving all around him. The faintest of whispers, shushing sounds, hushed voices grieving.

Sometime later, when he raised his head, the moon had slipped away, the water dark beneath the cliff that rose above it black as the wall of a pit.

In his hands his cheeks were wet.

The next morning the crisis response team came down from the board office. They met with teachers first – discussing grief counselling, warning about cluster suicides – then talked to individual classes and set up a counselling service in the guidance room. Anyone could drop in, just cut out of class and go. Brad told his grade twelves he was sorry about Angela, wished he could have helped her, knew it was hard for them too. Parker looking down the whole time, his arms folded on his desk, his head cradled in his arms. They should go see someone on the crisis team, Brad said, and in the future, if any of them had problems, any kind of problem, they should talk to Mr. Gunnars in the Guidance Office – or come and talk to him. Things could seem awful bleak sometimes, hopeless, if they didn't talk it through, but there was always a way out.

After that, he was glad to be busy, marking papers, preparing lessons, falling into bed at night exhausted, so fatigued there were even times he fell asleep right away. Most nights, though, he lay awake, wondering what he could have done to help her, trying anything that seemed as if it might make a difference, replaying that day after class when he'd said he had to talk to her, approaching her a hundred different ways, and nothing he imagined saying did a bit of good. He made it through his classes the best he could, going though the motions, like the kids, acting out the parts expected of them, no spark, letting the routine carry them toward the bell. Parker wasn't saying much in class – twice Brad had caught him alone, suggesting it wouldn't hurt to see the crisis team – eventually the kid had taken his advice. Brad had checked on that, and sometimes thought he should've gone for help himself.

Eight

The Halloween Dance. A warm fall evening, the gym packed with dancing kids, jerking, twitching spasmodically to an incessant rap beat, the air hot, stifling.

Too hot, one kid stepping away from her partner, turning this way and that, a lopsided shuffle toward the bleachers. He'd seen her from across the gym and he didn't think she'd make it. He started toward her, wondering who was behind the Bugs Bunny mask. She was sitting on the bottom bleacher now, her hands spread out beside her, clutching the plank. Something about the way she slumped against the next row of seats reminded him of Angela Maddox. He shuddered but kept moving. While he was picking his way through the dancers, the girl slid onto the floor, both shoulders beginning to jerk. He was afraid that she was throwing up, but all he could hear was the beat of drums.

When he knelt beside her, he smelled vomit. Leaning closer, he saw a dribble of vomit hanging beneath the chin of her mask. He set her up, supported her against the bottom bleacher and lifted the mask from her head. Vomit around her mouth, her nose. He wiped it away with a Kleenex, hollered for a kid to get the vice-principal. Up close, she didn't look at all like Angela Maddox. Wasn't anyone he knew. At least, he didn't think so. It was hard to tell with her eyes rolled back. Her forehead felt clammy. When she started to heave again, he leaned her sideways and tried to hold her with her head tilted away, but she sprayed her sweater anyhow.

Then Herb was there, and they got her to her feet, her arms around their shoulders. Herb looked around the gym, spotted Sue Burton by the stage, and shouted at a kid to bring Miss Burton to the office. The girl vomited once more as they walked her across the gym. After that, her legs stopped moving and they had to carry her, feet dragging behind. On the way, Herb hollered for Ollie, the caretaker, to get in there with a mop, but they didn't stop until they dropped the girl into a chair in the office.

Herb stood over her, shaking his head. "Cheryl Dunlop," he said. "You just never know."

"The minister's kid?"

"You got it. He's not going to like this call." Herb reached for the phone book.

Brad noticed sputum at the corner of her mouth. "Cheryl," he said, "are you okay?" When she didn't move, he said it again, louder. Nothing. He put his hands on her arms to give her a little shake. Her skin was damp and cold. When he shook her shoulder, her mouth fell open, releasing another dribble of sputum. He shivered. Angela Maddox wasn't the only kid who'd ever needed help. Got to do something here. But what?

That was when Sue arrived.

"She's passed right out," he said.

Sue lay her finger on the girl's eyelid, gingerly peeled it back. An opaque white, and he thought of the belly of a dead fish.

"I think she's in a coma," said Sue. "We need a medic."

"Shit." Brad heard the phone book bounce off the wall, heard three numbers dialed. "Schwitzer here. Vice-principal at Lawrence Collegiate. Can you get an ambulance over here quick? Got a kid in a coma. OD'd...No, booze by the smell of her." His voice was loud in the small office. "Yeah. Come in the main door on the crescent. We'll have it open for them." He hung up the phone. "She breathing okay?"

"Yes," said Sue. "So far." Quick, shallow breaths, but regular, Brad thought.

Herb nodded at Brad. "You can let them in. Wait at the crescent door and get them down here quick."

Walking down the hall, he thought how glad he was that Sue was there to help.

Later, when the ambulance had taken the girl away, he asked Herb if he'd gotten hold of Reverend Dunlop.

"Oh, yeah. Was not a happy camper. Didn't think his daughter drank."

"She did tonight."

"Could be her first time," said Sue, "one of her first times. She drinks too much too quick, then it hits her in the warm gym."

"Told him that," said Herb. "One thing. After it sunk in, kind of shape she's in, he thanked me for calling the ambulance. Most people, they give us hell when their kid is pissed."

They had a live band that night, West Side Raunch, playing a demented cross of rap and heavy metal. The music was both loud and awful, his head pounding almost as fiercely as the drums. It was one night he would have gone straight home to bed, but Kelly had caught him in the long break that morning and told him to come around for a drink when he got off dance duty. And when he was with her, he didn't have to think of Angela Maddox.

After he climbed the stairs to her apartment, he stood for a while on the outside landing, enjoying the fresh air and the silence. The air as crisp as autumn leaves in the dip where the pasture bordered on the home place. Be nice to walk through the trees right now, hear the leaves crackle underfoot, stroll into the pasture, stand there in the moonlight, the house lights off, look up and let the breeze wash over him. Stars so bright and close you could almost touch them.

Then the growl of a car cruising down Fifth Avenue. Still, the midnight air was like a cool washcloth on his temples. He should probably just stay right here on the landing, or go home – maybe his head would stop hammering – that might be the smart thing to do. He stood another minute in the cool air.

Yeah, tell her he had a smasher.

He tapped on her door. The door opened and there was Kelly, an oversized blue sweater hanging halfway to the knees of her jeans.

Oh well, maybe just for a little while. Wouldn't want to do something that'd make Workman happy.

She smiled up at him. "So how was your first dance duty?"

"One bad drunk," he said, "and a lot of bad music. Loud. Feels like a hammer in my head."

"Let's see if we can't do something about that." She took his hand, led him into the room, and set him in the easy chair that acted as the divider between her living room and kitchen. "Close your eyes," she said. "I'll get some ice."

He heard water running in the kitchen sink, the fridge door opening, closing, a clatter of ice cubes, was aware of a rustling sound, of footsteps padding back to him.

"Lean back," she said. "Get good and comfortable, then hold your head steady."

He felt a cloth being spread across his forehead, wet and cool, a weight placed gently on his head. Well, that would keep his cowlick down. "Ice," she said, "it's in a plastic bag." He shuddered when her fingers touched his temples. "Relax. It's the ice cubes made them cold." She stroked his temples, his cheekbones, the hinges of his jaw. "They'll warm up."

They did, smoothing his eyebrows, the hollows around his eyes, reaching under the cloth, eight fingers massaging his forehead, her thumbs kneading the tense muscles along his jawline. She must be standing behind the chair. Her fingers caressed, soothed, drew the tension from his head. One finger paused at the scar on his chin.

"What's that from?" she asked.

"Playing hockey," he said. What the heck, it was really nothing much.

He felt her thumbs on the back of his neck, kneading the tightness from sinew and muscle, dipping beneath his collar. A low humming sound by his right ear, tuneless but pleasant. She was leaning beside him, reaching around to undo his collar button, spreading his shirt, her fingers beneath the fabric, descending on his shoulders, pressing, releasing, pressing, squeezing, squeezing again, the firm compression of fingers at work, then gliding lower, fingers at play, skating across his chest, fingernails touching his nipples.

He reached up. Took the cloth, the ice from his head, dropped them onto the floor. "Come here," he said. He clasped her right hand in his and pulled her around, pulled her into his lap. Felt the shape of her breasts high on his chest, and kissed her.

Later his hands were under her sweater, her flesh sleek and warm on his palms, and he was reaching up, the wide strap, silk, it felt like silk, his thumbs under the silk, his fingers floating above, hooks and eyes, he thought, twisting the fabric, tugging at it, the smooth silk, the warm, warm back.

"Let me," she said. The sweater tightening over her breasts as she reached back, both hands below her sweater, behind her, working together, parting the straps. "Now the sweater." As she lifted her arms, he gathered the sweater into his hands, raised it over her head, pulled it free of her arms. Red hair tumbling out of the sweater, she slid her shoulder straps down, the bra falling away. Oh, man, he thought, she wants me doing this, me, and he leaned forward, his lips moving on her breasts. Warm and round and full.

"Headache better?" she asked.

"Mmm." His voice sounded strange, husky.

Later still, after they had shed all their clothes, he noticed the line on the soft flesh of her belly where the band of her panties had been a moment before, the white, white skin below, and her hair, tight curls, a red so dark it was almost black.

He reached for his wallet then, flushing as he grabbed his pants from the floor, groping for the hip pocket, finding the wallet, flipping it open, his bank card falling to the floor. He stretched to pick it up, got it, stuffed it back inside, and pulled the condom out at last, fumbling to strip the plastic wrap away, tearing at it with his thumb nail, feeling embarrassed as hell now, but it didn't seem to bother her. When they moved to the sofa, she said, "Wait. Just lie back." His head on the cushion, he closed his eyes, felt her straddle his hips, the solid weight of her on top of him. Like a dream, better than a dream. She began a rocking movement, slow and easy. When he opened his eyes, she said, "You lie there and just relax." She smiled. "If you can."

"Oh," was all he could say. He said it again after that, and louder, but not as often as she.

Later, much later, lying beside her on the sofa, his arm growing stiff beneath her head, his shoulder half-asleep and tingling, he found himself telling her how he'd failed Angela Maddox, how he'd told her he couldn't do it all, she had to help herself, and Kelly's arms were tight around him, her hands rubbing his shoulders, the small of his back, touching his forehead, his lips, her words like a soothing balm: "It's not your fault. It's not, Brad. It never was."

He fell asleep with her breath warm in his ear.

When he drove home a few hours later, he was surprised that he felt no guilt for sleeping with her. He was no womanizer, sex wasn't just a game with him, it had to mean something, had to mean a lot. And it did. He was sure it meant the same to her too.

Then he wondered, should he be so sure?

Maurie Pack was the first to talk about it in the staffroom, the guy who got it started, but everyone else seemed eager enough, as if they couldn't wait to join in.

"Administration wants to improve something around here," Maurie said one day at the long break, "first thing they ought to do is get Kelly Irving the hell out of the office."

"What?" said Brad. One word and his anger was showing.

"Make things efficient for a change."

"She's efficient," said Brad. That was when he noticed Vic Pendleton grinning at him. He glanced at Sue. She was looking at him too, but she wasn't smiling. What was going on here, he wondered.

"She's efficient – right," said Maurie. "But nobody else can do a lick of work in there. You try to get through the door, there's a mob of boys at the counter. Every one of them trying to sneak a look at her boobs."

"First thing we need is a new rule," said Dutch Van Hoek. "Nothing but turtlenecks in the office."

"You guys," said Myrna Belsey. She taught Home Ec on the top floor and seldom made it down to the staffroom.

"Bad enough all fall," said Vic. He grinned at Phil, who so far seemed to be the uninvolved observer. "A lot worse now."

"Damned rights," said Phil. Brad wondered why he was reminded of a relay runner taking a baton. "Nowdays, you finally push through all the kids, you think you might have room to do some work, and there's Cutler hanging on the end of the counter."

Every one of them grinning at him now.

Except Sue. She was watching him, no sign of a smile on her face. Nor anger either. He wondered what she was thinking.

"The guy's in love," said Myrna Belsey.

"Love?" said Sue. "Isn't that the only disease that cures itself?"

"Getting cynical, aren't we, Burton?" said Phil. But when Brad looked at her, she was smiling, no trace of cynicism on her face.

"Hey, you can hardly blame a young fellow," said Bruce Winslow. "Date with her be like having your very own

Playboy centerfold."

Brad knew his face was flaming, his ears turning red.

"No staple in *her* belly-button," said Phil. He paused for a beat. "So they say."

"You guys," said Myrna.

"Course, in *Playboy* they already come naked," said Maurie.

"Stick it," said Brad.

"You don't have to waste any time," said Maurie, "getting them out of their clothes."

"Over the line, guys," said Sue. "Time to change the subject."

For some reason he thought of the warning Sue had given him when he'd started taking Kelly out. "I don't know, Brad. Maybe you should think things through first."

He'd never seen her look so serious. Nor so flustered immediately afterwards.

"I asked her out for coffee. So what?"

"Nothing. Don't get me wrong." She had raised both hands, held them beside her face, palms toward him. She would've looked like a victim of a stick-up except that her face had flushed crimson.

"Seems to me it's no big deal."

"Yes. Of course. You're right." She noticed her hands then, floating in front of her face, and dropped them into her lap. "I need a refill." She grabbed her cup from the end table and started for the coffee urn. The staffroom was empty except for the two of them.

Brad watched her at the counter, jabbing the spiggot with her finger, filling the cup, splashing a spoonful of sugar into it, stirring it, glancing over her shoulder. Like a bird with a broken wing, fluttering along a fence wire while a cat patrols beneath.

He was surprised when she walked back and sat down again beside him. She glanced quickly at him, raised her cup and took a drink. Set it down. "Don't get me wrong," she said. "Kelly's a wonderful girl."

"My opinion exactly."

She took her spoon and scooped at something in her cup. She lifted the spoon, turned it upside down and tapped it into her saucer. "One of the nicest people I know."

Brad waited to see if she'd say more.

She lay her spoon in her saucer. Sat back in her chair, shoulders squared, her eyes straight ahead. "A real fighter for a cause. I think the world of her. Everybody does."

So that was it. "You don't think I should be...I'm not good enough for her. Is that it?"

Her head jerked toward him. "Oh, Brad. Of course not. She's on the rebound."

It was okay then, he had it all wrong. Nothing to worry about here. He smiled at her, leaned forward and patted her hand. "No problem," he said. "We're going for coffee. That's all. Or maybe I'll take her out and we can shoot some baskets, grab some rebounds."

Her face was crimson again. Red with anger this time. When she moved, he thought at first she might reach toward him and rake her nails across his face. But no, it was her cup she was reaching for, raising it from the coffee table to her lap, cradling it there in the palm of one hand, a little shimmer of movement within the cup before the coffee stilled, its surface flat as a tabletop.

"You're behaving like a kid," she said. "Adolescence, you know, isn't meant to stretch from infancy to death." She took a drink of coffee before adding, "And I've heard better puns in grade nine."

The razzing continued sporadically for weeks, most of the guys taking a turn. It bothered Brad, but not enough to make him stop seeing Kelly. On the morning of the American Thanksgiving, he sensed something even before he finished hanging up his coat. The briefest lull in the hum of conversation from the staffroom. He knew without looking toward them that something was going on. They were waiting for him. He knew it, though not one person in the staffroom looked at him as he walked past the washrooms and into the room itself. That was when the mailboxes caught his eye. A wedge of gift paper sticking out of his cubbyhole. Florist's wrap on a bouquet of flowers. He took the package in his hands. Yeah, it felt like flowers. There was a small card taped to the top of the package. "Brad, you really make me thankful," it said. "Love, Kelly." Typed. Probably wasn't her. Anybody could have done it. He began to open the package, ripping at the paper where it was taped shut at the top. The noise of paper tearing, the only sound in the room. He looked up, glanced quickly down. Everyone in the room was watching him. He gave the paper another tug, stripping it away, realized he was holding half a dozen thistle stems in his hand. A burst of laughter in the room. Yeah, and he was probably blushing too. He turned to face them, grinning, shrugging his shoulders. "You got me," he said.

Then he noticed the note attached by a paper clip to one of the stems. "Oh Brad," it said, "I wish that you could be my thistle, that you had just as many pricks." He looked up, furious. Some of them were already looking away, some of them still watching and smiling. Maurie Pack pretending not to watch, but grinning like a fool. You son-of-a-bitch, Brad thought, it's got to be you.

He flung the thistles in the garbage bag and started to stomp from the room, getting almost to the door before he realized he must look like an idiot, and he slowed down, trying to walk normally.

Maybe if he hadn't been such a blusher they would have let up. Yeah, and maybe not. At least, he only lost his temper once.

Fridays, the guys had taken to wearing ties, wildly coloured ties with animated figures on them, Mickey Mouse, Tweetie Bird, Bart Simpson, even James Dean and Humphrey Bogart, each of them trying to come up with something that nobody else wore. It was Vic Pendleton who walked into the school wearing a tie with a hula dancer who looked as if she might glow in the dark.

Phil whistled when he saw it. Brad noticed a look of surprise flash across Vic's face before he glanced down at his chest. Probably forgot what he was wearing.

"Oh, yeah," said Vic, "close as I'll ever get to Hawaii."

"Lookit the knockers on her," said Maurie Pack. Brad looked and saw that her breasts were barely defined, the nipples not even marked. "Must be about a 36 C," said Maurie. "About the same as Brad."

Here we go again, thought Brad. Damned if he'd say a thing.

"How's that?" asked Vic, who looked genuinely puzzled.

"You never noticed?" said Maurie. He was leaning back in his chair at the round table, a smug look on his face. "The way he holds his hands. Kind of cupped in front of his chest. A perfect 36 C, eh? Just praying he'll run into Kelly. Get a hold of –"

Three steps and Brad was across the room. He grabbed Maurie by the tie, hauled him out of his chair, leaned into him and shouted. "Shut your face! Shut your bloody face or I'll shut it for you." Maurie was grey as a shroud. Brad could hear breath rasping in the silent room. Wasn't sure if it was his or Maurie's. He looked at his fist clutching the tie, a drop of spit shining on his knuckle, another staining the bright blue fabric beside something that looked like the head of a golf club. He released the tie, brushing off the spit, the wrinkles falling away to reveal Donald Duck swinging a driver. Swinging and missing the ball.

"Sorry," said Brad, stepping back.

Maurie's face was still grey. He opened his mouth but didn't speak.

"So's he," said Phil Simpson.

Maurie dropped into his chair and turned to glare at Phil. "Like hell," he said.

"Bad behaviour's only repugnant in others, is that it, Maurie?" said Sue. Maurie gave her a dirty look, but he kept his mouth shut. When he thought no one was looking, he ran his fingers over his scalp, combing fallen hairs across his bald spot.

Even after that, the razzing didn't stop. Later the same week Vic Pendleton said, "Nice to be young and feeling your oats."

"Some people," said Bruce, "are feeling more than oats."

"Sowing them maybe," said Dutch. No names were mentioned, but the guys were looking at him.

Nine

December arrived that year masquerading as October, sunshine every day, warm winds, the school boilers shut down for repair. In three days the disguise was ripped away, winter glowering in its place, a chill working its way into the school, into all the classrooms, students huddled in jackets, shivering at their desks.

Live with it, the caretakers had said; by closing time we'll have the boilers ready to fire up again.

Maybe Eliot had it wrong and December was the cruelest month. Brad knew there was a baseboard heater in the office, wondered how to get one for his room. Walking into the staffroom, he heard Maurie Pack complaining about his grade tens.

"They come slouching in, coats eight sizes too big for them, nearly dragging on the floor. Think they can break the rules, they got another think coming."

Jerk, Brad thought. Some day, if Maurie didn't learn to keep his yap shut, he'd really get himself pounded.

"Exactly what rule would they be breaking, Maurie?" asked Phil Simpson.

"My rule. No coats allowed in the classroom."

"C'mon, Maurie, it's cold outside – in here too."

"Rules are rules," said Maurie. "Let them wear their coats, they drive you crazy, putting them on, pulling them off, hauling a dozen different kinds of junk out of every pocket."

"Maurie," said Sue, "that education degree on your wall's not a license to make life miserable for the kids."

"Screw you, Burton."

"Hey, back off," said Brad. "You're out of line."

"Mm," added Phil Simpson. "Interesting way to spend some time, though."

"Some day, Phil," said Sue, her tone thick with honey for just an instant before it changed, "some day you'll maybe hoist your brains above your belt."

Funny about these two, thought Brad, you'd never guess they like each other. But not Maurie.

And now Maurie was glaring at him. "Yeah, we know who's the real lover boy around here."

Brad ignored him. Better not get Maurie going. Uh-huh, be a good time to get out of here, maybe wander into the office, warm his bones before he went back to the basement. His room was colder than a tomb; they could lay Juliet under a shroud down there, nobody'd think a thing about it.

When he pulled the office door open, he noted the principal's closed door, saw Herb standing in front of the heater. The pleasure on his face gave way to a sheepish look. "Wouldn't want the computers to seize up in the cold," he said and hurried back into his office.

Kelly was at her keyboard, typing steadily.

"At least somebody's warm," said Brad.

She glanced up, nodded her head, kept typing.

Brad checked around the office. "I tell you, I could use

some warming up myself. How be we get together later on this evening? Around nine, maybe."

The typing stopped. "I've been meaning to – yes, nine would be fine. Meet you at Smitty's. On the highway." Staccato phrases falling like ice cubes on a steel counter.

"I can pick you up."

"No. I've got some running around to do. I'll meet you there." She bent away from him, typing again.

As he walked down to class, he shivered in the chill air of the stairwell.

B rad took a seat in the third booth, facing the door where he'd see Kelly when she walked in. Something was bugging her, must've been a bad day at work. He looked out the window. The weather was changing again. A gas jockey hurried out to the pumps, his head ducked against the rain that threatened to turn once more to snow. A half-ton at the pumps. No sign of Kelly's white Nissan.

He ordered coffee, told the waiter to check back again, he was expecting someone. Then he looked up and she was coming through the doorway, shaking her head, a mist of tiny raindrops falling away from that magnificent hair. "Make it two," he called to the waiter.

As she walked toward him, he knew people in the other booths would be turning to look at her. Some of them glanced up, noticed her, tried to appear casual, continued their conversations, but they couldn't keep their eyes off her. A few simply stopped talking and stared. Everyone envies me, he thought, an icicle growing somewhere in his stomach. What the hell was wrong with him?

She slid into the booth across from him. "Hi," she said.

Nothing more.

"Coffee's on its way. You want anything else?"

"No. No thanks." She glanced away from him, watching the waiter walk toward them and fill their cups, pouring too much, spilling coffee in her saucer. She took a napkin, folded it in two, lifted the cup, wiped its bottom and laid the napkin in the saucer.

Such fine hands, he thought, white fingers, long and tapered. He knew the feel of those fingers, the way they struck sparks along his spine.

"I don't know how to say this." She'd set the cup upon the napkin, was looking straight at him.

He should change the subject, get on to something else. If she didn't say it now, she might never say it, things could go on the way they were.

"What?" he asked. "What is it you don't know how to say." Oh Lord, and why did he have to ask her that?

His eyes on hers, imploring her not to say it. She looked down at her coffee cup, raised it slowly to her lips, sipped, a drop of coffee on that full lower lip before she raised her fingertip and wiped it off.

"Brad," she said. She set the cup on the table, folded another napkin and laid it in the saucer before replacing the cup. "You're a wonderful guy, somebody I really admire. I'll always think a lot of you." She picked up her cup, got it half way to her lips, set it down again. "We had some good times, didn't we?" She paused and looked at him.

He had to say something. "It sounds as if they're over." In his throat, a sliver of ice that coffee would not melt.

"I'm sorry, Brad. I really am." Her eyes glistened, tears welling on the lower lids, beginning to run. She reached for another napkin, dabbed at her eyes, her cheeks. "I didn't want it to be this way. I never meant to..." She wiped away some tears, smothered a sniffle with the napkin.

"What way?" His voice was too loud. He dropped it to a whisper and said, "I don't understand."

Once more she dabbed at her cheeks, then set the napkin on the table, placing both hands firmly upon it as if it might leap up and take another swipe at her eyes. The eyes that looked at him, and down at her lap, then returned to lock on his.

"Frank's back in town. Transferred to the base again." She was speaking quickly, an edge of panic in her voice. "He requested the transfer, but he couldn't get it right away. I didn't know I was still – I honestly thought it was over. Brad, I'm sorry, but he's the one for me."

It was Brad who looked away. The window beside him shaking a little in the wind, sleet beating against the glass.

"Oh," he said. It was all he could think to say.

"I didn't mean it to turn out like this." She took a breath. "It has nothing to do with you. It's me. If I'd only known, I never would have started up with you."

Outside, a sheet of newspaper was lifted by the wind and hurled against a gas pump, held there a moment, one edge slapping at the pump, before it was torn away, twisting across the pavement.

"Talk to me, Brad."

"What's to say?"

The paper caught in a puddle, almost lifted, then slowly collapsed into the water.

"I couldn't help it, Brad. Life doesn't always...it gets away on us sometimes." When he looked at her, she said, "I think a lot of you, Brad. I always will."

"Yeah, sure." He'd thought she loved him, but it must've been an act. That was it, sure. But it hadn't felt like an act.

How was he supposed to know the difference?

She reached across the table and took his hand, a sudden shock of warmth on his.

"I hope we can still be friends."

"Friends." He tugged his hand away. "Go. Will you? Just get the hell out of here."

She pulled back as if he'd slapped her. So that's it, he thought, we're done, but she was already out of the booth, hurrying toward the door.

Kelly had broken it off and, almost as if a referee had blown a whistle, the razzing stopped. They must've known. Hell, one look at him and anybody would've known. Still, he'd always wonder if someone had told them to stop.

Three days later, Workman spotted him in the hallway and walked over to him, a smile sliding across his face. A smile like a grimace. "Smart move, Cutler," he said. "Good to see you took my advice about the company dock."

Fury rose in his throat, hot and choking, and for an instant, Brad thought he might hit the man. Somehow he managed to turn away. "Yeah," he said, the sound like a grunt, but he kept walking.

The weather turned colder day by day. Although the streets were almost bare of snow, ice was thick on the river, and city crews had flooded all the outdoor rinks. Friday evening Brad dug out his skates from the back of his closet and drove down to the speed-skating oval in River Park. Walking from his car to the heated change-shack, he heard laughter and scanned the oval lit by streetlights; he saw kids playing crack-the-whip at the far end, others bent low over their skates, arms swinging as they raced along the straight-away. Half a dozen couples skating hand-in-hand.

He walked past the shack toward the river bank, gazed at the river, clear ice stretching from shore to shore and shining beneath a full moon. This was better. He didn't need anybody else around right now.

After searching along the bank, he found what looked like a raft pulled onto the sand. He sat down. Imagined kids poling it across the river in springtime, backs bending with their work, current catching them as they pushed away from shore. But it wasn't a kid's raft. Probably something the city had made for launching canoes in the summer.

And Huckleberry Finn, he thought, bet he never saw a river made of ice.

He laced up his skates, pulling them tight, liking the feel of the leather firm against his ankles. When he stepped gingerly onto the ice, there was no give beneath him. It really was frozen solid.

He struck out away from the oval and the lights, passing under a bridge, turning a corner, something swinging at him from the shadows, almost hitting him as he skidded to a stop, breath loud in his throat. But it was only a branch hanging low over the river. He pushed away from the bank where everything dissolved in a black smudge, and glided to the centre of the river where the ice picked up the moon's gleam. Skating beside the empty city campground, a few dim lights in the distance beside the River Park Road, he wished he had a hockey stick in his hands. It would feel more natural.

Stritch, stritch, stritch, his skates on the ice the only sound in the whole night, his legs pumping, getting into a rhythm, the skating easier now, and faster. He turned another corner, cruised beneath another, lower, bridge, heard a cooing on the girders above him, recognized it as pigeons, the explosion of wings startling him as they took off, alarmed by his sudden appearance beneath them.

He skated on, glad to be working his muscles. Around turn after turn in this, the river of turns, passing under a streetlight at the corner of a rusty iron bridge, then a black steel trestle like a giant's scaffolding against the night sky, next to it the massive pillars of the concrete bridge that carried the highway south of town, the whine of cars fading into the night. His cheeks stinging with cold, his breath quick puffs of white haze flowing behind him.

In places, the ice was almost like a freshly flooded rink. He kept going, the city on his right, the lights of houses shining above the cutbank that rose stark and sheer in the moonlight, the countryside on his left, a jumble of willows and poplars, their branches like ghostly, reaching arms, a field of grass stretching behind them, frosty and white. He kept skating, a slight ache in his shoulders and his quads, but a pleasant ache – the ache of muscles alive and working, a little rasp of breath in his throat to go with the sound of his skates as they stitched their pattern on the ice.

Another corner, and the city was behind him, the moon straight ahead, the whole white river unfolding before him, and he thought of Alfred Noyes and his ribbon of moonlight, the highwayman whipping his horse over the purple moor, riding to join the landlord's daughter, his lovely, black-eyed daughter, coming to her by moonlight, hoof-beats ringing through the frosty silence. Ah, but this was no ribbon of moonlight, just a frozen river, the moon's glimmer on the ice no more than a cold pallor, and there wasn't anyone ahead to wait for him.

No matter. It felt good skating.

On the wall beside the intercom he had hung a small cork board where anyone entering the class would see it. Though Larson had quit drawing his cartoons for newspapers years ago, Brad had collected half a dozen *Far Side* books. Each morning, he copied one cartoon he liked and posted it on the cork board. It never hurt to start the class with a smile. God knows, that was something they all needed. If he was watching when the kids came in there'd be the odd one who made a point of never stopping to look at the cartoons. Most of them, however, would pause for a quick peek on their way to their seats, and most of them sat down grinning. Some of them chuckled out loud.

Once, fifteen minutes into class, Walter Buchko had started to giggle. When Brad asked him what was going on, he shook his head and said, "Sorry, sir. That darned cartoon. It just popped into my head again – that silly cow reading poetry."

About once a week June Perkins announced, "I don't get it." Today, she stared a minute at a group of cows inside a barn, another looking in the window, being told there wasn't any room, she'd have to sleep in the house. "I just don't get it," June said. Then she grinned, unperturbed. "Goes to show you I'm not as warped as the rest of you guys."

That day after school, Brad was at his desk, staring at a set of essays that needed marking badly. No, he thought, misplaced modifier. The need is bad, the marking better be good. He was suddenly aware of people in the room. Looked up to see Willie Thornton standing just inside the door, his arm around a girl. Cheryl Dunlop, the one who'd been so drunk at the Halloween dance. He hadn't seen her since, although the next week he'd checked with her form room teacher to make sure she was okay.

"Didn't mean to bother you, Mr. C. Just wanted to show Cheryl today's cartoon."

"Sure. Go ahead."

The two of them stepped to the cork board, his arm still around her, her leaning against him, the two of them reading, chuckling together. He thought of driving with Kelly, putting his arm around her, the way she used to lean into him, the swell of her breast against his side. It was almost two weeks now, and he couldn't get her out of his head.

"...copy maybe?"

"Pardon me?"

"Her dad's a minister," said Willie. "We kinda think he'd like it. You mind if we make a copy?"

"No. Take that one. Everybody's seen it."

Willie released his hold on the girl, removed the cartoon from the cork board, gave it one neat fold and slid it into his pocket. He started for the door, then turned back to Brad.

"That Smith book," he said, "you know, I didn't think I'd like it, cowboys and all, but it really cracks me up. Especially that Ol' Antoine character. Wait till next year," he said to Cheryl, "you're gonna love it."

When they left the room, his arm was around her once again and they had to squeeze together as they passed through the narrow doorway. After they were gone, Brad sat for a long time staring down the empty hall.

It wasn't love, not with her anyway, that was for damned sure. Maybe not with him either. He was getting over her – wasn't he? – thinking of other things. Sure he was. No doubt about it. Anyway, he knew she'd liked him, liked him a lot, for a while at least, and then everything went down the drain.

He thought about how she'd told him Frank was back, it was all over between them, that was it, he could get lost for all she cared. Only she hadn't put it that way, hell, she'd come into the restaurant looking so sad you'd have thought she'd just heard all the rain forests in South America were burned off. Trying not to hurt him. Wanting not to hurt him. And he'd sat there like a lump, his mouth sewn shut till he told her to get the hell out of there.

Maybe he hadn't loved her after all, liking her so much he didn't know the difference, not when he was with her, in bed with her, Kelly so good at sex, so generous with him, he didn't know what to think. Didn't even know how he felt.

He couldn't very well go over to her apartment, take the chance of running into Frank. That would be real sweet, wouldn't it? The phone was no good. He had to see her when he talked to her. The last two weeks, he'd hardly stepped into the office, but when he couldn't avoid some business there, he made a point of not looking at her. Once when he did glance at her, he saw that she was ducking her head, studying something on her keyboard, just as concerned as he was to avoid eye contact. This was no way to live.

She deserved better than that. She deserved an apology.

٦ rked at the same school; they had to get beyond thi٢ e was the one who had to get beyond this, the on١ ٢ehaved like an ass.

١ : of times he strolled by the office after school, flir ck glances through the glass doors, but there wa a teacher at the cardex record file or a student at th . Once, the room was empty and he hurried in just about to speak, when he realized that a stu- de ٥ollowed him through the door. The student needed a copy of his marks for a job application. When

Kelly turned to get it, Brad ducked out the door.

The next day she came into the staffroom after school, poured herself a coffee and sat down in a chair four seats away from him, her eyes under that wild tangle of hair not once looking in his direction. The only other person in the room was Sue Burton who'd been sitting next to him. They'd been talking, but suddenly Brad couldn't remember what they were talking about.

"...not a bad kid," said Sue, "if you give him a chance." She paused.

Like a garden of red vines that's run amuck, red creepers tumbling over her forehead, her shoulders.

Sue was staring at him, a puzzled look on her face.

"Oh, yeah," he said. "Good kid." Who, he wondered, who the hell are we talking about?

Sue glanced to her left where Kelly sat. Picked up her coffee cup and took it to the sink. "I'll wash it later," she said and left the room. She knew. No doubt about it. Kelly watched her disappear into the hall, looked for a second as if she might follow her.

Brad stood up quickly and walked toward Kelly, hesitating a second before dropping into the chair beside her. He thought she shuddered when the springs creaked, but she was still looking toward the door. It was the closest he'd been to her in two weeks; he caught the scent of her, something better than perfume. He shivered.

"That night," he said, "when you told me we were through..." He leaned closer, tried to focus on the pupils of her eyes, vivid black in the midst of all that green – but they weren't black, they were charcoal, cobalt, dark brown, a mixture of colours. He looked away, saw the fridge across the room, a little gob of dried food stuck on the chrome handle. "I'm sorry," he said. "I behaved like a dork. You were..." What was the word he wanted? "...gracious. Perfectly gracious." What the hell did that mean? "I didn't want to swear – didn't know I was going to till it was already out." He should go over to the cupboard, get a knife and scrape the fridge handle clean. Oh, yeah. Then he could give the knife to her, let her finish the job, plunge it into his heart. Come on, cut the melodrama, get it done. "It hurt, is all. I know you were doing everything you could – trying to let me down easily. I apologize for my behaviour." She must be looking at him, he could feel the left side of his face getting warm. There was a stain beside the handle of the fridge, a pale orange stain running down the enamel and disappearing into the rubber that extended around the door. "Frank," he said, "he's a lucky guy. I envy him." Forget it, let's not get stuck on Frank. "I'll get over it." No, no, that wasn't right. "Friends, if we could still be friends..."

"Of course. We are." Her words so close it was as if she'd mouthed them directly into his ear.

"Good. I want to be able to come into the office and smile at you. Talk to you."

"There'll be other girls, Brad."

God, he must sound like some heart-sick wimp. "Other girls – yeah. I've got a date for Friday night. Who knows where that'll lead, eh?"

"Never can tell." The words like notes struck on a tuning fork. Then he heard a change in tone, huskiness entering her voice. "Thanks, Brad, thanks for telling me this. It makes everything so much better." Then she was leaning towards him. The sudden warmth of her breath, the feel of her lips brushing his cheek, the little puff of sound like a quick gust of static as she kissed him. "You're a good guy," she said, and he turned to look at her, found on her face the smile that he thought he'd never see again, like a sunrise after days of drizzle, sudden warmth after weeks of low cloud.

He felt something shift inside him, tried to keep from shaking. Another minute. He could hold it together that long, he had to. "You're not so bad yourself," he said. A dumb cliché, but it would do, sure, it would do just fine.

Later, after she'd reached towards him, touched his arm and given it a squeeze, after she'd taken her cup to the sink, washing it and Sue's too, drying them both and putting them back inside the cupboard, after she had smiled at him once more and turned away, walking back into the office, he continued to sit there beside her empty chair, wondering how he felt. His arm was still warm from the gentle pressure of her fingers. This was the way to do it, he thought, this was better than before.

He felt as if he were about to smile, nothing more than a little curl of the lips, but something like a smile. Now, where the hell would he get a date for Friday night?

Ten

The week before Christmas, he was sitting in the staffroom, looking glum, he guessed, still thinking about Kelly when he should be working, so many things to do before the holiday he wondered if he'd even make it. No plane booked for the trip to see his parents in Victoria, he guessed he'd have to drive.

"Cheer up," Phil said. "Best time of the year to be a new teacher."

"I don't know," he said. "So busy doing lessons, I'm way behind on marking. Sick of it to boot."

"Hang in there," said Vic. "First year is always tough." Good, old Vic, you could always count on him for encouragement.

"School Board knows it too," said Phil. "They appreciate the strain on new teachers. Which is why they waste money buying gifts this time of year for young punks like you."

"You're kidding?"

"Straight goods."

Brad considered Phil a minute, steady eyes staring back at him. He turned to Vic. "Straight goods?" he asked.

Vic shook his head. "Not for teachers new to the system," he said. "First year teachers period. New to the profession."

"Wouldn't you know it!" said Phil.

"Get over it," said Vic. "He taught a year in Herbert before he got accepted in the city. Still figures they owe him a turkey."

"You don't want yours," said Phil, "I'll take it off your hands."

"They deliver it to the school?"

"You kidding?" said Vic. "This system, they expect you to walk a mile for everything you get."

"Go up to the Board office after school," said Phil. "You have to ask for McAvoy."

"Wants to hand them out himself," said Vic. "Likes the chance to feel magnanimous."

"Right!" said Phil. "Likes making every first year teacher think he owes him one."

"Didn't work with Rutledge," said Vic. "Rutledge wanted to know if he could pick it up when it was cooked."

Brad laughed with the two of them, decided he could maybe quit early tonight, make it to the Board Office before it closed at five.

It was only his third time in the building. He'd been here once when he'd had his job interview with the high school supervisor, once more when the school copier had broken down and he'd desperately needed to run off exams for the next day. This time, as he approached the secretary, he glanced into the Board room. A long oak table, around it deep plush chairs on rollers. A shag carpet so thick he wondered if the rollers would turn.

"I help you?"

He wheeled around. "I was hoping to see Dr. McAvoy."

"Try his secretary. Two doors down."

His own secretary. Wow. Spread some of this money around, he could get another set of novels for his grade tens. *Of Mice and Men,* maybe. Knock their socks off.

The door was open, McAvoy's secretary working at a computer, the cord from a dictaphone running to her ear. "Excuse me," he said. No response. He gave the doorframe a sharp rap with his fist.

"One minute," she said. She kept typing, finishing a sentence, he guessed, then raised one hand to her ear, extracting the plug and holding it beside her head. She seemed to be studying her computer screen. "What is it?"

"I'd like to see Dr. McAvoy if I could."

"About?"

"What? Oh, getting my Christmas turkey."

Her eyes flicked up at him. "Another one," she said. Her right hand still hovered beside her ear. "Name?"

"Cutler. Brad."

"School?"

"Lawrence."

She turned away from him, pressed a button on her intercom, leaned toward it and said, "Excuse me, Dr. McAvoy. Cutler Brad from Lawrence is here. You want to see him?"

"Send him in."

She was sticking the cord back in her ear before the director had finished, but she did manage a curt nod toward his door.

When Brad went into the office, McAvoy was leaning back in his chair, waiting for him. He was a large jowly man, broad of shoulder and big of belly. Looked like a retired wrestler, Brad thought, somebody who'd been on the speakers' circuit and couldn't push himself away from the banquet table.

"Mr. Cutler, good to see you. Things okay? First year going fine? No problems at the school, I trust."

"No sir." All he needed to know was how to bring Angela Maddox back to life, how to handle kids like Bert Peale and Parker Stone. "I don't want to trouble you. They said I should see you to get my turkey."

"Oh," he said. "Yes, the Christmas turkey." He ran his hand across his mouth. "I don't think we even got the announcement out yet this year. Someone must've told you."

"Yeah, Phil. Phil Simpson."

"Good for him." He glanced away from Brad, fingered his desk calendar, picked it up. "The thing is, we're running late this year. Turkeys don't arrive until tomorrow." He set the calendar down again. "Tell you what. Soon as they're here, we'll send yours down to the school."

"I don't want to be a bother."

"No bother. You made the trip once for nothing. Should be there tomorrow morning."

The turkey was delivered midway through the long break. Brad was called to the staffroom door to pick it up, a big bird, fifteen pounds at least, frozen solid and wrapped in butcher's paper, an envelope bearing his name taped across the top. The guy from the meat market gave him a big smile as he passed it over. Brad needed both hands to carry it, had to open the door with his foot. When he walked back into the staffroom, the usual hubbub dropped away, silence spreading as he entered. He set the turkey on the big table and lifted the card off it.

"What the hell is that?" said Maurie Pack.

"My Christmas turkey." They were all staring at him.

"Where'd it come from?" Phil asked.

"Dr. McAvoy said he'd send it down."

"Come on," said Vic. "Couldn't be."

"What?" said Brad. He noticed Sue turn towards Phil, a bubble of laughter in her throat. He was such a bloody innocent. They were having him on. For sure. But the turkey was here, they were the ones looking puzzled. What was going on?

Brad got his fingernail under the flap of the envelope and ripped it open. Pulled out the card.

"What's it say?" "Who's it from?" Phil and Vic speaking at the same time.

Brad held the card above their heads so they couldn't see it as he read it to himself. He read it once. Read it again, grinning. Paused. Looked around the room. "I'll read you what he says. 'Dear Mr. Cutler. It's a pleasure to have someone young and energetic on our staff. They need a shot in the arm down there at Lawrence. On behalf of everyone at the board office, we're pleased to send you your Christmas turkey and wish you all the best for the holiday season. T. A. McAvoy.'" He glanced up, found himself the centre of a circle of perplexity. "There's a little more. I should probably read you that too. 'P.S. You can tell Phil Simpson we're sending him the bill for the bird.'"

A burst of laughter. They were all laughing, all of them but Phil. Then Brad was laughing too, real laughter, like an elixir bubbling in his throat.

They were still talking about it the next day.

"Christmas turkey's been suckering people for years," said Vic. "You're the first guy ever got one. Some time in the future – years from now – they'll be talking about you in the same breath with Rutledge."

Maybe, thought Brad, might be kind of nice, everybody going on about it, but he'd settle for getting along with Workman – sure, let the boss extend his contract, that would do just fine.

"Rutledge the one who started sucking people in?" asked Sue.

"Nope. Been going on longer than that. A legend in the system, eh? Rutledge got suckered too."

"Good story, though," said Phil.

"Had a hell of a time with him," said Vic. "Rutledge wasn't your normal trusting soul, but he sure wouldn't mind a free turkey. Eventually, we got him. Off he goes to the Board Office. Potter was director then. I guess Rutledge announces he's come to pick up his Christmas turkey. While the secretary's showing him into Potter's office, she and Potter have a hard time keeping a straight face. Rutledge catches them grinning, he knows something's up, just doesn't know what. Potter tells him that maybe the fellows in the men's staffroom have been stringing him along. That's all it takes for Rutledge. He's got it figured out. It's Potter who's trying to con him. Going to trick him out of his turkey. So he stands there and argues: other new teachers got a turkey, he bloody well better get one too."

"Interesting," said Sue, "but I think Brad's story's better."

"One thing about it," said Vic, "anybody new on staff next year, you can swear to them you got your Christmas turkey. No need to lie."

Yeah, he thought, if I'm here next year.

Then he remembered Christmas holidays, and he was felt good again.

He arrived in Victoria on Christmas Eve, making the whole trip in two days, tired from driving it alone, most of the Trans-Canada free of snow, but the Coquihalla Highway slick with ice. His mother buzzed him in, met him at the elevator, wrapped him in her arms, and held him as if she hadn't seen him for a decade. When he hugged his father inside their doorway, it was like squeezing a statue, body cold and hard as bronze, but then his father hugged him back.

His mother said she already had a turkey, she'd save his for the next visit. They had Christmas dinner in his parents' condo, exchanging presents around a Douglas fir, the first real tree they'd had in years. He was content to spend a few days on their chesterfield, a Gail Bowen mystery in his hand, his mind a million miles from school, but his father was soon prowling around the living room, wanting to show him the city and the ocean.

They left his mother on the balcony with her watering can, moving like a hummingbird from plant to plant. "I've got things to do," she said. "Go ahead – the two of you." He wondered about that, her setting him up to be alone with the old man.

They drove through streets where no snow lay, where shrubs still grew, boarded a whale-watcher in the downtown harbour. It looked too small for the ocean, too frail, little more than a rubber dinghy with wooden seats and a motor on the back. "Don't you worry," his father said. "It's a Zodiac, and it is going to fly."

Maybe this would be okay, they'd just do some tourist things together.

When the driver cranked the motor up, it responded like a speedboat, moving faster than he could believe, slamming over the waves like a snowmobile bouncing over winter prairie. Far out on the ocean there were still no whales in sight, but with the waves leaping beneath them, the spray in his face, he hardly cared. They rode beside an island where bald eagles nested, one of them soaring above them, circling on wings that barely moved, and near the shore he spotted a lone seal bobbing in the waves, its dark snout raised toward them. "Just wait," his father said, "wait till you get a look at the sea lions."

He's enjoying this, Brad thought, and so am I.

On their way back toward Victoria their driver cut the motor near a small lighthouse and they drifted alongside a rocky island where the sea lions lay, more than a dozen of them lounging in the sun, their hides glistening, most of them heavier than any cattle Brad had ever seen, one of them sliding into the water, waves rising from it as from a boat being launched. "Tons," his father said, "they must weigh tons. See the blubber on them."

Coming back through the harbour, Brad looked at the Empress Hotel in front of them, smiling at the sign advertising high tea in the afternoon.

"It's a whole different world," he said when the boat had slowed and it was easier to talk. "Nothing like Saskatchewan."

"You can smell the difference," his father said. "It's the moisture in the air. December – and everything is green." Brad thought his voice sounded lighter, younger than it had in years.

"You like it here, don't you?"

"I tell you, even a fool can grow things here." His father turned to him then, a sudden frown creasing his face. "The price of land is out of sight, and it's sure as hell not the home place."

Brad shrugged. He didn't want to get into it, but his father wasn't finished: "Living in a condo's not for me. The same bloody building as a dozen neighbours, like sleeping in a stack of boxes. Nothing like a farm. You can't even walk out onto your own land. Huh. Can't ever do that again. Thanks to you." He shifted in his seat, staring straight ahead. "Your mother likes it, though."

Yeah, thought Brad, and you do too, you old reprobate, but you'll never let me hear you say it.

Still, he knew that things were changing for the better.

January swept by in a haze, two weeks to get his classes finished, then final exams to mark, preparations for a new semester. On the last day of classes, when he was handing out review outlines to his grade twelves, Parker Stone looked up at him and asked, "You still going to be here next semester?"

"Not likely," said Bert Peale. "They got a new teacher coming in."

Brad felt a chill, nerves jumping in his stomach. He wondered if they'd heard something from the caretakers – the caretakers always knew what was going on – but no, that was crazy, Workman wouldn't tell the caretakers he was firing a teacher, they were riding him was all, grabbing another chance to make life tough.

He guessed the second semester would be just as hard as the first.

Eleven

"When a kid is away, you have three days to get a note from him," said Mr. Workman, addressing the staff at their February meeting. "No note in three days, you turn the matter over to Mr. Schwitzer. Understood?" He asked the question, but he didn't look up from his notes to check for a response. "At this point in time it's something I shouldn't need to explain."

Come on, thought Brad, *in time's* redundant.

"Something else," said Workman. "We have a few students disappearing in period five. Anybody doesn't show up in period five, you check the attendance sheet from period four. If he's not marked absent there, he's skipping out. Let me make this clear. You check your attendance at the start of period five; anybody who's absent then, but isn't absent on the sheet is skipping your class. You have to compare the two."

"Oh, brother," said Brad, but he said it under his breath. Beside him, Vic Pendleton raised his head to stare at him.

"Mr. Schwitzer will want to see anybody skipping school," said Workman. "Make sure they're sent to him." He swept the room with his eyes, swung back to the door in the corner of the room. "Miss Irving is here with the doughnuts. Two minutes to pick your choice."

Brad caught a glimpse of Kelly and joined the rush to the back of the room. She was gone when he got there. He stepped into the hall in time to see her shapely legs disappearing up the stairs.

When he sat down again with a cruller, Vic Pendleton leaned toward him. "Sure, he goes on a bit sometimes," Vic was almost whispering, but there was a knife edge in his voice. "Let me tell you something, though. He was vice-principal here for fifteen years. For a while, back then, it was a rough school. Everybody doing his own thing. No policy, no standard procedures. Hell, hardly any rules. He worked his ass off to get things straightened around. No wonder he likes to lay everything out."

"I didn't know."

"Okay. No problem." The knife was back in its sheath. "Maybe he does take it easy some of the time. He's tired, eh? I figure he's earned it."

Brad nodded his head – barely. He liked Vic, didn't want to offend him, but Workman, he didn't give a damn about Workman.

The principal was standing again at the front of the room, like a king who had no use for his subjects. "We've had some bad publicity lately," he said. Brad wondered if he were referring to the death of Angela Maddox. It had come up at the school board, probably had everybody talking too. "A variety of things," Workman continued, "the paper included. Damned foolish editorial, taking a stand against final exams. They ought to realize the benefits of finals. Kids having to study, bring together a body of knowledge. Good training for university, but I don't have to tell you that." He allowed a smile to cross his face. "One of the fellows at Rotary said we could use a public relations man like that school on the other side of Main. Cracking wise, you know."

Yeah, their drama guy was always talking to the paper, getting items printed on his school. Funny thing, thought Brad, Workman hadn't referred to Macoun High by name. Matter of fact, he never used the name. Rivalries ran deep. Must go back a long way.

"Well," said Workman, laying more weight on the word than it seemed to merit, "at this point in time I'd say we've got thirty-two public relations men – excuse me, ladies – *officers* in this very room. Mr. Van Hoek, this is important. Basketball practice can wait a few minutes."

Brad glanced at the back of the room where Dutch Van Hoek was sliding back into his chair, a sheepish expression on his face. Better watch it, Dutch. No sneaking off when the boss is standing on the dock, laying down the law.

"You too, Mr. Cutler." Brad spun away from Dutch. He knew his face was flushed. "I am not kidding about this. The best publicity in the world comes from students who like their teachers, who know they're doing a good job, and tell their parents about it. Consider that – the next time somebody gets on your nerves." He paused, staring down at them. Staring at me, thought Brad, giving me the gears. He's been listening again, hearing me go at it with Bert Peale. "Now, I've been studying something of late. I think what's needed at this point in time is a new policy for our institution."

On the other side of him, Brad noticed Sue Burton doodling, round, sweeping lines circling a series of dots. Uh-huh, he thought, points in time. She better not let Workman see her.

"This policy will require each of you to make four phone

calls this week and one every week hereafter. I see no reason for any groaning. Let me finish. Usually we phone parents when their children are misbehaving. It doesn't make them happy. Well, what the school needs more than anything else at this point in time is some good publicity. Every phone call you make is to be about something positive, a boy who's raised his average, a girl whose attendance has improved, someone who's participating in class, answering questions, doing homework. Those parents deserve to feel good." He looked up from his notes, studying his audience. "It's our job to make them feel good. Four times this week." He glanced quickly back at his notes. "Four times thirty-two teachers equals one hundred and twenty-eight sets of parents who are feeling good about this school. And, believe me, they'll talk to their friends. I can't begin to explain the value of such good feelings – especially at this particular point in time."

Before Workman had finished his sentence, Brad glanced at Sue who was silently mouthing the words of the principal. She grinned, though, when the word "particular" threw off her timing.

After the meeting, as the teachers filed from the room, a few of them were grousing about their new duty. "Something else to fill my days," said Myrna Belsey. "Four flights of stairs from the Home Ec lab to the nearest phone."

"With my luck," said Maurie Pack, "I'll be on the phone all week with busy signals."

"Come on, Maurie," said Phil Simpson. "Your problem's going to be finding four kids to compliment."

"Up yours."

"Whereas you –" Sue gave Phil a quick nudge "will, no doubt, be phoning the single moms, the good-looking ones, anyway."

"Come off it, Burton. They're the ones who phone me – even in Regina." Phil had been commuting to work for years. "Hell, I'm thinking of taking out an unlisted number."

"Got an idea," said Brad. "I can call Dr. Peale, tell him Bert is doing much better – only mouthed off once this week."

Hand it to Workman, Brad thought, to come up with some empty plan like this to waste his time. He didn't like phoning parents. It always took way longer than he thought it would. They were invariably out when he phoned or grumpy at being bothered at home. What the heck though, he didn't have much choice. He'd get out his day book, check kids' names, see which ones could use a boost, which ones deserved a boost. Jay Marsh, maybe.

He waited until the staffroom was cleared out before trying his calls. He wasn't sure how this was going to work, didn't need other teachers hearing whatever he had to say.

He chose Della Neudorf's parents for his first call. Back in September and October, Della had missed at least a class a week, sometimes two. The first time he saw her, she reminded him of Angela Maddox, an expression on her face that said she didn't care. But Angela had always looked kind of empty – yeah, hollow, finished, and no bloody wonder. Della never looked at him without a glower on her face. He didn't know what the trouble was at first, but he didn't want to fail with her too. He tried to combat her antagonism with frequent smiles, a quick use of her name every time he passed her in the halls. The problem, the way he eventually figured it, was really quite simple: she hated English, she hated English teachers, and she hated him. And he was already doing everything he could think of to make his classes interesting. Then one day in early December, when he was reading "The Devil and Daniel Webster," really getting into it, using a hellish voice for the judge from hell, the one who had never regretted his part in the Salem witch trials, he glanced at Della and noticed her give a little shiver of what looked like excitement, as the judge roared, "Repent of such notable wonders and undertakings? Nay, hang them – hang them all!" The next day, passing him in the hall, she gave him the briefest of smiles. Now her attendance was improving, her English mark rising.

He dialed the Neudorf number, listened to the phone ring. Four times. Five times. He was about to hang it up, when he heard the phone lifted, a voice saying, "Just a minute." A woman's voice. In the background, he thought he heard quick steps, a clatter of metal, more quick steps.

"Sorry. I'm in the middle of supper."

"I could phone back –"

"No, you might as well go ahead."

"Mrs. Neudorf, I'm –"

"This is Mrs. Phillips."

"Sorry." He'd gotten the home number from the cardex file. It was supposed to be kept up to date. "I thought I had Della Neudorf's mother."

"I'm Della's mother. Who is this?" Her voice was dark with suspicion.

"Brad Cutler from Lawrence Collegiate. I'm Della's English teacher."

"Oh. I see." A hint of crustiness. "What's she done now?"

"Nothing. I'm phoning –"

"Look. I tell her school's important, but she won't work. She got off to a bad start in grade one. She's always had trouble –"

The sentences were tumbling out; he had to set her straight.

"Mrs. Phillips! Excuse me. You misunderstand. I'm phoning to say how pleased I am with Della."

"What?"

"I think she's turning things around. She gets here a lot more often; her marks are going up; her attitude –"

"Yeah, it's always been a –"

"Is good, Mrs. Phillips. She's really trying. In fact, I think she kind of likes the class. I know I enjoy having her there."

"You're her English teacher?" A perplexed tone to her voice.

"Yes. She hasn't missed a class this month."

"Her English teacher. Every year she nearly flunks."

"You don't need to worry about that this year. Not the way she's been working lately."

"Working lately." The woman's voice sounded like an echo, a slightly puzzled echo. "She's going to make it then?"

"She's doing fine. You can be proud of her."

"Oh. Oh, I am. Yes. Thank you." There was a rush of warmth in the woman's voice. "I'll tell her what you said. Thank you very much." Before she hung up the phone, Brad heard her call, "Della."

For two months "sour" had been the one word that Della always brought to mind, the sullen face, resentment heating in her eyes, a sulky mouth, head often turned away, but more than once lately Brad had seen a smile that changed every aspect of her face. He guessed her mother was about to see that smile now.

Maybe Workman was on to something here. You had to hand it to the old goat. Not that this call was going to start some giant public relations coup that would change community attitudes to the school – not likely. Still, anything that made Della Neudorf smile was worth whatever trouble was involved.

He'd try the Marshes next, tell them that Jay was working well in class. Better wait till the supper hour was over though, before he made another call.

The second round of parent-teacher interviews arrived – the rough ones, according to Maurie Pack; second semester was when the parents really tore into you. Brad wondered about that. Maurie loved giving him a rough time.

After talking to a series of quite pleasant mothers, Brad looked up at the middle-aged man who was already pulling a chair back for the woman with him, sitting quickly beside her. He looked angry. "Bill Perkins," the man said. "This is my wife, Edna."

"Glad to meet you." Brad shook his hand, the grip strong, firm, held just a bit too long, the pressure meant to be noticed. Mrs. Perkins withdrew her hand as soon as he touched it. June, he thought, June in his first class after lunch. "I've got all June's marks right here." He turned three pages in his daybook.

"I know about her marks," said Mr. Perkins, his voice louder than necessary. He leaned forward, rested an elbow on the table. "June tells her mother she's going to have to make a speech."

"It's part of the course requirements."

"June's worried," said Mrs. Perkins. "She's never had to –"

"Scared is what she is." Mr. Perkins scowled. "Everybody have to make a speech?"

"Well, yes, that's the idea. When I announced speeches coming up, there were groans from maybe half the class. But the ability to get up and talk in front of people is important – a life skill." Oh, Lord, he was beginning to sound like a textbook. "Once they've made their speech, almost everybody is glad they did it."

"Glad it's over, you mean."

"Well, that too. But a lot of them have a real sense of accomplishment. Then when they're called on to make a speech later on in life, say, in the business world, they know they've already done one. It's not so harrowing."

"Yes, yes, of course," said Mr. Perkins. "What if they say, no, they won't do it – can't do it? That the end of it?"

"That's not exactly how it works," said Brad. Was there any point to going through the process, laying it all out for this guy? It'd be like pushing explanations at a pile driver. "If anyone's afraid to make a speech, I get them to write out the speech they'd make if they weren't afraid. Most kids – after they've done that much work – are willing to make the speech. If anyone's still troubled about it, I get them to make the speech to me after school. Good and loud. Looking around the room as if it were packed with a full audience."

"Uh-huh."

"I give them a little coaching, then they get to do it again. Actually, it only got to that stage once last fall. The boy finally decided he'd do it in front of everybody. Did just fine, too."

"June's nervous," said Mrs. Perkins.

"Scared," said Mr. Perkins. "She'll try to weasel out of it. I don't care how many times she does it after school; sooner or later I want her up in front of the class. Understand? No goddamn excuses."

"Uh-huh," said Brad. He'd sure read Mr. Perkins wrong, but darned if he was making any promises. "I'll work with her, do my best."

"Just make sure your best means she does the speech like

everybody else." He stood up, and stared across the gym. "C'mon, Edna. I told you you should've got in that lineup for Pack. Look at the crowd now."

Brad watched him hurry away, Mrs. Perkins scuttling behind him. Seems like June's problem isn't school, he thought, but someone else was already sliding into the seat across from him.

By 8:45 that evening, the gym was beginning to empty out, except for the line in front of Maurie Pack's table. Seven or eight people still waiting for Maurie, Brad noticed, but there were empty chairs in front of him and no one heading for his table. He knew he was far too tired to begin marking paragraphs now. Instead, he began adding the checkmarks he'd made in his daybook beside the names of students whose parents had come out for an interview.

Sixty-four of them. No wonder he was tired.

Inside the door of the gym, a man in a suit was talking to Herb Schwitzer, who pointed in Brad's direction. Oh, oh, he thought, not finished yet. Kenny Lowe's father maybe? No, he hadn't come last fall, he wouldn't bother now that Kenny was doing better.

The man strolled toward him. Distinguished looking, his grey suit a perfect fit, emphasizing his slim physique, the grace of his movement. Black hair, black moustache and eyebrows. A hint of grey in his sideburns. Square jaw, severe expression on his face. His eyes were as dark as his hair, and they were focussed steadily on Brad as he approached. Knows what he wants, Brad thought, but the man was smiling now, the severity gone from his face which, Brad could suddenly see, was actually handsome. He stopped at the table before Brad's, sat down across from Sue Burton.

"Good evening, Miss Burton," Brad heard him say. There was a slight emphasis on the 'Miss.' Brad wondered what it meant. "A flower unwilted. You certainly don't look like someone who's suffered through a day and night of interviews."

"Not much suffering involved," she said. There wouldn't be for her, Brad thought, she gets along with all the kids. Their parents too.

"No. Not for the good teachers. Not for you." The man was leaning toward her, but after a few seconds he pulled back. "So how's the boy doing this semester?"

"Fine, I think. He's in my homeroom, but I don't teach him."

"I know that, of course." The guy was talking loud enough; he didn't mind anybody hearing. Dr. Stone, could it be? "In a general way, I meant, what's your impression – he keeping his nose to the grindstone?"

"His marks are holding up," she said. From where he sat, Brad couldn't see her face, but something about the way she held herself, her head tilted, her backbone stiff and straight, not quite touching the back of her chair, something gave him the impression that she was embarrassed.

"Good, good. I guess I'm a little late. Busy night at the hospital." He smiled. "Checking patients must be a lot like checking students. Maybe we ought to compare notes on a long day, have a coffee, maybe try some flapper pie. The Uptown makes it fresh on Wednesdays."

"Well..."

"Good. As soon as we're done here. I'll drive us down, Sue. You can pick your car up later."

Brad was certain she was blushing now, but he watched

the man smiling down at her and stepping toward him.

The guy didn't look like Parker Stone, but it had to be his dad.

"Dr. Stone," the man said, and sat down without reaching to shake Brad's hand.

"Brad Cutler." He wondered if he should offer his hand now or just forget about it. Before he could raise his hand, he realized that Dr. Stone was looking at him as if he were slow.

"You have my son, Parker, in grade twelve."

"I do." What the hell was wrong here? He felt like a boy in front of this guy. A boy who'd been hauled into the office. "He's not your average kid."

"Damned rights, he isn't. I don't understand why his mark is only 78."

"That's not a bad mark," said Brad. "The class average was 67."

"Yes, but he's not your average kid."

You smug bastard, Brad thought. "Parker's almost always in the high 80s. What brought him down was one bad mark on an exam three weeks ago." Okay, you want it, I'll give it to you. "51 per cent. Wrote just enough to pass. My guess is he simply didn't care. It was about the time the football team took on the volleyball guys in a fund-raiser, half a game of volleyball, half of touch football in the gym. I think he was feeling too down to care, wishing he hadn't quit the team." How do you like them apples, Dr. Stone?

"Ancient history," said Dr. Stone. "What I'm concerned about is how he's doing now."

"93 on his last test. He's got a talent for English, writes a good sentence, explains himself well." Yeah, he can work when he wants to, thought Brad, he just doesn't like me very much.

"Anything more that I should be apprised of?"

What the hell, might as well apprise him. "I think he's a natural actor."

"Pardon me."

"We've been working on *Hamlet* two days a week for quite a while now. Dramatizing the odd scene in class. Parker's good at it. Has a real stage presence. When he's acting out a scene, it's so quiet in the room, you'd swear the other kids were holding their breath." It's good for him too, Brad thought, playing someone else is maybe what he needs right now.

"Better the arts than mayhem, eh, Cutler? Thank you very much." Dr. Stone was already turning as he rose from his chair. "By the way," he added, pausing to cast a stern glance down at Brad, "if he has another low mark, I'll expect an immediate phone call."

Yeah, I bet you will.

Brad watched him stop beside Sue Burton's table, his right hand falling gently to her shoulder, resting there an instant, the fingers moving then as if they were about to knead weary muscles. For some reason, Brad thought of a crab scuttling across a pristine beach.

"A massage," said Dr. Stone, "would take that tightness right away."

His voice was like music from a cheap computer, each syllable a perfect note, but mechanical.

Sue stood up, the chair screeching beneath her as it jumped back.

"Nine o'clock," she said, "then I can go." She glanced back at Brad, nervously, he thought.

"Oh, come on," said Stone. "It's one minute to nine; there's no one else coming now." His hand was at her elbow, steering her away from the table.

Brad knew there'd been something going on between them, but that was over and done with, wasn't it, last fall? He watched them walk past Herb Schwitzer, the two of them pausing to laugh at something Herb said. Then Dr. Stone put his hand on her shoulder and turned her toward the door.

You smooth bastard, you, keep your hands to yourself. Brad wondered why he felt so angry. Bugger got under his skin was all. Hell, Sue Burton was none of his business. He slapped his day book shut, slammed it into his briefcase. Looked around the gym. He might as well leave too. Seven of the teachers were still talking to parents; the only line-up was beside Maurie Pack where half a dozen parents sat looking bored or angry.

He glanced at the file folder of paragraphs still sitting before him. Hadn't marked a single one. He dropped the folder into his briefcase and buckled it shut. Tore the foolscap bearing his name from his table, crumpled it up and lobbed it toward a garbage can. A perfect basket, and he'd survived another set of interviews. He was almost at the door when he realized that Maurie Pack was there before him, caught in conversation with Herb Schwitzer. Their voices low, urgent.

"...people waiting," Herb said.

"Nine o'clock," said Maurie, "paper said we're done at nine o'clock. Way too late already. Nobody's paying me overtime."

"Lousy attitude. You can't just walk –"

"Listen. I told them to phone me after school. Tomorrow or the next day. Not to worry, it's all taken care of. Now I'm out of here." With that, he swept through the door.

Herb's face looked red, swollen. He was glaring at Brad now.

"I'm done," Brad said. "Mine are all gone."

"Stubborn son-of-a-bitch," Herb said. "Wants a go at administration and he wonders why no one'll recommend him. Causes more problems than all..." He looked at Brad, seemed to recognize him for the first time. His hand was suddenly raised between them, palm up, waving back and forth. "Yeah, go ahead. We're done here."

Brad stepped through the door and hurried along the gym hallway. Maurie Pack was already going down the back stairs to the parking lot. Too bad Stone didn't want a chat with Maurie. That might be interesting, watch the two of them go at it. Hell, he'd almost flattened Maurie once himself – after the razzing got too rough. But when he opened the rear door to the school and felt the cool evening air wash around him, the air as sweet as the end of harvest, he discovered he was thinking of Sue Burton. Well, Sue Burton and yes, admit it, Kelly Irving too.

The next morning in the staffroom he noticed Sue seated against the wall, idly stirring her cup of coffee. She was looking sharp today, in dark slacks and a purple blouse with billowing sleeves.

He took the seat beside her. "How'd it go last night?" he asked.

She stopped stirring, her fingers poised above her cup, shaking slightly. A drop of coffee fell from the stir-stick, splattering on her slacks.

"None of your goddamned business." She set her cup on the coffee table, pulled a tissue from her purse, began dabbing at her slacks.

Brad could feel one of the other teachers looking at them. Myrna Belsey, a shocked expression on her face.

"Sorr-ee," said Brad. "I didn't know you had a bad interview."

"A bad interview." She stopped rubbing her slacks and turned for the first time to look at him. "Yes." There were lines around her eyes he'd never seen before.

"You too?" said Myrna Belsey. She was the Home Ec teacher, the cookie teacher, according to Maurie Pack. "I bet it was Mrs. Atcheson. The grump. She told me her daughter's brighter than all her friends. Why weren't her marks higher? When I said it might be because she never does a lick of work, she got nasty."

"It wasn't Mrs. Atcheson." Sue stood, walked to the counter and dumped her coffee into the sink.

Ooh boy, thought Brad, I really did it to her there. Thought she was going to clobber me. Yeah, and wasn't that what he meant to do, get under her skin, shake her up a bit and see where that might lead?

When he came up to the staffroom after school that day, he found Sue at the round table in the center of the room. She was walking around the table, pulling a sheet of questions from each of ten stacks of paper, tapping their bottom edges on the table, stapling them together. Ignoring him.

"Sorter broken on the copier?"

She shoved another stack of sheets into the stapler. "Yes," she said, slamming her hand down on the stapler. It jumped beneath her palm.

She paused, examined the staple, which had collapsed without piercing the wad of paper. She plucked it out with her fingernail, flicked it toward the garbage can, set the papers back into the stapler. Leaned over it, pressing down, slowly, deliberately.

"You want some help?"

"No." She gathered another stack of pages, stapled them together.

"Nothing better to do at the moment."

"Suit yourself."

The two of them walked the circle around the table, collecting papers, stapling pages, dropping them in a pile. She never looked at him, never said a word. When they were finished, he took the two extra sheets and carried them to the recycle box, released them and watched them float down, landing on the mass of paper already there. Behind him, she was counting the stapled papers.

He waited till she was done. "Are you okay?" he asked.

She set the papers on the table in front of her. Slapped them down, he thought.

"How'd it go last night," she said. It was not a question. He saw the steel in her eyes, cold and grey. Lethal. No doubt about it, she was mocking him.

"I meant the interviews," he said, his voice tight on what he knew was a lie.

"Sure."

"Sorry if I embarrassed you."

"Stuff it." She picked up her stack of papers and walked past him toward the door. Just before she left the room, she said, "You want to know about somebody's night, ask Kelly Irving. I understand that's where the real action is."

Brad felt a little surge of pain across his chest. He kept his face straight, noncommittal as he watched her leave the room.

It was Monday morning when Brad turned into the staff parking lot and noticed a car idling at the edge of the lot, Sue behind the wheel. Waiting till the last minute, he thought, before starting another week. He pulled into space number fifteen against the caragana hedge on the west side of the lot, the hedge buried in snow. When he pushed his door open, it swung perhaps a foot, then stopped. He looked up. Sue was standing beside the car, both hands pressed against the window glass.

"This is embarrassing," she said. "You mind if I get in?"

"No. Hop in." What was this about?

She pushed the door shut, walked around behind the car, and got in the other side. She glanced quickly over at him, then stared straight ahead, sitting motionless. For all he knew, she could be looking at patterns of branches on the snow. He could hear a little clicking from somewhere beneath the hood as the motor cooled.

"What a crappy weekend," she said. "Thinking of you, didn't sleep worth a damn."

"Hey, wait a –"

"No, please. Listen." When she turned to face him, he saw that her eyes looked damp, fragile. "I wanted to catch you when there were no other teachers around. I'm sorry about Friday. It had nothing to do with you. Sometimes, when things go wrong, I can be such a bitch." She was speaking slowly, almost like an actress delivering a speech that she's rehearsed but hasn't quite memorized. "Taking things out on you – and Kelly. My God, I hope you didn't tell her."

"Course not." He paused, decided to go on. "We're not exactly an item, you know."

"I'm sorry, Brad." There was a little hitch in her voice. "What I said – it was just plain mean. I had no right saying those things, Brad. I apologize."

"Apology accepted." He said it quickly, knowing she had every right to be angry with him. He hoped she wasn't going to cry. "We better get moving or we're going to miss the first bell."

She didn't open her door, and neither did he.

"It's just...relationships, they...don't always...We went out for a while...last year...it wasn't working out." She paused, seemed to study him, looked suddenly angry. "He wanted me to know he was dumping me. Not the other way around." She blushed, as if she'd said more than she intended. "I didn't mean to take it out on you – I really am sorry."

"It's okay, Sue. I understand." But he wasn't sure he understood very much at all. Especially about what he was feeling now. Sympathy for her, he guessed, relief that she was done with Stone, sure, and – admit it – jealousy was what he'd felt before, when Stone's hands were on her shoulder, on her elbow. But that didn't make sense.

Twelve

"Dance duty," said Herb Schwitzer, walking into the staffroom at the noon break that Friday, "you guys know you're on tonight?"

"Not me," said Maurie Pack.

Brad looked up from his peanut butter sandwich and nodded his head.

"Tonight," said Herb. He raised his meaty arm and pointed at Maurie.

"Hell," said Maurie, "I thought I had the spring dance."

"You're on tonight. Check the schedule in the office."

Too bad, Brad thought. After their altercation, the less time he spent with Pack the better.

"Nothing I hate worse than dance duty," Maurie said.

"Twice a bloody year." Herb glowered. "Try doing five."

"Okay, okay. Who else is on?"

"Bruce, Sue, Vi."

Vi Isely nodded at Herb. The Physics teacher, she was always reading science journals and seldom spoke, seldom even showed up in the staffroom.

"You or Workman?"

"You have to ask? Workman's the boss, isn't he? Hasn't done a dance this year." He looked around the staffroom, checking faces. "I suppose I better put a reminder in Winslow's cubbyhole."

"Tell him," said Maurie, "to show up on time."

"Reminds me," said Herb, "this term we're opening the doors at seven-thirty."

"That's a half hour early." Maurie Pack looked angry. Like a fireplug about to blow its stack, Brad thought, he looked angry most of the time. "We'll close them at eight-thirty instead of nine. Maybe cut down on the number of drinkers that get in."

Brad thought of the dance he'd worked last fall, Cheryl Dunlop in such a drunken coma he didn't think she was going to make it.

"You ask me," said Maurie Pack, still frowning, "they ought to cancel all dances. Not our job to handle drunks."

"Fat chance," said Vic Pendleton. "Eight, nine years ago things got so bad, they cancelled one dance. That was it. Wouldn't you know, I'd traded that one for the bad one right before it – every time you turned around someone else was drunk."

"I don't like drunks any more than the rest of you," said Sue Burton. "But school dances are the only ones with any real supervision."

"So?" said Maurie. It sounded more like a threat than a question.

"Parents need to know what kind of place they send their kids. Not off to some rave getting high on Ecstasy. They trust us at the school." Sue was right, thought Brad. She usually was.

"Parents need to lock up their booze before they send

them out," said Maurie. "Show some responsibility."

"You want responsibility," said Herb, "I'll give you Mrs. Isaacs."

"Cam's mom?"

"Yes, she was something else. Rutledge pulled Cam out of the gym when he couldn't stand up straight. Hauled him past the lounge and told him to stay there. Instead, the kid takes off out the door. Running. Must've been 40 below and he doesn't have a coat on. Rutledge figures he's going to freeze to death out there, so he goes after him. Bunch of kids are crammed against the lounge windows to see what's going to happen. They're about half way up the hill when Rutledge catches him. Brings him down with a perfect flying tackle. Marches him back to the school. They come in the door, some smart-ass kid asks Rutledge if next year he's gonna coach the football team."

Rutledge was something else, Brad thought. He wondered if he'd have the nerve to go after a kid that way.

"What about the mom?" he asked.

"Oh, yeah," said Herb. "When I phoned her to come and get the kid, she said she couldn't do it. Was right in the middle of a cocktail party. You believe it? She couldn't very well abandon her guests. What about her son, I ask her, and she says she'll try to get down to the school by midnight. Christ, it's not even ten o'clock. The kid is already looking like he's going to puke. Rutledge goes right out of his tree."

Not much he could do though, thought Brad.

"He says he's tired of cleaning up puke, he's going to take care of the situation. You know how he was..." Herb paused, shook his head. "No, I guess you don't. Well, for him everything's a situation. He bundles the kid into his coat, walks him out to his car – Rutledge's car – tells him to keep his head out the window or he'll kick his ass. When he gets to Isaacs' house, he drags the kid up the steps, props him against the wall and rings the doorbell. Curtains open, he can see fifteen, twenty people standing around the front room, sipping drinks, trying to look classy. When Mrs. Isaacs pushes through the crowd and opens the door, Rutledge says he's got a delivery for her. She looks kind of puzzled, wonders what they ordered. 'It sure ain't pizza,' says Rutledge and he pulls the kid off the wall and gives him a little push into the room. Said the cocktail party got awful quiet all of a sudden. Said he hoped the kid made it to the can before he threw up, but if he sprayed a few guests, she damned well had it coming."

Brad laughed. "Rutledge was a real coyote type, wasn't he?"

"A trickster all the way."

"Most coyotes," said Sue, "do better in the wilderness."

Everyone was back at the school for dance duty by seven-thirty. Bruce Winslow was the last to walk into the staffroom, but he wasn't late. While he was hanging up his coat, Herb said, "Okay, we'll start with Maurie and I on the door, checking student cards. I'll do the elevens and twelves, Maurie the nines and tens."

"And if they don't have their student card?" asked Maurie.

"They can't bother to bring a card, we should say to hell with them, they don't get in. But if you know they're ours, we'll charge them double, donate the extra money to the food bank. Maybe next time they'll bring their cards. Let's see, Vi at the eleven and twelve table, Sue with the nines and tens. Student council kids will collect the money, you watch the kids coming in. Stamp their hands. See what kind of shape they're in. Bruce, I want you inside the gym door, making sure they all take off their shoes. Got you assigned there the first forty minutes."

"Jeez, it's deafening in there."

Brad could hear Nickelback blaring down the hall. He didn't know a deejay could get that kind of volume from a CD.

"Everybody gets forty minutes in the gym," said Herb. "It's all on the schedule."

"You got a schedule?" asked Maurie. "Getting carried away, aren't we?"

"Like to make things formal," said Herb. He was answering Maurie, but he was looking at Bruce. "Makes it tougher to slough things off. Going to try something else too. When we go down to the door, you'll notice there's a line of masking tape on the floor, stretches past the student lounge to the coat checks by the gym. That's where you come in, Brad."

Oh no, Brad thought, he's going to have me – no, surely he wouldn't.

"You make them walk that line."

"Give them a drunk test?"

"Yeah. Anybody can't do it, bring them back to me."

"What do I tell them?"

"What'd'ya mean – what'd'ya tell them? Tell them to walk the goddamned line." You'd think Herb had a hornet up his ass. He raised his wrist watch in front of his face, but Brad would have sworn his eyes never left him. "It's time to go. Let's move 'em out."

Lord, a drunk test. Not his idea of teaching. He wondered what his father would think – giving up the farm for this. For that matter, what would Mr. Roy think? Still, it was Herb telling him what he had to do. For Herb, he guessed he'd try it. If it was Workman pushing him, there'd be trouble, and that was crazy – trouble with Workman was the last thing he needed.

The student council kids were already at the school entrance, cash boxes set out on the tables they'd moved into the hall. Perhaps a dozen kids were peering through the glass doors from outside, waiting for them to be unlocked. When they were let in, their cards checked, their money paid, their hands stamped, when they finally got to Brad, he told them that something new had been added, a little check on their motor ability. He felt foolish saying it, but not as foolish as he would've felt telling them he was administering a drunk test.

"I haven't had a single drink," said Tim Hrenyk, one of Brad's grade elevens. There was a hint of belligerence in his voice. "I don't need to walk no bloody line."

"You want to argue about it, Tim, go talk to Mr. Schwitzer."

Tim glanced back at the door where Herb was checking the student card of a girl in grade twelve.

"He's busy. Ah, what the hell." He strolled slowly down the line of tape.

"What'sa matter?" said the next boy, whose name Brad didn't know. "You think I'm drunk?"

"I don't know," said Brad, "but someone usually is."

"Not me. Looket this." The kid was a little guy, scrawny as a ballpoint pen. He raised one leg, grabbed his ankle in his hand, and proceeded to hop the length of the line, every hop landing squarely on the tape.

Two girls, a blonde and a brunette, paused beside Brad to watch the boy take one last giant hop, landing on both feet.

"This is crazy," said one. "You're gonna make us hop?"

"No!" said Brad. He lowered his voice. "Walk is all you have to do. You can go together."

The two girls walked to the beginning of the tape and stood there, one on each side of it. They looked at each other, whispered something, their faces breaking into wide grins. They turned to Brad, the blonde with the button nose saying, "For you, Mr. Cutler, we'd crawl all the way along that line on our bellies." When he blushed, they began to giggle. Quick nods then, and they reached out to hold hands, raised their outer legs and began to hop along the tape. By the time they reached the end of the tape, they were both laughing.

"What's going on?" It was Willie Thornton who'd just had his hand stamped by Sue Burton. Even in slacks, he looked ready for the volleyball court.

"Nothing too serious, Willie," Brad heard Sue tell him, "a little test of your dexterity. Mr. Cutler will show you what to do."

The boy sidled over to Brad, his eyes on the tape. "I think it's a drunk test. Right, Mr. C?"

"Could be."

"I got to hop all that way?"

"No!" Brad took a deep breath. "For you, we'll make an exception. You can walk it on your hands."

"You kidding?"

"Of course, I'm kidding. Just walk the line, will you?"

Willie stuck out his hands beside him, and began stepping carefully, raising each foot almost to knee height as he brought it around in front of him, placing it exactly on the tape. He looked as if he were on a high wire. Just before he reached the end of the tape, he crouched down, placed both hands flat on the floor beside him and began to lift his legs. Moving slowly, carefully, he got both legs above his head, but he had to swing them back and forth to keep from falling. At last, he had a wobbly kind of balance. Then he raised his left hand and shoved it quickly ahead. His body teetered a minute. Then he collapsed on the floor, receiving a round of cheers from the three hoppers who had preceded him.

"Where do you teachers get these ideas?" It was Parker Stone at the head of a group of kids who'd just had their hands stamped. Parker looking angry.

"The Education Act," said Brad. "Section 18, subsection 14B. The prevention of alcohol-related problems in the small to medium-sized secondary school."

"You're putting me on. Right?" He wasn't exactly smiling, but at least he no longer looked angry.

"Walk the line, will you, Parker? They're starting to pile up behind you."

Parker stepped deliberately to the line, stuck his hands in his pockets, and did what looked like a soft shoe shuffle down the line. Give him an umbrella to swing, Brad thought, he'd look like Gene Kelly in *Singing in the Rain*. But there was something else there too. A hint of danger, maybe, like a violent music video, the shuffle of a rapper looking for someone to stomp. Well, he could accept a darker side from Parker ever since he'd learned the truth about the boy going steady with Angela Maddox, before she dumped him, before she hung herself.

"Bet I can do it on tippy-toes," the next boy said.

The girl with him gave him a little nudge in the ribs. "Backwards," she said. "Try it backwards."

Kids, he thought, you had to hand it to them. Still, it was going to be a long night.

When the doors closed at eight-thirty and he had finally watched the last kid walk the line, Brad was assigned door duty. That meant that he let nobody out or in. Except, of course, the kids going home and those on the late list. There were nine on the list tonight, kids working at fast food joints or at the mall, kids with legitimate reasons for being late. They'd all informed the office of their problem at least two days ahead of time and paid in advance.

He set a metal chair in the middle of the hall so he could watch the door and the washrooms and sat down. Music powered down the hall, the words and the tune indistinguishable, the bass shaking the walls. He hoped they'd play something quieter when he was in the gym. He didn't want another pounding headache.

Before it was time for Brad's shift in the gym, he did a quick check of the boys' washroom. Nobody in the cubicles, but a faint smell of marijuana in the air. Got to keep an eye on that, he thought, but right now he better stick to Herb's schedule for the gym.

The deejay was playing Bob Seger's "Old Time Rock and Roll" when he stepped through the door. Maybe it was the start of a golden oldies medley, songs he might listen to without blowing a hole out the back of his head. He nodded at Vi Isely who was standing just inside the door beside Ollie, the caretaker. She'd look a lot more at home in the physics lab with a journal, he thought. The music would drown out anything he might say to her, but she knew he was her replacement and quickly left the gym. Most of the kids were clustered near the stage where the deejay was at work, a bank of coloured lights suspended above his giant speakers, the lights flashing in various patterns, bouncing off the streamers that hung from the gym walls.

Brad turned to Ollie. "Any pukers so far?"

"What?"

"Any pukers?"

Ollie shook his head.

Brad pointed to the bleachers. "I'll check what's doing over there." If Ollie couldn't hear him, he'd get the idea. There was a group of kids at the far end of the bleachers, grade nine boys mostly, clustered together as far from the speakers as they could get. As Brad got closer, he could see they were grinning and talking together. A lot like me in high school, he thought, too shy to be caught anywhere near the girls. There were scattered couples lolling on the bleachers closer to the stage, holding hands, snuggling together. One boy and girl who were all over each other pulled quickly apart when they realized Brad was looking at them. Even in the half-light of the darkened gym, he could see that they were embarrassed. Beyond them, a boy sat alone in the top row, slumped against the cinder-brick wall, his head in his hands. "At the Hop" was playing now and Brad could see a few of the kids were trying to jive. He climbed up the bleachers and sat beside the boy, an aboriginal boy, he saw now.

"You okay?"

The boy raised his head, gazed steadily at Brad before speaking. It was no one he knew. Prominent jaw – like his own – and deep-set eyes. Looked a bit like Nelson Ahenakew, the only native in his classes. A younger brother maybe. "Okay – yeah," said the boy. "Just don't like this old-time crap." He said something more; it sounded like "moldy oldies." Brad shrugged and climbed back down. Bit of a loner there, he thought, wonder if I should stay and talk to him? Probably not at a dance, that'd be the kiss of death for sure.

Brad walked toward the dancers. Most of them were

dancing in pairs, couples facing one another, arms at their sides, gyrating. To his left, six girls were dancing in a frantic circle, hips shaking, shoulders quaking. At the center of a group of clapping kids, one couple was jiving, the boy spinning the girl, throwing her, catching her, rolling her over his hip. They knew what they were doing, looked, in fact, like they'd been taking lessons. Like his parents, he thought, his father swinging his mother around, a loopy grin on his face, still surprised that he could do this, the old man pushing seventy, the two of them taking lessons once a week, hitting every weekend dance in driving range of Outlook, and now the same thing in Victoria.

The music flowed without a pause into "Whole Lotta Shakin' Goin' On." Lori Campbell had left the circle of dancing girls, was shuffling in his direction, her feet moving to the beat. Tonight her hair was dyed a bright purple.

"You want to dance?" He wasn't sure if he heard it or simply read her lips. He glanced over his shoulder. Yeah, she was talking to him.

He leaned toward her. "I can't jive," he said.

She grabbed his hand, pulling him toward the dancers. She mustn't have heard him. He leaned closer, his mouth by her ear. "I can't jive."

She stopped pulling and looked up at him, grinning. "You can shake it," she hollered. She began to snap her fingers, her feet pounding the floor, heel and toe picking up the beat, body swaying, hips and shoulders jerking. What the heck. He began to step with her, following her moves, rather stiffly at first, knees bent, shoulders dipping, then feeling the beat, punching it out with his feet. Lori smiling up at him, he was really doing it. Letting loose a bit, actually having fun. A girl beside them pointed at him, began to clap. Two of her friends picked up the clapping. Brad wondered if he should feel embarrassed, but he kept his feet moving and smiled at Lori.

When the music stopped, she said, "Thanks," just as he said it himself. She stepped toward him, reached up and gave his shoulder a squeeze. A smile like a flower blooming, and she was turning back into the crowd. Amazing, he thought. When he was her age, he couldn't remember any kid who would dance with a teacher.

Thirteen

The set of oldies ended with Trooper's "Raise A Little Hell," then silence, the crowd thinning out. Brad was hoping for a long break, but five minutes later the dee-jay was back at it. Probably worried he wouldn't get the kids going again. The first song drew only a few to the floor, and faded quickly into another piece, something Brad didn't recognize. Sounded a bit like that new group from Saskatoon, Forearm Shiver. More kids jamming toward the stage now, hands above their heads, hips and shoulders bumping together. He glanced around.

A cluster of boys at the back of the gym near the fire-exit door. He saw that the door was open and walked quickly toward them. The door swung shut, boys spilling away from it, grade twelves by the size of them, and a couple of girls, purple hair, uh-huh, Lori Campbell one of them. Brad held up his hands, palms out.

Parker Stone stopped in front of him. Looking resentful – and maybe nervous too. Something was up.

"The door's supposed to be closed," said Brad. "What's going on?"

Danny Litowski stepped up beside Parker. "It was so hot in here. We just wanted some fresh air."

"We weren't drinking," said Parker, a frown on his face, "if that's what you think."

Brad strode to the door and swung it open. Nobody there. No sign of a bottle. He gave the door a firm pull to make sure it clicked shut and couldn't be opened from the outside. The boys were moving off, padding away on the sock feet that would never scuff the varnished hardwood. Sock feet and a pair of shoes.

"Hey," Brad shouted. The shoes stopped walking, turned toward him. Hell, it was Bert Peale. "No shoes in the gym," said Brad. "You know that."

"Yeah. I forgot," said Peale, who turned quickly away and started toward the gym hallway.

Nervy bugger, thought Brad. "Take the shoes off, Bert."

Peale stopped walking, but he didn't turn around. He stepped on the heel of one shoe, pulled it off, and did the same with the other. He bent to retrieve them, picking them up in one hand, his other hand reaching for the glasses which had slid down his nose when he bent. As he stood, he turned to glare at Brad, his middle finger pushing at his glasses.

You little snot, give me the finger, will you? Brad started toward him. Easy, he thought, easy does it. Peale with his shoes on, but had Peale walked the line when the doors were open? Not a chance. He'd remember Peale.

Brad caught him just as he stepped into the gym hall, flinging his shoes against the wall. It was quieter here; he wouldn't have to yell.

Brad stepped in front of him. "You came in through the fire escape door, didn't you, Bert?"

A look of scorn on his face. "No way." He shook his head, and turned back toward the gym. Brad thought he caught a whiff of beer on him.

"Just a minute," said Brad. "Let's see the stamp on your hand."

Peale's sneer wasn't quite so big. "They forgot to stamp me," he said, "but I paid to get in."

"Maybe. I suppose Mr. Schwitzer will remember checking your student card. What say we go talk to him?"

The boy did not look scared. "Sure," he said, "why not?" There was a strange look in his eye. He was speaking slowly, enunciating precisely. "Where we going to find him – Shitzer?"

"Watch your mouth." Brad took him just above the elbow and started him down the hall toward the office.

"Get your dirty hands off me." The words snapped at him, nasty, violent.

Brad shrugged and pointed to the office. They walked side by side down the hall, neither of them speaking. The odour of beer went with them. When they passed the outside door, Brad noted that Peale paused, glancing outside. Brad wondered if he might bolt, and knew all at once that if necessary he'd chase him down, yes, even tackle him if he had to, but the boy stepped ahead, continuing toward the office.

When they arrived at the office door, Brad could see Herb sitting at Kelly's desk, feeding coins into the plastic change sorter. Brad tried the door, but it was locked. Herb looked up at the sound of the door handle, his expression hardening when he saw Bert Peale with Brad. He strode to the door, flung it open.

"Here we go again, eh, Peale?" He glanced at Brad. "What's the problem this time?"

"I think he snuck in the back door of the gym." Brad

wondered if the kid would give him the finger with Herb looking on, but the kid never took his eyes off Herb.

"Not me. I paid."

Herb looked at him a moment before speaking. "Funny, I didn't see your student card."

Peale didn't hesitate. "I must've got in the wrong line."

"With all the nines and tens, eh, Peale?" Herb sat down again at the desk.

"I guess so."

"Tell me: who was working that line?"

"Somebody – I don't know. I must've been looking down at his feet."

Herb leaned back in his chair and smiled at him, a tight smile devoid of humour. "Sure you were, Peale. And then you wondered how come he was wearing high heels."

"What?"

"You don't have a clue who was checking student cards."

"Some woman – okay?" He dropped his eyes under Herb's dark glare. "So you caught me – big deal!"

Herb waved his finger at the boy. "No, Peale, Mr. Cutler caught you. I just proved you were lying." He drew a deep breath through his nostrils before continuing. "I suppose that makes you a liar as well as a drunk."

"I'm not drunk." The boy almost shouted.

"You smell like a brewery."

"Bloody well am not – *do* not."

Brad wondered if he should go back to the gym, but the air in the room felt charged, as if an electrical storm were about to burst. He thought he'd better stay.

"Been suspicious three times before. This time, I've got you." Herb picked up the telephone.

"What're you doing?"

"Wouldn't want your parents to miss the opportunity of getting a whiff of your breath."

"You don't need to phone them."

"Oh, Peale, but I do. It's school board policy."

"Fuck school board policy." For just an instant, the kid looked surprised at what he'd said, and Brad almost felt sorry for him, but then Peale stepped toward the desk. "Fuck you too." He lunged forward, placed both hands on the desk and leaned into Herb's face. "No fucking wonder everybody calls you Shitzer." His face was only inches from Herb's. "You're just a big fucking shit."

Herb's face was red, his right hand shaking. When he stood up, the kid flinched and jerked backwards. Herb lunged across his desk, grabbed the boy by the front of his shirt. Brad stepped forward. "Mr. Schwitzer!" he said, but Herb didn't seem to hear him. The fingers of his right hand were curled into a fist, the fist coming up. Herb looked away from the boy then, looked at his right hand, watched the fingers slowly unclenching, the hand relaxing, dropping to the table between them. He released the boy's shirt, lowered his left hand, began rubbing his hands together. It was as if he were brushing dirt from his fingers.

When Bert Peale saw that Herb was not going to punch him, he leaned forward again. "Fuck you, Shitzer, you dumb fucker. And fuck your fucking wife too."

"You're lucky, Peale," said Herb. "Twenty years ago, I would've ripped that filthy tongue out of your mouth. Then stuffed it down your throat." He stepped back from his desk. "Today, I'll just recommend you do something to improve your vocabulary."

"Fuck you."

"Even a cheap thesaurus would help." Herb reached

for the phone on his desk.

"Fuck you." Peale wasn't quite as loud this time.

"I'm phoning your parents. Get used to that idea. You're not getting out of here till they come to pick you up." His voice softened, became almost gentle. "You might as well sit down and wait."

Peale opened his mouth to speak, but apparently thought better of it, for he closed it again and slouched over to a chair against the wall and sat down, a sneer on his face, his whole posture a sneer.

"Mr. Cutler," said Herb, "I'll ask you to stay till they get here. If you don't mind."

When the Peales arrived fifteen minutes later, Brad heard them coming. He stepped out, holding the door for them. Mrs. Peale, looking harried, was right behind her husband who was marching down the hall, long purposeful strides, his expression severe. He looked like someone who knew what he wanted.

When he saw Brad, he said, "What's the meaning of this?"

"Your son," said Brad, "he –"

"Where's Schwitzer?"

Brad nodded through the open door.

"Derek," his wife said, but he was already stepping into the office. Brad thought he smelled liquor on her breath. She glanced quickly at him, turned again to her husband.

"Just what the hell is going on here?" Peale asked.

"Dr. Peale," said Herb. "Ma'am," he added when she followed her husband through the door. He glanced at Brad. "Thanks, Mr. Cutler. Maybe you should check that gym door again. If I need you, I'll let you know."

When he started down the hall, he was surprised to find his knees shaking, a hard weight in his stomach. It was as if he'd been through this before – or something like it. He was glad when he saw Sue at the school door letting in two kids on the late list. He waited till they were in, then walked with her toward the gym.

"Wasn't that Bert Peale I saw you taking to the office?" A simple question, yet her voice was a river lapping over the stone in his stomach.

"It was." He shook his head. "God, I thought Herb was going to kill him."

She stopped walking. "What happened?"

"Kid told him to fuck himself – about ten times."

"Oh, oh."

"I swear to God Herb swelled up twice his normal size, veins sticking out of his forehead, fists on him like war clubs. He wanted to smash that kid."

"But surely he didn't?"

"No. He got himself calmed down. Somehow. Told Peale he needed to broaden his vocabulary."

Sue laughed. "Sometimes you've got to hand it to Herb." She glanced back toward the office. "So those were the Peales I let in the door. They didn't look happy."

"No. They'll be going at it right now." He shook his head. "Coming in here drunk and cursing – it beats me – you're bound to get caught. It's just not common sense."

"Common sense?" Sue smiled. "It's not as common as the cold, you know."

When the dance finally ended at eleven-thirty, Brad had to help out in the coat check where the lineup of kids brandishing tags and shoving toward the counter threatened to turn into a scrimmage. It was after twelve by the time the last coat was collected. Brad walked back to the staffroom, a nerve drumming in his head. He saw Sue coming toward him, her coat already over her shoulders. A Linda Lundstrom parka, classy, he thought, just right for her.

"Good night, Brad," she said. That voice like liquid honey.

"Night, Sue." He turned and watched her walk down the hall, moving with the fluid grace of a figure skater, the parka swirling around her calves as she swung through the door.

The lights were off in the staffroom when he entered, but in the dim light from the hall he could see that his was the only coat on the hangers. The door swung shut behind him as he slipped into his coat. That was when he noticed the red glow in the corner of the room. A long pull on a cigarette.

"Want one too?" Herb's voice.

"Oh, no. No thanks."

"Not to worry. I'll flush the butt away. Wouldn't want a blemish on our smoke-free environment."

"No," said Brad. "I just don't smoke." His eyes were growing accustomed to the darkness, dim light seeping between the curtains from the streetlight down the block. He could make out Herb slumped on the corner of the sofa. Brad walked toward him, stepped around the coffee table and sat down. "How did it go with the Peales?"

The cigarette flared again. The air here was heavy with smoke. There were seconds of silence before he heard the sigh of Herb exhaling more smoke.

"Not so hot. The good doctor thinks I'm picking on his son."

"What a load. He was drunk."

"Not the way they see it. Somebody spilled beer on him."

"Crap. You tell him what Bert said?"

"Uh-huh. Didn't believe me, of course. Kid's got his parents wrapped around his finger. I told them, be in here first thing Monday morning, we'll meet with Mr. Workman. See if he's expelled or just transferred to another school. The bastard said by Monday morning he'd have my job." He took another pull from his cigarette.

"He can't do that. Can he?"

"No." Brad could see the smoke now as Herb exhaled. "But he's used to getting his way – especially about the boy. He'll phone the director, make it as miserable as possible."

"But McAvoy will back you, won't he?"

"He's good with school finances. I don't think he likes controversy." Herb reached to his left, picked up a coke that Brad hadn't noticed on the end table, took a quick sip. "Then there's Workman. Well known for his love of conflict. Huh. Not much fire left in him since that fiasco with the board two years ago. Might not be able to boot the kid out of here."

"He's lucky you didn't just strangle him."

Herb took another sip of coke before setting his can down. "Luckier than he'll ever know." Through the smoke, the severe line of his chin looked softer than usual, his features pliant, malleable. "Monday morning, might need to call on you if things aren't going well."

"Of course."

"Run along now. I'm going to have one more cigarette."

Brad left him there, glancing back when he heard the match strike, Herb's face rising from the shadows like a death mask about to be torched.

At home in his basement suite Brad poured himself a whisky, turned the stereo on low, the guitar of Liona

Boyd, "Chariots of Fire" so quiet he could barely hear it. Her fingers plucking the strings, better even than silence, he could almost feel her fingers moving. It was a tape his mother had made for him. "Play it when you need to relax," she'd said. "Music soothes. Even your dad agrees with that."

He glanced at his bookcase. Planks he'd stained with Watco Danish Oil and set up on the cheapest bricks he could find. Books overflowing everywhere and nothing he could bear to look at now.

He turned the lights off and sat down in the wicker chair. Glanced out the window, nothing to look at but the neighbour's board fence. Couldn't even see the sky from here.

He took a sip of whisky. Held the liquor in his mouth, the taste both bitter and comforting.

Poor Herb, having to sweat it out till Monday. At least he hadn't hit the little bugger. That would've been a real problem. Peale was in the wrong, swearing up a storm, definitely in the wrong. Even Workman would see that, he had to.

That cigarette, its lonely glow in the dark staffroom.

He swallowed. Took a longer drink from his glass. Rolled the liquor around on his tongue.

Last fall, he thought, last fall after the dance, he'd gone over to Kelly's, been invited over to Kelly's. His head throbbing, her hands on his temples, massaging the back of his neck, moving over his chest, electrical sparks on his chest and her rocking above him. He closed his eyes, the red blaze of her hair, the bursting match, the cigarette bright in the shadows.

He was distracted throughout his first class on Monday, waiting for a call to the office. When none came by the break, he went up to the office, taking the steps two at a time. Kelly looked up when he came rushing into the room. The principal's door was closed.

"Herb still in there?"

She nodded her head, frowning.

There was no call during his period two study either. When it ended, he hurried back to the office, saw immediately that the principal's door was open a crack, caught a glimpse of Workman spreading papers on his desk.

"Where's Herb?"

Kelly nodded toward the vice-principal's office, her face grave.

As Brad stepped through the doorway, he could see Herb behind his desk, staring at the bookcase on the opposite wall. Brad pulled the door closed behind him. It was some time before Herb looked at him.

"Are you okay?" Brad asked, immediately wishing he hadn't phrased it like that.

Herb nodded his head.

"The meeting – how did it go?"

Herb stared at Brad a moment before answering. Maybe he shouldn't be here; maybe this wasn't his business.

"McAvoy joined us part way through. Had to go over everything again. Didn't much matter. Workman went along with him."

"He wouldn't back you?" Brad knew he should be keeping his voice down.

"Kid's suspended for three days."

"That's all?"

"Three days. Got himself a nice little vacation."

"After what he said. Christ, I could've told them what he said."

"Wouldn't matter. Seems Dr. Peale has more weight

around here than I do. He admitted the boy was out of line. A natural reaction when I'm always on his case, out to get him, watching his every move, no wonder the boy blew up."

"Crap. I was there, I can tell them –"

"Forget it, Brad. We had it out – they made their decision. They're not going to change it now." Herb was no longer focusing on Brad, but looking at a blank paper lying on his desk.

"Dumb-ass decision."

"Uh-huh, but it won't bother them. Just makes my job a lot tougher. Down here in the trenches, we'll pay for it again and again." He looked back at Brad, suddenly reached across the table and shook his hand. "Thanks for your concern," he said, but now he was looking beyond Brad's shoulder.

The door, Brad thought, he wants me out of here.

After lunch, while his period four students were working on their *Hamlet* questions at the end of the class and he was walking the aisles, giving them a hint here, a prod there, he quietly asked both Parker Stone and Danny Litowski to stay a minute after the bell.

He watched them while the other kids were folding up their books and filing out the door. Danny had his head bent toward his *Hamlet* text, but his eyes were darting around the front of the room. Parker was staring right at him. Brad waited until everyone else was gone and shut the door.

"Friday night," he said, "we had a problem with Bert Peale. Not only was he drunk, but he snuck in the gym door." He waited, studying their reactions. Danny's eyes were on him for an instant, then dropped away. Parker continued to stare at him, no expression on his face. "I think you two already know that." Danny ducked his head over his work. "You and half a dozen others." Brad paused. "But you were the ones I talked to." He glared down at them both, hoping that somehow he looked ferocious. Parker never blinked, but Danny finally raised his head above his book, his eyes immediately shifting toward the door and back again at Brad.

"It was so hot in there," said Danny, "I just wanted to cool off." His head jerked down again. "When I got there, Bert was already inside with the other guys. I didn't know he done something wrong."

A likely story. "How about you, Parker?"

The boy continued to stare at him for a full twenty seconds before he answered. "I said we weren't drinking. It was the truth."

"What about Bert? He was drinking."

"I guess so, yeah. Before he came to the dance." Something about Parker's expression seemed to change. "You never asked me about Peale."

"No, I suppose I didn't." He wasn't getting anywhere. "Next time," he said, "I'd appreciate it if you told me what was really going on."

"Yessir. For sure." Danny's head was moving up and down in a series of little jerks. Parker said nothing. If he nodded, the motion was imperceptible.

When Brad dismissed them, Parker waited till Danny was through the door. "I couldn't tell you," he said.

"Why not?"

Parker shifted, seemed to be inspecting his feet. "Look, I'm sorry. I didn't exactly lie, but this has nothing to do with Peale. A friend of mine was out for a smoke."

"A friend of yours."

"That's all I can say."

"Smoking pot?"

Parker looked startled. "Pot? No. A cigarette. That's all."

Brad studied him a moment. Head up now, looking a little sheepish, but staring right back at him. You had to hand it to the kid. "Okay, Parker, you better go ahead to class."

Lori Campbell, Brad remembered, she was there and then she was gone. Was Parker protecting her?

Usually when Brad came to school, he walked from his car past the side door by the gym and on to the main door on the crescent, getting as much fresh air as he could before he entered the building. The fresh air, really, it was all he missed about the farm – no matter what his father claimed. Well, that and the quiet, yeah, and the sunsets that stretched for miles at dusk. Thursday morning he bent his head against a bitter March wind that blew from the east, whipping ice crystals against his face. He ducked through the side entrance, walked down the gym hallway and past the lounge where kids were already congregating. It seemed noisier than usual in the corner of the lounge by the coke machine. Cheers and laughter, half a dozen boys crammed together, high fives, "Yeah!" they said. "Yeah!" and in the middle of the group, Bert Peale, a smug grin on his face.

And now he gets to be the hero, thought Brad. Hardly seemed fair. Sure, and when was life ever fair anyway? Wasn't that what he told his students when they complained that something wasn't fair? "We do our best; we believe in fairness here," he said. "But out there, if you expect that life's always going to be fair, you're in for one big shock."

What the hell, let him smirk. Just makes him look more homely than usual.

Two of the boys noticed him watching them and stepped quickly back from the others. Brad continued down the hallway beside the lounge. Although the warning bell had not yet rung, some students were already straggling out of the lounge by the entrance nearer the classrooms. He saw Lori Campbell glance over her shoulder in the direction of the coke machine. She looked angry. Another girl was shaking her head. A boy in front of him – he wasn't sure who – said, "Bunch of turkeys."

Kids. It was a mistake to jam them all into one category. Shouldn't forget that. Peale might be a hero to some, but not everybody. No, not by a long shot. Might be worth mentioning that to Herb.

Fourteen

A week later, while straightening his desks after school, Brad noticed a note scribbled on the corner desk, the one that nobody used at the back of the room.

It was printed neatly in red marker pen: "Power to the students." It was followed by six exclamation marks. He glanced across the room at the other unused desk. Something there too.

It looked like different printing, a black marker this time. "To find out the truth about Schwitzer," it said, "go to page 1333 in the *The Oxford English Reference Dictionary.*"

Brad moistened a kleenex with spit and obliterated both notes, leaving only a faint smudge of black on one desk, red on the other. He walked to the front of the room, looking down at the dictionary on the corner of his desk. The page was easy to remember. He opened it, turned to page 1333, read the line highlighted in yellow. "shat *past* and *past part* of SHIT." Some smart-ass kid, Peale maybe. There was an arrow running down to the bottom of the page where someone had scribbled, "Proceed to school library. Check *The American Heritage Dictionary* (Second College edition), page 1131. It'll be worth the walk."

Might as well see what this is all about, thought Brad. He jotted down the page number.

The library was almost empty, Rita Croft, the librarian, busy with the vertical files, Nelson Ahenakew stamping paperbacks on the counter, a couple of boys at the computers, probably on the Internet. He pulled a blue volume from a shelf of dictionaries, opened it to page 1131. The same yellow highlighter, the word, "shithead," glowing on the page, and with it the definition, "a highly contemptible or objectionable person." There was small, neat print in the margin which said, "Schwitzer? Maybe so. Maybe not. Proceed to page 136 of *Cold As A Bay Street Banker's Heart* – if you can find it." What was going on here? This didn't sound like Peale.

He found it on the computer, a prairie phrase book by Chris Thain. Catalogue number 427.971 Tha. On the language shelf. The word "Shitepoke" was highlighted, a bittern, he saw, but only part of one sentence was highlighted: "it comes from the use of the term shite as a more acceptable expression for shit." At the top of the page the same neat printing said, "The next step is easy. Go to page 83 of this same book." On page 83 Brad found the heading, "Hockey Pucks." Four paragraphs followed, but only a couple of lines were highlighted: "the frozen horse droppings, or road apples, that so many of us played hockey with..." In the space at the bottom of the page was written: "Does Schwitzer look like a goalie? He's big enough to stop a puck. Continue to page 326 of *The MacMillan Dictionary of Contemporary Slang* by Jonathan Green." Couldn't be Peale. He'd never go to this much trouble.

The book was only a shelf away. "Take a dump" was

highlighted, and its definition, "to excrete, usu. in sense of incontinence." Oh, come on, thought Brad. The printing at the bottom of the page began with a felt marker, but the paper was cheap, the marker spreading as if onto a blotter. Black ballpoint completed the note: "If Schwitzer's incontinent, it's at the other end. Now go to page 124 of Lewin & Lewin's *Thesaurus of Modern Slang.*" There he found "Dung" highlighted, plus one of the synonyms that followed it, "moose nuggets." That was one he hadn't heard before. The note said, "Is that really a moose nugget Schwitzer has on the end of his watch chain? Wonder how his French is? See *The Concise Oxford French Dictionary,* page 347."

Brad figured he could guess this one. Yes, there it was: "merde: excrement, shit, turd." Beneath it was printed: "Mange de la merde." Uh-huh, getting rough, are we? Then the note: "Is Schwitzer a turd? Better check this out by going to *The Oxford English Dictionary,* Volume XV (Ser – Soosy) page 287."

Brad walked to the counter in the center of the library where the encyclopedias and all twenty volumes of *The Oxford* were shelved. Definitions for "shit" ran from page 286 to page 288, but only a few words were highlighted: "shit-work: work considered to be menial or routine." The note said, "Does Schwitzer do the shitwork for Workman?" Hey, what was going on here? This kid was up to something. Who the hell was he? Or she maybe? Lori Campbell, Pam Wheeler, they'd be sharp enough to like this game. The directions continued, "Things get a little tougher now. Dos Passos the author, 70 the page, one the clue."

Midcentury and the *U.S.A.* trilogy were the titles he thought of at once. Maybe not so tough after all. If "one" meant volume one of the trilogy. He went to the fiction section, picked up the thick Modern Library edition which contained the three volumes in one. There it was on page 70 of *The 42nd Parallel:* "We're up shit creek now for fair." and the note: "There's nothing fair about it at all." Was this a comment on the dance and its aftermath? Sounded like it, but would a kid think that way? Herb sure, but a kid? There was another line of precise black printing in the margin. "And next a test of your tenacity." Not every kid would use a word like that. Must be someone with a decent vocabulary. "If you want more," the note continued, "take a trip to the public library. Try Robert Chapman's *New Dictionary of American Slang,* page 384."

This was getting crazy. It wasn't worth the bother, of course, but the kid had him going. What wasn't fair, what did that mean? It might not have a thing to do with Bert Peale and Herb. Well, shit-a-damn, he said to himself, grinning, it was only a five minute sidetrack on his way home. He wasn't ready for supper anyway.

A t the downtown library he looked up the title on the AcerView computer system, discovered there was one copy, in the reference department. He found it behind the row of filing cabinets that held the vertical files. Waiting for him on page 384 were the words with the yellow glow: "shit on a shingle: n. ph. WWII Army creamed chipped beef on toast." Interesting phrase that, he could see how it would appeal to a kid. The note was interesting too. "Beef is right," it said. "Schwitzer's got a big beef. You have to drop down for the next one. *The Collins English Dictionary,* page 1409."

He found it on the bottom shelf, found the highlighted phrase: "in the shit: *slang* in trouble" and the note that accompanied it "In big trouble (i.e. deep shit) Can the man survive? Can *you* go farther? Yes, if you remember Jenny Fields and Roberta Muldoon: page 217."

He had no idea who Roberta Muldoon was, but Jenny Fields was familiar. Somebody he should get. Not a real person. Fiction. He knew he'd read it. Come on, come on, it was almost there. Wasn't she a nurse? Of course. Garp.

He hurried to the fiction section, the only John Irving book without a dust jacket. A line of conversation by Roberta Muldoon was highlighted: "Oh, I never knew what shits men were until I became a woman." The note said, "Even a teenager can see what man is the real shit here. You too may discover the truth – if you can find page 115. You're almost there. Hint: refer to the foolscap of Rachel."

Rachel, Rachel, that might be it. The movie title for *A Jest Of God.* But what did foolscap have to do with anything? It was only a few steps from John Irving to Margaret Laurence. What kid would be reading Irving and Laurence – and Dos Passos too? Did he have any students like that? He opened the book to page 115. No highlighting. It must be something else.

The foolscap of Rachel? It didn't mean a thing.

He went to the computer, pulled up a stool and sat down. This could take a while. He brought the cursor up beside "Subject KeyWords," clicked the mouse, typed the word "foolscap," and clicked the "Search" order. His answer was immediate: "Search returned no hits." All right then, let's try "Title KeyWords." He typed the same word, received the same immediate response. How about Rachel then? Definitely worth a try. This time when he clicked "Search," the response took a few seconds. A list of books appeared before him. He scrolled thirty-eight of them across the screen, everyone of them with "Rachel" in the title. Sure, there was *Looking for Rachel Wallace,* another Spenser mystery, should be lots of shit in that one. Foolscap, though, it wasn't the stuff of hard-boiled detective novels. Better scroll down the list again, study every title.

Then he knew he had it. Of course, that was it, it had to be. *The Rachel Papers.* As he hurried back to the stacks, he would've sworn that his pulse was racing. He found three books by Martin Amis, none of them the right one. Damn. Somebody'd checked out the only one he wanted. Bloody hell!

Wait a minute, could be misfiled on this very shelf, alphabetical order shot to hell. Better take a look. Come on, Rachel baby, be here somewhere.

And there it was, shoved between two Kingsley Amis titles. Father and son together, thank the Lord.

Was this the final note then? As he flipped through the pages to 115, he could feel a little shaking in his fingers. A yellow glow on dark print: "'Why,' I wondered, 'did old shit-face come round?'" A longer note in the margin: "Schwitzer may sometimes be a Shitzer, but he's not the old shitface. You'll find him in the inner office, sitting on his ass. The all-time, all-star shitface, shithead, shitheel, the non-supportive Mr. Trevor Workman. Now you know."

My God. Well, how about that? The kid was right on target – nailed him to a T. What kid, though? The swearing sounded just like Peale, but surely he wouldn't let Herb off the hook. And "non-supportive," now that was interesting. The kind of thing Herb would think himself. Wait a minute, surely Herb wouldn't go through this charade. No, of course not, couldn't be him.

Then he noticed a second note scrawled in the lower

margin: "Please, turn page." Please, eh? When he did turn the page, he nearly dropped the book. The note said, "Hi, Mr. Cutler. I figured you'd get here sooner or later." He glanced over his shoulder, immediately felt foolish. This was crazy; nobody'd be there, watching him.

Who had led him here though? It had to be one of his students, that was clear enough. But what kid would spend the time setting up all the clues, would bother laying the trail from book to book, from dictionary to novel and back again, from the school library to the public library? Hell, what kid would do all that reading? That should limit the possibilities. A reader then, it sure as heck wouldn't be Bert Peale. Nor Parker Stone, either. He was sharp enough, but not the guy to have his nose buried in a book. Lori Campbell, maybe; she was a reader. Not likely to get hung up on all that shit though. Well, somebody sharp, somebody who liked word games, who would get off on the idea that he was dropping clues for someone else to follow, somebody with the imagination to picture a teacher on his trail. Hell, that might appeal to a lot of kids. But how many of them would have even heard of Martin Amis, let alone read the right book?

Wait a minute.

He strode back to the reference department. They should have them here too. There they were at eye level, the twenty dark blue volumes of *The Oxford English Dictionary*. He selected Volume XV. He couldn't remember the page number, but it was easy enough to find, the notations for "shit" stretching over three pages. Yes. Following each definition, examples from the world's literature, dozens of them. There among them were Dos Passos, J. Irving, M. Amis, with titles, pages, quotations.

Somebody could have stumbled on it the way he had. Somebody – hell. Anybody. Anybody who could find "shit" in the dictionary.

He shook his head and shoved volume XV back on the shelf. Interesting the way the trail seemed to be following Schwitzer, then suddenly changed course and nailed Workman. Too bad the old bugger wouldn't stumble on it himself, get a shock he deserved.

Now, whose mind would work like that? He wondered if he'd ever know.

During the long break the next day, Brad went into the office, noting Workman's closed door. He pulled out some student records on the cardex file, glanced at them, shoved them back, withdrew another, while Kelly took care of three kids at the counter. Anything to seem busy so she wouldn't think he was waiting for her. That jungle of hair above all those curves. She was beautiful all right, but it was finished – nothing stirred inside him.

She was done at the counter, turning back to her desk, when she saw him at the cardex. "Brad," she said.

"Kelly, I want to ask you something." That wasn't the way to put it. He watched how she dropped into her chair, already looking uncomfortable. "About Mr. Workman."

She looked up, just the touch of a smile on her face. "What about him?"

"In the last couple of months or so," Brad asked, "he have run-ins with any kids?"

She pointed towards his door. "It's usually shut."

"So how would you know, eh?"

She shook her head. "Not what I meant. As far as I know,

he hasn't come face-to-face with a kid in weeks – except, of course, the Gourmet Club."

"No run-ins?"

"I would have heard." She looked perplexed, her eyebrows like twin flags raised over the deep green of her eyes.

"I suppose so." It felt good talking to her again – like an ordinary person, a friend, but just a friend. Why not tell her that somebody had Workman figured out exactly right? No, maybe not. "I found a note the other day. Seems like some kid's really got it in for Mr. Workman."

"Oh, yeah? I couldn't guess why. Since the board cut him down, he tends to let things slide." Her fingers were on the keyboard again. "Except for awards night, he has Herb handle the assemblies. I doubt if most kids would even recognize him."

"Uh-huh." He could see that she wanted to get back to work, and he had no reason to linger. That was quite a change, he thought, and not a bad thing either, not bad at all.

Fifteen

A couple of minutes before the noon bell, Brad heard a sputter of static on the intercom followed by Workman's dreary voice, a reminder of a meeting of the Gourmet Club though he didn't hear when, something else he didn't catch at all in the sudden noise of students shutting books. "Wait for the announcements," he said, the noise easing off a bit. You'd think someone who'd been around as long as Workman would know that announcements right before the bell were useless. The second they began, every student in the room knew the class was over, started closing books, shuffling feet, chatting with neighbours. Workman finished twenty seconds before the bell, and Brad watched them, most of them chatting, a few sitting quietly, their eyes on the clock.

Shawna Carter, he noticed, was neither talking nor eyeing the clock. She was looking right at him. Last fall he was pretty sure she'd had a crush on him for a week or so, but then she'd found herself a boyfriend and she'd forgotten all about it. He was glad that was over. Say, maybe she was the one who'd laid that trail of shit through all those library books. No, not likely. Smart enough, though. Must want to talk about something. Bet she waits till the rest of them are gone.

Sure enough, she lingered at her desk, fiddling with her books until the room was empty. He hoped she wasn't going to start hanging around again. As she walked up the aisle toward him, she began to talk, her voice loud at first, then suddenly quieter. "Mr. Cutler, would you mind waiting a minute before you go up to lunch?"

"No problem. What is it?"

"Oh, it's not for me. June's got a class on the third floor. It'll take her a minute to get down here. If you can just wait a bit." Shawna was edging toward the door.

"What's this about?"

"She needs to talk to you." Her voice dropped into a whisper. "When there's no grade twelves around." Shawna glanced over her shoulder toward the door.

"I'll wait for her. You go ahead."

A minute later, June Perkins rushed into the room. Brad could see that she was out of breath as she abruptly stopped inside the door, then swung it closed behind her.

"You wanted to see me?"

"I need to talk," she said. She was beside his desk now, shifting from one foot to the other as if she had to go to the washroom. "You know when you were talking about speeches? You said there was nothing to worry about." She smiled at him, but her smile didn't quite look real. "If anybody started winging tomatoes, we could protect ourselves with your lectern."

He'd been horsing around, of course, trying to slip in a few points about public speaking, but keeping the message light. He'd even demonstrated, lifting the top of the lectern off its stand, waving it around in front of his face as if knocking away a hail of rotten vegetables.

"Nobody's going to throw tomatoes."

"I know that." There was a hint of disdain in her voice, but she was too nice a girl for it to persist. "My speech though, I *am* worried about it."

"Somebody who can discuss things in class the way you can shouldn't have much problem making a speech."

"I'm scared." With that admission, she suddenly reminded him of a fawn he'd once seen poised beside the highway, ready to run for the bush.

"Your father said as much at interviews. There's no –"

"This has nothing to do with my father." There was a snap in her voice. She paused, sat down in the front desk and continued, "Give him his way, I'd be speaking in front of thousands."

Something was really bothering her, and Brad was suddenly uneasy. Every time he had a troubled kid to deal with, he thought of Angela Maddox and the way he'd screwed up with her. He tried to smile at June. "What I was going to say is there's no reason for you to be afraid. You've got a lot of friends in the class. Look at them when you speak. They'll help put you at ease."

"It's not my friends I'm worried about."

Brad rose from behind his desk, walked toward her, took a seat in the student desk beside her. "This isn't like you, June. What's the problem?"

"The guys are going to laugh at me."

"No, they won't. I'm sure they won't."

"They laughed at Nelson."

"I guess they did – a little." Nelson Ahenakew had offered to go first; he'd said he wanted to get it over with so he wouldn't get nervous waiting for his turn. He hadn't seemed nervous, had got off to a good start, in fact, looking at his audience rather than at his notes, but then he'd raised his head in the air and done most of his speech staring at the ceiling. The class got an excellent view of his nostrils. There had been some giggling from the front of the room. "People must've thought it funny the way he had his neck craned at the ceiling," said Brad. He'd been at the back of the room, watching, listening, jotting tentative marks onto the chart he'd worked out ahead of time, trying to scribble comments, a few suggestions for improvement. Damn, he should have been suspicious. "What was going on there?"

"I...I can't say." He thought again of the fawn about to bolt.

"June, if there's something I ought to know about, I need you to tell me." He reached across the aisle and laid his hand on hers. "Please."

He could hear her breathing in the empty room, quick shallow breaths. Followed by a longer one. "On the front desk – the one right in front of the lectern –" she paused, her eyes flicking away from him, then back again, "they were hanging something." When she said "they," her voice had taken on a strange intonation. Hell, Bert Peale sat at that desk. She didn't want to mention his name.

"What were they hanging?" He tried not to emphasize the "they."

"Something." Her eyes were flicking away again, a rosiness slipping into her cheeks. "You had to be at the front to see. That's why Nelson kept staring up the way he did."

He thought a moment. "This happen with anybody else?"

"Parker. He went right on like it didn't bother him."

No use embarrassing her any more. "I'll talk to them

both," he said, "find out what's going on. Put a stop to it."
She sat there, studying his feet. What did she need to hear?
"You go ahead, June, make your speech. I swear to God
nobody's going to laugh at you."

She stood up. "You wouldn't need to tell anyone?"

"Of course not." Was that what was worrying her?

She glanced at the bulletin board where the speech schedule was posted. It was a typed list of names and dates, too
small to read from here. "One more Thursday before it's my
turn," she said. "I'll be ready."

He could have asked Parker in period four that day, but he
doubted that Parker would tell him a thing. He'd try
Nelson first. Maybe get it out of him. Nelson helped out in
the library two days a week. He'd catch him there, have a little talk – yeah, if nobody else was around. No need for anyone to see him quizzing Nelson. You never knew who might
want to give a native a rough time. There was a book he
needed anyway.

The library looked empty from the entrance. When he
pushed through the turnstile, he could see Nelson shelving
books in the 800s, four computers at the back of the room
with students on the Internet. Nobody he knew. He stopped
a few yards from Nelson, studying the shelves. *The Cow
Jumped Over the Moon* by Earle Birney. That was the one Vic
had recommended. He lifted it from the shelf.

"You want to sign it out?"

He nodded, handed the book to Nelson and walked with
him to the counter. Nelson passed the wand over the bar
code on the back cover, turned the book over and read the
title. "You into nursery rhymes, Mr. C?" An impish grin.

Nelson might be aboriginal, but if he'd been around in Elizabethan times, Shakespeare could have used him as the model for Puck.

"Mr. Pendleton says it's one of the best books he knows on poetry. A whole section about 'David'." Nelson looked puzzled. Of course, if he hadn't taken the poem, there was no reason the title would mean a thing to him. "It's a poem I really like. Perfect for grade eleven." Brad glanced around the library. Still just the four kids at the back of the room. "Nelson, I've been wanting to talk to you."

"How so?" Nelson leaned into the counter, looking interested.

"Your speech. It...well, it was kind of disappointing. I figured you'd blow us all away."

Nelson grinned. "I was kind of disappointed myself."

"Hard to do a good job when you're mainly trying to keep your eyes on the ceiling."

"Yeah." Nelson paused, deliberated briefly, continued, "I was nervous...afraid I'd...start giggling."

"You want another try at it? When there's nothing hanging over the front desk?"

"You knew about that?"

"Not then. I do now. What was hanging over that desk, Nelson? What was it you didn't want to look at?"

Nelson leaned closer across the counter, his face serious, then cracking into a smile, then serious again. "Aw, hell," he said, "there was a cardboard penis hanging right in front of me, a big hairy one with drooping balls. I was afraid I was going to bust a gut." By the time he finished, he was grinning again.

"Thanks, Nelson. Might have guessed it'd be something like that. You want another go at your speech, I guarantee it won't be hanging there next time."

"Maybe. I'll let you know."

Period four the next day, and there was Bert Peale right under his nose in the front desk where he had to look at him all the time, where he himself had put him just three weeks ago to keep him out of trouble. Well, today they were going to have a little talk. That meant he'd probably go whining to his old man tonight, and tomorrow he'd have Dr. Peale to deal with, too. And then Workman on his back. No matter. It had to be done.

He waited till they were taking up the questions on *Lord of the Flies,* waited for the tough one that Bert Peale wouldn't bother to do.

"Number three, Bert. What's the significance of the parachute and corpse vanishing at the very moment that Simon is killed?"

"I couldn't get that one."

"Couldn't or didn't?"

The boy shrugged, his voice filling with malice. "Pretty much the same thing, isn't it?"

"No, Bert, there's a vital difference. Which I'll explain to you at 3:30."

Bert half-turned his head, making sure the row of students beside him could see the sneer on his face. "Ah, you're just out to get me."

"Right, Bert. Out to get you to do some meaningful work for a change. In here. 3:30."

But for a second he wondered, was he being fair to Bert? No, this wasn't just about Bert. It was the other kids, they had enough to worry about, hell, they didn't need distractions in their speeches.

Feeling crappy after his talk with Peale, he went up to the staffroom for the break between classes and took a seat beside Sue. He figured he'd be feeling better soon.

"Got a story for you," he said. Her eyes never left him as he told her about the trail of clues that had begun in his room and taken him to the public library. He could tell she was enjoying the tale. "I figured it was a guy at first, but then I had to wonder. There was a line marked in *The World According to Garp,* something about not knowing what shits men were."

"John Irving's quite astute."

He knew she was kidding him and pushed on. "If it was a girl horsing around, it was someone who didn't mind spending a lot of time at it."

Sue was nodding her head, still smiling. "Last year, I kept finding notes hidden on my desk. Messages from Middle Earth. Signed by Bilbo Baggins at first, later on by Frodo."

"You recognize the writing?" .

"They were printed – the neatest calligraphy. Made me think it was a girl. Pam Wheeler maybe, or Lori Campbell. They were witty little notes, some of them about the better school we'd have if only hobbits ran the place, if they had –"

The bell rang before she could finish.

"It made me think of Parker Stone." She rose, winked at him, and headed for the door.

Parker Stone, could he really be the one?

It was almost ten minutes after the final bell of the day when Bert sidled into Brad's room, dropping into a seat by the blackboard.

Brad looked up from his desk. "I was beginning to

wonder," he said.

"Didn't feel like coming, eh? But I came."

"We'll try to get you a medal for that." Oh sure, give him a dose of sarcasm. That'll really help. "Let's have a look at your notebook." Brad slid his chair back from his desk and walked over to the boy. He took the Hilroy scribbler from the desk, found the section devoted to English, glanced at the answers in it. There was something written for all of them now, in most cases not very much. Brad read the ones that had been due today. "You're on the right track with these. You just need to go a bit deeper."

"All's you care about is getting me in trouble. You're just mad cause I come through the gym door, and you couldn't get me expelled."

He spoke quietly, calmly. "If you'd been expelled, it wouldn't have been for sneaking in, but for swearing at Mr. Schwitzer."

"Neither one of you likes me."

"I don't know about Mr Schwitzer, but I like you a lot better when you're doing your work. When you're not assing around." Oh, oh, better take it easy.

That smirk on Peale's face again, the one he'd like to wipe off with a hunk of sandpaper. "You shouldn't be talking that way," said Bert. "My dad wouldn't like it."

He was right about that. His dad had the reputation of being a good Presbyterian, but the talk in the staffroom said he was a prude. Which made everyone wonder, after Bert swore at Herb, what had happened when his father got him home alone with no teachers listening in. Surely, the man didn't really believe that Herb was exaggerating. He was a snob, but he wasn't stupid.

"How would he like to know that his son was hanging a

cardboard penis over the front of his desk?"

The boy looked up, his mouth slightly open, a slim string of saliva stretching from his upper to his lower lip.

"How would he like to know that that's what you do when the others are trying to give a speech?" Bert looked down, wiggled his butt in his seat.

Brad wouldn't wait for an answer. "Next Thursday, when the kids are doing their speeches, I'm sending you to the library to work on an essay."

The boy's head snapped up. "What kind of essay?" Already, his tone was surly again.

"An essay about what you did, how it affected the others, why you won't do it again." Before he could protest, Brad added, "You do a good job, I won't mention it to your dad. The whole thing ends here."

Bert Peale glared at him for what must have been a full thirty seconds before he spoke. "Yeah, sure. Okay."

After he shambled from the room, Brad sat back at his desk. He picked up a leaf of foolscap, began to fold it into smaller and smaller rectangles. When he looked at the tiny wad in his hands, he saw that the paper was damp.

A week later, when June Perkins stepped to the lectern, she smiled at her audience and delivered an animated speech about her experience as a candy-striper at the Union Hospital, her head swinging back and forth, making everyone a part of what she said, the words rolling from her tongue like silk thread from a silver spool.

"You need to pay attention to detail," Brad told his grade elevens. "If you notice the little things, it makes a difference."

"That in reading or real life?" Tim Hrenyk, his voice drenched with sarcasm.

"Reading is real life. But either way, notice the little things, you'll get more out of life."

"Sure." Tim again. Except for his hair which he kept shaved to the skull, he sometimes looked just like Bert Peale. The same sullen mouth.

"I'm trying to make a point because of what's coming in the next chapter." The students were well into their study of *To Kill a Mockingbird*. He wanted them to get all the details, to love Scout and her older brother, Jem, as much as he did. "If you pay attention, you won't miss what's going on here. Something you'll maybe get a charge out of." He grinned. "The thing is, I'll know if you get it."

"How you going to know?" asked Shawna Carter.

"Teachers always know." He grinned more broadly. He didn't want them to think he really meant it.

As they began reading chapter six, he leaned against the wall at the side of the room and watched their faces. Heads bent over their paperbacks, notebooks open beside them, faces serious, eyes looking for details. Tim Hrenyk had his head down, his brow furrowed. He was like Bert Peale, yeah, but there was a difference too, admit it.

Maybe, thought Brad, the difference is in the way I handle him.

He looked at Skye Wilson, who was concentrating hard, the tip of her tongue just visible at the corner of her mouth. Usually, she made a point of sitting sideways in her desk so that the boys behind her would have a good view of her breasts, but she was lost in what she read, had forgotten for a while that she was stacked. This was more like it. Last fall, she'd taken every opportunity to hang over his desk, shoving her bust towards his face. Thank God, he'd had Kelly then, to keep his mind occupied. Now Brad scanned the class. After a minute he saw the smiles begin to appear, first on the face of Joan Washburn who was a fast reader, then at opposite sides of the room, Jay Marsh and Shawna Carter breaking into almost simultaneous grins, both of them nodding their heads. Shawna looked up at him and winked before returning to the book. Yes, right on. Beside her, Wilson Wong noticed her reaction and looked perplexed. Wilson could make algebraic equations jump through hoops, but English was his second language. The subtleties of the passage would be too much for him. As they would be for others in the class. But there were soon half a dozen people with smiles on their faces. Brad glanced at Tim Hrenyk. His mouth was slightly open, just enough that he might be breathing through it, his lips barely moving. No sign of a smile. Some of the slower readers were getting it now, the passage tugging at the corners of their mouths. Jill Parini looked up at him, her eyes wide, a huge smile on her face. Good for her, Brad thought, bet she didn't think she'd get it. He waited a few minutes more.

"Let me interrupt for just a moment." Heads popped up around the room. "A lot of you certainly got it. Right?" Nodding heads. "So, Jay, how did I know you got it?"

"Probably saw me – I nearly cracked up." He was smiling still – yeah, that wide smile, those crooked teeth, he did look like Huckleberry Finn.

"Right. Because it was an interesting passage – one you wouldn't want to miss. Could anyone explain exactly what's going on there?" Half a dozen students were looking about them, heads swivelling from face to face, wondering what they'd missed. Perhaps two-thirds of the others were grinning, but not a single hand was raised. What was wrong here? Of course.

"Who could tell us? Expressing it in genteel terms, you understand. We wouldn't want to offend anyone's finer sensibilities."

Immediately, six or seven hands were in the air. Jay Marsh was actually waving his hand above his head.

"Well, Jay?"

"They're having a contest." He began to chuckle. "To see who can pee the farthest."

Tim Hrenyk raised his hand, laughing now. "Jem and Dill are," he said. "Not Scout."

"Exactly," said Brad. "Because Scout doesn't have the necessary plumbing accessories to compete." Way to go, Tim, he thought, and then he wondered if he would have been as pleased if it had been Bert Peale with the right answer. Maybe not. Got to do a better job with Peale.

He noticed Wilson Wong then, squirming in the middle of the chuckling students, a bemused look on his face as if he had been suddenly set down among aliens. Probably wonders what plumbing has to do with anything, Brad thought. Better catch him at the end of class.

Sixteen

"Just in talking to Mr. Workman," said Herb Schwitzer. "We're wondering about Friday's lit. Browning's turn, isn't it?"

Brad raised his head from his lunch and nodded. He was the staff adviser for Browning. Lawrence Collegiate had a house system for intramural sports and other in-school activities, all students being assigned to either Browning, Tennyson, Shelley or Keats. Each house was expected to put on one "lit" per year, lits having begun, Brad gathered, somewhere in the darkness of antiquity as literary programs, but now having degenerated into variety shows made up largely of songs and skits lifted from television.

"Last one was pretty much a waste of time," said Herb. "Lot of dumb noise and running around."

"Hey," said Maurie Pack, "don't be looking at me now. We got athletes in Shelley, not actors and singers."

"Was I looking at you, Maurie, or you just feeling guilty for what you put us through?"

"It wasn't that bad."

"So, Brad, your kids got something planned that'll justify

an hour and a half of school time?"

"Should be better than the last one," he said, grinning in Maurie's direction. Be nice to stick it to the jerk.

"Can't even have a meal in peace around here," said Maurie.

"Mr. Workman's concerned," said Herb. "Not much quality the last year or so. Wouldn't mind cancelling the things altogether. What have you seen so far, Brad?"

"There's a skit about a motorcycle gang. An original – pretty good too. Let's see. Wilson Wong plays the piano, something classical – goes over my head – but that kid is so good, you'd have to be cooling in the grave not to be impressed." He glanced at Maurie. "Then we've got a couple of numbers by the Hammerhead Band."

"No," said Maurie, "they were in our lit."

"Two of them from your house, two from ours. They qualify. I think they've been practicing since the last lit. Sometimes now you can even hear a tune."

"Should have more than that," said Herb.

"I haven't finished," said Brad. "We've got a couple of Monty Python skits – kids are hooked since they put it back on cable." One of those skits, he knew, wasn't going to win any votes from Workman, but the kids liked it, and so did he. He shrugged. "Should be pretty good. There's a Shania Twain bit too, and a big joke finale. They're going to pile a heap of mats on the stage, a bunch of kids lying there, each one bounces up and tells a joke."

"Kind of pointless, eh?" said Herb. "You checked out the jokes, I suppose?"

"I heard them, sure."

"Okay. Maybe there is enough for a full lit. We'll take fifteen minutes each for period four and five, then down to the gym without a break."

Maurie groaned. "What we going to do in fifteen minutes?"

"Take up an assignment, give one – you figure it out. The lit's an hour and a half."

Monday morning in the staffroom they were still talking about it.

"You should've seen Herb," said Myrna Belsey. "He's standing at the back of the gym, the only light's on the stage, but his face is so red he's glowing in the dark. Looks like his wiring's got a short-circuit."

"They changed the jokes," said Brad.

"And Workman's in the gym. Snuck in the back door to check things out. Been there the whole time. I figured it was stroke time for sure."

"Workman was there?" Brad felt panic, like a blade at his throat.

"Yeah," said Maurie, "and he wasn't laughing."

"They were different jokes," said Brad.

"I don't think Herb even noticed him," said Myrna. "He was heading for the stage, going to throttle the first kid he reached."

"I didn't know they'd change the jokes," said Brad. God, but he was in deep trouble now.

Maurie gave him a knowing smile. "What about the bed?" he asked. "They change that too?"

"Mats. It was supposed to be gym mats."

A few minutes later, when the announcements began at the start of classes, they heard a rather subdued Herb

Schwitzer reading off the day's schedule of meetings and practices. He sounded tired this morning. When he finished with the junior badminton games at six-thirty in the gym, he paused. Everyone knew he wasn't finished because the slight buzzing from the intercom meant it hadn't been shut off.

"This morning," he said, "we're going to hold the bell for a minute. Mr. Workman has something to say."

This is it, thought Brad, now it comes.

The students were sitting alertly in their seats, throwing quick glances at one another, sitting straighter, as if at any moment Workman himself might step into the room. Most of the year he simply ignored them; if he had a message for them that meant something was up.

A sharp click and the intercom's buzzing ceased. Ten seconds later it resumed, followed immediately by a voice ripe with anger.

"People," it said, "this is Mr. Workman here. I can't begin to tell you how disappointed I am at this point in time. That performance Friday afternoon was absolutely disgusting. In all the years I've been at this institution there's never been such a thing. Such an outrage. Your parents – the public – they demand better than this. They have every reason to be affronted."

I should've gone to see him Friday, Brad thought. He wouldn't be so mad – chewing out the whole school over the intercom.

"Let me make one thing absolutely clear, what happened last week will never happen again. You've sunk to a new low, you've insulted your teachers, you've stained the good name of this institution."

Institution, thought Brad, he makes its sound like a federal prison. He shuffled away from where he was standing behind his desk and leaned against the wall opposite the intercom. As far away as he could get. Pointless, he thought, if Workman didn't nail him now, he'd do it later.

"Here we are, taking children from almost every grade school in the city, trying to raise you up, transform you into young ladies and gentlemen, the kind of people that society will welcome. Let me tell you, it's a bigger job every day. This morning, if you hear your name on the intercom, it means Mr. Schwitzer will see you in the office right away. Immediately."

Brad glared at the intercom, realized he was scowling and quickly looked away.

"Let me emphasize, people, there won't be one lady, not a single gentleman in the names you hear. Oh, yes, one thing more. This institution has seen its final sordid display. All future lits are cancelled."

The students were staring at the intercom, every one of them silent, waiting for the names of those in trouble. But the intercom clicked off.

Then it snapped on again, the buzzing louder. A call meant for this room, Brad thought, not the whole school.

"Mr. Cutler, I want you in my office. Now."

Brad had been enjoying Friday's lit from the stage wings, where he was helping out by working the curtain. Even some of the silly bits that went on a tad too long were funny. Like the belly button with the bright red lip-sticked lips around it that filled a tiny spotlight on the darkened stage while the stomach behind it heaved and gyrated in an attempt to mouth the words that Shania Twain's voice sang through the loudspeakers. Pam Wheeler, who was the MC, had announced it as a performance by the essential Shania Twain.

This was good stuff, Brad thought, satire, over Workman's head if he didn't know the singer, but nothing he could complain about.

Next was the dead parrot skit from Monty Python with Parker Stone and Arnie Jordan arguing over something which, more than anything else, resembled a rubber chicken. When Parker returned the dead parrot to the pet shop owner and was told that it was merely sleeping, his frustration was palpable. Then there was the wonderful moment when he slammed the parrot onto the counter, its rubber head breaking loose and bouncing into the air where it seemed to hang an instant exactly at eye level between them. Both boys looked shocked. It was Parker who ad-libbed, "Ah yes. Now I see that it *is* just sleeping."

The kid's a genius, Brad thought.

When he heard Wilson Wong at the piano, he knew he was right, the boy could really play – and the audience was smart enough to be impressed. As Wilson left the stage, Brad reached out from behind the curtain and patted him on the shoulder. "Good work," he said, and pulled the curtain shut.

The second Monty Python skit was the one that made him feel uneasy. There was really nothing wrong with it, but he knew Workman wouldn't like it. Sure, he could have told the kids to can it, but it was okay, it was funny. He wasn't going to cut it just because there was a chance Mr. Workman might not approve. A damned good chance.

In the dim backstage light, the boys took their positions in a semi-circle behind the curtain. A stagehand shoved a cardboard tree beside Danny Litowski, who steadied it till the branches quit vibrating and then nodded at Brad. He pulled the curtain rope, felt it bind once on the pulley, yanked it free and got the curtains open. Six boys in blue jeans and red plaid shirts, their faces stubbled with dots of mascara or a few days' growth of beard, their leather boots pounding the beat into the floor as they sang out to the world that they were lumberjacks, and they were okay. They could really sing too, every one of them on key. Maybe Workman might think it was all right. When they hit the line about liking to dress in women's clothes, they opened ranks and there behind them was Walter Buchko prancing about in an outfit made entirely from bras. The audience roared and hooted for two minutes. They knew it was funny; maybe Workman would too.

Then the lights went down and the music came up, "Born to Be Wild" thundering over the loudspeakers, the Steppenwolf snarl almost lost in the roar of motorcycles. This was one the kids would love. And in another minute here came the biker gang, Parker Stone, Walter Buchko, Arnie Jordan and the others in black leather jackets, stomping toward the front of the stage, every one of them with a beer bottle in his left hand, the right hand coiled around a chain, a knife, a gun. Suddenly, in a move that Brad had helped them choreograph, all spinning simultaneously, they turned their backs on the audience, revealing their crests, skulls and crossbones on each of them. Beneath the skulls, the makeshift crests said simply, "Heck's Angels." Another choreographed move and they faced the audience again, each of them with a globe of pink bubble gum swelling from his mouth. They stood absolutely still, the bubbles growing and growing. When the bubbles exploded it was like a series of shots. Panic struck the biker gang. Bottles and knives, guns and chains clattered to the floor. They turned to run, eyes wide, some of them with gum stuck to their cheeks and chins. They collided at the center of the stage, falling backwards, grabbing one another, tugging and twisting to be free. A moment of chaos and they fled to stage right, disappearing behind the curtain.

Wild applause – which ended with the thunder of motorcycle engines – and here they came again, this time on children's tricycles, pedalling frantically, heads bent over front wheels, ungainly legs pumping, elbows out, knees jutting awkwardly. Parker, who led the pack, looked over his shoulder with terror, but his wheel turned sharply, and he spilled from his bike, tumbling to the floor in a heap which caused a chain reaction as the other bikers ploughed into him, all toppling to the floor. They rose as one, reached for their bikes, tucked those bikes beneath their arms, and – in steps that never stretched beyond six inches – they ran from the stage.

Brad found that he was laughing just as hard as the audience. He leaned forward, peeked around the curtain and saw the kids in the far side of the front row, all of them clapping and laughing. It was a good lit, the best he'd seen so far. He bet Herb would love it. Maybe even Workman.

He didn't change his mind until the last skit.

By then the microphone had broken down, and Parker had come to him, looking worried.

"It's been a great lit," Brad said. "Doesn't matter if we have to end it right now."

"We don't need a mike. Really. Let us finish. We can project good enough. They'll still hear us."

Why not, thought Brad. "Sure, let's give it a whirl."

"You could help us though," said Parker. "If you'd go out to the audience and stand by the back door where the exit light is. We'll be able to see you there. Just raise your hand if we need to talk louder, okay?"

"Sure, but I was working the..."

"Danny'll run the curtain."

Brad hurried out the stage door, trotted down the hall and pushed through the door at the back of the gym. The curtains closed, they must still be setting up the mats. He glanced up at the light. Yeah, they could see him here all right. When he looked back at the stage, Pam Wheeler was stepping between the curtains, blinking in the spotlight.

"Next, and last – but sure as heck, not the least," shouted Pam, trying for a good, long dramatic pause, he noted, but cutting it short, being too anxious to get on with the skit, "direct from the Sin City Motel, we bring you 'An Orgy of Humour – and More.'"

What? This wasn't right.

Pam leered at the audience. "Right here on the Lawrence stage we've got the scene that was too hot for the Jerry Springer Show." The curtains rolled back to reveal what could only be described as a bed fit for giants. But it wasn't supposed to be a bed. Even from here you could see that the bed was really just gym mats piled one on top of the other, three piles of mats placed side by side. On top of the mats he saw what looked like three bedspreads stitched together. This wasn't what they'd planned. Beneath the bedspreads were the reclining forms of at least eight figures. What the hell?

Suddenly, Walter Buchko's head appeared. When he sat up and began to flex his muscles, everyone could see that he was naked to the waist. Naked, oh, man, no. All at once, Sara what's-her-name popped out from the covers, rising up beside him in what looked like a black negligee. "Don't you just love a hunk?" she said directly to the audience. "This one's got such a great body: broad shoulders, huge biceps, wonderful hands, a stomach of steel, and balls –" she hit a climax and paused, "he balls all night long." Immediately, they ducked beneath the covers which were suddenly alive with bodies pumping up and down.

No, my God, they can't be doing this.

There was a second of silence, a murmur running through the audience, then shrieks of laughter, the roar of a great wind shaking the gym.

Brad took a step, felt his knees waver, thought for a second he might go down. No, he had to do something. He took another step toward the stage, started walking faster, hurrying down the side aisle.

Another head was thrust from beneath the covers. A boy again, someone Brad didn't know, sitting up in bed, also bare-chested. A second girl in black sat up beside him. Jan Hewitt, he saw, one of his grade elevens. She had to wait for silence. Then she turned away from the boy, shaking her head, a look of disdain on her face as she spoke, a flurry of words: "I says to Ted, I says, 'You got to know how to treat a lady, you got to do a better job,' and he says, you know what he says, 'Screw you!' he says." Her nose was in the air now, a shocked look on her face, her voice haughty, pained. "'Well!' I says, 'Now you're talkin'!'" A sudden sensual smile as her arm snaked out, snagged him by the head and dragged him underneath the covers. Then four couples humping beneath the spread.

A tornado's howl filled the gym, whirling from the students seated in metal chairs to those in the bleachers against the wall, the roar booming back again, pounding against Brad as he rushed up the aisle. He had to get to the curtain. There was a hand on his arm. When he looked around, he saw Sue Burton beside her class in the front row, shaking her head.

"Easy," she said, her head still shaking, "it's okay."

"No." It wasn't okay, and she knew it.

"There goes Herb. He's going to shut them down."

Brad looked across the audience. He could see Herb charging up the center aisle, gaining speed as he went. He'd been moving in a deliberate walk, but he was soon trotting, his trot breaking into an awkward gallop. On stage two more figures were sitting up in bed, the boy – it was Parker, my God, he was part of it – saying that he was a salesman who'd been stuck in a blizzard, the girl saying that she was Snow, the farmer's daughter, she knew exactly where he could sleep, yes, he could sleep with her. Parker was about to say more when he froze, his mouth open for his next line but unable to deliver it, his eyes wide and focused straight ahead. The girl beside him saw where he was looking and ducked beneath the covers. Parker finally got his mouth closed and snapped back into action, his head swinging to the right, his hand waving wildly. The curtains seemed to jerk, paused, jumped ahead, then began a speedy progression across the stage. Just as they swung shut, Herb reached the front of the gym. He laid both hands on the stage, hoisted himself upwards, getting his left leg onto the stage, heaving himself upright. He was moving so fast he was off-balance and staggered into the curtains, almost falling. Then his arms were flailing at the curtains, grabbing at them, trying to find the opening. Finally he had it and disappeared from sight, the curtains falling closed behind him.

That was when the stage lights went out. In the dim glow from the exit lights over the gym doors, Brad could see that the curtains were still shaking. He better get up there too. In the distance, he heard an angry voice – or voices – but he had no idea what was said.

The gym was quiet now, everybody listening, the only

sound his footsteps as he trotted to center stage.

The curtains jumped suddenly, something striking against them; they shook and parted, a hulking figure pushing between them, stepping to the apron of the stage. It was Herb, of course. He stood with feet splayed, his hands on his hips as he looked down at the audience, at Brad standing right in front of him. Brad thought he must be pausing to catch his breath, to let his nerves settle down, but when he spoke – and he spoke almost at once – his voice was calm.

"Mr. Cutler," he said, "would you step over to the side wall and give us some light in here?"

Brad nodded, hurried to the electric box by the side door, glad to have something – anything – to do. He pulled the metal door open and began flipping breakers, the overhead lights breaking into a dim glow, then beginning to brighten. Some of the students were watching him, he noticed when he turned around, but most of them had not taken their eyes from the vice-principal.

"Now," Herb said, "as you may well have gathered, this lit is over. In a minute you will commence to exit the gym in an orderly fashion. The grade nines first, then the tens, followed by the elevens. Not yet! In a minute." He paused. "Today grade twelves will stack the chairs – boys and girls both –" his voice was suddenly angry "and make darned sure you do a good job."

When Brad closed the door on the electric box, it rattled beneath his shaking hand. Parker, he thought, Parker set me up.

Seventeen

Workman was waiting for him outside the inner office. "Get in there," he said, and he followed Brad in, almost stepping on his heels, the door slamming behind them.

This is it, thought Brad, I'm finished now. Let Workman get behind his desk, then explain. But Workman was right beside him.

"I had no idea –"

"You call that a lit! You're the staff advisor – and you let them put on that rubbish!"

"I didn't know –"

"Sit!" Workman pointed at the chair in front of his desk, but he made no move to sit himself. Brad hesitated, then slumped into the chair. He felt like a kid again, trying to explain something to his father when the old man was roaring mad. "You sit right there and you listen. There's some crap I won't put up with. Not from you or anybody else. I had three phone calls Friday night. At home! More on Saturday. Parents calling, absolutely disgusted, dirty jokes in my school – I won't stand for it." Workman was leaning over him, his face like hot metal. Brad could feel the heat. "You think gutter humour's right for my school, you think it's okay kids screwing on stage, you're out of here." He was waving his hand now, looking as if he might strike Brad across the face. "I don't put up with that crap. I won't put up with you. You get me? I can do it. One call to Dr. McAvoy and you're gone. You understand what I'm saying?"

"Yes." He could phone the Teachers' Federation, sure, but they wouldn't help him – couldn't help him without tenure.

"You better believe it." Workman suddenly wheeled around, slid behind his desk and sat down. Brad could hear his breathing, quick and heavy. His face still red, like a pot that had boiled itself dry on the stove.

Brad opened his mouth to speak, drew a quick breath instead. Tried again. "Can I explain?" His voice was so quiet he wondered if Workman had heard him.

Workman nodded then. "You damn well better explain."

"I had no idea they were going to tell those jokes. Honest to God!" he said, and felt like a fool saying it. "They had different jokes at rehearsal – clean ones – and they didn't have a bed. Each kid jumped up on the mat, said a joke, then did a bellyflop down again. There wasn't any bed. If I'd known what was coming, I'd've put a stop –"

"You *should*'ve stopped it. The second you saw that bed."

"I couldn't. I was out in the audience."

"You're supposed to be backstage, making sure everything goes right. That's your job."

Workman had him there. "I know, but...there was this problem."

"Damned rights there was a problem." Workman leaned towards him, his fists on the desk.

I can tell him about Parker, Brad thought, let the kid take

some shit. He looked down at Workman's hands, fists like sledge-hammers about to pound the desk. Wondered if he should do it. For some reason, an image of Angela Maddox flashed into his head, Angela with Parker beside her, blank eyes, dead eyes staring through him. It was crazy, it made no sense, but he knew he wasn't going to do it.

"The mike quit working. I...I thought I better get out front, make sure they could be heard."

"Make sure everybody heard the dirty jokes."

"I...never knew." He winced. He didn't know what else to say. "I'm sorry."

Workman sat back in his chair, glanced down at his hands, and lowered them into his lap.

"All that homosexual crap wasn't much better."

"Pardon?"

"Gay lumberjacks, young Buchko strutting around, decked out in brassieres." Workman's voice was louder now. "The kids sneak that one by you too?"

He could blame it on them. Sure, get away with it, he'd be okay, off the hook and clear.

Except he couldn't do it.

"No, I guess I let that one go myself."

"You let it go." Each word like a drop of acid.

"It was the only thing in the whole lit that seemed questionable, I thought –"

"Except for dirty jokes and a bit of public screwing."

"I didn't know about those." He shrugged. "The lumberjack skit was my fault."

"Whole lit was your fault," said Workman, but his voice was quieter, as if something had changed. Brad stared at him, his suit jacket hanging slack from his shoulders, his face almost emaciated. "I warn you," said Workman, "anything else like this ever happens, I'll see you never teach in this town again. You understand?"

Brad nodded his head.

"One more chance, and that's it. Now you get down to your room, make sure those kids haven't knocked the walls out by now."

Somehow he got through the morning, running on empty, his teaching hollow, mechanical, no better than a robot stuck in front of the class. Let him get a hold of Parker Stone, there'd be some emotion in his voice.

At noon he forced himself to stay in his room for a minute counting the essays he'd taken in at the end of the last period, one paper missing, what the hell, he'd figure out who it was later on. When he walked into the hall, he was struck by the unusual quietness of 110, the lunch room across the hall. Were the kids up to something? As he walked toward the door, he realized he could hear a hum of conversation. When he stepped through the doorway, he saw kids at their desks, talking seriously, their heads bent together. Yeah, he knew what they'd be going on about.

He backed out and, turning to the stairs, almost bumped Parker Stone.

"Parker," he said, "we need to talk. Now."

"I was looking for you."

Brad led him into his room, stepped behind him and slammed the door shut. He didn't get a chance to speak before Parker turned to him and said, "Mr. Workman reamed us out. Mr. Workman! You should've heard him going after Walter. Man, Walter really caught it." Parker gasped a quick breath. "We've got to see Schwitzer after school about how long we're in detention, and I need to talk to you."

"You figure I'm going to help you?"

"No. Of course not. I...I just want to apologize. Getting you off the stage, out of there...it was my idea. We knew we had to do something – you'd never let us get away with that bedroom scene."

"What about the broken mike?"

Parker looked down at his feet, scuffing one running shoe against the other. "Ah hell, it was working. I just unplugged it." He raised his eyes. "I lied to you, Mr. Cutler. I never should've done that. I'm sorry."

Brad had been waiting all morning to tear into Parker. Now, he was surprised how calm he felt.

"You ever think you'd get me reamed out too?"

"You? You're a teacher." Parker's expression shifted. "You're kidding, right?"

"The hell I'm kidding. You ever think about consequences?" He was suddenly furious. "About who else is going to catch it? Your dumb-ass dirty jokes could mean my job."

"No," said Parker, backing away from him, "they wouldn't –"

"Damned rights they would."

"I'm sorry," said Parker. He was sandwiched against the chalkboard now. "I never thought –"

"You never thought? Son-of-a-bitch, that's some bloody excuse." He knew he was yelling, yeah, roaring just like his old man. "What the hell got into you?"

"I don't know. Honest to God." Parker paused for a breath, looked relieved when Brad took a step backwards. "It was like this. Bunch of us were sitting around at Pam's and she said, sure she'd MC, but we had to come up with a big finale. Pam told us about this sex movie she'd seen on the late show, kind of a group grope, I guess it was, and then – Don't get me wrong. I'm not saying it was her idea – the whole thing just kind of grew on us, everybody sticking in ideas, we could do something the kids'd be talking about for months." He had glanced over Brad's shoulder a number of times as if the door might open and he could escape, but now he was staring right into his eyes. "We got carried away, I know. It was all kind of crazy. We were having so much fun dreaming up the things we'd say, we kind of forgot about what was going to happen afterwards. I guess we went a little crazy."

"I guess you did." Brad had almost lost it there before, but this was better, it was him again, he was in control.

"Yeah, I know I've got it coming – detention, I mean. I just wanted to apologize to you. Lying like that – it never should've happened."

"You've got that right." Brad was leaning toward Parker again. He stepped away. "You had to figure you'd be in deep – trouble." He'd almost said "shit," but he stopped himself in time. Barely.

Parker had a weird expression on his face, a little grin twisting his mouth. "In shit with Shitzer's what everybody calls it, sir. Sorry. Didn't mean that." Parker grimaced. "The only thing is, they've gone and cancelled lits."

"Too bad. It was a pretty good lit – until the end anyway." Brad paused; something was nagging him. "That dead parrot skit was a riot, Parker – you really made it work."

"Thanks, sir." Another grin, but this one was different. The last one was quick, but cock-eyed, something off-kilter there. Of course.

"It was you, Parker. I should have known."

"What?" The kid was still grinning, but he looked nervous.

"That trail of shit clues. From my dictionary all the way to the public library. You're the one who laid the trail."

"I wouldn't know about that, sir." Parker shook his head, but his grin had broken into a smile, rare and full.

"It's a scene you don't actually see in the play," Brad said to Lori Campbell and Parker Stone, who were standing in the hall outside the closed door to his classroom. "Polonius just describes it. Olivier did it in his *Hamlet* film though, and I'm pretty sure you two can bring it off." Ophelia would have orange hair today, but that was okay. He settled his eyes on Parker. "If you don't mind looking a bit weird." This was maybe pushing it, but the kid owed him one.

Lori leaned into Parker, giving him a quick poke in the ribs with her elbow. "Nobody'll notice the difference."

"Doesn't matter," said Parker, his voice gruff. He nodded at Brad. "I can do it. It's all just acting."

Yeah, thought Brad, and every time you do it, something changes for the better.

Then he noticed Parker's eyes averted from Lori. How about that? He's blushing – and pretending not to. Uh-huh, for sure something going on here with these two.

"Let's see. Roll your pant legs up and we'll pull your socks down – there, 'downgyved to the ankle,' like Shakespeare says. Muss your hair, yeah, let it fall in your eyes, and we'll pull your shirttail out, redo a couple of buttons so they're crooked."

"What's this all about?" Parker asked.

"The look of a lovesick man – at least that's how the

Elizabethans saw it. And Polonius, of course, after Ophelia describes her meeting with Hamlet." Brad took off his sport coat and handed it to Lori. "You're supposed to be sewing in your closet. Maybe pretend the sleeve is loose and go to work on the seam." He demonstrated, with exaggerated movements of his hand, drawing an invisible needle through the fabric and plunging it down again. "I'll pull my chair up beside the desk, and you can sit there in plain sight." He glanced at Parker, who looked suitably rumpled. "What you have to do, Parker, is walk slowly into the room, staring at her. Then grab her wrist, hold it a bit, then stretch it out with your own arm at full length. Put your other hand over your brow and study her face. As if you're trying to figure out whether you can trust her or not. Take your time about this. Then give her arm a little shake, nod your head three times, and sigh – good and loud, something everyone can hear – then you let her go. After that, you go back out the door, but – and this is important – keep your eyes on her the whole time. Shakespeare says, 'He seem'd to find his way without his eyes.' Lori, you have to look really worried while all this is going on, kind of freeze, then stare at him till he's out the door. As soon as he's gone, you run the other way to tell your father about it. You two okay with this?"

"Sure," said Parker, Lori nodding at the same time. "All right if we run through it a couple times out here?"

"Of course. It only takes a minute or so."

He watched them do it, the two of them suddenly transformed into young lovers locked in a relationship that wasn't working out.

"Looks good," said Brad. "Just stare at her a bit longer before you nod your head. You two run through it once more. I'll go back into the room and set the class up for what's coming."

He opened the door on a gentle hum of conversation, heads turning toward him. "Okay. Parker and Lori are going to try a little scene for you – one that doesn't actually occur in the play. It's something we just hear about, a meeting between Hamlet and Ophelia. The whole thing is done without any words. See if you can figure out what's going on. Any questions?"

"Yeah," said Walter Buchko, "which one plays Ophelia?"

Brad rolled his eyes while a chorus of groans answered Walter's question. Brad grabbed his chair and set it in full view beside his desk. He was about to tell the class that this was Ophelia's sewing room when he heard a burst of static followed by Kelly's voice on the intercom.

"Excuse me, Mr. Cutler. Sorry to interrupt your class, but Mr. Workman would like to see Lori Campbell in the office."

"Now?" He knew he was glaring at the intercom, glanced at his students, hoping his voice hadn't been as loud as he thought it was.

"That's what he said." She sounded defensive. "As long as she wasn't writing a test."

"No test," he said, "but we are in the middle of something. Can't it wait?" He hoped she wouldn't think he was angry with her.

"He said he'd like to see her now."

Bloody hell. "We were just going to do a scene from *Hamlet*. Ask him if he can wait till we're done, would you?"

"One moment, please." The intercom ceased buzzing. Brad stared at it, waiting till it snapped to life with another burst of static. "Mr. Workman says he needs her in the office now."

"Damn!" Brad glanced quickly at his students, most of whom were wearing various stages of grins on their faces. "Forget I said that." He meant the last remark for them, and

Kelly too. "I'll send her up." He tossed the words toward the intercom as he stepped into the hall where Lori and Parker were waiting for their cue to enter. "I guess we're going to have to can it," he said. "Too bad, Lori, but Mr. Workman wants you in the office."

"Damn," said Parker.

"What for?" asked Lori.

At least she doesn't look worried. "He didn't say."

"What about our scene?" Parker asked.

"We'll have to read on today," said Brad. He saw the disappointment on Parker's face. "We can do it tomorrow though. Just won't be as effective when we've already read the scene."

The next day Brad took Parker and Lori into the hall at the beginning of class. While Parker went to work on his clothes, pulling his pant legs up and his socks down, Brad turned to Lori. "Yesterday," he said, "I hope you weren't in any trouble with the principal."

"Oh, no. Not at all." She was standing poised, ready to go, busily watching Parker rumple his clothes.

"None of my business," said Brad, but he couldn't help himself. "What was going on there?"

She kept staring at Parker. "Mr. Workman called six of us in." She paused, studying Parker as he messed his hair. "He wanted to plan our next meeting – the Gourmet Club."

"Son of a bi –"

She was looking at him now. So was Parker. Bloody hell, when would he learn to keep his mouth shut?

"Sorry," said Brad. "Just an expression. Didn't mean him."

"Right," said Parker.

"I'm sorry, Mr. Cutler," said Lori. "I wanted to do the scene. There really wasn't much reason to pull us out of class."

"I guess there wasn't." Smarten up. It wasn't her fault. It was Workman again, the bugger.

Although Brad felt like pounding up the stairs to the office at that moment, he knew it would be a big mistake. He waited until the five minute break after class. When he threw open the office door, he noticed Kelly glance at him, her eyes widening. He nodded at the closed door. "Anybody in there with him?"

"Maybe you should wait," said Kelly, her hand leaping to her mouth.

"He free?"

"Brad...yes, he's free."

Brad strode to the door, raised his fist, caught himself and tapped the door, twice. Better be careful or Workman would fire him out of here. Yeah, but hell, this wasn't just a lit, this was important, the school principal was screwing up his class. It had to stop.

"Come in."

For most of the last hour he'd been trying to figure out what he should say to Workman and doing a lousy job of teaching *Hamlet*. He couldn't just keep quiet, but what could he tell him without getting himself into more trouble?

He still didn't know what to say. He stepped inside, swung the door shut behind him. Stay calm, that was what mattered.

The principal was leaning back in the soft chair behind his desk, looking like a cadaver still slightly puzzled by its own death.

Brad edged toward a chair, then decided not to sit. "Mr. Workman," he said. "There's something I need to talk to you about."

Workman slowly raised his right hand to his face and began to stroke his lower lip with his index finger. "Well," he said, "I suppose this would be the time to do it then." There was an instant when his mouth opened that Brad thought he was going to bite the tip of his finger. "Why not get on with it?"

"Yes, right. Yesterday, when you called Lori Campbell up to the office...well, I really needed her in class."

"I see." That finger was still stroking his lower lip, moving slowly from the left side to the right.

"We were doing a scene from *Hamlet*. She was in it."

"Uh-huh."

"I'd really appreciate it if you didn't pull students out of my class." Did he sound kind of pushy? "Unless it's something important, of course."

The finger stopped moving. "It was important."

"The Gourmet Club?"

The finger was stirring again, moving away from the lip, pointing directly at him. "Mister Cutler, how long have you been teaching? Not even a year, right?" His voice, at least, was calm. Brad nodded his head. "Perhaps, you should consider that at this point in time some of us have been around a lot longer than you. Some of us might know just a bit about how to run a school." His volume was up, the words coming faster now. "A bit more than you do. About what's important. What's important in this institution. Don't you. Don't you ever tell me what to do."

The finger was pointed right between Brad's eyes, Workman staring along it as if aiming a gun. Brad saw the anger in his eyes, the eyes beginning to cross, focusing on the finger, the hand dropping to the desk. "Instead of worrying about what I do here in the office, you might be wise to give some thought to your own performance. In and out of the classroom. Especially after that ungodly lit you organized. You might do well to remember that I'm the one who decides who gets hired and who gets fired. Before the term ends." Workman's voice was softer now, his expression sinister. "Please, close the door on your way out."

As the door clicked shut, Brad remembered Herb Schwitzer saying he should get himself a reputation. He guessed his reputation was better with the students than it would ever be with their principal.

"Not to worry," said Sue Burton. "He likes the sound of his own voice." It was the end of the day's classes, an hour after Brad's meeting with Mr. Workman, the staffroom filled with teachers drinking coffee.

"Firing, though," said Brad. "It was a definite threat."

"You questioned him," said Sue. "He's not particularly fond of being questioned, but I don't think he's going to let you go for that. You're too good a teacher."

"Not to worry," said Phil Simpson. "Rutledge used to push him a lot harder than that."

"Uh-huh, and he's gone, isn't he?" said Maurie Pack. "You could be right behind him."

Brad glowered at Maurie. The jerk never missed a chance to make him sweat. Then he noticed Vic Pendleton glancing uneasily from him to Maurie and back again. "What is it, Vic?"

"I don't know. I guess he almost caught it that time with Ellie Kent."

"Not the only time," said Maurie.

"Who was Ellie Kent?" asked Brad.

"Best artist in the school," said Vic. "She knew it too. Rutledge used to set up this art gallery in the main hall – recent work from his best students. Ellie figured most of the paintings should've been hers. Used to go sashaying by them, glancing at them, you know, a big sneer on her face; you could almost hear her sniffing at the lesser works." Vic laughed. "Rutledge told her he'd seen her studying the paintings. Said she looked like a bloody snob. Either that or she had a pole shoved so far up her ass it was pushing her nose into the air."

"Workman didn't approve, eh?"

"Workman was not impressed," said Vic. "Her old man was on the school board."

Brad whistled. "He talk to Rutledge about tenure?"

"I don't know what he said. His door was closed. The office door was closed too. But you could hear him in the main hall – an angry roar that went on and on. When Rutledge came back into the staffroom, he sat down and never said a word."

"He was bleeding," said Phil. "A strip torn right off him. Don't worry though, he healed. After that he used to ride Workman every chance he got."

"The winter coat," said Vic.

"Yeah," said Phil. "One of those long black overcoats, hung down to his ankles. Like the outlaws used to have in western movies. Johnny Cash is wearing one on his 'American Recordings' album cover."

"Johnny Cash," said Sue. "You're a Johnny Cash fan?"

"So? Connie Kaldor's not the only singer in the world."

"I thought your taste in country ran more to women with big boobs."

"Stuff it, Burton. This coat – Rutledge's, not Johnny Cash's – had shoulders on it would make Arnold Swarzenegger look like a shrimp. And burn marks all over it. Rutledge was not a neat smoker."

"Rutledge wasn't neat. Period," said Vic. "In that coat he looked like an evacuee from an explosion – only thing survived was a canvas tent, and he'd made his coat from that."

"Every year on Halloween he put it on," said Phil, speaking quickly, reclaiming his share of the story. "Wore it each and every day until the fifteenth of March. Herb said he looked like a bed after an orgy."

"Workman hated that coat."

"With a passion. One day he's in the staffroom when Rutledge comes to work. Rutledge walks in, sees him sitting there, frowning at him. Half the time he never did the buttons up, just threw the coat over his shoulders. So he strolls by Workman, kind of shrugs his shoulders and he walks right out of the coat, lets it fall in the middle of the floor."

"Which is exactly where it stays the whole day," said Vic.

Sounds like Rutledge could get away with anything, Brad thought. Be nice maybe, but he'd settle for a job next year.

"It's the last time Rutledge hangs up that coat," said Phil. "Every morning after that, he shrugs out of the coat, lets it lie where it falls. Till he puts it on to go home at night. Workman could have killed him."

"Never said a word, though. Couldn't stand us knowing Rutledge got to him. One day he walks into the staffroom, he's talking to somebody, not thinking about the coat, and he damned near trips on it."

"Yeah, he looks down to see what he's hit, and there's that damned coat. 'Ignoramus,' he says, and he boots it up against the wall. That was all. Left it right there."

"Every day," said Vic, "until it disappeared."

"My story," said Phil. "This goes on all winter. Till one day in early March – nice day, snow's melting, must be ten above. Rutledge comes up from the art room about quarter to five, his coat's gone. No sign of it. Except right in the middle of the round table's this pile of junk, a wad of crumpled-up kleenex, a couple of long butts, an empty DuMaurier package, three or four books of matches, some change, keys, three gloves – none of them match. Course, it's the stuff from Rutledge's pockets. Nobody ever saw the coat again."

"Workman threw it out?" asked Brad.

"Burnt it," said Phil. "At least that's what everybody figured. Except maybe for Rutledge. He thought Amy might have done it."

"Amy?" asked Brad.

"His wife," said Phil. "She hated the coat even more than Workman."

Sue leaned over and nudged Brad. "Feeling better now?" she asked.

But when Brad started down to his room to mark papers, Maurie was right behind him. "That was it," said Maurie. "That's when Workman decided to get rid of Rutledge."

He's just kidding, Brad thought, trying to make me worry. That's all it is. Sue's the one who's got it right, I should be feeling better. But he just wasn't sure.

Eighteen

Today was the big scene from *Hamlet*. Brad had picked his cast three days before, given them abbreviated scripts, keeping the action, but cutting much of the dialogue.

The first thing he noticed after lunch was that all his grade twelves were present. The next was the anticipation on their faces. As they shoved the desks to the back of the room, everyone pitched in to help. His chair and another borrowed from the next room would serve as thrones. Yesterday they'd read as far as the play's last scene; today they'd see how everything ended. Brad wasn't sure himself as to exactly how this was going to go. Parker Stone and Arnie Jordan, who were playing Hamlet and Laertes, had hung a huge towel – a tapestry, they said – from under the ceiling tiles near the side of the room and insisted that his desk be pushed against the wall behind the towel. He wondered what that was all about. Nothing crazy, he hoped. They'd rehearsed the scene the day before with foils he'd borrowed from the City Fencing Club. Foils and masks. He didn't want anyone getting hurt. Still he'd been feeling uneasy ever since Parker had said, "Arnie and I, we practiced again last night, added a few details."

The cast was waiting in the boiler room next door, so the

other students hadn't seen them in costume as they came into class. Claudius and Gertrude were dressed in bathrobes and the crowns that were usually reserved for the Mr. and Miss Lawrence elections. Walter Buchko, as Osric, wore a wooden sword stuck through his belt and a hat with so many feathers half a dozen ostriches must be walking around with depleted tails. For once, his wispy goatee looked appropriate. Hamlet and Laertes wore jogging suits with long sleeves, and leather gloves to protect their dueling hands. Horatio was dressed simply in jeans and T-shirt.

When the students were seated at the back of the room with a row of empty desks between them and the action, Brad set them up for what was coming. "Today," he said, "I think you're going to get an idea of why Elizabethans thought the theatre was fun. The big scene that everything's been leading to." He noticed Bert Peale frowning at him, but he pushed on. "Now, you're in it too because you're the audience at court, called together to see what's supposedly a friendly duel between Hamlet and Laertes. Of course, we've been reading the play so we know that treachery's afoot. What kind of treachery?"

Half a dozen hands shot up. Brad nodded at Della Neudorf who said, "Laertes has got poison on the tip of his sword."

"Right." Brad went to the desk where the swords and masks lay. "They look pretty much alike, but notice this sword with the tape on the end. The button on it's fake. He can cut Hamlet with that – and poison him. Notice how that sword gets to Laertes. But maybe Hamlet's too good with the sword and Laertes can't break through to stab him. What's the backup plan?"

More hands shot into the air. "The drink! The king's got a poisoned drink for Hamlet."

Brad nodded towards a wine bottle that sat on the desk beside the swords. Next to it was a plastic goblet. "The king isn't going to want anybody thinking about a poisoned drink. See if you can decide how he makes the drink look innocent and how he gets the poison into it.

"So we're watching a duel in court. You lords and ladies will be expected to rise for the king and queen and – of course – to applaud at appropriate moments." Brad looked at the class, students hunched forward in their seats, every eye on him. Except for Bert Peale, who seemed to be inspecting patterns on his desk. "Our cast is going to provide the action – and a few of the words. When we're done, we'll listen to the tape of the last scene and you can try to put together words and actions in your heads. Be right back."

Brad stepped into the hall and was about to open the door to the boiler room when he saw the principal walking toward him.

"I heard there was something going on down here," said Workman. "Thought I'd better sit in."

"Oh. Well...I don't know. I mean, well, I wouldn't want to throw the actors off."

Workman scowled at him, then turned toward the classroom. "I'll just grab a seat at the back," he said. "They won't even notice I'm there."

Damn. That was all he needed, the principal staring at his kids from the back of the room, giving them that scowl of his, making them self-conscious, screwing up the whole scene.

Better warn them though. Wouldn't do to have them spot him part way through – the shock might freeze them altogether.

He opened the door to the boiler room. They turned to him, nervous, he could tell, but excited too, eager to get started, the room charged with energy. "Listen, gang," he said, "there's been a bit of a hitch. Mr. Workman's going to be sitting at the back of the room. He wants –"

"No way!" said Walter Buchko.

"What gives him the right?" said Parker.

"Hey, he's the principal." Brad shrugged. "Don't worry. He's checking up on me – not you guys. There's no reason it should throw you. Don't let it."

Parker frowned at him, then nodded his head. Neither he nor Walter looked happy about it, though.

"I know you can do it," said Brad. "It's going to be fine. Just give me a chance to grab a seat, then you can start. Take your time, and remember: you can still enjoy it."

He walked into the room, noting Workman folded awkwardly into a desk at the far corner of the room. A sour expression on his face as if he were expecting something painful. When Brad was seated on the cupboard in the other corner of the room, he watched his actors enter. First came a guard wearing what looked like a Boy Scout hat, with a long pink feather stuck into it. He carried a six foot lance and marched across the room, clicked his heels as he came to a stop, raising the lance and slamming it onto the floor where he then stood at attention. Next came Walter as Osric, who pranced into the room, turned back to the door, caught a glimpse of Workman and began to blush. Still, he managed to sweep his hat across the floor in a magnificent bow that must have dusted at least six feet of flooring tile. He remained crouched in his bow while King Claudius and Queen Gertrude entered, the crowd following Brad's lead, rising and clapping as Claudius led his wife to her throne and took a place beside her. Danny Litowski and Annette Federko looked startled by the applause, but only for an instant. Brad checked Workman from the corner of his eye.

He wasn't clapping. Hamlet and Laertes entered next, Laertes flinging dirty looks at Hamlet all the while, Horatio walking behind them, looking protective of Hamlet.

Suddenly, the king rose, clapping his hands together. "Come, Hamlet, come," he said, "and take this hand from me."

Hamlet pulled off his glove and stepped towards Laertes, reaching for his hand. Laertes looked reluctant, but shook his hand, his glove still on. With his left hand, Hamlet patted Laertes on the shoulder. No sooner had he turned away than Laertes was rubbing at his shoulder as if he might erase a stain. They were doing just fine; Brad hoped that Workman would see it.

"The foils, young Osric," said the king. Osric swaggered to the desk where the foils lay, picked them both up and flourished them above his head, then wheeled toward Laertes who chose the one with tape on it, leaving the other for Hamlet. The two duelers began to warm up, flashing strokes through the air, Laertes taking a great cut which made the air sizzle. Beside him, Brad heard one of the students say, "Ooh." When the boys felt at ease with their swords, they pulled on their masks, which went over the back of the head and hung down in front to protect the throat. Surely Workman would see that nobody could get hurt here.

A quick, sharp clap drew everyone's attention back to the king who was motioning for the wine. Osric immediately poured the goblet full, spilling a little over his fingers as he did. When he raised his head, he was looking straight at the principal. He hesitated, the goblet wavering in his hand. Come on, Walter, thought Brad, don't let him throw you, you can do it. Walter frowned at Workman and slammed the bottle down. He's going to be okay, thought Brad. You could almost hear him thinking, Yeah, to hell with you, Workman. He raised his wine-covered fingers to his lips and began to suck them, his eyes immediately crossing, a slight wobble taking his whole body. The kid had guts. Walter might not be a perfect Osric, but he wasn't going to let anything stop him from injecting some humour into the role. When he brought the goblet to the king, Claudius rose and addressed the audience in pantomime, his right hand punching the air again and again. Good, thought Brad, Danny's overdoing it just the way a nervous Claudius would do it. Yeah, but is Workman going to know that? Then Claudius spoke, loud and pompous: "Now the King drinks to Hamlet!" As he sipped from the goblet, Brad noticed two students on his left nudging one another.

The goblet, still nearly full, was returned to the table by Osric, who drew his wooden sword and prepared to referee the fencing match. First Hamlet and Laertes raised the hilts of their foils to their chins, bowing to the king and queen, to the audience, and to each other. Then they crouched with swords raised and extended, sword tips crossed. Osric flounced once around them before swinging his sword with a limp-wristed motion that still somehow managed to knock their foils apart.

The match was on, Osric wheeling and running for the wall, one hand disappearing into a forest of feathers to hold his cap on his head. Hamlet and Laertes sparred gingerly, swords reaching out, parrying, jabbing again. Suddenly, Hamlet swept aside his opponent's foil and hit him in the side.

"One," said Hamlet, lowering his sword.

"No," said Laertes, his voice angry as he turned away. Arnie could act too. He was almost as good as Parker.

Osric stepped between them, minced between them, Brad thought, enough mincemeat there for a dozen pies. The boy swung his right arm in the air, his pinkie finger raised, circling, pointing to Hamlet. "A hit," he said, his voice high and fruity, "a very palpable hit." Around Brad, the students were giggling. Giggling and clapping. He hoped Workman knew that Shakespeare meant Osric to be funny.

"Stay," said Claudius, bawling out the order, his hand raised, palm outward. Immediately Osric was strutting between the duelers, his arms outstretched between them, making sure they waited for the next match. "Hamlet," continued Claudius, "this ring is thine." He raised his left hand, where a gold ring shone on his finger. It was Brad's college ring, the only ring he owned. He hoped no one would wonder why there wasn't a fake pearl on it, a pearl filled with poison. After Osric brought him the goblet, the king drank some wine, toasting Hamlet, then dropped the ring into the goblet and waved for Osric to carry it to Hamlet. Beside Brad, the students were stirring, murmuring. "Bet there's poison in the ring," he heard Melinda Harper whisper. Sure, she'd want everyone to know she knew.

As Osric approached him with the drink, Hamlet took off his mask to wipe sweat from his brow. The classroom was hushed, everyone waiting to see if he would drink. Looks good and thirsty, Brad thought. But no, he shook his head and pushed the goblet away. "Good," someone murmured.

Osric shook his head and turned to carry the goblet back to its table. "Look at Osric," Lori Campbell whispered. When Osric set the goblet down, his index finger was inside the glass, dipping deep into the wine. He raised it casually to his lips, was about to slurp the wine from his finger when his expression suddenly changed and he gave his finger a violent shake, flicking drops of wine onto the floor and prompting an outbreak of cackling from his classmates. Brad glanced at Workman. He was glaring at the kids – who abruptly ceased laughing. Damn him, anyhow.

After daintily drying his finger on his sleeve, Osric started the second match, this time sweeping the swords apart with a huge flourish of his hat. As the two began to fence, a small feather was lifted from the hat, wafting between them. Before it floated to the floor, Hamlet's foil had connected again.

"Another hit," said Hamlet, "what say you?"

Laertes slapped the foil aside. "A touch, a touch, I do confess it," he said, scowling first at Hamlet, then at Claudius.

The Queen rose from her throne, walking toward Hamlet, who raised his mask, letting it ride on top of his head. Brad had never thought of Annette Federko as being queenly, but she moved like royalty, gliding towards her son. Workman should like that. She pulled a silk handkerchief from her sleeve. "Here, Hamlet," she said, "rub thy brows." As Hamlet wiped the sweat from his forehead, Queen Gertrude reached for the goblet of wine, raising it to toast Hamlet. Claudius, still on his throne, waved his arm to attract her attention, but when he spoke his voice was just a whisper, "Gertrude, do not drink."

Gertrude threw in his direction a look that might have been a sneer. When she drank, a buzz ran through the students. Brad wondered if Workman would know what was going on. After the Queen had taken her seat again, Osric began the third match, Hamlet and Laertes exchanging blows until their foils were crossed above their shoulders and pinned against the chalkboard. Immediately, Osric strutted between them, raising his pinkie finger to part the foils. Next, he took two quick steps toward the audience, his nose in the air. "Nothing, neither way," he said, and around Brad the audience was laughing. Walter was really good – they were all good. Surely, Workman would see it.

Then Brad saw Parker glare at Workman – it was Parker, all

right, not Hamlet. Parker stepped toward Osric, cupped his hand and grabbed him by the left buttock, staring all the while at the principal. What the hell, if Workman saw that, they were dead.

"Look," someone said. Laertes, his hands gesturing as if to ask, "What now?" had turned to the King, who stabbed his finger toward Hamlet.

"Have at you now!" roared Laertes as he struck Hamlet in the right shoulder. He pulled back then, almost as if he'd shocked himself by what he'd done.

Workman hadn't stopped them yet. Maybe, thought Brad, we're going to be okay.

Hamlet's hand clasped his shoulder, came slowly away, paused before his eyes. Even with the mask hiding his face, you just knew he was seeing blood on his fingers. Suddenly, he attacked Laertes. Three quick strokes and Laertes' foil was on the floor, spinning in a circle around its hilt. When it stopped turning, Laertes, his eye on Hamlet, reached for the hilt, but Hamlet cleaved the air with his own foil, Laertes' hand jerking back. Brad heard gasps around him in the crowd. Hamlet picked up the sword and walked away from Laertes, felt its tip with his finger and nodded his head.

"The pointed sword shows treachery," Brad announced, "but he doesn't know about the poison." Shut up, he thought, they'll figure it out.

Hamlet stood beside the towel that hung from the ceiling. What was that for anyway, Brad wondered. He hoped they weren't going to try something stupid – surely not with Workman here. Hamlet turned to Laertes, shaking his head. He raised his own sword and tossed it to Laertes who caught it just in time to parry Hamlet's first drive with the sword that Laertes knew could kill him. Before Hamlet drove again for Laertes, Horatio grabbed his arm, but Hamlet flung him off, flung him away like a soiled shirt. There were none of the niceties of formal fencing now. Their dueling was rough and awkward, but somehow realistic too. Hamlet was furious, and Laertes was fighting for his life, foils slashing as they forced each other back and forth across the room. Brad could hear gasping breath, grunts rising from the depths as they heaved and struggled. Wonderful, he thought, anyone would know it's a fight to the death. There was something happening here, something he couldn't quite explain.

Now Laertes was backing Hamlet toward the side wall, pinning his sword there. As Hamlet struggled to free his sword, Laertes leaned into him and kneed him in the balls. Brad gasped. Holy shit, and Workman was halfway out of his desk. A louder noise around him, half the class gasping too. Hamlet bent to clutch himself, his sword clattering onto the desk. Laertes stepped back, laughing. He raised his sword to drive it into Hamlet, but at that instant Hamlet reached for the towel that hung from the ceiling, sweeping it over Laertes' head. Lord, thought Brad, they're trying so hard – and they aren't just acting now. They'd set loose something more, drawing on a raw energy from deep inside.

Hamlet vaulted onto the desk, retrieving his sword just as Laertes threw aside the towel and saw the prince rising above him. Laertes lunged forward, slashing at Hamlet's legs, but Hamlet leapt straight up, the foil slicing the air just beneath his feet. More gasps from the class. "Wow," someone said.

Then Hamlet jumped from the desk, his foil flashing faster and faster, sweeping Laertes' weapon aside, stabbing him, the foil running neatly beneath his armpit so that he looked as if he'd been run through the chest. Laertes stumbled back, sliding down the wall, the foil still in him. Hamlet stepped toward him, raised his foot, placed it on Laertes' chest and held him against the wall while he withdrew the foil. Then stepped away, allowing Laertes to collapse on the floor.

At that moment, the Queen half rose from the throne, her hands reaching for her throat, her face contorted in pain. She remained motionless, frozen in horror, just long enough for every eye to focus on her, then fell to the floor.

In the seat beside her, Claudius was shaking his head, groping for an explanation. "She swounds," he stammered, "to see them bleed." But Gertrude raised her head to say her last words, "No, no, the drink, the drink! I am poisoned."

Hamlet whipped across the stage, his voice ringing with the command of royalty. "Let the door be locked. Treachery! Seek it out."

The guard stepped to the door, his lance raised to prevent anyone from leaving. Brad heard a creaking sound from a desk beside him, glanced down to see Melinda Harper rocking back and forth with excitement. Workman now was slouched in his desk.

"It is here, Hamlet." Laertes was gesturing from the floor, his body twitching in agony. Overdoing it a bit, Brad thought, but not bad, it'll hold. "The drink, the sword – poisoned!" He had one arm beneath him, pushing his upper body off the floor, the other arm pointing at Claudius. "The king, the king's to blame."

Hamlet glared at his stepfather, his expression raw with hatred. Brad was shocked at the thrust of black rage he felt toward his own father, a sudden return of the fury he'd known in high school when his old man had told him he'd be quitting school and that was it. Then the rage was gone, and he was watching Parker again.

Hamlet took his time now, his thumb sliding slowly down to the point of his foil, flicking it three times. "The point envenomed too." He turned slowly from Laertes to Claudius. "Then, venom, to thy work." He charged the throne as Claudius rose, a dagger in his right hand. But Hamlet was quicker, driving his foil into the king's stomach, doubling him over, dropping him back on the throne. Lord, he better not have hurt him. Danny looked stunned for an instant as he clutched his stomach, but he stayed in character.

This wasn't acting. This was energy and passion, all the dark and twisted feelings that had shaken them with turmoil, every shock and flurry of emotion they'd never found the words for, unleashed now by Shakespeare and, yes, thought Brad, by him too.

Hamlet flung his foil to the floor, turned slowly, his eyes coming to rest on the goblet of wine, a smile licking the corner of his lips. He strode to the goblet, picked it up, and turned back to Claudius who was still bent over, clutching his stomach with one hand, the other gesturing toward the guard for help. Hamlet grabbed him by the hair, knocking off his crown, pulling his head up, his mouth falling open. Then Hamlet poured the wine, dumping it into his open mouth, onto his chin, his cheeks, his neck, a torrent of wine showering down his chest. Beside Brad there was a small tumult of sound, gasps, squeals, a voice saying, "Yes! You scumbag!" The whole experience – it was alive in all of them.

Brad cast another look at Workman. He was shaking his head. To hell with him, this was how the play should work.

Hamlet held the king's head upright for a moment, then dropped it, the king sprawling from his throne, one hand snaking out toward his crown but sinking before he clasped it.

On the floor not far away, Laertes was gesturing to Hamlet. "Exchange forgiveness, noble Hamlet," he said, but his voice was trailing off, his head falling dead on his chest.

Hamlet took half a step toward him, nodding. A little shiver took his body, his legs not quite steady. The poison working in him, thought Brad, wonder if they'll get it, if Workman will. Hamlet turned toward Horatio, his legs wobbly now. "I am dead, Horatio," he said. "You got to tell my story." A line Shakespeare had never written, but it didn't matter.

Horatio's hand was at his eye, wiping tears away. He shook his head, saw the goblet by the thrones. "No," he said, "here's yet some liquor left." He reached for the goblet, grabbed it, but before he could get it to his lips, Hamlet wrenched it loose, the goblet falling to the floor, spinning away. "Tell my story," he said with what seemed to be the last of his strength as he stumbled back into Horatio's arms, straining a moment to stand upright before allowing his friend to lower him to the floor. His eyes swept the room before him, bodies strewn everywhere, settled on the audience, seemed to focus for an instant on Workman, then slowly closed. A loud sigh and his head sank against Horatio's shoulder.

Horatio waited a second before he spoke. "Now cracks a noble heart," he said, and he froze with Hamlet wrapped in his arms.

"That's it," said Brad. "We should give –" but the class was already applauding, hands beating together, pounding their desks, whistles, cheers filling the air.

Workman left the room as the students were shoving the desks back into rows. At first Brad thought he was going to slip out without saying a word, but then he sidled over to Brad. "Shakespeare's probably rolling in his grave," he said. "I'll see you in my office at the break." When Brad looked away, he saw Bert Peale smirking at him, enjoying his uneasiness.

Nineteen

"For a while there," said Workman, "I thought there might be some hope for you." He looked tired, even thinner than usual as he leaned forward in his chair, his knobby elbows on his desk.

Brad shrugged. He didn't know what to say. Might as well tell him what he felt. "We were trying to get Shakespeare off the page – make it live. I thought the kids did a good job."

"Yeah, you would. Young Buchko flouncing around like he's some kind of gay musketeer, might as well be a bloody transvestite –"

"That's how Shakespeare wrote the part."

"Don't tell me what Shakespeare wrote. I've read the play, you know."

"It's a legitimate interpretation."

"It's *your* interpretation. Boys kneeing each other in the groin, grabbing each other by the ass."

Oh, hell, he'd seen Parker after all. What was the use?

Workman's face was red, a thin patina of sweat shining on his forehead. "Well, what have you got to say for yourself?"

Brad couldn't let Workman get away with this. He had to say something. He felt his hands shaking and braced them on his knees. "Mr. Workman," he said, trying to keep his voice steady, "some things happened there today that weren't supposed to happen, but a lot of what those kids did was darned good. They just...kind of...got carried away on a few things."

"Carried away is right. I'll be damned surprised if your king doesn't have a hole in his stomach."

Brad had to stop himself from nodding. Danny probably would have a bruise.

"And the reason they got carried away," said Workman, "may have something to do with a teacher who doesn't know how to keep order."

"It was a tough scene. It had to look spontaneous." He could feel his voice getting smaller, as if he himself were shrinking in front of Workman, diminished now and expendable. "I did the best I could."

"I'm afraid your best isn't good enough." Workman looked at ease now, leaning back in his padded chair, relaxed and smiling. "I'll have Dr. McAvoy come down one day soon and watch you in action. See how he feels about letting you go."

The three boys must have rushed down to his room as soon as they heard the final bell. They looked flushed and breathless.

"We did okay," said Arnie Jordan, "eh, Mr. C?"

What could he tell them? No matter what Workman said, they *had* done okay – more than okay. It wasn't their fault that he'd got another chewing-out, that Workman wanted to get rid of him. Well, Parker's fault maybe. He had to talk to

Parker, keep him there when the other two left.

"You guys were terrific." He glanced at Walter Buchko standing beside Arnie, grinning like a pup. "Jim Carrey couldn't have made Osric any funnier, Walter."

"The kids liked it," said Walter.

"Loved it," said Brad. Parker was looking intently at him, his expression unreadable.

"How about Workman?" Parker asked.

"Mr. Workman," said Brad. "He was...well, let's just say he was less than enthusiastic. He figured we let ourselves get carried away." He saw the way Arnie and Walter seemed to sag, their enthusiasm sucked away. "Look: not to worry. It's the best thing that's happened in class all year."

"Not just the funny stuff, either," said Walter.

"The sword fight," said Arnie, "it look real?"

"It did. But when you kneed Parker in the groin, I don't know, I wondered what was going on."

Parker was still studying him.

"Yeah, we worked that out on our own," said Parker. "Figured it might surprise you."

"It did." No, he wasn't going to wait till he had the kid alone. "Grabbing Osric by the ass – you work that one out on your own too? That supposed to be another little surprise?"

Walter and Arnie looked shocked. Parker glared at him, then looked down at the floor.

When Parker didn't answer, Walter said, "No. We didn't plan that. It just sort of happ –"

"Parker?"

Parker looked up, rage in his eyes. "Get off our backs, eh? You didn't see him, sitting there like he's the king of the world or something. We're trying to make this play work and he's looking down his nose at us. Big sneer on his ugly face."

"What?"

"Workman. Walter had Osric down pat – perfect – and every time he moved there's Workman looking at him like he's a piece of shit."

"So you grabbed his ass!"

"Yeah, let him suck that one up. See how he likes it." Parker was poised in front of him, swaying a bit, his hands doubled into fists.

"Him – or me?"

"What?" Parker looked puzzled – genuinely puzzled, but then he was an actor, wasn't he?

"I'm the one who was up in the office getting reamed out." Yeah, Workman threatening to fire him, wanting McAvoy to help him do the job.

"Jeez," said Walter.

Parker seemed to flinch. "I never thought about –"

"No, you're not much for thinking ahead." Brad knew his voice was filling with sarcasm. "Haven't we had this little conversation once before?"

"I guess so. Yeah." Parker looked glum – glum and sullen.

Walter was shaking his head. "We never meant to get you in trouble, sir. No way." His words erupting on a thin spray of spittle.

"No, I don't suppose you did." Not Walter, for sure, nor Arnie either. Parker maybe.

The three boys stood self-consciously before him, Walter awkwardly shifting his feet. Parker's eyes on him still. Something was going on here; they weren't finished with him yet. But the conversation had ground to a halt, Arnie and Walter glancing at Parker.

"We had this idea," Parker said at last.

Uh-huh, here it comes, but Parker was hesitating. He reached up with his right hand and began to massage the back of his neck.

"Go ahead. Shoot."

"That scene," he said, "even if Mr. Workman didn't like it, it was well-done, right? Well-done and entertaining too?"

"Of course."

Parker allowed a stunted smile to crawl across his face. "We want to do it again," he said, "for the whole school." He quickly added, "We'd leave out anything you didn't like."

"Oh," said Brad. He sat down behind his desk.

"You said it was good."

That kid. You had to admire his nerve. "It *was* good. Not just because you guys did it well. Though – obviously – you did. It was good because the class's been studying the play. Everybody knew who the characters were, what the conflicts were, everything that led up to that ending."

Arnie and Walter looked at each other, then at Parker, who was glaring at Brad.

"Since the lits got canceled," said Parker, "there's nothing going on around here. They'd like our scene."

Sure, give them a chance to really make a fool of him. "All the other grades – they wouldn't get it." Three faces staring at him now, two of them almost expressionless, the other hostile. They were so enthralled with what they'd done, they couldn't see it. "The other English teachers wouldn't want their students knowing how things end before they even start the play." Which was true. He wouldn't want his own students to see the big finish before they began reading.

"The other teachers," said Parker, making it sound like a curse. There was something dead about his eyes. "C'mon. Let's get out of here." He was already turning away.

Arnie glanced at Walter and started after Parker. Parker with that sullen look he'd seen before. Walter shrugged at Brad and turned to leave the room. They're dying to do it, he thought, but it wouldn't work, it really wouldn't, not for the whole school, not the way it had in class. Still, he owed them something for that. Was he just afraid they'd start grabbing ass again?

"Wait a minute, guys."

The three of them stopped inside the door, turned slowly around.

"You really want to act in front of the whole school?"

Arnie and Walter nodding their heads, Parker staring at him, an expression on his face that might have been chipped from a block of ice.

"Then the thing to do is pick a play and do it. Something everybody will like. Self-contained – no study necessary before the audience sees it."

Arnie was grinning, Walter nodding. Brad studied Parker, wondering if the ice might be starting to melt.

"Pick the right play and it could be a lot of fun," said Brad, "but a lot of work too. Even for a short one. A lot more than a scene from *Hamlet*."

Parker shook his head. "Work's nothing," he said. "Who's going to direct it?"

"I'm no director," said Brad. "Never done a play in my life." He looked at Parker, felt the chill of another ice age coming on. Oh, what the hell. "I guess I directed your scenes in *Hamlet*. I could try something more."

"Way to go, sir," said Arnie. Walter looked ready to slap him on the back.

"You need to find a play the kids will like," said Parker. "A one-act maybe. Something we can do."

"I'll check around," said Brad. He watched the three of them leave the room, Walter and Arnie exchanging high fives behind Parker.

Oh, man, he'd set himself up again, given Parker another chance to show him up, and in front of the whole school. But he'd lost Angela Maddox, he didn't want to lose Parker too. Yeah, and where was he going to find the one-act play that was right for them? Or the time to look for it? There was a stack of marking half a foot high on his desk. And what did it matter anyway if Workman let him go? He shouldn't jump into things, should always think them through before he opened his big mouth. He pushed away from his desk. Now he'd have to go up to the library, see what he could find. What the hell was going through his head?

It was supposed to be another routine staff meeting, but shorter than usual, the kind that Workman liked, simple agenda, no contentious issues, everything laid out ahead of time. A quick meeting – get it done and go home. No mention yet of staff cuts, nothing about the one teacher Workman planned to fire. Uh-huh, must be waiting till McAvoy had a look at him.

They hadn't bothered going down to the meeting room, had just stayed in the staffroom. But before Workman could call for a motion to adjourn, Dutch Van Hoek raised his hand.

"We've got to do something about the dishes in the sink," he said. "I come in after practice, there's such a pile of dirty dishes, you can't hardly get near the water tap. Some days there's not a clean cup to use."

"Well, Dutch," said Maurie Pack, "that would seem to

indicate you should've washed your own cup the last time you used it."

"Crap! I look in the cupboard, my cup's never there."

"My point exactly," said Maurie.

"The microwave's worse than the sink," said Myrna Belsey. "Gobs of dried food all over. So many stains on the door, you can't see through the window. I wouldn't put up with it in the Home Ec lab."

"People who use the microwave ought to clean it once in a while," said Phil Simpson.

"People ought to wash their own dishes," said Myrna, "instead of piling them in the sink."

"Ought to, sure," said Herb Schwitzer. "End of any long break, you watch what happens, bell rings, most people drop their dirty cups in the sink and run for class."

"Cups are nothing," said Myrna. "I'll bet right now there's half a dozen plates in there, haven't been washed for days. Haven't even been scraped."

"What we need," said Workman, "is a work detail to clean things up, keep them clean."

"Right," said Phil. Brad noticed him throw a quick glance at Sue. He could guess what was coming. "Women's work. I suggest the ladies set up a rotation to keep the dishes cleaned."

Brad watched Sue raise her head, nostrils flaring, a filly about to gallop. She was really something.

"Stuff it, Simpson. Enough women's work around here already – just trying to keep certain guys from jamming their feet inside their mouths."

Brad wondered about that night that Dr. Stone had dumped her. He bet she'd told him to stuff it too. He hoped she had.

"A little decorum, please," said Mr. Workman. What an oaf.

Sue was right most of the time, thought Brad. That other time, for sure. Trying to warn him, and he hadn't seen it. Too busy playing the smart-ass. What an idiot he'd been. Yeah, and still was. He was staring at her, but looked away when he saw her head turn toward him.

Maybe there was something else he hadn't seen.

"Mr. Schwitzer could make up a schedule," said Vi Isely. "Names in alphabetical order – everybody takes a turn."

"Not me," said Maurie Pack. "I go home for lunch."

"Coffee cups are the problem," said Vi. "Plates don't amount to much."

"Not my problem," said Maurie. "I drink coke."

"That's another thing," said Bruce Winslow. "Every year the staff fund's in trouble because the coffee fund loses money. You suck all the profit from us coke drinkers."

"Off the topic," said Workman.

"Make a list of coffee drinkers," said Maurie. "Let them take turns washing dishes."

"Hey," said Phil. "I wash my own dishes. Be damned if I'll wash someone else's."

"The sink's a mess," said Workman. Oh oh, thought Brad, he's starting to look angry. I better keep out of it. "We have a guest speaker in the school, I'm almost ashamed to bring him into the staffroom."

"Caretakers should keep it clean," said Bruce. "Not a job for professionals."

"We hardly sound like professionals," said Sue. "You tell Ollie to clean it, we'll have a real problem on our hands."

"Right," said Phil. "Don't want to cross the men who really run the school."

Brad watched Workman who looked as if he might speak, but changed his mind and simply glared at Phil. You had to hand it to Phil; he was never afraid to say something he knew would bug the principal.

"Obviously," said Herb, "we've got to do something."

"We deal with serious problems in here," said Bruce. "You'd think we could solve something as simple as this."

"Simple?" said Sue. "Surely you jest?"

She was sharp, Brad thought. He could listen to her anytime, talk with her for hours. It wasn't like being with Kelly, he had to admit it; even last fall, when they were going hot and heavy, there were times he just wanted to sit down and talk with Sue.

"We could make a point of doing our own dishes," said Myrna. "Every one of us. Every time we use a cup or plate – wash it on the spot. That would solve the problem."

"Tried that twice in my years here," said Vic Pendleton. "It worked fine both times – for about a week. Then the sink was full again. Pretty soon, people were pretending they didn't notice."

"Yes, but if people agreed to do it," said Myrna.

"They agreed last time," said Vic. "Hell, they swore they'd do it."

"We could throw out the coffee urn," said Maurie. "Make everybody drink coke." There were groans from all sides of the room.

"Sure," said Bruce, "cut out the freeloaders. Let the staff fund turn a profit."

"Screw the staff fund," said Herb. "Here's what we're going to do." He strode to the coke machine, lifted a plastic case that had a few empty cans in it, and dumped the cans onto the counter. "This case," he said, "is the new home for dirty dishes. It'll be up there." He pointed to the top of the cupboard above the sink. "Up there where you can't reach it without a ladder. When I go home every night, I'll stop off in the staffroom. Anything in the sink ends up on top of the cupboard." He had sounded angry when he began to speak, but his voice was calm now and he smiled at the staff. "Now, I don't expect this is going to do the trick either. One good thing, though – won't have a sink full of dirty dishes."

"Should make for some interesting mornings," said Brad, "watching to see who's after their cup, climbing on the counter."

"You gals'll be straining to reach up there," said Phil. "Should be quite a view."

"We women," said Sue, "will get our cups from the lower shelves. Where the clean dishes go. Same as usual."

She's always got an answer, Brad thought. The thing he liked about her was the way she seemed at ease in any situation – no, that wasn't quite it – at ease with herself. Sure, she had a hot temper, but when she lost her temper, she got over it. Even that time he'd been smart with her, sounding off after interviews, giving her a rough time about her date with Stone, she'd eventually recovered.

"Motion to adjourn," said Herb. "Fifteen minutes and I check the dishes."

Brad wondered if people would rush for the sink, but, no, they sat talking for a few minutes, one after another walking casually to the sink, washing and drying a cup, setting it on a shelf in the cupboard. Though nothing seemed to have changed, he noted that within ten minutes the sink was empty. Sue sat at the round table, still doodling, the sheet of foolscap beneath her right hand almost entirely filled with cups and saucers. On the way to the door he hesitated when he passed her table. She looked up from her doodling, saw him pausing there, seemed to scrutinize him, then began shading in another saucer.

Deciding Kelly was the one, man, he was a bigger idiot than he knew. He recalled Sue warning him that Kelly was on the rebound, and his response was just a stupid pun. When she was thinking of him, taking a chance, saying more than she wanted to say, maybe, concerned that he might be hurt.

Yeah, last fall, there he was, a smart-ass making jokes, and she was right all along, had Kelly figured to a T. But maybe there was more than that going on, a lot more in fact. Kind of weird, he thought, but it really didn't matter how old Sue was — at coffee breaks, in the staffroom after school, she always was the one he had to talk to. He guessed sometimes he just wasn't smart enough to listen.

Twenty

When Brad walked into the staffroom at noon the next day, he was thinking that Dr. McAvoy still hadn't been down to check him out. Maybe the director was just too busy for that. Quit worrying about it. He'd grab a quick bite and then go to the library and start checking for plays. His usual peanut butter sandwich. Made the night before at bedtime. Two slices of bread thick with peanut butter, the crunchy kind. Just peanut butter. Add a little jam and the bread would be soft and soggy by the time he ate it.

The round table in the centre of the room had one empty seat, between Wallace Sloan and Sue, who was nibbling on carrot sticks. Brad took the empty chair. It felt good to walk in like that, look around the room, then stride right over and grab the seat beside her. Except for Sue it was all men gathered at the round table and sitting against the far wall. On the east wall, the easy chairs and sofas were completely filled by women. Looking up from his bowl of soup at the round table, Vic Pendleton saw him survey the room.

"You'd think we were divided into sections by sex," said Vic.

Beside Vic, Phil Simpson raised his head above a baloney

sandwich. "How's that?" he asked. Brad looked at Phil, an easy grin on his face.

"Male and female," said Vic. "The old days – before they redid the school – we had a common room, plus a men's staffroom, and a women's staffroom."

"Must've been nice," said Phil. "Have some peace and quiet then."

Brad glanced at Sue, but she wasn't biting today. This close beside her, he could catch a hint of her perfume. Something light and fresh, lavender, he thought.

"Nice – hell," said Dutch. "Men's staffroom was so full of smoke you could hardly breathe."

"Maurie smoked a pipe," said Wallace. He taught music and usually had rehearsals at noon.

"Still do," said Maurie Pack. "Smoking fascists won't let me do it here."

"You could stroll out to smokers' row," said Brad. "Stand in a snowbank with the kids."

"Like hell. I need a smoke, I go out to my car." Maurie gave him a dirty look.

"I noticed," said Dutch. "Last week this kid came running into the gym, wanted to use the phone. Said there was a car on fire in the teachers' lot."

"Yeah, yeah."

"Lucky you overheard him," said Sue, smiling at Dutch. Brad hoped her smile was meant for him too.

"Damned rights. I grabbed the phone, managed to stop the fire department before they got more than one truck out the door."

"Yeah, sure." Maurie noticed Brad laughing and fired another scowl in his direction.

"I thought Rutledge cured you of the pipe," said Vic.

When Maurie rolled his eyes and shook his head, Brad decided to probe a little deeper. "What did Rutledge do, Vic?" If Rutledge gave the gears to Maurie, he wanted to hear about it.

"Nothing much. Filled his pipe for him."

"Smart-ass," said Maurie. Brad wasn't sure if he meant Rutledge or Vic.

"Chalk used to come in boxes packed with sawdust," said Vic. "Rutledge put a layer of pipe tobacco on top, but he had that sawdust underneath. These pipe smokers, hell, they claim they can distinguish fine tobacco just like connoisseurs testing a wine's bouquet."

"Crap."

"Crap is right. You smoked sawdust. Never noticed a thing."

"I knew. Didn't want to give you guys the satisfaction."

"Ha! Underneath the sawdust, Rutledge had this layer of cut-up rubber bands. Maurie thought he was smoking a new blend of Old Briar."

"Bullshit. I noticed the rubber right away."

"Sure you did. We could smell burning rubber for five minutes before you said a thing."

"Bullshit."

Sue leaned toward Brad. "One thing about Maurie," she whispered, "he enjoys any joke that isn't on him."

Brad grinned, nodding his head. He could feel her shoulder firm against his, the heat of her bare arm through his shirt sleeve. He didn't pull away.

"You retire," Maurie said to Vic, "you can always get another job. With the bloody smoke police."

"Smoke all you want," said Vic. "Just don't use the air I have to breathe."

"Room's heating up without smoke," said Brad.

"To hell with you," said Maurie, his voice loud.

"It is indeed," said Sue, shifting in her seat. Brad's arm was still warm, tingling from the weight of her shoulder leaning into him. When he glanced away from Maurie, he noticed Phil Simpson staring at them, no longer chewing, though his mouth was full, yeah, staring at him and Sue, a puzzled expression on his face. What was that all about?

Workman didn't usually appear in the staffroom during the lunch hour, but suddenly he was there, pouring himself a coffee, pausing to survey the room. Brad wondered if he'd heard them riding Maurie Pack, watched him walk towards the round table where they sat. Wonder what I've done now, Brad thought, when Workman stopped beside him. The principal stood between him and Wallace Sloan, stood without speaking. What the hell did he want? Brad guessed he'd better acknowledge the man. Glanced quickly up, but Workman wasn't even watching him. Then Wallace noted Brad looking over his shoulder and half-turned in his seat.

"You ready for tomorrow night?" Workman asked.

"Yeah, should be a good concert."

"Rehearsals going okay?"

"Sure. We're ready."

"Fine. Good performance means a lot of happy parents."

Brad was surprised to see Workman bend towards Wallace and briefly lay a hand upon his shoulder. A pat on the back, he supposed. A rare thing for Workman.

Sure, thought Brad, my kids do a great job with *Hamlet* and all he does is ream me out. Which reminded him: he still had to pick a play, somehow get permission to stage it in the gym.

He noticed Vic Pendleton across the table watching

Workman through the door, then turning to Wallace.

"Probably worried about their shoes, eh?"

"You guys," said Wallace. He shook his head, but he was grinning. Vic and Dutch laughed out loud.

"What?" said Brad. Why not get them going, forget about other things? "Something else before my time?"

"Yeah," said Dutch, "Rutledge."

"And Vic," said Wallace. "Don't forget Vic." He leaned back in his chair, shaking his head at Brad. "I should've known something was up. Band's getting ready in the gym, I hustle down here for a quick coffee, and Vic wants to talk. Course, I want to get going. I mean, how often do we get the gym for rehearsal, eh?"

"Not my fault," said Dutch. He rose and walked to the sink. "Where's my cup?"

"Ha," said Wallace, pointing to the plastic case on top of the cupboard and not missing a beat in his story. "But Vic is into some long-winded spiel about this new music teacher at Macoun High. Supposed to be one hot number." Wallace looked at Sue who was leaning toward him. What the heck, she was here, Workman was gone – Brad was feeling good again. The library could wait a minute.

Wallace shrugged at Sue and said, "I was single then. Anyhow, I got up once to leave. He actually hauls me back down, says this girl –" he glanced at Sue "this young woman, she was a friend of his, he could maybe line me up. Then, out of the blue, he says, shouldn't I be getting off to band practice? He's been working his butt off to keep me in the room, and now he wants me gone. I should've known, eh?"

"You would've," said Vic, "if you'd seen Rutledge come back into the room."

"That bugger," said Wallace. "He'd been down talking to

the band. Told them Workman had been complaining about the way they looked."

"Didn't have uniforms in those days?" asked Brad.

"Same as now," said Wallace. "Red and gold. Problem was the uniform didn't include shoes. We have a concert, the kids'd turn up with every kind of footwear under the sun: oxfords, loafers, cowboy boots, a lot of running shoes – every brand name you can think of, socks even. Looked like hell – least that's what Workman said. He was always yammering about the band should have uniform footwear. So Rutledge is down talking to them while Vic here has damned near got me hog-tied to keep me in the room." Wallace reached for his coffee cup and took a long drink.

Knows he's got me hooked, Brad thought. "Well?" he said. Sue was smiling at him – with him.

"That night, junior band finishes their last number, concert band comes filing in. Uniform footwear all right, everyone of them barefoot." Brad laughed with the others at the table, but Wallace wasn't finished. "Got him back though, the same night. I asked for a volunteer to conduct the last number. Man, I was just staring at Rutledge. He knew I wanted him."

"He volunteered?" asked Sue. She might be asking Wallace, Brad noticed, but she was looking at him.

"Yep. Came right up and grabbed the baton like he's Leonard Bernstein or something. The band's all primed – we do the guest conductor bit maybe every second year. Usually get a parent. Course, Rutledge doesn't know this – first concert I'd ever seen him at. The program says we're going to play Ralph Vaughn Williams' 'English Folk Song Suite.' Rutledge steps up on the podium, stands poised for a minute. Poised, hell – *posed* is more like it. You'd think he really was Leonard Bernstein up there. Then he gives the baton this magnificent flourish, and nothing happens, the band's just sitting there, staring at him. Rutledge sneaks a look over his shoulder, kind of worried, you know. Audience starts to giggle. So he tries again. An even bigger flourish. Nothing. Except the audience is laughing and he's getting really worried now. He glances around, looking for me. I just shrug, so he tries again. Only this time, he turns right to the audience.

"Ladies and gentlemen," he says, "for your edification and enjoyment, we are now going to play Williams' 'English Folk Song Suite.' When I say 'we' I mean the concert band – these very people assembled here before you. The ones with the silent instruments in their hands." Well, sir, everyone in the brass section raises his horn to his lips. So he swings around on the podium, lifts his baton, roars, 'Now!' and sweeps it down." Wallace paused, grinning. "Not a sound. They could've all been frozen. Rutledge looks puzzled, he takes his baton and starts to scratch his head. That's when they start. 'The Old Gray Mare Ain't What She Used To Be.' What a hoot."

"Tell 'em the rest," said Vic.

"Yeah, well. You know Rutledge. He's stunned for maybe three seconds. Then he turns to the audience, gives them a little bow and starts doing a jig right there on the podium. One of those Celtic stepdances. Faster they play, faster he goes." Wallace shook his head, grinning. "And man, he's good – the guy can really dance. Got the loudest applause of the night."

What a character, Brad thought. That was fine for Rutledge, he was dramatic, flamboyant, a guy everybody had to notice – kind of neat maybe, but all Brad wanted was to be a good teacher, with a job for next year.

"You had to hand it to Rutledge," said Vic.

"You sure did," said Sue. "The man wasn't afraid to take a risk."

Brad kept his eyes on Wallace who was still grinning. He didn't need to look at Sue to know she was gazing at him. Was there a chance for him, he wondered, was that possible?

"Any luck so far?" asked Parker Stone. Brad looked up from the stack of familiar essays he was marking – personal incidents, most of them, light and entertaining. He saw that Walter Buchko had followed Parker into the room.

"Grade elevens – some of them are pretty good."

Parker gave him a withering glare. "Not what I meant."

Walter glanced at Parker and jumped in: "Any luck finding a play?"

"Oh. Not yet, no."

"You even look?" asked Parker.

"Yeah, I looked. Don't have a lot of time for it right now, either." Impatience flooding his voice, and it sounded like an excuse, even to Brad. "There are only six anthologies of one-act plays in the library. I skimmed through them – nothing seemed right for us."

"We already looked at those," said Walter. "Kids wouldn't like them – they're pretty old."

"Old shouldn't matter," said Brad, "as long as we get something good."

"A comedy would probably be best," said Walter, "something to get the kids laughing."

Brad nodded his head, noted Parker studying him. "What

is it, Parker? You have an idea?"

"You're really going to do this, are you? You're not just waiting for us to forget about it?"

So that was it. The kid didn't trust him.

"Somehow, Parker, I don't figure there's any chance of you forgetting." Brad smiled, hoping his frustration wasn't showing. The problem was so many of the one-acts were flat and dated. Characters out of sync for these kids. Maybe there was something else he could try. Something bigger, something right for them.

"Listen," he said, "I'll keep looking. You guys do the same. Sooner or later, we'll find a play we can do."

"Sooner would be better," said Parker.

Twenty-one

When Brad went up to the staffroom after his second day of marking familiar essays, he was thinking about the play. He'd had an idea there, part way through an essay, something lifting dust on the backroad of his memory, something they might try, and then it was gone. Now he saw that the history meeting was over, Phil and Sue still at the big table, a few other staff members beginning to drift in for the day's final coffee, Kelly on her way back to the office, cup in hand.

Wait a minute. He'd taken Kelly to it. Sure, *Out of the Frying Pan,* just the kind of play he needed. Might've thought of it sooner, but it was so darned long. He wasn't ready to jump into a full-length play. That would be getting in way over his head. Maybe he could try the funniest scene though, isolate that, it might just work by itself – if he could get a copy of the script.

"Blackhead!" Sue was glaring at Phil.

"Goobies," he shot back at her.

They seemed to be in the middle of an argument, nothing unusual there. He sat down on the other side of the table.

Sue's right index finger moved beneath her ear, began to massage the side of her neck. Thinking, Brad thought, digging deep for this one.

"St. James Within," she said.

Phil's response was immediate. "St James Without." He smirked at her.

"What the hell?" said Dutch. What the hell, was right, thought Brad.

"Jerry's Nose," said Sue.

"Sop's Arm," said Phil.

"Tickle Cove."

"Sweet Bay."

Oh, he had it now.

"Heart's Desire." She seemed to know he had it, and flung a smile his way.

"Heart's Delight," said Phil.

"Great Paradise."

"Happy Adventure," said Phil, who was suddenly leering like a fool. "Dildo."

"Not your turn," said Sue. "South Dildo."

"That's a cop-out," said Phil. "Blow Me Down."

Brad had to hurry to beat her. "Come By Chance," he said.

Sue picked up her notebook and snapped it shut, the sound like an exclamation mark on a quiet page. She stood up, looking first at Brad, then at Phil.

"Seldom!" she said. "I suspect that goes for both of you." She smiled broadly, then headed for the door without another glance at either of them.

He never would figure her out. Yeah, he thought, Witless Bay. Little Heart's Ease.

"You know something?" said Dutch. "You're all crazy."

Phil grinned. "You may be right," he said.

When Brad was sure that Sue wouldn't see him, he hurried down the hall to the library. Rita Croft was stacking books on a trolley.

"Got a map of Newfoundland?" he asked.

"Vertical file," said Rita, "under 'L.'"

"What?"

"Labrador and Newfoundland."

He pulled out the map and spread it on top of the file case. He ran his finger down the index; there it was, in the second row under S, third from the top: Seldom........E16. That was okay then, it was a real place.

Fat lot of difference it made. He'd been horning in, and she was telling him something. Or maybe Phil. Was that possible, he wondered, the two of them? Was he so slow to catch on?

Sure, that was it. Phil was the one. Had been all along. The one for her, uh-huh.

He suddenly felt like hell. Looked down at the map in his hands, folded it and filed it away. There were things he had to do. "Say," he said to Rita Croft, "you wouldn't have a copy of a play called *Out of the Frying Pan,* would you?"

"We don't have many plays," she said, but she stepped to the computer, typed in the title and waited. "Sorry. It's not one of ours."

B rad sat in the staffroom, reading the battered playscript he'd borrowed from the Scarecrow Theatre. It was almost as funny as he remembered it – and most of the cast were young. Good parts for his kids and sure, Norman would be a perfect role for Parker. There had to be a way he could use part of it, the second act, say. It was really funny. Might stand on its own if he changed some things. Picked up a few lines from act one. Worked in the necessary exposition. What about an ending though?

"Go home."

He looked up from the script. Phil Simpson was strolling into the room, shaking his head as he came. Brad glanced down at his watch. Six-forty-five. "You're still here too," he said.

"Tonight, yeah. Not all the time – like somebody I know."

Brad shrugged. "Things to do," he said.

"I'm hungry," said Phil. "You want to split a pizza?"

"I don't know," he said. He was ready to say no, but then he thought, why not, nothing good in the fridge at home. No need to rush back to his basement suite. He could maybe have a talk with Phil, check things out about Sue. He had to know for sure. "Yeah, sounds good."

After they had decided on Hawaiian and Phil had phoned the order in, Phil took a seat across the table from him. "It'll be ready in half an hour." They were both silent a moment. Better get something started, Brad thought. He didn't usually feel awkward with Phil, but this was different. Sue made it different.

"I figured you'd be back in Regina by now," he said.

"Usually am. Had a lot of things to run off tonight. Course, that's always when the copier jams."

"Uh-huh." Brad could hear a gurgling in the coke machine. He watched it vibrate, the whole machine shuddering ever so slightly.

How to get around to it? "You been commuting long?"

"Eight years now. Ever since I came to Lawrence."

Might as well find out. "Girl friend in Regina, I'll bet." Brad tried to keep it light.

Phil didn't answer. He looked at Brad a long time, his eyes hard as flint. "Nope," he said finally.

That was it, then. He should have known before, should have known it all along. The way they were always joking around together. Yeah, and maybe he did know – just couldn't admit it to himself. He felt something hollow opening inside him, something pizza wasn't going to fill.

He tried to smile. "I guess I know," he said.

"You know, do you?" Phil stared at him, sparks snapping off the flint in his eyes.

No need to get mad about it, Brad thought. Well, might as well get it said. "It's you and Sue, isn't it?"

He thought something changed in Phil's expression, a spark dying, maybe, a slight shift in the intensity of his gaze.

"Yeah," said Phil, "we're friends. *Good* friends."

Brad felt the hollowness expand, thought it might swallow him. Phil's gaze never wavered. He seemed to be studying Brad, his eyes calm now, calm and deliberate, appraising him. "Interested in Sue, are we?"

Brad shrugged. He couldn't very well deny it.

"What the hell," Phil said. "Might as well tell you. I'm gay."

"What?"

"You heard me."

"Yeah, but –" God, no more mincemeat cracks from him. "I thought you and...Sue know this?"

"She knows."

"But you two – you're always horsing around."

"So? We like to banter." Phil's voice was low and hard. He turned away from Brad, watching something outside the staffroom window.

It was okay then, he still had a chance.

"Don't get me wrong," Brad said. "I just never knew." He

was rattled, didn't know what to say. "I suppose everybody knows but me."

"Sue does." Phil was still looking out the window, but when Brad turned to follow his line of vision, he saw nothing but an old station wagon parked half way up the hill. He heard Phil take a deep breath. "And now, you." Phil was still staring out the window, but after another moment, he gave his head a little nod and looked at Brad. "Maybe, that was a mistake."

"What? You think I'm some kind of homophobic creep?"

"Not what I meant."

"What then?"

"You can keep your mouth shut, can you?"

"Sure."

Under Phil's steady gaze, Brad lowered his eyes. The coke machine was vibrating more loudly now, a rattle of glass as the metal trays shook the bottles they held.

"You think I'm ashamed of what I am?" said Phil. "I ought to let everybody know?"

"No. I –"

"Look. I tried that already. In Herbert. Wasn't going to hide a thing. Right away, there's a bloody controversy – and I'm at the heart of it. Then a regular smear campaign. Filth on my blackboards, 'faggot' scratched on the hood of my car, grown men carrying on like I was some kind of wild animal out to get their boys. Christ, but it got nasty." Phil paused, glanced away from Brad, then back at him. "Eventually I told them I wasn't coming back. Yeah, just quit. Saved them the job of firing me." He moistened his lips before continuing. "I'm not exactly keen on being in the closet, but I tell you, there's no way I'm going through that crap again – not ever."

"No. I can see what you –"

"Most people on our staff could handle it just fine. Most

people."

"I don't know," said Brad. "I wouldn't be in any rush to tell Maurie." But he was thinking, it's okay, there's still a chance for me with Sue.

"My thoughts exactly. He was on your case long enough – over nothing. Besides, you tell anything to this staff, the next day every kid in the building seems to know. Nothing but trouble that way. I tell you, they wouldn't've named the school after Lawrence if they knew the man was gay."

Lawrence too, he hadn't known that, wondered what to say. "Just as well Workman doesn't know. You'd be in real trouble."

"You're sure of that, are you?" Phil studied him an instant. "He knows all right. Said it's my business and no one else's."

"Workman said that?"

"Uh-huh. 'Kids don't need to know what they aren't mature enough to handle.' His exact words." Phil checked his watch. "Shit. I better get that pizza."

Man, this put Workman in a new light.

When Phil stood up, Brad pushed back from the table. "You don't mind," he said, "I'll ride along with you."

It took him two days to work up his nerve about seeing Workman. He thought about the principal's anger at the gay lumberjacks in the lit, at Walter's mincing Osric – maybe Workman was just looking out for Phil, maybe he wasn't so bad. Still, Brad didn't want to give the guy another chance to yell at him, to threaten him, but there was no other way. God knows, he'd rather spend an hour with Bert Peale than five minutes in that office.

Brad had asked Herb about it first, of course, hoping Herb

would give permission, but Herb had said he'd better check it out with the big guy. Herb's term. Workman was big if you thought of height, shanks on him like two-by-twos, long ones. If you got him on a scale, it would be a different story. Yeah, and when Brad walked in, Workman looked up at him, no more warmth than another two-by-two.

"Mr. Workman," he said, drawing a deep breath, then rushing into it, his words floating on a long breath of air. "I wonder if I could ask you a kind of personal favour."

"I know Dr. McAvoy hasn't had his little visit with you yet. But he's still coming."

"Oh, no, that's not it." Workman caught him with a fast ball there, but he had to hang on. "How would you feel about giving up some school time for a play?"

"Sit down." The principal waved his arm toward one of the three chairs before his desk. "Globe Theatre starting up their school tours again, eh?"

"No, no. Just a play with the kids." He better be careful how he put it, didn't want to get Workman going. "Comedy – something everyone should enjoy – grades nine to twelve. Wouldn't take more than forty minutes. I thought we could afford the time – be a good replacement for a lit."

"The lits are cancelled – thanks to you."

Let it go, careful now, keep your voice down. "Of course. But this wouldn't be anything like a lit. No horsing around." Workman sat behind the desk, his face as expressionless as a sheet of gyproc. "No ad libs. We'd be working from a script."

"We?"

"The kids and me – I."

"You'd be directing this play, would you?"

"Uh-huh."

"Ever direct a play before?"

"No, not really. Sort of." Oh, that sounded great. "You saw that duel scene in class – I directed it." He knew Workman wouldn't consider that a good thing and rushed on: "We did other scenes from *Hamlet* too – better ones. The kids want to try something a little more ambitious."

"More ambitious than *Hamlet*?"

Workman could make him feel like such a dork. "Not exactly. We just did bits and pieces from *Hamlet*. But the kids liked it."

"And you'd like to do something more?"

"I would – yes." This guy was on Phil's side. Why couldn't he give him a break too?

Workman sat without responding, as if waiting for something. Man, he wants me to beg.

"I'd consider it a privilege," said Brad, "to have the chance."

Workman continued staring at him, a smug look on his face, something shifty about his eyes. Then his expression changed. He was actually smiling now, looking completely satisfied with the situation. The guy must be having a good day. "You've got a play in mind?"

"I thought I'd try *Out of the Frying Pan*; it was a minor hit on Broadway, back in the fifties, I think. We'd just do the second act though. A couple of little changes and it should work pretty much like a one-act play."

Workman was no longer smiling. "Another bloody bedroom scene," he said, "and that'd be three strikes and out."

"It's harmless – nothing but good, clean fun."

"I'd need to see the script."

Was that his way of saying yes? "Of course," said Brad, "I'll bring you a copy after school."

"Nothing untoward, and I suppose you can go ahead." He

shoved back his chair and stood up. "Be nice to have something on stage won't be an embarrassment to watch. You remember though, everything I've said before goes double for this one."

Uh-huh, he figured as much, but he couldn't stop now. "Just one other thing," he said. "I don't have any budget." He was speaking quickly now. "There'll be a royalty, we'll need to purchase scripts."

Workman stepped around his desk, looking down at Brad. "Miscellaneous," he said. "We'll find the money in a slush fund and debit miscellaneous." He reached down and laid his hand on Brad's shoulder, his fingers like five dry twigs. Brad thought he heard a rasping sound deep in Workman's throat. It might have been a chuckle. "Sometimes," the principal said, "you have to give out a little extra rope, see if a fellow's going to hang himself."

He's just kidding, thought Brad, has to be.

B rad knew he had to get started with rehearsals, but he kept having the uneasy feeling that Workman had outmaneuvered him. Maybe so, but if that was true, he – Brad – had set the trap himself, then stepped inside and closed the gate for Workman.

Can't be thinking this way. Got to push on with it.

He placed a sheet of foolscap on the desk in front of him and drew the floor plan on it. He was no carpenter. They could use dividers for the walls, but there had to be a door. A curtain, maybe. That might do the trick. A chesterfield against the wall upstage left, a couple of chairs opposite. Lots of open space downstage where the actors rehearsed Mr. Kenny's Broadway play. That part was easy.

He reached in his pocket for the coins that were always rubbing on his thigh. Separated them on the desk beside the foolscap. Got to keep them straight, he thought. He rummaged through the top drawer till he found a marker pen. Printed an "N" on a quarter. The ink ran together, sat like beads of crimson dew on the coin's surface. It wasn't going to work. He opened the side drawer, took the masking tape from its place beside the tin box of chalk ends. He tore off squares of masking tape, applying one to the top of every coin, then labelled each coin with an initial to represent a character in the play. He opened the script to page one, began reading the play, noting the action, moving the characters around on the set. He had to have a good idea of where everyone should be before he went on stage with the actors to block the play.

The auditions had been disappointing. He'd been thinking of the play as a class project, but not everyone who'd acted in the *Hamlet* skits was interested in a play that involved rehearsals after school. Parker Stone and Walter Buchko, of course, Arnie Jordan and Lori Campbell too. But not Annette Federko who'd been so good as Queen Gertrude. She was busy with piano lessons after school, taking them and giving them too. Even so, he thought she might have read for a part if she hadn't had a fall and cracked a bone in her ankle.

They'd had to open up auditions to the whole school before they got enough actors.

Twenty-two

Brad was in the library, stacking books of Canadian poetry on a trolley for a mini-anthology project he'd planned for his grade elevens. Workman wasn't going to have the chance to claim he'd eased off with his classes while he was working on the play. His students would each have to choose eight poems they liked by at least six different poets, then write brief commentaries on them all. Thanks to Vic Pendleton who was always hounding Rita Croft to order more books, the library had lots of contemporary poets, local poets too. Brad wondered if maybe Vic didn't write a little poetry himself.

Let's see now, Alden Nowlan, his wry sense of humour should appeal to kids. Lorna Crozier, for sure, a landscape they knew. Margaret Atwood, somebody'd probably go for her. Patrick Lane, yes, a hard edge to his work. Al Purdy, his idea of hockey a mix of ballet and murder. They should like that. Two books Mr. Roy had once loaned him: Stephen Scriver's hockey poems and *Just Off Main*, by Gary Hyland, another era sure, but every poem about a kid. Raymond Souster. Anne Szumigalski. What was that poem about the man and the woman – a wire stretched between their heads? He sat down and began to flip through the pages of *Woman Reading in Bath.*

He looked up when he heard the door open. Sue Burton waved to him on her way over to the magazine rack, raised the shelf on which the latest copies were displayed and lifted out a stack of old *Maclean's.* You might not notice at first, but when you got to know her a bit, she was amazingly attractive. There was a certain grace about her as she slid onto a chair and laid the magazines on the table next to Brad's. Grace, yeah, that was the word. She was wearing a sleeveless blouse, her bare arms moving over the magazines, her hands opening the one on the top of the stack, a finger running over the table of contents, her other hand closing the magazine, turning it upside down, laying it aside. He looked at the smooth tight skin where her arms met her shoulders, imagined the cool touch of the silk blouse, warm skin moving beneath the fabric. He felt himself begin to blush. Looked down. *Woman Reading in Bath.* No help there.

He slid the book back onto the trolley, fumbled for *Rhymes of a Rolling Stone.* Nearly every kid would pick a poem by Service. Suppose he took Service off the list. How would that change their reading?

He watched Sue's hands, her tapered fingers efficiently turning pages, rejecting magazines, stacking them neatly in chronological order. Her hands pausing, hanging motionless above the last few issues.

She was looking at him. He felt something catch in his throat, swallowed hard. She smiled at him, a smile like a heat wave, a fire storm – man, the automatic sprinklers would be on any second. He nodded and smiled back, knowing that his smile was quick, awkward. He saw her smile gradually fade, felt the air begin to cool around him. She watched him for seconds more, then lowered her eyes to her work and quickly sifted through the last three copies. She shook her head.

"Not here," she said.

"Waste of time?"

She stood up, lifted the stack of magazines, cradled them against her breasts. "Not at all," she said. "November 15th is missing. It'll be the one I need – they'll have it at the public library." That smile again. He could feel the temperature rising. "Some things are worth the effort." Her voice like a song. "You never know where they'll lead."

He watched her walk back to the magazine rack, stooping to lift the display shelf, her skirt drawn tight around her hips as she slid the magazines back on the shelf. Sudden heat in his groin.

He opened the Service book to its table of contents.

That was it. Enough. He wouldn't watch her out the door.

She doesn't look that old, he thought. Nobody would guess she's older than me. Well, hardly anybody. It was only a few years.

What did it matter anyway? He was interested.

Still, try to start something with Sue, he'd have Workman on his back again, no fishing from the company dock, eh? Yeah, and all the others, Maurie too – which was a hell of a lot worse.

He and Sue were the last ones in the staffroom one afternoon a few days later. Dr. McAvoy still hadn't been in to see him, but he wasn't going to think about that today. It was the first warm day this spring; half the kids had their shorts on already, but right now he was content to sit and forget about how nice it was outside. He was nursing his coke, making it last, wondering if she were doing the same with her coffee. She was whistling something quietly, almost inaudibly, something he'd heard her whistle before. He liked the tune, its fluid quality.

"What is that?" he asked.

Sue looked up from her coffee, looked around the room. "What?"

"That song."

"Oh, that. 'Wood River,'" she said. "One of my all-time favourites." She whistled a bit more of the song, then surprised him, singing: "The heart is bigger than trouble, the heart is bigger than doubt, but sometimes the heart needs a little help to figure that out." She stopped, blushing. It was almost as if she'd surprised herself as well.

"Nice," he said. "Who sings it?" He grinned. "Besides you, I mean."

"Connie Kaldor. She's wonderful." Sue shook her head. "You'd think the local stations would play her more, but no, they're always stuck on country or golden oldies. Thank God for the CBC."

She was smiling back at him. He felt like talking, hoped she did too.

"How did you get into teaching?" he asked.

"I was a small-town kid," she said. "No more experience than a stone-boat. Figured I had about three choices. Be a nurse, a teacher, maybe a farmer's wife. Had a squeamish stomach. That took care of the nursing."

"What small town?"

"Dafoe." She saw the look in his eyes. "No, most people don't know it. On the Yellowhead west of Wynyard. The town's got one of those huge concrete elevators, but it's still getting smaller every year."

"I suppose the only residents left'd be a bunch of unhappy farmers dreaming about the girl who got away."

"Oh, yes." She laughed. "Or thanking their lucky stars."

The girl who got away. Funny. It didn't bother him any more. Hadn't for quite a while.

"Teaching seemed a natural choice – I was always a reader – just like you, I gather."

"Uh-huh," he said. Had it been lust with Kelly, maybe? With her, anyone would understand. But no, it was definitely more than that; still, he guessed it hadn't been love.

"We both read an awful lot," she said.

"Yeah, I can't remember a time when I didn't have my nose stuck in a book. Hockey coach chewed me out once for having a paperback in my gym bag on a road trip. Back in high school there was a teacher took the trouble to notice, said I'd make a good English teacher." He smiled at her. "I guess I told you that."

"You told me," she said. "He was right too."

"Thanks. Some of my kids you wouldn't convince."

"Kids," she said. "Sometimes they don't know they've had a good teacher till years later. Back in Wynyard – they bused us in for high school – we had this one teacher used to make us write essays. The only one who did – everybody groused about him, always whining about the work he put us through. But some of us went to university – my God, we'd learned something. That first essay assignment, we knew what to do, where to look, we were miles ahead of everybody else. Heck, the prof. mentioned 'bibliography,' most of them figured he was talking a foreign language." She paused. "Place the size of Wynyard, you couldn't help running into

Mr. Lowick – he was the teacher. One time I stopped him on the street and thanked him. You never saw a man look so pleased."

Her voice was like a familiar tune, but a tune played on some exotic instrument, a xylophone, say, something that transformed the notes, made them new and vibrant. Go on, he thought. Maybe he could keep her talking.

"When you were a kid," he said, "you remember the first book you ever really loved?"

"Easy. *The Wizard of Oz*. I figured Dafoe was a lot like Kansas, I wanted to be Dorothy. No, that's not quite right. For a while there, I thought I *was* Dorothy. Every time the wind blew, I used to pray for a tornado." She laughed, a little crescendo of laughter. "What about you, Brad? You have a favorite book?"

"Huckleberry Finn."

"When you were just a little guy?"

"Yep, *Huck Finn*. My mother read it to me, a chapter every night at bedtime. The old man, he figured it was a waste of time, but he could never convince her of that. When she was finished, I got her to start all over again. Read it myself later on, half a dozen times, I bet."

Sue was nodding her head.

"I noticed something kind of funny, though. You know how Twain called Jim a nigger?"

"Sure. The way people talked back then."

"Uh-huh, but not when Mom read it. If somebody got tough with Jim and said, 'Listen, nigger,' in her version it always came out, "Listen, black man."

"Your mom into political correctness?"

"Oh, no, that wasn't it. She just wanted her only child growing up a reader – a non-racist reader. First time I read the book myself, I happened to mention something about Jim and used the term "nigger." She set me down then and there, gave me a talking to about the power of negative language, the way racial slurs can hurt people – every bit as much as sticks and stones."

"Your mom sounds like a neat lady. I'd love to meet her."

"Oh, she'd like you." Anybody would. Animated, he thought, that's what Sue was. Always. Enough life in her for three people. Hell, he could talk to her all night. "You want to go for pizza?" he asked.

"He's a drunk," said Bert Peale, "plain and simple." It was the first time in ages that he had deigned to speak in class. Brad wondered if the fact that Dr. McAvoy was wedged into a desk at the back of the room had anything to do with Peale speaking out. Everybody else seemed uneasy, a bit tight. Maybe they thought McAvoy was staring at the backs of their heads, wanting to check on them. Instead of being here to get the goods on him, doing Workman's dirty work. He kept his text on the lectern so no one would see his hands shaking.

They'd been reading the poem "Mr. Flood's Party," had been asked to draw some conclusions about Eben Flood. Brad glanced quickly at McAvoy who had a notebook open on the desk. Damned if he was going to change his approach just because the Director of Education was inspecting him. So what if Workman sent him? He still had to do what he thought best.

"Evidence?" said Brad.

"He's singing, and there's two moons listening. Seeing double, eh? Swacked out of his head."

"Hey, two moons – neat," said Danny Litowski. Then he closed his mouth, sharply, glancing nervously at the back of the room.

"So he's drinking all right," said Brad. "Does that mean he's just a drunk?"

"Come on," said Bert. "He's out there in the middle of nowhere, just him and his bottle." That edge to his voice, always pushing.

"Somebody else want to jump in here?" Brad looked around, but no one raised a hand. Surely, they weren't going to clam up on him now.

"He's got a friend," said Della Neudorf, finally. "Somebody who offers him a drink. Calls him Mr. Flood."

"He's talking to himself, Dimbulb," said Bert. Della sank down in her desk, her head low over her text.

Smartass kid, thought Brad. "Easy, Bert. No need for that. You're so quick to judge, you might jump to the wrong conclusion sometime."

"Not likely." He graced both Brad and Della with his sneer.

McAvoy was leaning forward in his desk.

"I'm afraid Eben Flood *is* talking to himself. But Della's got a point too. Notice how often he's referred to as *Mr.* Flood in the dialogue. Why might that be?" He prayed the kids wouldn't shut down with McAvoy here; they had to help him out.

Parker glanced up but didn't speak.

"Maybe that's how people used to address him," said Lori Campbell. "With respect."

Della raised her head above her book and smiled at Lori.

"Sure," said Bert, "before he became a hopeless drunk." He grinned quickly, half-turning his head toward McAvoy, then settled back into his desk, the grin fading to his customary sneer.

"Let's go along with Bert for a while here," said Brad. And here he was, handling Bert with kid gloves again, wondering as usual if that was the best way. Probably was, this time anyway, with McAvoy watching everything, just waiting for a chance to jot something down. "Any other signs of Mr. Flood's drinking?"

"It says he had to go a long way to fill his jug," said Walter Buchko. "Must've needed that drink pretty bad." Bert gave his head one dramatic nod.

"Good," said Brad. "Anything else?"

"He raised the jug again – and again," said Melinda Harper. "He sure wants more than one shot." Another sharp nod of Bert's head.

"Uh-huh. Anything else?"

"The jug must be pretty important to him," said Lori Campbell. "He sets it down as tenderly as a mother lays her child down."

"Right. Anything more?"

No one was looking at him except Bert who now wore something like a cross between a sneer and a triumphant smile on his face. Wait, McAvoy was watching too, staring at him from the back of the room, his expression non-committal. The others had their eyes on their books. Brad let them read a few moments before he spoke again. They had to see it. "Now you're probably starting to notice some little things that suggest maybe he isn't just a drunk."

Bert glared at him and said, "Not a chance."

No one else spoke.

"Come on," said Brad. "You can get this." Every eye averted, and he could feel them dropping away, leaving him to handle it himself. Then Parker raised his head and looked at him. Would Parker help him out with McAvoy sitting there, with Bert sneering at everyone who had a different answer? Did he dare to try him? He could hear a desk creaking, McAvoy shifting in his seat. Someone nervously tapping a foot on the floor. Not another sound.

"What do you think, Parker?"

The boy studied him a moment. "A drunk wouldn't care who heard him singing," Parker said at last. "But Mr. Flood makes darn sure there's no one else around before he starts to sing." Bert turned toward him and shook his head.

Walter jumped in immediately. "He says, 'No more. That will do.' I always figured drunks kept drinking till the last drop was gone."

Bert directed a pitying look toward Walter.

"Perhaps this poem is about something more than drunkenness."

"Not likely," said Bert, but he said it quietly.

Brad decided to ignore him, hoping McAvoy would think that the right approach. "What else do you notice about Mr. Flood?"

Della's hand shot up. "He's old. First word of the poem." She flung a look at Bert's back as if to say, let's see you argue with that one.

"Uh-huh."

"He's a hermit," said Nelson Ahenakew.

"Does the poem say that?"

"No, but he lives in a hermitage."

"Good. What else?"

"He used to live in the town and people liked him," said Annette Federko. "His friends honoured him."

The kids were really coming through for him. And Parker

was the one who got them started.

"He was a drunk," said Bert. "They slammed the door in his face."

"Strangers," said Lori. "They didn't know him."

Brad looked down at Bert who was no longer sneering, but frowning. "The man drinks," said Brad. "We're not arguing about that, but trying to get beyond it." He thought about the dance, Bert foul-mouthed and drunk, his father furious – but at the wrong guy, his mother with liquor on her breath. Did that have something to do with the way Bert was going on? "What else is the poem about?"

"Intoxication," said Bert, grinning when a few of his classmates laughed. "Inebriation," he added.

"Thanks, Bert, for adding to the discussion." Oops, better watch the sarcasm. McAvoy's not going to like that. "Try this: why's he drinking?"

"Cause he's a drunk."

"Bert!"

He noticed Parker turn and cock his head to look at Bert, who was back in his old seat, directly behind him. "He's lonely," said Parker.

"Proof?"

"He's talking to himself because he's got no one else to talk to."

"His friends are all dead," said Lori. "That's why he hears that phantom salutation."

"It'd be an awful thing," said Melinda, "if all your friends were dead and you had to go on alone."

"Because he's old," said Pam Wheeler.

"There's not much ahead for him," said Walter, "and 'nothing in the town below.'"

"Kind of like 'Death of the Hired Man,'" said Pam.

"'Nothing to look forward to with hope.'"

"Exactly," said Brad. Man, these kids were sharp when they got going. "Anybody know that song he's singing – 'For Auld Lang Syne'?"

"Bet it ain't rap," said Walter. "Nothing for the home boys."

"Maybe it's New Year's Eve," said Pam.

"Oh, sure," said Bert.

"It's the song they sing at midnight," said Pam. Her look at Bert was almost enough to wither him, but not quite. "Could be, this guy is all alone on New Year's Eve. That would be really tough to take."

"Sad," said Melinda, "real sad."

"Everybody gets drunk on New Year's Eve," said Bert.

When Parker spoke, his voice was cold. "Maybe not everybody. The last time Mr. Flood raises the jug he does it 'regretfully.' Then he shakes his head and he's alone again. That's it, eh? The liquor doesn't work."

"Doesn't prove a thing," said Bert.

"What do you notice about the fourth verse?" asked Brad.

Bert spoke before anyone else could. "He loves the jug. Lays it down tenderly."

"What do you notice that we haven't talked about?"

"I got it," said Danny Litowski. "The jug sits on firm earth. The uncertain lives of men do not."

"Meaning?"

"Well, it says 'most things break.' Life is tough, eh? Things don't always work out the way you want them to."

"And in the case of Mr. Flood?"

"He used to be honoured and respected in the town," said Danny. "Now he's old and all alone."

"And drunk," said Bert.

"Probably never guessed he'd end up like that," said

Melinda. "Look at us. We all figure we're going to be a big success."

"It used to be his town," said Pam, "but all the people there are strangers now." Her face was shining. "Like Willie Loman. 'They don't know me any more.'"

Brad brought his hands together in two quick claps. "Good stuff, Pam." My God, she was better than he was at spotting parallels. "All of you, in fact. I'd have to say you've pretty well nailed this poem down. Anybody any questions?"

Some of them, he noticed, looked pleased. He hoped McAvoy was pleased too. Bert just looked glum. Melinda was leaning over her text, running her finger down the page. Brad knew she wanted to get in at least another word. He waited till she raised her hand.

"Yes?"

"What's this about the ghost winding a silent horn?" She pronounced it 'wine-ding.'

"Good question. Only it's wind-ing. Anybody get it?" Blank looks. A few heads ducking away from him. "It means 'blowing.'"

Parker put up his hand, almost reluctantly, it seemed. Then he glanced over his shoulder at Bert who wasn't looking at him – or anybody else. Yeah, Bert's probably going to like this. Well, it's part of the poem, it should come out. Brad nodded at Parker and said, "Give it to us, Parker."

"You got to picture him," said Parker. He was seated sideways in his desk, half turned toward Bert. Was that gleam in his eye antagonistic – or conspiratorial? Brad wasn't sure. Parker curled his fingers around an imaginary jug and raised it to his lips. "Sucking on that jug. Looks like he's blowing a horn."

"Like I told you," said Bert. "The guy's a drunk."

Damn, but that kid knew how to get under his skin. Let it go, he thought, just let it go.

At the back of the room, McAvoy was hunched over the desk, scribbling in his notebook.

No doubt about it though – except for Bert – things had gone really well. The guy had to be writing something good. Had to be.

Twenty-three

The first call was for Brad. It came shortly after the final bell one day in late May, less than two weeks before the play was to be performed for the students.

"Am I speaking with Mr. Cutler?" the voice said, strong and sure. A voice he'd heard before, someone he ought to know. "This is Dr. Stone calling. I understand you're the one directing this little play. 'Bloody Murder,' is it?" He sounded awfully serious. Was he confused about the subject matter?

"That's what we're calling it. Right. It's really just the second act of an old Broadway play, *Out of the Frying Pan*. A comedy."

"Nothing too serious then?"

"No, no. There's not a murder in –"

"Fine then. It shouldn't be a problem when you tell Parker he's going to be replaced."

"What?"

"That you're getting someone else for his part."

"Why would I do that? Parker's wonderful."

"You don't seem to understand." The supercilious tone that must've made life miserable for a generation of nurses.

"I want Parker out of that play."

"You're right, I don't understand." His voice rising. Easy, easy. Find out what's going on here. Take a deep breath. "Is there some kind of problem with the play?"

"It's not exactly *Hamlet*, is it?"

Arrogant bastard, Brad thought. Give him a shot. "No. We've already done that."

"The play is piffle. Nothing my son needs to be a part of."

"The play's fun. We're having a ball with it. The school's going to love it."

"That may be. But not with my son in it."

"Look, Parker's the best thing about this play. The guy who brings everyone else up to his level. He's a natural actor."

"No doubt. He has many talents."

"I don't get it. What's this all about?"

"I'm sorry you're so slow, Mr. Cutler. Let's draw a picture, shall we?"

Up yours, Brad thought, but he managed to keep his mouth shut.

"Parker's always been good at everything he tries. That's the problem. He has a tendency to spread himself too thinly. Doesn't concentrate on the things that really matter." He paused as if that explained everything. Brad could hear his breath in the receiver.

"I suppose you're saying that the play doesn't matter."

"Precisely. Parker doesn't have time to waste. He needs to direct his efforts toward medical school."

"Dr. Stone, we rehearse twice a week after school. No more than two hours at a time. Parker's a sharp kid. That's not going to affect his marks."

"I'll be the judge of that."

"No sir. I'm his teacher. I know exactly how he's doing."

"You're impertinent, Cutler. I expect you to drop him from the play."

"It's just a few more practices and we're on."

"I want him cut."

The bastard, he really meant it.

"I can't do that. It's too late to replace him now. We've got a dozen other kids counting on him. They've all been working hard."

"I'm not concerned about the other kids. Cut him."

"Look. This isn't going to drop Parker's marks one iota. We need him in the play."

"I want him cut. You understand? Today."

Was that what he should do, take the easy way, go along with Stone? But it wasn't fair to the other kids; hell, it wasn't fair to Parker.

"No. I'm sorry. I can't do that."

"Cutler, I'm ordering you to cut him."

"And I'm telling you, it's not something I can do."

"You can do it all right – and you damned well better do it."

He could hear Stone's breath rasping in the phone. Of course, he knew he should listen to the man, do what he wanted, but then he thought of Parker, never missing rehearsals, working hard all the time, the first one in the cast with every line memorized. "You want him out, tell him yourself." Oh damn, now he was in for it.

"No, sir." The voice so loud that Brad lifted the ear piece away from his head. "I'll have Workman tell him."

But he hadn't hung up.

It wasn't too late to say yes. Sure, that would keep Workman off his case. Uh-huh, and what would it do to

Parker? He could see the kid's reaction, his eyes as dead as Angela's.

"Your last chance. Shall I have Workman tell him?"

Brad took a deep breath. The decision was his. "All right then," he said, "you go ahead and do that."

"Damned rights. And I'll have him deal with you too."

A click, and he was left with only dial tone. He slammed the receiver down, slammed his fist into the palm of his hand. This was crazy, getting Stone fired up, giving Workman another reason to get rid of him, but it was what he had to do.

The second call must've come immediately. Brad was almost down to his room for rehearsal when the hall intercom crackled and snapped into life: "Mr. Cutler, report to the office as soon as it's convenient." Herb Schwitzer, sounding tired. At least, it wasn't Workman blurting an order to get there on the double.

Brad stuck his head into the room. The kids already had the desks cleared away to make rehearsal space. "Start when Mr. Kenny comes to watch the kids' play, and run it from there," he said. "I'll be back as quick as I can."

When he got up to the office, he saw that Workman's door was closed, that Herb was standing in the doorway to the vice-principal's office. Herb waved him in and shut the door behind him.

"Just had a little talk with Dr. Stone."

"So did I," said Brad. "I thought he'd be calling Mr. Workman."

"Out. I took the call. Maybe a good thing. For you. Probably not for me. Seems incensed about your play."

"He wants me to drop Parker from the cast."

"So he said. Claims you wouldn't do it. Have a seat."

Brad took the chair in front of the desk, waiting till Herb was seated behind it. "He seems to think Parker's marks are going to suffer," said Brad. "That's a crock. Parker can ace anything he wants to."

"Play's next week, right?"

"Next Wednesday."

"No reason to cut him then?"

"None that makes any sense."

"Not in the kid's best interests, eh?"

"It sure isn't."

Herb leaned forward, his elbows firmly planted on the table, his hands together in front of his face. He leaned his chin on his thumbs, the tips of his fingers rhythmically beating together. His eyes were closed. "Don't know if we can ride this one out or not," he said. His hands were drawn toward his face every time he opened his mouth. "The bugger said he'd have your job."

Brad knew it was coming; still he felt a shiver of dread.

Herb laid his hands on the table, and Brad could see that he was smiling. "I told him he was a fine surgeon, but he wasn't qualified to teach." Brad heard a distant rumble somewhere deep in Herb's esophagus. It sounded like a chuckle. "Should've known better, I suppose, but it was a pleasure to hear the good doctor sputter. Probably be off your back for a while anyway. Yeah, on mine now. He called me impertinent. Used to having things his own way. Maybe not this time." He had ceased grinning and looked almost stern. "Mr. Workman's off to Vancouver for a big administrator's conference." Another grin. "Director's going with him. I didn't mention that to Stone."

"I can do the play with Parker?"

"Up to Parker, I'd say. Stone can order him to quit. I don't think he wants to though. Let him do his own dirty work."

"Uh-huh." Brad wondered if any of it would matter. "He quit football because of his dad."

"Wasn't happy about it." Herb stood up. "Probably still mad at his old man. Stone's a piece of work, all right. Son-of-a bitch said he'd have me fired too. I don't think so."

In the dim light of the room, Walter Buchko was draped over an easy chair, his right hand hanging in an ash tray on the floor, a knife still quivering in his back. Behind him on four metal chairs drawn into a line, Lori Campbell seemed to be sleeping quite sedately on her back, except that her head was tilted at an awkward angle and a knife was plunged into her chest. Beside the chairs was a table, tipped onto its side. Hanging over the table was Pam Wheeler, a knife jammed between her ribs. Near her feet lay Jill Parini, her body curled around the knife that had been driven into her stomach.

Utter silence. Then a movement in the shadows. Parker Stone walked slowly into the room, stepping carefully over Jill's feet. He glanced at the bodies, took a long drag from his cigarette whose sudden glow revealed the sardonic grin on his face. He inspected the tip of his cigarette, the ember fading, turning to ash, and flicked the ash into the skull he carried in his other hand.

"Strange," he said, "they're all dead." He admitted he'd been wrong about the sinister butler; the guy was innocent – and dead. So were the Crystal Gazer and the two mysterious sisters. Of course, it had to be the nervous young man. Parker again stepped over Jill's feet and strode to the closet door, flinging it wide. Staggered suddenly backwards, a look of horror on his face. Arnie Jordan toppled to the floor in front of him, his white hands brushing the legs of Parker's pants as he fell, a stiletto in his back. Parker knelt beside him, grabbed his wrist, held it while gazing at his watch. A quick shake of the head. The nervous young man was no longer nervous; he was dead.

Parker bolted to his feet, terror washing over his face, his head shaking in little spasms. Of course. He should have figured it out when he found the bloody cap in his suitcase.

"I should have known," said Parker. "I walked in my sleep."

"Curtain!" said Brad. "Good job, Parker. Exactly the right amount of corn that time. The rest of you guys were great. You actually looked dead."

"Very first time," said Walter, "I got through it without giggling."

"I don't know about that," said Parker. "The knife was quivering in your back."

"Hey. I gotta breathe, eh?"

"That's it for today," said Brad. "Knives in the prop box, please. Can you stay a minute, Parker?"

"No problem."

"Knife's stuck again," said Walter, backing toward Parker. Parker reached through the slit in the back of his shirt and removed the wooden knife which was glued onto a small square of cardboard, which had been stuck to Walter's back with duct tape. "Thanks. See you guys tomorrow."

When the others were gone, Brad sat in a metal chair, motioning Parker toward another in the line of four chairs that represented a sofa.

"Something wrong?" asked Parker. "You're looking pretty serious."

"Could be. I got a call from your dad."

"Shit! Sorry. What's the hell's he up to now?"

Brad wasn't sure how to put it, didn't want to lay too much on the boy's father. "I get the feeling he's not happy about your being in the play."

"You can say that again. He figures I should quit."

"I guess he thinks you're wasting your time."

"Yeah. Anything doesn't lead to an MD is a waste of time."

"You thinking maybe you should end your thespian career?"

"No way! We're doing this play. He can shove his MD."

"Another week. I don't think it'll keep you out of med school."

"He can shove med school too."

"Parker, I don't want to cause you troubles with your dad."

"Screw him. I'm doing the play."

Brad stayed in the chair for a long time after Parker had left the room. He wondered if he should change his mind, if he should maybe call Parker, tell him to think it over a bit more before he made his final decision. Funny thing, he thought, his old man's a doctor, mine's a farmer, and the two of them are just about the same.

Walter Buchko was waiting in the hall outside his room the next morning when he came down the stairs for his last class before noon.

"Parker's been away all morning," said Walter. "I phoned his house at the long break. No answer."

"Maybe he's sick."

"He was fine yesterday. We've got rehearsal today. He wouldn't miss rehearsal."

"Well, maybe he'll show up then."

It was their first rehearsal on the gym stage. They'd spent the noon hour – all of them but Parker – lugging furniture and props up to the gym, arranging dividers to look like the walls of a cheap New York apartment, marking key spots they had to hit and taping them on the floor. They even had a chesterfield that Walter and his father had brought from the rumpus room at home. Everyone was there on time and in costume – everyone but Parker.

"Where's Parker?" asked Arnie.

Brad shrugged.

"What's going on?" said Pam.

"I don't know," he said. "We'll take it from the top. I'll read Parker's lines, but I want to be out front watching. You know his moves. Try to play it as if he's there. Look at the spot where he'd be." He knew it wouldn't be the same, of course, but it would have to do.

When practice was done, he phoned the Stone residence. In his receiver, the phone sounded as if it were ringing somewhere in a distant tunnel. There was no answer.

He tried again at supper time. The phone was picked up before the first ring was finished.

"Yes."

"Could I speak to Parker, please?"

"Not here." Then, dial tone buzzing in his ear.

He tried again at ten, counting a dozen rings before he

hung up the phone.

Half an hour later his own phone rang.

"Hello."

"Sorry to bother you so late, sir. This is Walter."

"No bother. What is it, Walter?"

"I saw Parker. He said to tell you he's sorry he missed practice. It won't happen again."

"What's going on, Walter?"

"He had a fight with his old man. His old man kicked him out."

"Oh, oh. That's not so good. He staying at your place?"

"He wouldn't tell me where he's staying. Said he's okay though, not to worry. He'll see you tomorrow, be there for sure. Bye."

Brad held the phone in his hand, staring at it, the distant buzzing like a fly stuck between two panes of glass in a far-off window. He'd like to phone Sue, tell her what was going on, maybe talk it over with her. She knew more about Stone than he ever would. But not at this hour. It was too late. He set the receiver down.

He glanced out the basement window, staring at the shadow of the neighbour's fence, dark as the walls of the ravine that ran from behind the barn at home down to the South Saskatchewan. Cutbanks and a tangle of willows, the bend where he hid his raft. It was the place he used to go when his old man was on the warpath. Getting out of the house, away from the barn, just sitting on the raft sometimes, his feet dragging in the water, staring for hours as the river slid by, tiny swirls on the surface, undertow beneath, the whisper of waves soothing the currents that seethed within him.

The poor kid. All for a play that was definitely lightweight, mainly for laughs, sure, but it did say something about kids doing what they had to do. A lot of fun too. And what did that matter? It wasn't worth it, causing problems for Parker, breaking up a family. Some family.

Hell, they'd get over it. The play wasn't the problem anyway. His father was the problem. Parker was seventeen years old. He had a life to live. He wasn't in medical school yet, probably never would be. Oh, great, his father'd love that. Parker's choice though. Too bad his mother wasn't alive, bet she'd stick up for him. Kid's got a right to make a choice. To make his own choice, make it by himself.

Yeah, that was how it ought to be. Except, of course, in Parker's case that meant trouble.

Twenty-four

The next morning Sue was sitting in her usual chair on the east side of the staffroom, a coffee cup on the end table next to her. Brad poured himself a black coffee before he sat beside her.

"Got a problem," he said.

"Awfully early for problems." When he didn't respond, Sue turned and looked at him. "Go ahead. You need to talk."

"I had a call from Dr. Stone. He's not happy with me. Or Parker either." She listened without a word while he told her the details.

"Where's he staying?"

"I don't know. Some friend's, I guess. Right now, his dad's the one who worries me."

"The man has a temper, all right," she said. "But he's no fool. He'll settle down, forget about getting you fired."

Brad wished he could believe that. "He threatened Herb too."

She let out a low whistle and shook her head. "Not wise. He's just too used to having things his own way. Comes from being a single parent, I suppose."

"I guess you know him pretty well." Brad paused when she didn't reply, then stumbled on. "I mean, you used to go out with him."

She looked at him a moment. "Used to," she said. "Not for long."

"Of course." Why couldn't he just keep his mouth shut? But no, he wasn't done with it, either. "I know you're the one who called it off."

She was no longer looking at him. "That's not how he'd remember it." When she took a sip of coffee, Brad thought she was finished with him. But she spoke again. "Oh, the man was a charmer. As long as everything went his way. He always had to be the winner. Took me a while to figure that out." She gazed at her coffee cup, sipped another drink and set it down. "Seems to me, it's Parker you should be worrying about."

"I guess you're right. Walter – Buchko – said he'd be back today. We'll have a talk." He slumped in his chair, his eyes closed for an instant, praying Parker would be back, but what he was suddenly thinking about was Angela Maddox, the way she'd quit coming to class, and that was it, no one ever saw her alive again. Parker moping around for weeks after that. Thank God, he'd gone to see the crisis team.

Brad was staring at his classroom door when the attendance sheet was slid under it fifteen minutes into the first period that morning. Usually, he didn't get around to picking it up until his students had filed out at the end of the period. Most of the sheets on his spike had footprints on them. Today he was bending for the sheet almost before it settled to the floor.

There were two absentees in 4D. He was relieved to see that Parker wasn't one of them.

Walter Buchko caught him in the hall just before he got to the staffroom for the long break.

"Parker's back," said Walter. "He'll be at play practice tonight."

"Good. You look relieved."

"Yeah, I guess so."

"What is it, Walter? You're grinning like a madman."

"Guess where he slept last night."

"Not at your place, eh? I don't know."

"In the park. He slept under the bridge."

"No."

"Sure did," said Walter. "Under the bridge. In his sleeping bag. That'll teach his old man."

"His father's probably worried sick. I better talk to Parker."

"Don't worry. He'll be in class this afternoon."

"Thanks for letting me know." Brad started for the staffroom, hesitated, turned around and walked into the office. There were two grade tens at the counter, gazing at Kelly. He stepped between them and her desk, speaking softly.

"I need a favour, Kelly."

She raised her head from her typing, a puzzled look on her face. "Sure."

"Could you phone Dr. Stone's office? Tell him Parker's back in school this morning."

"Can do. He skip yesterday?"

"Could be. Don't worry. Herb'll catch up with him."

"He usually does."

Brad waited outside his room a few minutes before his first afternoon class began, hoping to grab a word with Parker, but he felt awkward, students hurrying by, glancing at him, wondering why he was hanging around in the hall after the warning bell. Still no sign of Parker. Come on, he thought, come on, Parker. When there were no more stragglers on the stairs he went inside and pulled out his attendance forms. One empty desk at the front. Parker's, of course. Where was he? Surely there was nothing to worry about, not really. They just had to talk. What the hell was going on with the kid, though? Well, he wasn't officially absent till the final bell rang. He might still show up. Maybe.

He did, hurrying into the room just as the bell began, striding directly to his seat, not even a glance at Brad.

At least he's here. I'll catch him after class.

Brad sent the attendance form up to the office with Neil Wallace. A trip up and down the stairs might get his circulation going, keep him from dozing off in class.

Parker was motionless in the front seat. He had *Modern Canadian Stories* with him though. The right book.

"We'll take up the questions on the Margaret Laurence piece," said Brad.

They dealt with factual questions first, interpretations next, no sign of anyone who hadn't done his homework, Brad throwing in extra questions as they went along to keep them on their toes.

"How come the grandma's voice is compared to a silver teaspoon tapping on a crystal goblet?"

"That's how she used to call the servants," said Annette Federko. "In the good old days. She thinks she's high-classed."

"Delusions of grandeur," said Pam Wheeler. "She won't

admit those days are gone."

Man, these girls were sharp. Ask almost any one of them and they'd nail the answer every time. Brad glanced down at the assignment sheet. "Question five," he said. There was no way of avoiding it; he had to ask it. "The signs that Ewen may not be leading the life he wants?"

Parker had been sitting with his head down, staring glumly at his book. Now he raised his head to stare at Brad, but his expression never changed and he made no gesture to answer.

Bert Peale lazily raised his hand. "He put out his brother's eye with a BB gun. Then got him into his company in the war. To watch out for him, eh? When he died, Ewen felt like it was his fault."

"Good. You're right on target, but there's a bit more," said Brad. "You want to take it a little further?"

"Not me," said Bert.

Always jerking me around, thought Brad. Knows, and won't say. "Anybody else?"

Neil Wallace lifted his head. "After the war he came back home and went into his father's medical practice."

"Go on, Neil."

"Instead of his brother. Sounds like that's what the brother would've done if he'd lived. Doesn't say it, but it sounds that way."

"Good. That's the implication, all right."

He noticed Bert Peale lean forward and whisper something to Parker. Parker started to turn around, but sat forward, resting his head in his hands.

"Anything else?" asked Brad. He couldn't very well drop the question yet. A week ago when he'd assigned "To Set Our House in Order," it had seemed like just another question. Now everything had changed.

Bert gave Parker a poke in the shoulder.

"Bert?" Brad said it loud. Bert flinched in his seat, jerked his hand away from Parker. "Well?"

Bert shrugged. Somehow he could make even a shrug look like an obscene gesture.

"There's his library," said Lori Campbell. "All those books about far-away places. That's what really interests him."

"Right." No problem there. They might get through it yet.

Pam Wheeler raised her hand. "Ewen's father used to read Greek. The only one in town who could. Ewen says he must have been a lonely man. Kind of a parallel there." She paused and added, "Takes one to know one."

"Right on, Pam." Not bad. They had most of it now. Enough, anyway. He could go on to the question about Vanessa.

Melinda Harper raised her hand. He glanced away, caught Bert whispering to Parker. "Bert!" The kid drew away. Melinda was waving her hand now, those behind her grinning at her. He couldn't very well ignore her. "Yes, Melinda."

"Ewen's father was a doctor because that's what *his* father was. Ewen too. They all had to follow in their father's footsteps. Had to. Every one of them, I bet." She sat back in her seat, nodding her head.

"Uh-huh," said Brad, glancing quickly at Parker. He was just in time to see Bert flick a finger against Parker's neck. "Stop that!"

"Lay off," said Parker, half-turning in his seat.

"He's stopping right now," said Brad. "Question six." He glanced down at his notebook. "What's Vanessa learning about life from the adults around her?" When he looked up again, Bert was coiling away from Parker and Parker was springing from his desk, its legs screeching on the floor.

Before he knew what was happening, Parker drove his fist into Bert's stomach, Bert landing a round-house right on Parker's shoulder at almost the same instant.

"Stop it!" Even as he shouted, he knew that neither boy would listen. Bert's glasses went spinning onto the floor, but Bert didn't pause. The two boys were standing toe to toe, hammering at each other.

The kids in the rows beside them were leaping out of their seats, falling out of their seats, backing off. Annette Federko, the girl closest to Bert, had a cast on her ankle. As Brad wheeled around his desk, he was aware of Annette stumbling, Annette screaming.

Before he could get to them, Bert gave a little feint with his left hand, striking Parker full in the face with his right. A spray of blood. Brad felt it on his arm as he reached between them, got a hand on each boy's chest, tried to hold them apart. Like trying to separate attack dogs. "Stop!" he said again, the word little more than a quick gasp. Parker knocked his arm away, stepped forward and hit Bert in the face. A trickle of blood from Bert's mouth. Brad got his hand on Parker's chest again and shoved. He felt Bert slide off his other hand, move beside him, reaching over his arm. Another spray of blood as Bert again struck Parker in the face. More screaming. It wasn't just Annette.

He couldn't keep them apart. Wasn't strong enough.

He spun away from Parker, got both palms on Bert's chest, lunged toward him, drove him backwards. Behind him, Parker was shoving at a desk, trying to get around him. He stepped into Parker's path, blocked him, felt him step back to go the other way. Brad wheeled around, grabbed Parker from the side, got both hands around his waist, his fingers clasped together, swung him away from Bert. He felt his feet slipping, staggered backwards, got a grip and yanked at Parker. "It's over," he said, and felt Parker hesitate. He backed toward the door, dragging Parker with him. He could see Bert standing in the middle of a twisted row of desks, wiping blood from his lower lip with his fist.

"Someone open the door," he called.

No one moved. Then Lori Campbell ran past him and pulled the door wide. When he heaved Parker outside, he saw Lori leaning away from them, squashing herself into the chalkboard, the fingers of her outstretched hand white against the open door. He could feel Parker coming with him now, following along. He hauled him to the foot of the stairs and let him go. "That's it. It's over." He wasn't sure if he said it or only thought it. Parker turned toward him, shaking his head, a dazed grin on his face. Blood poured from his nose.

Brad opened his mouth to speak. Took a deep breath instead.

"You're bleeding," he said finally. "Go up to the boys' washroom. Stuff some paper in your nose. I'll be up in a minute."

He watched Parker on the stairs, saw him start to wobble. "Wait," he said, but Parker got his hand on the railing and went quickly up to the main floor. Brad walked back into the room. Bert was half-sitting on the top of a desk, his glasses in his hand. His lip had stopped bleeding. The other kids were scattered in a semi-circle around him, closer to the walls than to Bert.

"You okay, Bert?"

Bert nodded his head, but didn't look at him.

"You better sit down." Brad took him by the shoulders, eased him onto the seat of the desk. "Stay there till I get back." All the kids were watching him. "The rest of you..."

He paused, looked at their faces, some of them strained, all of them serious. "I kind of think the class is over for today. How be the rest of you go up to the lounge?"

He turned toward the door, felt his right foot begin to slip. Looked down at a smear of blood beside his foot. He felt his hands start to shake. "Walter," he said, "get a caretaker, will you?"

Then he was out the door and running up the stairs after Parker. He thought he heard sobbing through the transom above the washroom door, but when he opened the door Parker turned on the tap, water gushing into the sink. Parker ducked his head under the tap and held it there. Brad hesitated beside him. "You're going to be okay," he said and laid a hand on Parker's shoulder. The flesh quivered beneath his touch like a horse's flank shaking off a fly. The water in the sink was pale pink. Parker let the water run on the back of his head, down his neck, then groped for the tap and turned it off. When he raised his head, Brad saw two red clumps of paper shoved into his nostrils. Brad reached for the towel dispenser, pulled out half a dozen sheets and handed them to Parker. After Parker had wiped his face and the back of his head, he stepped into the cubicle and tore off a strip of toilet paper. He pulled the bloody wads from his nostrils and replaced them with clean paper.

"Always was a bleeder," he said, his voice gruff. He backed out of the cubicle and started for the door. Wavered and stopped in front of Brad. His eyes were wet. "I'm in trouble," he said. "God, but I'm in trouble."

No, thought Brad, I'm the one in trouble. "I guess so," he said to Parker. "But nothing that can't be worked out."

"They're gonna boot me out of school."

"I don't think so." No, not you, Parker. Me.

He heard the washroom door open behind him, swung around to see Herb Schwitzer.

"Bell's going to go any minute," said Herb. "You two best get up to the office before the halls are full of kids." He held the door for them. "Other fella's there already."

Coming out the door, Brad saw some of the students from his class standing in the lounge, staring at them, looking worried. He knew they'd watch them all the way down the hall to the office. Brad was just pulling open the office door when the bell rang.

Bert was seated in front of Herb's desk, his head bowed, his hands clasped together between his knees. Brad took the seat beside him, making sure Parker wasn't next to Bert. Crazy maybe. A look at each of them and he knew he wouldn't be straining any more to keep them apart.

"This is unacceptable," said Herb. He was standing behind his desk, almost leaning over it, glaring at the three of them. Oh, hell, thought Brad, he's going to have to report this to Workman. Fighting in my class, that'll be the end of everything, I'll be gone for sure.

"Totally unacceptable," said Herb. "Fighting's bad enough in the yard. Worse in the hallways. We won't put up with it in the classroom. Hitting a teacher's intolerable."

"What?" said Brad.

"Look at you."

He noticed his shirt then. A splatter of blood on his right sleeve, dark stains on his chest.

"Oh," he said. "No. No one hit me. I think the blood came from Parker. Most of it."

Parker turned to him and nodded. The wads of tissue in his nostrils looked red and moist. "I'm a bleeder," he said, a nasal drone to his voice.

Herb seemed to recede from them. He was no longer leaning over his desk. "Good thing no one hit Mr. Cutler. You'd both be out of here. That understood?"

Brad glanced to each side. The boys seemed to be studying the grain in Herb's oak desk, but they were both nodding their heads. Bert looked briefly at Brad, then lowered his head again.

"I'm sorry," said Parker. "It never should've happened."

"You've got that right," said Herb. "Floor looked like a slaughter-house when the caretaker called me down. I want to hear what happened. Now."

The boys looked at each other, then at Brad. That was when the bell rang.

"Damn," said Brad. "I've got a class."

"I guess you have," said Herb. "Come back after school. I want to make sure I get the truth out of these two." He watched Brad stand up and start to leave. "There's a lab smock behind my door. You might want to cover up that shirt."

"Yeah. Thanks." He reached behind the door for the smock. Stiff, white fabric, a few acid burns on one sleeve. It would do. He pulled it on and headed for his classroom, wishing that he had some idea what he was supposed to teach this period.

Twenty-five

At three-thirty he took the long way up to the office, going by Sue's room at the other end of the basement, hoping she'd still be at her desk. She was there, a stack of papers piled in front of her, but she was staring at the window that three art students had painted on her back wall, the only window in her room. They'd do that for her – not for just anybody. Brad watched her a moment from the doorway. Absolutely motionless, as still as an artist's model – and just as beautiful.

He stepped into the room. "Hi," he said.

Her head jerked toward him, but she smiled. "Caught napping." She gave her head a little shake, dark brown hair bouncing on her collar, a shimmer of shadows. "A hundred miles away."

"Seventy kilometers sounds better."

"Pardon."

"Been a rough day. I need to get out of town. You wouldn't want to drive down to Regina for a movie this evening?"

"No," she said, but she was giving him that smile, the one that could defrost a fridge in seconds flat. "I *would* want to."

"Great." He knew he was grinning like a fool. He'd better say something more. "There'll be lots of choices at the Southland. Pick you up at eight." He backed toward the door. "Got to run. Little appointment with Herb."

The smile dropped from her face. "Oh, Brad," she said. "The fight. The kids were talking about it when I came down to class. You're okay?"

"Fine."

"You sure?"

"Sure."

"Suspended," said Herb, "both of them. Unless you've got something to change the picture. I talked to some of the other kids from your class. Asked why no one helped you get them apart."

"They were swinging hard. A lot of wild punches."

"Yeah, kids said they were scared. Hell, Annette Federko was terrified. Thought she might break her other leg, I guess. Well, now, couple things to check. Parker threw the first punch?"

"Yeah. He was —"

"Bert bugging the hell out of him?"

"Yes. I'm not sure what was going on there."

"Bert's still pissed about Parker quitting football. Let himself get carried away. Told him he was quitting the play too, he was nothing but an effing quitter." Herb paused, cleared his throat. "Felt sorry for Parker. Kid probably wouldn't have lashed out weren't for problems with his old man. Pretty worked up."

"Yeah, but I think there was something more going on too."

"They lying?"

"No. Sounds like you got the straight goods. A bit more to the situation though."

"Tell me."

"We were doing a Margaret Laurence story, taking up the questions. Part of it's about an unhappy man – seems he became a doctor mainly because his father was a doctor before him. We were discussing that about the time Bert started yammering at Parker. Probably sent his stress level over the top."

"I bet it did. Doesn't change things though." Herb was suddenly grinning at him, speaking in his best redneck voice: "You gonna teach them there Canadjun writers you gotta expect trouble, eh fella?"

Brad smiled. Briefly. He didn't feel like smiling.

"Go ahead," said Herb. "I know you've got a question."

"How long are they suspended for?"

"Three days. Don't worry. Parker'll be back on Wednesday just in time for your play."

"The suspension begins tomorrow morning?"

"Yeah," said Herb, a growl in his voice. "Friday, Monday, Tuesday."

Brad wondered if he should say it. "We're supposed to be rehearsing in a few minutes."

"Okay, okay. Suspension starts tomorrow. He can go to rehearsal."

Might as well try for one more. "There's dress rehearsal Tuesday." He quickly added, "It's after school. Tuesday night."

"You never told me that, understand?" said Herb. "Now get the hell out of here."

"Thanks. It'll mean a lot to Parker."

"Go."

When Brad went down to the gym, he saw Parker seated by himself, his legs dangling over the front of the stage, his fingers drumming on his knees. The kid was no Huck Finn, but right now he looked as if he might be on a raft, his feet trailing in the water, his eyes on the river, hoping it would wash his cares away.

The other kids were sitting quietly on the set furniture, waiting for him. They all looked as ill at ease as Parker. When he saw Brad coming, Parker stood up.

"Let's do it," he said.

Yeah, thought Brad, get right into something safe. "Scene two was a bit rough last time. Let's start with it."

They immediately took their places for the scene where the aspiring actors prepared for the arrival of Mr. Kenny, the famous Broadway director. They seemed tight at first, standing awkwardly in their places, but soon relaxed as they began to move and speak. Parker fell into character at once, his voice firm, snapping orders as he led the others through the start of Mr. Kenny's play.

Probably relieved, thought Brad. A lot easier being Norman right now.

By the time the cops had discovered the stage littered with dead bodies, threatening to have them all arrested, Mr. Kenny included – and outraged because of it – Brad found himself laughing out loud.

"Much better," he said when they were done. "The timing's really working now. Especially the interruptions and the surprise entrances. Dress rehearsal at six-thirty Tuesday. We've got the gym the whole night. That includes you too, Parker."

The boy nodded, then vaulted off the stage and headed for the gym door.

"Hold on a second, Parker." Brad jumped down and caught him halfway across the floor. The house lights were off, and he couldn't read Parker's expression in the shadows. "Your nose looked fine on stage. You going to be okay?"

"Sure." Parker turned toward the door.

"Parker."

"Yeah."

"You want me to phone your dad?"

"Mr. Schwitzer already phoned him." Parker began walking toward the door.

"He handle it okay?"

"Schwitzer?"

"Your dad."

"I don't know. Guess so. I'll find out on Wednesday."

Brad was beside him now. He looked at his face, wondering if his nose was beginning to bleed again. No, it was just a red glow from the Exit sign above the door.

"Wednesday? You won't see him till then?" He knew what it was like to be so furious with your old man you could hardly stand to look at him.

"Better that way."

"Parker, I don't know about this." He wasn't sure what to say. The kid couldn't hide from his father that long. "I think you need to go home, try to talk with your dad. Work things out." That wasn't exactly what he wanted to say, but he couldn't very well tell him not to do anything crazy.

"Wednesday. Then we'll talk."

"Parker, this isn't —"

"I'm not going home till then." Parker's voice was loud, echoing in the empty gym.

"Where're you going to stay?"

"It's taken care of."

"You can't be sleeping in the park."

Parker looked startled. "Sleeping over at Walter's," he said. "Now."

"You're sure about that?"

"No sweat. Your play's gonna come off just fine."

"Forget the bloody play. It's you I'm worried about."

Parker stepped past him and pulled the door open. "Get off my case, will you?" Then he was out the door, yanking it shut behind him.

She was whistling, the song he'd heard before, "Wood River." They were driving back to town.

"You sure like that song," he said, his eyes on the highway.

"Uh-huh. Always gives me a lift."

"You need one?" he asked. "I thought it was a good show."

She was leaning against the car door, half-turned in her seat, looking at him. "The show – or Julia Roberts?"

"She was okay too."

The car bucked as they hit rough pavement. Brad glanced into the rear view mirror, then pulled into the left-hand lane.

"I talk you into a show you didn't want to see?" he asked.

"No. It was as good as any other."

"You're not a Julia Roberts fan?"

"You've got that right."

They were beyond the broken pavement and he switched lanes again. She was still leaning against the door.

"Let me guess. You didn't like Pretty Woman."

"Hollywood crap. Hooker falls for a rich, handsome john and he carts her off to live happily ever after." She was sitting up now, her back rigid, her eyes bright in the gleam of the dash lights. "Too many kids believe that crap." She sat back against the door.

Brad glanced at her. Noticed the grin on her face.

"You knew what was coming," she said, "didn't you?"

"Oh, I thought you might say something like that."

"Am I that transparent?"

"Not at all. Almost a year together in the staffroom. I know you pretty well."

They were on new pavement now, the hum of the tires deepening.

"You think so?" She bent away from the door and reached toward him, poking his arm with her index finger. "And how well do I know you? You love teaching, your mom got you interested in books, you have some problems with your father. That's about it."

He checked the rear-view mirror, glancing quickly at her.

"The two of us," he said, "we get along fine – now they're in Victoria."

"See what I mean?"

"No. I'm serious. Last Christmas, I went skiing on the way home, sure, but I spent some time with them first, touring around the island. We were doing just fine. Well, except once, when he got started about the farm. He ran down pretty quick though. Now that it's gone, there's nothing new for him to get mad at me about."

"The farm was the problem?"

"In spades. It's kind of weird, though: I always loved the countryside; I just couldn't stand farming. Wasn't cut out for it, either – I knew it by the time I started high school. Dad couldn't handle the idea that there wasn't going to be a fourth generation Cutler on the home place."

"So you fought about it?"

"All the time." He wondered if he should tell her. Didn't want to be melodramatic about it. "This once, fall of grade nine it was, he was really on my back a lot, telling me grade ten was plenty, two more years and I'd be quitting school for good, time then to shoulder a man's load – that was his term – he wanted me to start taking over the farm. So I ran away."

"Really?"

He turned his head toward her, saw by the light of an on-coming car that her eyes were wide. "You better believe it," he said. "I grabbed my sleeping bag, a canteen of water, a loaf of bread, half a dozen cans of beans and headed for the river." He snorted. "Like Huck Finn running from his Pap. Only my old man never beat me, never even drank. I guess I read the book one too many times. Jack, a friend of mine, and I had built this raft. Had it tied up in the shallows where the river swung into the ravine back behind the barn. Nighttime when I took off, but a full moon shining, no problem picking my way down the ravine trail, and then through the bush I see this dark square that I know is the raft, and beyond it, the river, covered in mist."

Yes, mist rising in the cool air, like something breathing, looked like a pale ghost lying there, a little stirring of ripples where it shook out the sheet before it settled down and fell asleep. He could still see it.

"I untied the raft, pushed off right away. Didn't know where the hell I was going – but I was going, that was all that mattered. Drifting at night so my old man wouldn't spot me and drag me home." He turned his head again, and grinned at Sue. "Second night out, I was floating along, lying on my back, looking up at all those stars, seemed like they were way brighter than usual, lower too, hanging there just for me." He shook his head. "I fell asleep and ran aground. River so shallow there at the bend, nothing but sand bars and mud, I was stuck. Couldn't get near the main channel. Huh, the old man didn't have to drag me home. I walked out to the grid road myself, guy from town gave me a lift back."

"Your parents must've been worried."

"I guess they were," he said. "Didn't think about it then though. My dad was hopping mad, I'll tell you, but Mom got him quieted down. He even shut up for a while after that about my quitting school. Till I hit grade ten anyway. Guess I was lucky she was there." And now he was thinking of Parker again.

"Nothing like a woman to smooth the rough spots," said Sue. She leaned toward him in the seat, laid her hand on his where it rested on the steering wheel. "Thanks," she said. "I think I already know you better."

"Could be. But *I'd* like to know *you* better." Forget about the kid, enjoy his time with her.

He eased his foot off the accelerator and looked at her. A long look.

"Hey," she said, "I never sleep with a guy on the first date."

"Not what I meant." He coughed, glanced in the rear view mirror, headlights coming fast behind him, looked across at her, her mouth crinkled in amusement. Sure, playing the mouthy broad, putting him on. As usual.

"What I think," he said, "is we better go out again tomorrow night."

The next morning he was whistling as he entered the staffroom. He glanced at Vic filling his mug from the coffee urn. No need for that today, he thought, already felt as if he could lick the world.

"I don't know," said Vic as he walked to the table where the guys were seated. "Some days I need an extra cup just to get me started."

"Should expect that," said Maurie. "Comes from being the oldest guy on staff."

Phil nodded his head. "Maybe Burton will donate her Geritol."

Brad looked at Sue in the corner of the room, a smile breaking over her face. Man, she was pretty. "Geritol?" he asked.

"Last year," said Phil, "on her birthday, we gave her a chocolate cake and a bottle of Geritol. Had it wrapped in the most expensive paper. She figured she was getting Chanel Number Five."

Sue laughed. "You guys, if you ever bought a woman real perfume, you'd know it doesn't come in clunky bottles weighing half a pound."

"Come on, Burton," said Phil. "We had you going – thirty candles and a spray of Geritol."

What the – she was thirty-one now? Eight years, Brad thought, she's eight years older than me. That wasn't possible, was it? Two or three, he'd guessed, maybe four. But eight?

Hell, it didn't matter anyway.

Sue was watching him, her smile slowly fading.

He hoped she hadn't seen surprise on his face. No, the joke was over. That was all it was, nothing more to smile about.

He was walking the aisles, giving his students a prod here and there, keeping them at work creating narrative incidents about Grandpa from "The Great Electrical Revolution." There'd been lots of laughter when he'd read the story to them – they'd liked Mitchell's flamboyant Grandpa – but it was Friday afternoon and now they just wanted the period to end.

Lori Campbell was writing a scene between Grandpa and his wife. Brad paused beside her desk and read a few lines. He laid his finger next to a line of dialogue that began, "By the holy nose-hairs of Noah!"

"Sounds like Grandpa, all right," he said.

When he got to Walter Buchko's desk, he read a description of Grandpa pulling a box over his head so that he could make it across an empty lot without an onslaught of agoraphobia.

"Good stuff, Walter." He leaned over and whispered in his ear. "Must've been tough getting up this morning, eh? Bet you and Parker talked half the night."

Walter's head popped up, almost clipping him on the jaw. "What?"

"Isn't Parker staying at your place?"

"Sure. Arnie too. For the week-end. We're setting up the tent-trailer in the driveway."

"He wasn't there last night?"

"No. But he will be tonight."

"What bridge was he under, Walter?" His voice was louder than it should be. He noticed some of the students raising their heads to look at him.

"The one in Crescent Park." Walter remembered to whisper, but Brad wondered how many others had heard him.

"I don't do it the second date either," she said, laughing. They were parked in front of her bungalow. After Friday evening in Regina, browsing in the Book and Briarpatch, dessert in their cappuccino bar, drinks at The Keg.

"You bring it up a lot," he said. "Probably spend way too much time thinking about it."

"Touché."

"It's your brain I'm after." He gazed at her forehead, then lowered his eyes. "Course, your body's okay too."

"Thanks." She wasn't smiling. "It isn't Kelly's."

"Hey. That was a compliment." He wondered, was this the age difference getting in the way?

"Sorry. I wasn't sure."

"A compliment." It shouldn't bother her – not when he could handle it.

"Hard to know what to expect," she said, "from a guy who takes you out to a book store. Nobody's ever done that before."

"I thought you liked books."

"I do."

"Moi aussi. Two of my favorite things the same night."

"Two."

"Oh, yes."

At her door, he took her in his arms and kissed her, felt the compelling warmth of firm lips, no thought of breathing for an instant there while she kissed him back, her hands on his shoulders to hold him close. When she didn't ask him in, he was disappointed – but kind of relieved too. He wanted to check on Parker.

As soon as he got back to the car, he fished into his wallet for the piece of paper on which he'd jotted Walter's address. He held the door open and read it by the overhead light. 1120-11th Avenue.

He drove off Main, and along Oxford, cruising past the

big homes standing solid in the shadows of huge pine trees.
A quiet night. Only a few cars moving. A jog at 9th Avenue,
then along Carleton to 11th. He paused at the stop sign long
enough to roll down his window before turning the corner.
He drove slowly up 11th, saw the tent-trailer in the driveway,
a light shining dimly behind the canvas, shadows moving on
the walls. As he pulled abreast, he could hear low music
drifting across the street. He didn't recognize the song.
Probably something kids would like, he thought. Good. It
was okay then. Everything was okay. Parker was there,
Walter hadn't been stringing him along.

Saturday night, she invited him in. An older house, a slab
bungalow, and she owned it, too, hardwood floors shining from the ceiling light, book cases on one wall, a bay window on another. Oil paintings on both sides of the window,
one a prairie scene, a thin line of land at the foot of the picture, a huge sky heaving with clouds, you could almost hear
the wind howl. A dusky night club in the other painting, a
shining trumpet blown by a black man with swollen cheeks,
smoke hanging in the air, the rest of the band in shadow, but
the light around the trumpet shimmered, seemed to vibrate
with music.

"These are wonderful," he said. As good as his Group of
Seven reproductions – and these were originals.

"I think so too. They're presents." She laughed. "From me
to me. A couple years ago in June I decided to reward myself,
to celebrate getting all my finals marked. What better way,
eh? I'm thinking about a McLaughlin this year."

"Who?"

"Grant McLaughlin. He's a local artist. Does these clay

sculptures about a foot high. He's got a twisted sense of humour. The one I like has William Shakespeare in a hot tub out on a sheet of ice. Shakespeare's looking glum, but he's fishing through the ice, a line tied around his toe, and working on a manuscript, *Love's Labour Lost.*" She nodded towards an empty shelf on the bookcase. "I've got a space reserved for it."

"Sounds interesting," said Brad. He walked to the bookcase, surveyed the shelf at eye level. Half a dozen Alice Munros, what looked like the complete works of Graham Greene, Jane Austen's novels too, and a boxed set of George Orwell's non-fiction, five volumes with grey images from period photographs decorating their spines.

"You're an Orwell fan?" he asked.

She nodded her head. "Any time the marking piles up and I get to thinking life is tough, I just read a few pages from *Down and Out in Paris and London.* Orwell slaving in those hot Parisian kitchens, bad as working in an oven. It's the perfect cure for feeling sorry for yourself." She had followed him to the bookcase, but now she stepped away. "There's something else you ought to see." She led him to the hall and pointed.

A quilted wall hanging, a mass of gorgeous colours, shelves of books, he saw, but the top row was sky, rich blue fabrics on the covers, the bright light of morning, the darkness of a storm rolling in. On another row the books were full of branches, a dozen different kinds. Below them, vegetables and fruit, a trail of pea pods, carrots in a cluster, berries bright as blood. The bottom shelf had scenes of childhood on the books, stuffed animals, frogs on lily pads – kiss-me frogs with crowns, a collector's jar of lady bugs, laughing kids at play.

"This is marvellous," he said.

"It really is. But I didn't invite you here to look at art." She was smiling at him, a strange gleam in her eye. "You want to see the bedroom now or later?"

Man, she didn't fool around. "Now," he said, trying to hold his voice steady, "now would be nice."

She was rolling in his arms, her breath, his breath hot in his throat. He felt her arc against him, felt the shock, the charge running deep inside. "Sue," he said, "Sue."

"What?"

He caught his breath. Excitement like he'd never known, and yet it seemed so natural – and utterly amazing too. "Didn't know it'd be like this."

She pulled away from him, hoisting herself on one elbow, studying him. He could see her luminous smile in the darkness. "I knew," she said. "You might've asked me."

He leaned toward her, kissed her again, her tongue connecting with his own.

She pulled away once more, turned over, settled onto her back, gazing at the ceiling. He heard a chuckle, low and sexy.

"What is it?"

"I could've told you months ago."

He reached toward her, laid the palm of his hand on her cheek, began to trace the shape of her lips with his index finger. Felt them open.

"Months ago," she said. "I was dropping hints all the time. Afraid everyone would know. Everyone but you."

"Oh, come on now."

He felt her roll toward him, press hard against him. "Mm," she said, "good idea. Right now."

Monday would be the same as usual, except that everything was different now. A class, a study room, another class to get through in the morning, up the stairs for every break and down again, the whole noon hour with the staffroom full of people, other people, two classes in the afternoon, stacks of tests to mark after school. He'd never be able to concentrate, not when all he wanted was to be with her, alone with her. Then the evening flying by.

He couldn't wait till Monday.

She was whistling again, the sound almost lost in the hum of tires on pavement.

"You only whistle if you're sad?" he asked.

"If I'm sad." She looked at him and smiled. "If I'm happy."

When he'd phoned to ask her out Sunday after supper, she'd seemed pleased, but on the way to Regina, he'd felt tension in the car, the conversation strained the way it never was with her. He'd wondered about the wisdom of another trip out of town – it might give her the wrong idea – but now, coming home after the show, she seemed fine.

When they dipped toward the bridge a mile outside of town, she leaned toward him and said, "Look at that moon. You could drive without your lights." Her shoulder was warm against his. "Want to take the bypass, stop for a bite at the All-Nighter?"

He kept his eyes on the road, the first turn-off into town coming up on the left. The All-Nighter was where the guys from work hung out. He didn't want to be running into them, to have them on his back again. Wasn't sure how to put it. "Kind of late," he said. "Still got some things to do for tomorrow." He felt her pull away from his shoulder.

"You wanted to go for coffee in Regina. It would've made us just as late."

"That was an hour ago. I'm kind of tired. The drive, I guess." He flipped on the left-turn signal, listened to its blink, blink, blink. Thought he heard her take a breath beside him.

"In town you're tired."

"What?" He was off the highway now, slowing as the car pulled beneath the overpass.

"Never mind."

He drove up the slope and turned into town.

"We could drive around a while if you want."

"Or park," she said, the last word ringing through the dark car like a slap.

"That wasn't what I meant."

"It doesn't matter, Brad. Not a bit." Her words struck like shards of rock.

"Look. I'm sorry I'm tired." Shit, he couldn't very well tell her.

"Forget it," she said. "I've got you figured out."

"What?" They were on Athabasca now, her face visible for an instant in the glow of the first streetlight, her expression a mix of anger and something else – humiliation maybe. "What are you talking about?"

Shadow again, and he couldn't see her face.

"I'm good enough for strangers, eh?"

"What – I'm tired is all – still got a pile of work to do."

"Come off it, Brad. You don't want to be seen with me."

"What do you mean?"

"You know damned well what I mean."

"Bullshit I do."

"The only bullshit here is coming straight out of your mouth. You know it too."

"What the hell?" He was losing it. "I don't even know what you're talk –"

"Enough, Brad. I'm too old for this kind of shit."

"Too old is right! Too old to talk sense." He knew he was screwing up, but he was mad – he couldn't stop himself. "Too old for me, that's for damned sure."

She didn't answer him at first. When she did speak, her voice was surprisingly calm. "Drive me home, will you? Right now. It's obviously way past your bedtime."

On Monday morning he decided to skip breakfast and get to work early.

He had driven her home last night in silence, furious with her for cutting him down, raging at himself, knowing he had to apologize, planning to say something when they got to her place, but she opened the door and was stepping out before the car rolled to a stop. He drove quickly home afterwards and phoned her, told her he was sorry, but she said she didn't want to talk, if he couldn't stand to be seen with her in town, there was nothing left to talk about. She hung up at once.

He'd been wrong – sure, he knew it too – he should have levelled with her right away, but he couldn't very well tell her he was afraid of what the guys would say. God, and then he'd lost his temper, but she kept jabbing at him, hell, yeah, jabbing at him like he was just a kid. Till she pushed him into it. Then he'd called her old, and there was no way to get that one back.

He might catch her now in the staffroom before the others arrived.

Driving toward the school, he decided to turn down 11th Avenue. He noticed immediately that the tent-trailer was gone. When he passed the house, he saw the trailer folded down at the head of the driveway. Damn. He wanted to talk to Sue, but he knew he'd better get down to Crescent Park.

When he went past the school, he slowed the car and looked to see if her Nissan was in the parking lot, but the caragana hedges were fully leafed out, blocking his view. He gunned the motor then, wanting to get back to school as soon as he could. He left his car beside the public library and took the winding path along the creek. Two white swans watched with imperial disdain as he walked by. Beneath them, the water was muddy-coloured and dotted with bits of fluff from the cottonwood trees. He stared up at the wooden bridge. It looked as if it might once have had a redwood stain, but it was faded now, though not yet the grey of prairie fence posts. Before he got to the bridge, he cut up the hill. The grass was long and wet with dew; it needed mowing. A lilac bush at the top of the hill kept him from seeing what was beneath the bridge. He stepped around the bush, looked over the cross-hatch of wooden beams. No one there. The perfume of lilacs heavy in the air. Then he noticed the grass beneath the bridge where nothing grew. Long grass torn from the ground and piled in a narrow pad no longer than a man's body. Piled and flattened.

He placed the palm of his hand on the grass and immediately felt foolish. Of course, it wouldn't feel warm to the touch. He hurried to the top of the bridge and walked part way across it. Beneath him the creek curved away into a semicircle. From this height it seemed to hold the sky in its still waters, looking almost blue. He gazed downstream at a sharper bend in the creek where his attention was caught by a small branch, hardly more than a twig really, drifting beneath the bank, although there didn't seem to be much current – perhaps the breeze that stirred the water was pushing it along. At the bend the water was shallow, a ridge of mud stretching down from the bank, and the branch turned sluggishly and stopped moving, stuck in the mud. For a long time he stared at the motionless branch.

He looked away then, studying the paved walks beside the creek, the wide lawns, the dirt paths through the grass, the shadows beneath the trees, gazing back towards the library, across the park toward the swimming pool. Nothing moving anywhere.

She was sitting in an easy chair against the wall, the chair beside her empty. Ten or twelve teachers already in the room. He went to the urn and got himself a cup of coffee. Took a quick sip. Realized he was hungry. Stupid, skipping breakfast. Still, worrying about Sue – and now, Parker – he didn't think he could've eaten anyway.

He walked to the big table and pulled out a chair next to Dutch. He didn't want her getting up the minute he sat down beside her.

"The last day of classes," said Dutch, "if you get tenure your first year, the Board gives you a summer ham."

"Sure," said Brad, "I go for that, next thing you'll sell me the Fourth Avenue Bridge." Tenure, he thought, fat chance of that. He'd be finished as soon as Workman got back and heard from Dr. Stone. But the man had looked after Phil. Maybe there was still some hope.

"Nobody who fell for the turkey ever goes for the ham," said Vic. He studied Brad. "Don't look so bloody serious. Another year and they'll give you tenure."

"I wish."

"Long as nobody gets murdered in your room," said Dutch.

Brad glared at him. "Shove it," he said.

"Sorry. Didn't mean the fight." Dutch looked hurt. "I was joking – thinking of your *Hamlet* duel."

"Oh, okay. Sorry."

Maurie Pack was watching Brad. "Tenure didn't do a hell of a lot for Rutledge," said Maurie, "now did it?"

"What do you mean?" asked Vic. "Better wages in Alberta, his choice to go to Calgary."

"Crap! That was Rutledge's story. Saving face was all, so we wouldn't know Workman fired him."

My God, thought Brad, if Workman fired Rutledge, what chance was there for him?

"Workman couldn't fire him," said Vic.

"Same thing as being fired. Gave him such a lousy timetable he had to quit."

"You don't know –"

"Took half his art classes away. Didn't give him any choice."

Brad looked from one man to the other, both of them angry, their jaws thrust forward like mirror images of one another. Tension filling the room. He could feel it in his chest, his heart beginning to race. They'd gotten rid of Rutledge. The man was a legend – with tenure too – and he was finished, done for, just like that. Was there any hope for Brad, a first year teacher? No, he was as good as gone.

Vic slumped back in his chair. "I didn't know that," he said.

"Should've."

"Oh, to hell with Rutledge, and you too!" Vic swung his head away from Maurie. "Listen. Don't be worrying about tenure. They maybe do some dumb things in the office. They're not crazy."

When Brad turned to Vic, he caught Sue watching him,

but she quickly looked away. "Hope so," he said, but he figured Vic was just trying to make him feel better. Workman would love to get rid of him. He glanced at Sue who seemed to be studying her coffee cup. When Workman was done with him, that would be it, he'd never have a chance to set things right with her. She was motionless, gazing at her cup.

No, he couldn't let it end this way; he'd try again after school.

Might as well go down to his room now, he thought. See if he could get something done there; got to finish off the rest of the year somehow. Maybe Walter'd come by with news of Parker.

That afternoon he waited ten minutes after the final bell for the halls to empty out.

When he came into her room, she was just rising from her desk.

"Can I see you a minute?"

She paused, but she didn't sit back down. "I've got some things to copy." She picked up a stack of papers from her desk.

"I need to talk," he said.

"I need to get some copies made."

"You could listen a minute. I need to explain something."

She was almost past him when she stopped. If he reached out, he could touch her on the shoulder.

"Forget it, Brad." He thought for a second her eyes were damp, but she looked steadily at him and he knew he was wrong. "You're ashamed to be seen with me – what's the point?"

"That isn't it. It was just all the crap I had to take – last fall, I mean, it got me all screwed up. I was wrong – I'm sorry."

"No. You're absolutely right. It's not a good idea. On the

same staff, it never is. Too many complications. It's just not worth the trouble."

"I think it is."

"For you it's not."

"No, Sue."

"To hell with you," she said. "I'm not spending my weekends hiding in Regina. We'd be no better off than Phil Simpson."

She turned toward the door, but he stepped in front of her. She didn't raise her head to look at him, but kept moving, side-stepping away from him.

"Find someone else," she said, her voice harsh. "A kid maybe – someone young enough for you."

He stepped back. When she passed him at the door, she didn't look at him. Wouldn't look at him. He could only guess how much he'd hurt her.

It was the age thing, wasn't it, and he still hadn't leveled with her.

Twenty-six

He waited till it was almost dark that night before he drove down to Crescent Park. Damn, maybe he should just camp out under a bridge himself. He was in no better shape than Parker.

To hell with her, he thought.

That was what she'd said to him, of course, but he knew *he* didn't mean it. Though *she* did. Or was she just hurt?

The trouble was she could read him like a book. She knew he was running scared, didn't want the bastards on his back again. Or Workman telling him what he couldn't do. Wanting to be with her all the time for sure – as long as no one knew. No, as long as the guys didn't know. Well, forget about them, write them off – who needed them anyway? He liked them though, some of the time. Most of the time. Except for Maurie Pack. And Workman, yeah, he'd always be there, giving orders, saying no.

What the hell was he supposed to do?

Then there was the age thing, hanging there in the back of his mind, nagging away. Could it really work when she was so much older? Was he smart enough to make it work? Was that what she was thinking too?

Forget about it. Parker was the one who ought to have him worried.

He left the car by the west entrance to the park and walked directly toward the bridge, stepping off the paved walkway and down onto the lawn, picking his way slowly around the bushes. He didn't want a twig snapping under his foot. The lilacs were dark against the bridge and the dusky sky, the scent strong. He stepped carefully around the bush and underneath the bridge, peering into the shadows beyond the wooden beams.

It was dark here, but he could still make out the bare dirt, the torn grass spread on the ground.

Was there any point in waiting?

He stepped over a beam, sat down on the grass, a piece of gravel poking him in the left buttock. The grass wasn't much of a cushion. He closed his eyes and lay back. Wiggled his hips. Better than nothing, he guessed, better than the hard ground. He could hear a steady hum of cars a block away on Main Street, an occasional twittering of birds in the trees around him. Something splashed in the creek. He opened his eyes and looked up. A line of sky glowing faintly between the boards above him. Not much protection here if it should rain. He tilted his head, looking farther up, saw spaces repeating themselves at regular intervals between the boards. Something dark at the end of the bridge. He rolled over, hunched to his knees, and crept into the darkness. Reached out. Felt cloth beneath his hand, cloth jammed into the space above a bridge support. He knew it was a sleeping bag before he pulled it out.

Must be coming back. Lord, I hope he is. Parker's a bright kid, too bright to do something stupid. He's got to be.

When he went to replace the sleeping bag, he felt

something stiff beneath a fold of cloth. None of his business really, but he pulled it out anyway. The script of their play. That was a good sign, had to be a good sign.

He stuffed the script back, set the sleeping bag above the beam and sat down to wait. Maneuvered his back against another beam and got himself comfortable. More or less.

Dr. Stone was a prick, all right, but the kid would have to go back home eventually, try to work something out. Find some way to survive in his father's shadow. Stone had one thing right though. The kid was sharp enough for med school. No doubt about that. Hell, maybe some day he'd think about it, even want to go to med school.

Some day, maybe, not today.

He crossed his arms over his chest and felt goose bumps above his elbows. The air was cooling off. Even in June the nights could be chilly.

He looked down the hill at the creek. It was dark under the bridge, but twenty yards to the south there was a warm glow beneath a park light. In that halo of light the paved walk had a sheen like oil. Beside it the grass looked as if it had been painted green. Where the light fell on the water, he could just make out the small branch stuck in the shallows.

It was quite a while before he wondered what time it was. Here, under the bridge, it was too dark to see his watch. Where the hell was Parker? He waited, the wooden beam hard against his back, his buttocks sore from the ground beneath. He considered pulling out the sleeping bag and folding it up for a cushion. No, it wouldn't hurt him to sit and take it for a while. He probably had it coming.

What a jerk he'd been, shooting off his mouth like that, screwing up with Sue. But eight years was more than just a bit; it took some getting used to.

What about her? She knew how old she was. How old he was.

Maybe it was just as tough for her, going with a younger guy. Yes, it probably was. Imagine her discomfort, wondering if she should take a chance on him, arguing about it with herself, maybe, trying to get used to it, deciding it's worth any trouble it might cause, and then the guy shoots off his mouth and proves how wrong she is.

For a long time he stared at the black creek below him.

He closed his eyes then, sat motionless, thinking that he might doze off, he was tired enough, the hum of cars a lullaby, distant and soothing, but something was floating before him, something round and shadowy, wavering, sliding into focus, dark eye sockets staring from the empty face of Angela Maddox. His head jerked up, bounced off the beam behind him.

Must've dozed off. He braced himself against the beam, stared hard at the park light shining through the trees. Have to stay awake.

When his butt was numb, he stood up, felt as if his bones were creaking, stiffness in his back and legs. He stood motionless, listening. Occasional traffic on Main Street, but the park was quiet. He stepped out from under the bridge and walked across the lawn toward the light, his left hand held out before him. When he could read his watch, he stopped. Eleven-ten. He'd give it fifteen minutes more.

It was after midnight when he finally drove home, wondering if Parker had found another bed that night. Praying it was just a bed he'd found. Brad wasn't going to think of Angela Maddox trying to solve her problems on the end of a rope. No, that was crazy, Parker didn't have that kind of problem, he was better off than she was, he had to be.

"Not to worry," he said. "It wasn't a disaster. Dress rehearsals never go well. Nobody expects them to." Yeah, as if he'd ever been at one before. Say something helpful. He'd been so relieved when Parker had walked onstage in costume, he had trouble getting into the play at first, couldn't focus on their practice. He hardly knew what to say.

"Some pauses we could do without, two late cues on the lights, one slow entrance. And a couple of dropped lines – which nobody would ever notice. Not bad, I'd say. You all get into character; you're doing a good job of reacting – really listening to everything that's said. Problem is you've said your lines so much, you've forgotten this is a comedy. It is, and don't worry – people are going to laugh in the right places. One other thing, then you can go backstage and take off the makeup. One thing you are lacking – the only thing – is an audience. We get that tomorrow afternoon."

They looked more relaxed now, a few of them smiling as they got up from the places they'd taken at the front of the stage when he'd called, "Curtain."

"Wait a minute. I was wrong," he said. "One other thing you need to know. We'll put in an extra row of chairs at the back of the gym. Any of your parents want to come, there'll be a place for them. Tell them they won't have to sit in with all the kids."

Later, he caught Parker coming out of the change room and walked with him toward the door.

"Good job, tonight," he said. "I think you're going to love working in front of an audience."

"Hope so."

"Parker, I have to ask you something."

Parker stopped walking. "Sure," he said, "go ahead."

"Where did you sleep last night?"

"In bed. What do you mean?"

"Parker!"

"What?"

"I went down to Crescent Park last night." Parker looked straight at him, his eyes steady in the glare of the fluorescent lights that lit the hall. "Under the bridge, there was a sleeping bag shoved in between the beams. I think it was yours."

"Maybe it was. So what?"

"You use it last night?"

"After I got tired of hanging out – yeah."

"You shouldn't be sleeping in the park. No telling who could come along."

"I can take care of myself."

Brad looked at the boy, feet firmly planted, legs apart, broad shoulders facing him, muscled arms hanging tense by his sides. Like a gunfighter in a western movie, poised to draw. Yeah, probably could take care of himself.

An adult body, sure, but he was still a kid.

"You better go home."

"Not yet."

"Your father must be worried sick. You talked to him lately?"

"What the hell for? All I'm s'posed to do is listen."

"Parker."

"I'll phone him. Okay? I'm going home tomorrow night anyway."

"That's good to hear." Brad paused, relieved, something shifting in his belly. Decided to suggest it anyway. "Why not go home tonight?"

"Nope. After the play. Not gonna fight about it any more."

Brad studied the boy's face, his eyes dark, intense, his jaw thrust out like someone daring a foe to punch him in the face. "Okay," said Brad. "You better come home with me."

Parker shook his head. "Now that would start some talk. Not a good idea, Mr. C." He smiled at Brad, reached toward him and tapped his shoulder, like a parent with a child. "One more night is all. I could do it standing on my head. Then I'm back at school, we do the play, and I go home. Don't worry. My old man and me, we'll work things out."

Brad watched him walk away, shoving the glass door wide, watched him through the door as he moved beyond the reach of the school lights and disappeared in darkness.

Be nice for a change if someone could work something out.

"We get close to the end of the year," said Vic Pendleton, "there's more interruptions than classes."

"Thank God for that," said Maurie Pack. "Kids don't feel like working. Me neither."

"Yeah," said Bruce Winslow, "but they work some of the time."

"Pot calling the kettle black."

"If I'm the pot," said Bruce, "the kettle's a hell of a lot blacker."

"I got a course to finish," said Vic. He turned to Brad. "This play going to be worth our while?"

"Hope so," said Brad. "Think so." He didn't feel like arguing. "A one-act play. It won't be long."

"Hate losing time this close to finals," said Vic.

"They're shortening both classes. Twenty minutes from each one. That's all you'll lose – then we're off to the gym." He noticed Sue in her usual chair. She didn't seem to be listening.

"Better than losing half your kids to the track meet," said Myrna Belsey. "No offence, Dutch. What can you do with so many gone the same day?"

"Anyhow, it sure beats another pitch on drunk driving," said Maurie.

"That wasn't exactly a beer commercial," said Rita Croft. "They're trying to prevent it. Besides, the kids enjoyed it."

"Right," said Maurie. "They would've clapped too, but the noise was hard on their hang-overs."

"Sounding bitter, aren't we?" said Phil. As usual, right on target with Maurie. Same as always, Brad thought, they'd never guess he was gay.

Maurie shrugged and said no more.

"Don't you worry, Brad," said Myrna. "We're looking forward to your play."

"Some of us," said Phil. Then he grinned at Brad. "You want to hear some real grousing, all you have to do is threaten to cancel."

When the house lights went down, Brad was standing in front of the set. If the play was really good, if enough people told Workman how good it was, maybe, just maybe.... He waited till the spotlight hit the curtains, pulled them apart and stepped out before the audience, blinking, trying to focus in the glare. A chorus of hoots arose from the senior grades. "What a body," someone yelled. He held up one hand and waited for silence. Lifted his other hand over his eyes so he could see the audience. Good. There were teachers positioned here and there among the students. Ought to keep down the rowdiness.

"Ladies and gentlemen," said Brad, hoping he didn't

sound too much like a sideshow barker, "today you're going to see a play called 'Bloody Murder.' It's part of a longer play by Francis Swann called *Out of the Frying Pan*. Since you don't have programs, I thought I'd better say a few words about the play."

"Think again," he heard someone shout, but there was an immediate shushing sound.

"What you'll see when the curtain opens is a suite on an upper floor of a big apartment building. It's evening in New York City. The suite is rented by a group of young actors hoping to break onto Broadway. The cast is made up entirely of your fellow students." He began listing the parts and the actors. When he said that Norman was played by Parker Stone, he heard a murmur run through the audience. A murmur and a hum spreading from row to row. He wondered what it meant. "They've all worked hard on this play. We hope you enjoy it."

He stepped back to the curtain, groped for the opening, and slipped through. He heard laughter behind him. Well, it was a comedy. Let them laugh. He signalled for the curtain to open and, as the lights dimmed, headed for the wings.

He thought he heard gasps when the lights came up revealing four bodies strewn across the stage. Utter quiet. Then Parker strode through the door, the skull in his hand. Alas, poor Yorick – it seemed right somehow for the kid who'd found himself playing Hamlet.

Brad held a script just in case someone needed prompting from stage left. He looked down. The script was shaking in his hand. It was up to Parker now. The kid had worked so hard on this, surely he wouldn't goof around and take the chance of screwing something up. Brad hoped he wouldn't. Knew he wouldn't.

A few minutes later he heard a snicker, then a chuckle. A belly laugh. Scattered laughter from farther back in the gym.

The audience seemed to understand a group of actors wanting to lure a famous producer to their suite so they could do his play for him and show him their stuff. They liked the idea of slipping him a Micky Finn to keep him there. When Parker paused, a disdainful look flashing on his face, then nailed his line, "I said calm him – not embalm him," there was laughter everywhere. Brad leaned against the wall, turned the page, hardly needing to look at the script. Every line, every bit of business, every shift in expression – Parker was hitting every one just right. This was going to be fun.

After the actors lured Mr. Kenny to their suite by feigning an interest in his culinary experiments, after he'd borrowed their flour and set his Gumbo Z'herbes simmering on the stove in his suite below, they finally convinced him to watch their rendition of his Broadway hit. The gym was quiet as the fortune teller leaned over her globe, ordering the frightened girl to walk to the bed and pull away the blanket. As Pam Wheeler took a hesitant step toward the bed, Brad heard a chair leg scrape the floor out front. It was the only sound in the gym.

Pam reached for the blanket, pulled it by the corner and screamed. A terrifying scream that shook the spot lights. As Parker rushed into the room, the corpse sat bolt upright, wondering what was the matter. The laughter rolled from the back of the gym. Mr. Kenny was not amused, but the actors swore they'd get it right and begged him to let them try again. Another scream and Parker dashed into the room, this time with the landlady right behind him. Howls of laughter. They were doing it, they had the audience with them all the way. More apologies to Mr. Kenny and another try. The fortune teller at her globe, another scream from Pam. Footsteps at the door – then silence. No sign of Parker. Pam looked worried, glanced frantically around the room, screamed again, even louder than before. Nothing. Another scream. At last the door opened, revealing Parker with a cop hanging on either arm. This time the laughter was so loud and long, the actors had to repeat their lines twice before they could be heard. And on it went, pratfalls and surprises, corny lines and dumb cops, a disappearing corpse, Mr. Kenny forced by the police to sit and watch his own play. When the play – the real play – ended, the gym was quiet for just a second. Before the lights went up for curtain call, the applause began, first the clapping, then, as the lights brightened over the row of bowing actors, whistles, cheers, shrieks. The actors raised their heads, looking at one another, surprised and pleased. Lori Campbell was blushing. She glanced at Brad and waved for him to join them. He shook his head and stepped backward. They were the ones who'd earned it. Let them enjoy it. From where he stood he could see perhaps a fifth of the crowd. They were on their feet now, most of them still smiling, all of them pounding their hands together.

Afterwards, when he considered the way the applause went on and on, he wondered if much of it hadn't been for Parker. Tossed out of school, fighting with his father, sleeping in the park. Making it to practice anyway.

The kids would know, of course. They always knew.

Twenty-seven

When they'd removed their set from the gym stage so that the weight-lifters could use it again, when they'd folded their costumes away and were cleaning off their makeup, they were still giddy with euphoria. Brad had never seen them look so happy, so sure of themselves.

"Listen up," he said. He had to say it again before everybody heard him. "Ten minutes and we meet at Pizza Hut. Treats are on me."

A burst of cheers.

"You'll be sorry, Mr. C," said Walter Buchko. "I can eat an awful lot."

On his way up to the staffroom for his keys, Brad saw Sue in the hall. "Good show," she said. It was all she said. He had to find some way to get through to her.

Herb Schwitzer darted out of the office and pumped his hand. "Don't mind saying I laughed just as hard as the kids. Those cops! Had me in stitches. Landlady couldn't've looked more stunned if you'd clobbered her with a hammer." He looked down at Brad's hand, released it. "Had a few parents pop into the office, said they liked it too. Mr. Workman be glad to hear that when he gets back." He turned toward the office, pulled the door open, and spoke over his shoulder. "Oh, yeah. Mrs. Campbell – Lori's mom – said we should hang on to you."

Nice, he thought, hope somebody listens to her. What the hell, might as well say it. "Pass that on to Mr. Workman, will you? It'll help a bit when he hears from Dr. Stone."

"Relax. We'll ride that one out together."

At least Herb was with him. That was something all right, but was it enough? "Kind of worried about next year," he said. "I need all the help I can get."

Herb stared at him a second, then shook his head, let the door swing shut behind him. "Sorry," he said. "It's been a long time since I was new at this game. Some things you tend to forget." He reached out and laid a firm hand on Brad's shoulder. "Listen, Brad, Mr. Workman doesn't always listen to me – board concerns sometimes get in the way – but it'll sure be my advice to keep you on."

"Thanks," he said. "That's got to help." But would it really? Was there any chance Workman didn't have his mind made up?

There was something else he needed to know. "I don't suppose Dr. Stone showed up."

Herb paused in the office doorway. "You got it. No sign of the good doctor."

B rad decided to leave his car in the school parking lot and walk the two blocks to Pizza Hut. To savour the victory – yes, it really was a victory. The first play he'd directed in his life and it had worked the way theatre was supposed to work, the actors winning their audience at the start, the audience forgetting themselves, getting into it, anticipating the next twist, the next chance to laugh. The kids had done their job – every one of them.

And Sue had said it was a good show. That was all, but it was the first time she'd spoken to him since Monday afternoon. Probably the last time too.

Oh, get off it. This was no time to be feeling sorry for himself. Herb was going to put in a word for him; it probably wouldn't help, but he knew at least he could get a reference from him, and that might mean another job somewhere. What more could he want?

Sue. Sue was what he wanted. Without her, the job didn't seem to mean as much. He knew that now, didn't care how old she was. If only she would listen to him, maybe he could find some way to get through to her, to apologize and tell her what an ass he'd been, but no, talking wasn't going to do it. He'd need something more than that.

While he waited for the light to change at Main Street, he looked across the parking lot and through the restaurant windows. The kids were crowded together around what looked like three or four tables pushed together. They were leaning toward the centre of the tables, laughing and talking, arms gesturing, going over the big moments, he bet, reliving every one of them.

They didn't need a teacher dropping in to squelch their fun, make them feel awkward, the conversation suddenly unnatural, strained. Maybe he should just drop off some money at the till and keep walking.

He crossed the street, thinking he didn't have much cash, but he could use his credit card, leave a credit with the cashier. A coke each and a couple of slices of pizza. This could cost him something. Well, that was okay; they deserved a celebration.

When he opened the door, he wondered what was wrong. Reverberations like distant thunder, like dozens of drummers hammering on bongo drums. From the entranceway he looked over the partition toward the body of the restaurant, the kids pounding the tables with their palms, Pam and Lori bolting toward him, each taking a hand, pulling him in, slipping their arms through his, walking him to the table. People in the booths turning, craning their heads, wondering what was going on, a few of them with disgusted expressions on their faces. He knew he was blushing. The girls took him to the head of the table where Walter and Parker sprang to their feet, almost knocking heads as they pulled out the one empty chair. Cheers, a great roar of cheers as he sat down, cheers continuing as he shifted in his seat, grinning – yeah, he knew it, he was grinning like an idiot – holding up his hands, waving them off, the cheers finally ebbing. He looked around the table at their open faces – none of them worried about who might be staring at them, judging them noisy, rude, obnoxious. All of them happy for him and to heck with what other people thought.

It was then that he realized what he would have to do.

He didn't know if he could pull it off, though. Hell, he was basically a shy person. Had a problem introducing himself to strangers, never at ease with people he didn't know, people he wasn't sure of. Always a little nervous walking into class till he got the students warmed up. His students, kids he already knew. He'd hated the beginning of the term, one new class after another, every class packed with kids whose names he didn't know. Blank faces staring up at him. How would he do in front of a new class at the end of the year? Tomorrow morning.

Or in the afternoon maybe, the next day for sure. He

couldn't put it off much longer.

The readiness is all. That was what Hamlet said to Horatio as he faced his final challenge. Yeah. And that was what he'd told Bert Peale when the kid had insisted that there was no point to the play. You had to be ready for whatever life flung your way, and not just in ancient Denmark; the good, the bad, betrayal by a friend, a parent, you had to take it all. Yeah, had to be bigger than trouble. Bigger than doubt.

She'd said she wouldn't spend her weekends hiding in Regina. She knew, all right. He'd been running scared, worried about what everyone would say, the crap he'd have to take, unsure about himself because he was so much younger and sometimes felt like such a kid. He was unwilling to admit it, yes. But she thought he was ashamed of her, of how old she was, and then he'd gone and called her old, and that had clinched it. Another humiliation. He had to deal with all of that, had to show her he could deal with it. Take the chance. Only trouble was he wasn't ready.

He had to type his final exams, four sets of them, run them off, get them stapled, bundled up and locked away in the office. Collect all the books for the extensive reading kits, get back the sets of stories he'd photocopied, assign marks for contributions in class, do his averages, tally up his attendance sheets, figure out recommends for the junior grades, type out study guides for every class, something to help them organize for the finals, give them every chance he could. Then map out the seating plan for the Grad banquet. So many things to do, so little time. It was easy to work away at them, to put off what he knew he ought to do. Had to do before it was too late.

Convince her.

Workman was waiting for him in the staffroom the morning after the play. All he said was, "In my office – right now."

This was it, thought Brad, he was finished now. He could feel the eyes of the other teachers on his back as he left the room. A minute later he was slumped in the chair before the principal's desk. Workman took a deep breath, hovering above him.

"I go out to Vancouver for a conference, and that's your chance – right away you're piling stones on my coffin lid."

Workman was glaring at him. His eyes, sunken above the cheekbones, were dark and fever-bright. He continued to glare without another word.

"I don't quite know what –"

"Fighting in your class. Blood all over the floor." Workman stomped behind his desk and slammed into his chair. No sign that he was ready for the coffin. "The Board's on my back again. Kids brawling in the school."

"Just two of them," said Brad. "It was so sudden. Took me a minute to get them stopped."

"No discipline. That's your problem." Workman leaned forward. "One of your problems."

Was the man enjoying this? "How do you mean?"

"Dr. Stone's been giving me an earful. Complaining about you. I've heard a lot of that this year."

Brad shrugged. "He's not an easy man to –"

"He tells me you're leading his boy astray, advising him to forget about medical school."

"That's not true. He was in my play is all – and didn't want to quit."

"I heard you wouldn't let him quit."

"It was up to Parker. But I sure wasn't going to make him

quit – not when the other kids had worked so hard – not when there was no reason to quit."

"No reason? His father wanted him to quit."

What was the use? He'd been through it all with Herb. Nothing was going to make Workman see the light. "His father should have told him, then."

Workman shook his head. He glared at Brad as if he were a piece of gristle he'd just pulled from a sandwich he'd been chewing on. "You're something else, you know that? And here's Mr. Schwitzer recommending we keep you on another year." Workman paused. "Dr. McAvoy too. Huh, good men taking leave of their senses." Workman leaned toward his waste basket, looked as if he might spit, then seemed to change his mind. "I guess you get another chance – one more year and maybe then we'll let you go." He waved a bony hand toward the door. "Go on; you're done in here."

Brad stood up and turned away from him.

"And don't think," said Workman, " that you're going to get any cushy timetable with all English classes."

Brad opened the door and closed it quickly behind him. Leaned against it, breathing deeply. He didn't know whether he should celebrate or mourn.

That afternoon, he drew Parker aside after class. "How did you make out at home?" he asked.

"Got yelled at, grounded for a week." Parker hesitated. "Ah, it's not so bad. I have to study for finals anyway."

"He must have been pretty worried."

"Sure. Worried about me getting into med school."

"I think he was worried about you – where you were, how you were."

"I doubt it."

"Parker, let me tell you something about fathers." Listen to him, going on like some kind of expert. "Took me a while to figure this out. They love you, they want what's best for you – they really do – sometimes, though, they just don't know what that might be."

"Sure as hell isn't med school."

"Maybe not. But you can decide that later." Might as well tell him. "My father always figured I should stay working on the farm, but it just didn't interest me. He was furious when I went into education. His only son refusing to carry on the family business. It still bugs the hell out of him, but I can understand that – and he's starting to change. We're going to work things out." The boy looked annoyed. "Your father hasn't cooled down yet?"

"I guess he has. He blew off some steam at me." Parker ducked his head. "I know he phoned Mr. Workman. Probably blew off some more at him." Parker raised his head, looked him in the eye. "I hope he didn't get you in any kind of trouble."

"No need for you to worry." No, he could do enough of that himself. "They're keeping me on for next year. I'm fine. How about you? Your dad ready now to forgive and forget?"

"Oh, he'll ride me for a while, but eventually he'll get over it."

"Good." Eventually, yeah, but not for quite a while.

"Got to run," said Parker, turning away, but hesitating, turning back again. "I knew they'd never fire you. Even Workman's too smart for that."

Workman had been smart enough to rid himself of Rutledge with a lousy timetable. Well, maybe he could hang in where Rutledge couldn't. Maybe he had a better reason. Because this was where Sue was, where he wanted to be. But somehow he had to get through to her. And the days dwindling down and down. Time was running out; it would soon be too late. He knew she'd be gone to Europe for the summer.

The last day before exams, there were desks to clean and number, have carried to the gym, laid out in rows where all the grades would write together.

"I want my essay back."

Bert Peale was standing in his doorway that last day at noon, glowering at him.

Brad shrugged his shoulders, puzzled. "I explained in class. We have to keep everything for six months – until your marks are official and we're sure there's no screw-up with the Department of Education."

Bert shook his head, sneering.

"After that," said Brad, "you can have all your creative work back. The exams, we keep."

"You don't get it, do you?" Bert's tone was both patronizing and angry.

"No, I don't." He felt suddenly tired, worn out. "There's a lot of things I don't get."

"That's obvious. I'm talking about the essay I had to write in the library."

"Oh, your apology." That was months ago. The kid had apologized for flashing his drawing of a penis, admitted he'd been wrong. Whether he meant it was something else.

"Yeah, the one you made me write when I should've been listening to speeches – like everybody else. I want it back."

Brad looked at the boy, hostility hanging on him like a coat of armour. He could try again, he guessed, but was there any point to it? He got up and walked to the filing cabinet in the corner of the room. Unlocked it and pulled open the second drawer, fished through his files until he found Bert's essay. Decided to try one more time.

"You're a good writer, Bert, when you want to be."

"Yeah, and I'd ace this class if it wasn't such a waste of time."

Brad handed him the essay without another word.

"Bet you'd like to keep it," said Bert. "Show it to my old man."

He wondered if he could find the energy to speak. "To tell you the truth," he said, finally, "I forgot I had it."

"Yeah, sure! You teachers are so full of crap." Bert spun away and headed for the door, but he wheeled around just as he got to the hall. "Four exams – then it's Grad, and I'm out of here. Good riddance."

He was gone before Brad could answer him, but what did it matter, what was there to say?

Brad looked at the door. It was such a long way off. His lunch was in the staffroom, up all those stairs, two flights of stairs. He slumped into the chair behind his desk, and looked across his room – five rows of empty desks.

He remembered his first meeting with Herb Schwitzer – it was just last September, but it seemed years ago. You've got to like them all, Herb had told him, every last one of them.

He guessed that was more than he could do.

After he sent the afternoon attendance sheet up to the office, he got a pail of soapy water and a can of Comet from the caretakers' room and set them on his desk. Laid half a dozen rags and a roll of paper towel beside them.

"Clean up time," he told the students. "Get rid of all the ink. Then wash them off. Real well. Before we move them to the gym for finals. You may be writing on these very desks. Be sure you wipe away the cleanser grit."

Well. Forget about his conversation with Bert Peale. Now was the time. Now or never.

Sure, and hadn't she said it herself? The thing she admired about Rutledge – the man wasn't afraid to take a chance.

Well, Brad wasn't flamboyant, wasn't much like Rutledge, he thought, but he was here every day, getting the job done, and he could take a chance too.

"I'll be back in a minute. I've got to run an errand." His voice felt tight in his throat. He saw Lori Campbell look up at him, a puzzled expression on her face. Must've heard something different in his voice.

He walked down the hall, wondering if it wouldn't be smarter just to turn around, go back to class, start writing his room number on the corner of every desk when it was cleaned.

Or go ahead, make a total ass of himself.

He felt his heart hammering in his chest, realized he was barely inhaling, drawing his breath in quick, little puffs. Oh, hell, he'd never be ready.

Then he thought of Phil Simpson admitting he was gay, taking the risk, confiding in him. Letting him know that Sue might be available.

He kept walking.

His hand was on the knot of his tie, making sure it was

straight. Usually, he didn't bother with a tie, but today might be special. He hoped so.

Some of them would know him, he supposed. Might be a few he'd even taught. Mostly strangers though. Hell, every class was different, even if you'd had every kid somewhere before, they were different till you got to know them as a class, till you'd taught them at least a couple weeks. These kids, he didn't know, didn't have a clue how they'd react. But that was the point, wasn't it? The only thing she'd understand.

As he came down the hall, he could see that her door was shut. He heard a roar of laughter inside her room, then Sue's voice, cheerful but muffled, followed by another roar. She sure knew how to handle kids. "Even politicians catch on eventually," he heard her say. "Natural consequences are inevitable; they're not unusual punishment." Scattered laughter.

If he paused any longer here outside the room, he might never make it.

He gave two loud raps on the door, opened it and stepped inside. A large class. More than thirty kids. Turning to stare at him, wondering what he was doing here.

"Excuse me," he said. "Sorry to interrupt." He had to get it done. Right now. "I've got something to say to your teacher. And I need witnesses."

Their heads were turning, quick glances at her, at one another, then back at him.

She was beside her lectern in the middle of the room. He walked toward her, catching a glimpse of white blouse, of long, denim skirt, but he kept his eyes on the students, noting the way they sat quietly, following him with their own eyes, puzzled expressions on their faces. He could feel a wobble in his knees when he stopped beside her. He didn't dare look at her.

"Here's the situation." His voice sounded deeper than usual, but it wasn't his voice; it was someone else's, speaking through him. A ventriloquist maybe, and he was just a dummy. Yeah, a dummy – another minute and everybody'd see it.

"Your teacher," he said, still looking at them and not at her, "she's someone special. You probably know that already. It's something I've learned this last year working with her." He was running out of breath. He paused, took a quick breath. "The trouble is – I said something stupid to her, something I didn't mean. I apologized, but, man, she doesn't think a whole lot of me. That's fair enough. I can handle that." He was babbling now, the words tumbling out. Never mind. He was going to get it said. "What I couldn't handle is her having it wrong. Going away for the summer with the wrong idea. You guys have got to see it. I want the whole world to know. The way I feel. The thing is, I love her."

Except for a little gasp of breath from a pug-nosed girl in the side row, there wasn't a sound in the room.

Then he turned to Sue.

She stood there motionless, her eyes wide – with shock, maybe, but aflame too, fire and tears, he thought, his gaze falling on her mouth, one eyetooth digging at her lower lip. But then she leaned against him, raised her lips to his and kissed him.

After his desks were moved up to the gym, after he'd said goodbye to his grade twelves, wishing them well in their exams and all good things for the rest of their lives, he carried the last box of extensive reading novels into the book room. He'd have to tape the covers of *They Shouldn't Make You Promise That* and *The Lark in the Clear Air,* make them last as long as possible. It would be worth the trouble; some of the kids loved them as much as he did. He found a space on the top shelf between sets of *The Stone Angel* and *Who Has Seen the Wind,* edged the box into the space and pushed it home. The shelves were full, some of the boxes falling apart, the titles scrawled on the sides in marker pen, a few crossed out and written over. They needed new boxes – and a good sorting. Maybe, when his exams were marked, he'd have some time to come in here and work through the ones he used.

He switched off the light and pulled the door shut behind him. A sharp metallic click. He gave the handle a twist. Good, it was locked.

When he turned away, he bumped a Slurpee container on the floor, almost kicked it over – it was more than half full, ice cubes shaking in the drink.

"Don't worry, sir. I'm gonna finish it."

He recognized the voice at once. Parker Stone grinning at him from where he leaned against the wall. Right beside him, Lori Campbell, a grin on her face too.

"You two look so happy, you'd never guess finals start tomorrow."

Parker shoved out his hand, his whole face now breaking into a smile. "I never would've guessed."

Brad wasn't sure what to do. Couldn't very well leave him standing there, his hand hanging out. He took the hand and shook it, felt Parker pumping back.

Lori stepped beside him. She actually reached out and slapped him on the back. "Way to go, Mr. C," she said.

"Right in front of everybody."

"You heard."

"Everybody heard," said Parker. "The whole school's talking." A quick frown. "My God, what if she'd told you to get lost?"

"I don't know, Parker. I was hoping she wouldn't. It was worth the risk, you know."

"She kissed you," said Lori. "She really kissed you – right there in front of everybody."

He was blushing and he didn't care. "Hey," he said, "I kissed her back."

"You sure did!" said Lori.

"We heard!" said Parker.

"Better than the movies. The kids in Miss Burton's room, they thought it was awesome."

Parker let out a low whistle and rolled his eyes. "Man! What a kiss! Man, oh, man!" He balled his right hand into a fist, gave Brad a quick tap on the shoulder, then stepped back and picked the Slurpee off the floor. "See you Tuesday morning," he said. He ran his index finger across his throat and made a slicing sound. "Don't make it too tough, eh?"

"You'll both do fine."

Brad watched him slip his arm around Lori as they walked toward the glass doors on the landing. They each wore backpacks stuffed with books.

"Bet you'll need a lot of practice," he heard Lori say as she leaned her head on Parker's shoulder, "before you can kiss like that." And a tinkle of laughter skipping back to him, a deeper chuckle joining it, until the glass door swung shut and cut them off. Looked like Parker had a date for Grad.

Brad stood for a moment in the silent hall, watching their legs grow shorter until their shoes disappeared up the stairs.

Nice kids, he thought. The school's full of nice kids. Well, better get up to the staffroom. See how bad it's going to be in there. Yeah, and when Workman gets the news, it'll be like heaping boulders on his coffin lid – or on mine.

He started down the hall. Paper everywhere. The students had been told to empty their lockers, get rid of everything they didn't want. Four garbage cans sat at the end of the rows of lockers, but they were full, overflowing, crumpled papers strewn around them. As he walked down the hall, he glanced at his room, the lights off, the door open, shadow and darkness, a gaping maw. Well, it hadn't swallowed him.

On the floor in front of him he noted three apple cores, a shrivelled sandwich with its corners curled and grey, five crumpled paper bags, two gym shoes without shoe laces, another with a hole in the toe, a grimy pair of socks balled together, a ripped t-shirt with "Strictly from Hunger" painted on the chest beneath bared fangs, a scattering of peanut shells, half a dozen sheets of unmarked graph paper, a wrinkled poster of Bart Simpson, four squashed soft drink cans, an empty cigarette package, a torn map, a paperback without a cover, a ball of what looked like aluminum foil.

He paused, eyeing the ball, lined it up and booted it over the garbage cans – yes, a perfect field goal! The ball of foil bounced off a locker and dropped to the floor. He stooped and picked it up, stepped back, faked once, swung around and hooked it toward the garbage can. He couldn't miss today. Sue had said she'd be waiting for him when he was finished in the book room.

He trotted up the stairs.

Notes And Acknowledgements

Readers – and especially English teachers – may note that in writing this novel about a high school teacher and his students I have on occasion switched around the poems, stories and books taught in particular courses. I would like to assure them that this was done, not out of ignorance, but for artistic reasons. Some readers, knowing that I was myself an English teacher, may study the characters of this novel in an attempt to discover real people lurking behind fictitious names. Let me state that the characters who appear in this book grew in my imagination; they never worked in the schools where I taught and were never meant to resemble particular living teachers or students. Even real incidents, when they occasionally crept into the plot, were used fictitiously.

I owe a great debt of gratitude to Edna Alford for her editorial insights; she must surely be one of the finest editors in this country. Thanks, also, to the members of my prose group (Byrna Barclay, Pat Krause, Dave Margoshes, and Brenda Niskala) for their encouragement and chapter-by-chapter comments over a period of many months, to Sandra Birdsell, Barbara Sapergia and Geoffrey Ursell for their generous responses to early drafts with detailed notes and wise advice, and to the members of the Poets' Combine for their continued support and friendship.

Special thanks to Connie Kaldor for permission to use the chorus from her Canadian classic, "Wood River." Connie says she likes to see her songs go to different places, and her words have been singing in my head throughout the writing of this novel, being, in fact, a part of its inception.

Quotations from "Out of the Frying Pan" by Francis Swann, a comedy which is great fun to produce with high school students, are used by special permission of Samuel French Inc.

Additional thanks to Anne Warriner, Karon Selzer, and the staff of the Moose Jaw Public Library – especially those in the reference department – for their assistance, encouragement, and provision of a friendly place to work and think.

I want to thank, as well, the editors of *NeWest Review* who published an excerpt from Chapter Four in the final issue of that fine magazine. Would it were still with us.

Finally, I would like to express my appreciation to the Writers' Union of Canada for their support of Canadian writers and to that most important of organizations, the Saskatchewan Writers Guild, whose staff and members have helped sustain me through many years of writing.

What was said about *Things You Don't Forget*

"Robert Currie has a wonderful ability to create characters who remember their pasts in ways that enlarge a reader's own private memories." – T. F. RIGELHOF

"In Robert Currie's *Things You Dont Forget*, a new and splendid collection of 11 short stories, nobility of spirit is dramatically pitted against the realities of existence. . . . [This] is to my mind the best book of stories published in Canada in the past decade. It's a memorable accomplishment, one that makes you impatient to read more." – LEN GASPARINI IN *The Toronto Star*

"The prairie wind breathes across the pages of Currie's 11 stories, set in Saskatchewan.... [Currie] has an excellent eye for detail, the writing is clear, the characters are well delineated, and in each tale an event occurs that forever changes people's lives." – W. P. KINSELLA IN *Quill & Quire*

"Like life itself, these stories run the gamut of human behaviour and experience. Currie likes to see the humour in everyday life and he's generous with his funny touches.... There's something for every taste in this highly accessible collection." – VERNE CLEMENCE IN *The Saskatoon StarPhoenix*

"At last we have a new story collection from Currie.... I always remember Toronto novelist Austin Clarke's pronouncement in a Creative Writing class: 'Dialogue is the smell of the story.' No one understands that better than Robert Currie, who gives his scenes dimension – an appealing aroma, if you like – with crisp and authentic dialogue." – DAVE WILLIAMSON IN *The Prairie Fire Review of Books*

"Robert Currie's *Things You Don't Forget* is indeed an unforgettable collection, evoking with powerful gentleness ineradicable hesitations in the lives of his characters." – ARITHA VAN HERK FOR *the Saskatchewan Book Awards*

about the author

Robert Currie's short fiction collections *Things You Don't Forget* and *Night Games* were both published by Coteau Books. He has also published four chapbooks and four poetry collections. *Teaching Mr. Cutler* is his first novel.

Born in Lloydminster, he spent his teen years in Moose Jaw before attending the University of Saskatchewan. He returned to Moose Jaw where he taught high school for 30 years, and where he continues to live. He received the Joseph Duffy Memorial Award for excellence in the teaching of language arts.